Little Wishes

Michelle Adams

First published in Great Britain in 2021 by Trapeze
an imprint of The Orion Publishing Group Ltd
Carmelite House, 50 Victoria Embankment
London EC4Y 0DZ

An Hachette UK Company

1 3 5 7 9 10 8 6 4 2

ISBN (Mass Market Paperback) 978 1 4091 9504 7
ISBN (eBook) 978 1 4091 9505 4

Typeset by Born Group
Printed and bound in Great Britain by Clays Ltd, Elcograf S.p.A.

MIX
Paper from
responsible sources
FSC® C104740

www.orionbooks.co.uk

*To Dad, without whose life and loss this book
would never have been written. I miss you.
And to Christine. Nobody taught me more about
what it means to love than you.*

Now

On her favourite day of the year, Elizabeth Davenport awoke alone, as she had done every day for the best part of five decades. Home was a small cottage nestled on the very cusp of the Cornish coast, north of Land's End and south of just about everywhere else. If you looked at the cottage from the outside, which she doubted many people did, it seemed too small to house two floors and a set of stairs which ran straight up through the middle. It was almost as if it was hunkered down, fearful of being swept away by the Atlantic currents that simmered only feet away. But it offered Elizabeth more space than she needed, and a perfect view from which she could paint the mercurial scenery without ever having to open the front door. Few reasons existed to venture far nowadays, and little in the outside world concerned her anymore. But today was a different story. Today she cared about what was out there, because it was the one day each year when Tom came back.

Her eyes adjusted to the sunlight marbling through the lace curtains as a few cheerful voices rose above the lull of the ocean. Being careful to keep her body under the warmth of the covers, she let her hand drift to the empty side of the bed, stroking the sheet, crisp as the day it was ironed. Although Tom had never slept in this bed, she was struck by the feeling that somehow, he was missing from it. And while his absence remained a lifelong void that she could never fill, it was eased by his annual return to Porthsennen, when he came to leave a blue crocus on her doorstep, a wish attached to the pot with a length of garden string. It was always for something they would have been doing if they were together on that day, like lounging in bed, eating at a restaurant, or seeing their family grow. And although they had never fulfilled any of those wishes, his return meant that for a short time each year, their lives coalesced. It was a day when everything felt right, when she felt truly like herself, in a way that for the remaining three hundred and sixty-four days, she did not. And what Elizabeth knew, what made her heart beat each time she saw that little blue flower, was that to go to such effort, to never once fail in all that time, meant that they loved each other just the same now as they had done on the day they first kissed. With her head on the pillow and her eyes closed, she recalled that first wish:

1969: I wish that today we could lounge in bed all morning, listening to the sound of the waves.

After a while in bed, Elizabeth rose, her feet cool on the bare wooden floor. Reaching for the pink silk robe hanging on the back of her door, she couldn't help but smile as she slipped her arms into it. That was something else Tom occasionally did too, left other gifts along with the flower. One year it was a pair of hiking boots, another year a bottle of champagne to celebrate a decade of love. So many years had passed that she was no longer sure if she could remember when exactly he left that pink robe, but she knew she had worn it every day since. And today marked fifty years since he'd made that promise to love her for the rest of his life, when he gave her the very first crocus flower; her stomach was somersaulting at the mere thought of what he might bring for a day as special as this.

Pacing carefully down the stairs, Elizabeth drew back the curtains and light flooded the small living room. A view along Whitesand Bay filled the alcove window, and ahead, just above the rooftops of the old fishing stores, the vast grey of the Atlantic Ocean surged and receded on the tide. A breeze brought forth the scent of white caps breaking offshore, and Elizabeth could just hear the clatter of fishing boats rocking as waves danced against their wooden hulls. Cookie, her British Blue, purred for his breakfast, all the while nuzzling against her legs. Getting a cat was certainly one of Tom's better wishes; Elizabeth and Cookie had enjoyed seventeen good years together now, and his presence was often the only thing to ease the relentlessness of being alone.

Sunlight catching at the mirrored edge of a photo frame drew Elizabeth's attention to the windowsill. The image of Kate as a child stared back at her. To think of such happier times with her daughter was bittersweet, painful now to think how long had passed since they had last spoken. Of how she missed her. Overcome for a moment, she placed the frame back on the sill and wiped the corner of her eye, lost as to how to help her daughter forgive the most terrible mistake she had ever made as a mother.

'I suppose you're hungry, aren't you?' Elizabeth said at last, following the welcome distraction of the fluffy bundle still fussing at her feet. Cookie's tail rose poker straight in appreciation as she stroked her hand along his back. Elizabeth set a plate of fish on the floor, then located a half bottle of champagne that she had placed in the fridge the night before. Although she could never bring herself to open the bottle Tom had left on the doorstep many years ago, each year she bought a replacement to toast their memory. It was difficult with her arthritis, but she managed to send the cork flying across the room with a loud pop. Cookie didn't even flinch. 'You must be going deaf,' she told him, laughing to herself as she poured herself a flute. It was too early for it really, and the alcohol didn't agree with her blood pressure tablets, but it was just one day out of the year. This was how their special day began, she thought, remembering the wish from 1978: *I wish we could sip champagne for breakfast while we sit and gaze at the ocean.* Each year she tried to realise Tom's wishes in whatever way she could, but every year she was reminded that some were easier fulfilled than others.

Bubbles fizzed from the flute as a pan of water came to a steady boil on the stove. Soon enough, she had prepared a plate of poached eggs on toast. Stooping to retrieve a small wicker basket from the cupboard alongside the fireplace, she set it down on the table, along with her breakfast. As she took her seat at the table, an old Elvis Presley LP began to play – a scratchy version of a song she loved, one she only ever listened to on this day.

'Ah yes,' she said aloud, fingering through the little blue slips of paper in the basket until she came across one she liked. 'This was a good idea, wasn't it?'

On the little note it read: *1993: I wish that you would*

read my diary, so that you would know every day of this year I was thinking about you. That diary was still in the cupboard along with the unopened champagne, delivered that year along with the wish. True to his word, every daily entry was about how he had been thinking of her. Forty-eight more wishes remained in that basket, each one a testament to something they had missed, to a part of their lives they hadn't really shared. After reading his diary she had wanted to find him and tell him what a mistake it was that they weren't together. But the reality of their lives had stopped her, for it wouldn't have been fair. Knowing that he was married, and that technically so was she, meant that to be together was impossible. Still, the thought of everything they had missed out on, coupled with the strength of his commitment to honour his promise each year was something difficult to digest; his wishes and gifts were enough to make her wonder what kind of life they might have been able to share had they stayed together.

Tom had been her first love, her only love, and a man she could never forget. In his presence she had felt so much like herself that when he left it was almost as if he had taken a small part of her with him. That was why she looked forward to this day so much; his annual gifts awakened those parts of herself, and for a short time each year she felt as if she was still that same girl who fell in love all those many years ago.

Pushing her empty plate aside, she stood up; her head light with bubbles and excitement. Cookie returned to his favoured spot, a small basket in one of the windows where he could, should the mood take him, imagine a hunt of the local gulls without having to move too far.

For now, he seemed content to have a good wash and settle in for a rest. Replacing the wish in the basket, Elizabeth raised her glass in the air.

'Here's to us,' she said, looking at Cookie and thinking of Tom. Her eyes flicked to the door; should she look already? The excitement swelled inside her like a great big inflatable balloon. Even though she knew that a reunion was never on the cards, she had always wondered if one day he might just knock on the door and be standing there with the crocus in his hand rather than left on the doorstep. Especially this year, the fiftieth and most important as she could see it. That would be her wish this year, she thought, just to have him back. But if those wishes were all they had left, it was enough for her to know that he still cared enough to come. And at least this way, she supposed, they had never suffered the difficult years of marriage, the arguing or disappointments that every couple she knew had experienced along the way. Instead they remained for ever young, their relationship one of eternal hope.

Setting the empty champagne flute back on the table, she moved towards the door. Her anticipation had got the better of her, and she couldn't wait any longer. The key turned with a clunk in the lock, the handle creaking as she pulled it. A gust of sea breeze picked up the edges of her silk robe as she opened the door, the chill of the air taking her breath away as she looked down to the step. But despite all her hope, expectation, and all the ways that she relied on the arrival of his gift, when she looked down there was no little flower or wish waiting to be found. This year, the step was empty.

Then

The first Elizabeth knew of the accident was when she woke to the dull thudding of her father's boots on the stairs. The dark sky was broken by the glimmer of moonlight as it fussed at the edge of a break in the clouds. The clock ticked at her side, and she saw that it was a little after 1 a.m. Somewhere in the distance a door slammed, followed by the faintest ringing of a bell. Was that a voice she could hear too, calling out? Pushing the covers aside, she jumped from the bed, moved towards the window. As she peered into the street, she saw her father rushing from their home in the direction of the sea. His shoes were untied, the blue and white stripe of his pyjamas flickering underneath the tails of his coat. There had been calls for such urgent departures in the past, but even in the direst of emergencies he always got dressed. Leaving in his nightclothes was unthinkable.

Elizabeth pushed her feet into her slippers and opened her bedroom door. With her father gone, the responsibility for her mother was left to her. Even at the age of seventeen she knew it wasn't good for her to wake alone. Ahead, a thin slither of light shone from the door of her parents' bedroom, left ajar in an otherwise tenebrous house.

'Mum,' called Elizabeth as she moved along the landing. They tried to keep her accompanied since the cruelty of the confusion had set in about a year ago, yet still there were unpredictable moments like this when she ended up alone. Alzheimer's disease, her father called it. The name didn't mean much to Elizabeth, but she hated the disease all the same. Only last month they had found her mother trying to take a boat out, with seemingly little idea about where she was and devastatingly unprepared for what might have lain ahead. Her condition was getting steadily worse, just a little bit every day; her presence in their family like a rock ground down by the constant weight of the tides.

As she pushed open the door to her parents' bedroom, an empty bed presented itself, the sheets turned in both left and right. Elizabeth thought she heard a noise then, something in the kitchen perhaps. Her mother must already be downstairs. Turning to leave she almost missed it, but there, sitting alongside the chest of drawers was her father's black doctor's bag. A fresh worry surfaced; he couldn't work without his bag, and if there was an emergency great enough to rush from the house still dressed in his pyjamas, Elizabeth had to do something. Not long had passed since he'd left, she thought, and wondered if perhaps she could still catch him. Snatching up the bag, she hurried down the stairs. 'I'll be back as quick as I can, Mum,' she called, locking the front door behind her.

The winding streets of her small village were imprinted in her mind, and she used that knowledge gained through years of childhood play to get to the coast as quickly as she could. The wind bit at her ears, and through the thick coastal dark she could hear the increasing intensity of the sea breaking ground as she inched ever closer. Then overhead a bright light filled the sky, an arc like a comet, followed by the accompanying boom of a maroon as it was fired from the lifeboat station. Her fears grew as half-dressed men whizzed past her, en route to answer the lifeboat's call. Following the commotion of harried voices, she took her first steps onto the sand behind the lifeboat station. It was then that she heard the chilling shriek of her father's cry, and saw him down at the water's edge.

Arms flailed as a small crowd did what they could to hold him back. Mr Bolitho, and another man whose name she didn't know splashed their way into the water ahead, each of them in a state of half-undress. Torchlight picked out a figure emerging from the water, pulling with him another person, as lifeless and heavy as a wet ragdoll hanging at the rescuer's side. His face was familiar, a young man named Tom whom she once knew from school. He had changed, grown broad in the shoulders, different from the boy Elizabeth used to know. Then her eyes moved to the body hanging limply under his arm. Her father's bag fell from her hands as she watched her mother peel away from Tom's grip, forming a lifeless heap on the sand.

Stumbling forwards, Elizabeth saw Tom pressing his mouth against her mother's, filling her lungs with his breath. Her father was still screaming, helpless in a way she had never witnessed before. Why wasn't he doing anything? Wet sand hit Elizabeth's knees as she fell to her mother's side, just as a jet of water came spluttering from her mouth.

'Oh, Catherine,' her father called as he scrambled to reach her. Her skin had been touched by ice, a sheen of glacial blue that shimmered in the light of the moon.

'Will she be all right?' Elizabeth asked, as she held her mother's hand, her skin so cold it was almost painful. Gazing upwards into the crowd, she searched the desperate faces for an answer.

'She'll be all right, miss,' Tom said. He reached across, placed a wet hand on Elizabeth's shoulder. Somebody draped a blanket over his back, and then another over her mother. His breath was warm as he leaned in close. 'But we need Dr Warbeck.' Dr James Warbeck was Elizabeth's fiancé, and they were due to be married next year. Tom glanced briefly at her father, then lowered his voice to a whisper. 'Your father is in shock. He's no help here.'

Dr Warbeck was already on his way, having woken to the sound of the maroon. He was still getting used to coastal life, but it had been a busy summer for the lifeboat crew, and the need for urgency when he heard the call for help was as familiar to him now as it was to hear the trundle of buses passing his window when he'd lived in London. Dropping down onto the beach, sand filling his shoes, he hurried towards the crowd, still unsure what lay before him. Moments later he saw Elizabeth, then her father, next to her mother still lying on the shore. Elizabeth's breathing was as quick and short as his own.

'James, do something, please,' she begged.

'She's very cold,' he said after checking Catherine's body. 'Lizzy, go on ahead, get the fire going. And you,' he said, pointing at Tom. 'I suspect you are suffering a little from the exposure. Go with her. The run will do you good. Now come on, gentlemen,' he said to the crowd of local fishermen who had gathered to help. 'We need to get this good lady back to the warmth of her home. Who will help me carry her?'

Elizabeth burst through the door to her home, looking left and right as if she had arrived in a place she didn't know. Her knees still felt cold and damp as she knelt at the fireplace, no idea what to do. The logs seemed too heavy, the coal insufficient as she tried to build the fire. All knowledge of a task she knew well had been lost in the confusion of the night. No matter what she tried, the fire floundered.

'Let me help,' Tom said, taking the pot from her when a third match went out. His voice broke the silence, reminded Elizabeth that she wasn't alone. The warmth of his body next to hers evoked the memory of just how cold her mother had seemed at the beach.

'Do you really think she'll be all right?' Elizabeth asked as the earliest sparks engulfed the wood. But before he could answer they heard the crowd arriving with her mother, the slam of the door, the shuffle of feet. By the time they got her in the chair the first flames of a decent fire were licking the sides of the chimney.

Elizabeth stood aside to let James work, watching as he measured her mother's blood pressure and listened to her chest. Her father sat at her side, tears welling in his eyes, his cheeks pinched pink by the fire. Elizabeth had never known him look so helpless. A single tear broke free and streaked across his wrinkled cheeks. The room was silent, her mother too, everybody waiting on James's verdict.

'Miss?' Elizabeth heard a whispered voice coming from behind her. Tom was standing alone, his drenched clothes dripping saltwater to the floor. 'I'm sorry,' he said, pushing his wet hair from his face, 'but do you have a towel I could use?'

With James taking care of medical matters, she knew that the best thing she could do would be to help the person who had saved her mother. 'You'd better come with me,' she said as she beckoned Tom to follow her towards the stairs.

Under normal circumstances it would have been inappropriate to ascend the stairs as they were together. Eyebrows would have been raised at the disappearance of two youngsters like that, especially in a small place like Porthsennen. Yet on that night nobody noticed as he followed her in silence. He waited at the top of the stairs while Elizabeth rooted around in her father's cupboards. Moments later she emerged carrying a well-worn jumper and a pair of dress trousers that tapered at the ankle.

'Thank you,' he said as she handed him the pile of clothes, adding a pair of brown brogues that she knew her father didn't wear anymore.

'I should be thanking you,' she said as she stood back. 'For what you did, I mean. You saved my mother's life, no doubt.'

With the top of his forearm, he brushed his floppy wet hair from his face. 'Anybody would have done the same, miss.'

Elizabeth had so many questions buzzing around her head. She wanted to ask what he had seen, and how he'd ended up being the one to help. About how her mother fell. But she didn't know where to start, because she was sure on some level that she knew the answer to at least one of those questions. And her father was very specific; they were not to divulge any details of the illness that had claimed her mother, not a word about her memory problems, or the strange things she sometimes did around the house. Elizabeth didn't want her inquisitiveness to fuel the fires of speculation.

'Perhaps,' she eventually said, agreeing. 'But you were the one who did. I would like to say that I am very grateful.'

'My pleasure.' Silence descended again. Tom glanced down at the puddle of sea water forming under his feet. 'Where should I change?'

The floorboards creaked as she moved towards the bathroom, pipes rattling as they delivered warm water to the sink. Tom held back from following her, but when she looked up to see he wasn't there, she moved to beckon him through. For a moment all she could do was stare at him as he stood in the doorway to the bathroom, the man who had saved her mother. Gratitude swelled inside her, and she wondered if there was anything she could ever do to repay such a thing as saving a person's life. 'There's plenty of hot water, and soap in that dish,' she said after a while. 'Take as long as you like.'

As Tom stepped into the bathroom Elizabeth looked away, suddenly aware of their proximity in such a small and private room. Edging past him, she made her way to the door. Just before he closed it, he held up the clothes and shoes and said, 'Thank you again for this. I appreciate it, miss.'

The urge to rush back in, reach out and hug him came to her, but she stifled it, and instead smiled and pointed to the sink. 'Get washed and changed before you catch a chill, and come down when you're ready.' Steam billowed towards her as he turned on the taps. 'But just before I go, could you do me a favour?' It seemed wrong to her that somebody who had done something so great should have to refer to her so formally. 'Please stop calling me miss. My name's Elizabeth.'

Tom just smiled, nodded his head. 'I know that,' he said, before closing the bathroom door.

Elizabeth's fingers tingled against the hot mugs of tea which she'd made for the people who had stuck around after the accident. Once those drinks were in the hands of the helpers, with a rag she found under the sink she set about mopping up the patches of sea water that Tom had left behind, then swept up the sand which crunched underfoot as she walked. It was another fifteen minutes before folk began to leave, reassured by the fact that Catherine Davenport was in bed and out of danger. Elizabeth returned to the living room to find it almost empty.

'You're leaving?' she asked James when she saw him buttoning his coat. Her father was finishing up what looked to be a large measure of brandy. Judging from his rosy cheeks, it was unlikely to have been his first. His eyes were still red and swollen from tears.

'I am going to leave you both in peace,' James said, reaching to stroke Elizabeth's face.

'We need to get some rest,' said her father as he stood up from his chair, setting his glass down on a small table. Elizabeth couldn't bear the thought of how terrible he must be feeling. He swept her up in a tight embrace.

'Stop worrying now, eh? She's going to be fine.' It was the safest place Elizabeth had ever known, yet still her father nodded to James who was hovering next to them. 'Tell her, won't you? She'll listen to you.'

'Your father's right, Lizzy. She's going to be just fine.' As James went to continue they heard the creak of the staircase, the plod of heavy feet. They turned to see Tom arriving in the hallway. Elizabeth's father stepped forwards, reaching for Tom's hand.

'Hello, young man, or should I say the hero of the hour. I believe you are the person who saved my wife.'

Tom nodded.

'I don't know how to thank you enough,' her father said. 'Please, tell me your name.'

Tom remained quiet, his fingers fussing at a fray in the jumper. 'This is Thomas, Daddy,' Elizabeth said, stepping in. 'We actually used to go to school together.'

'Well, we are very grateful to you, Thomas,' her father said. 'But I'm surprised to hear you were at school with Elizabeth. You look older.'

'A little bit, sir.'

'So, are you working now?'

'When I can. Mainly pollack and mackerel, plus a bit of netting for crayfish.' Fishermen populated both Tom and Elizabeth's family trees as far back as anybody knew. 'I have been working for Mr Cressa for the last three years, and where I can during the winter.'

'Three years?' Her father shared a glance with James. 'How old are you? Twenty-one? Twenty-two?'

'Eighteen, sir.'

Elizabeth's father appeared puzzled. 'You didn't choose to continue your education?'

Tom couldn't maintain his gaze then. 'I learnt what I had to, sir. Now I help my family.'

'Well,' said Dr Davenport, giving Tom a pat on the shoulder. 'That is very admirable. You must tell me your father's name so that I can congratulate him on having such a fine young man as a son.'

'It's Pat Hale,' said Tom.

Her father took a moment, a heavy breath in. 'Pat Hale, eh? You're his eldest son.'

'His only son, sir.'

'Yes, of course. I remember the unfortunate incident with your brother. I'm afraid I didn't recognise you.' Elizabeth watched her father, his mind elsewhere. 'Well, I do hope that in some of your father's sober moments he finds the time to be proud of you.' Elizabeth noticed Tom's cheeks flush, and just for a moment she wondered what had transpired, and why her father had said something so cruel. 'Now, if you'll excuse us, Thomas.' He patted him on the shoulder, guided him towards the door. 'We'd best get ourselves off to bed. Thank you once again.' James followed Tom from the house, kissing Elizabeth on the cheek just before he left. It came as a relief when her father closed the door.

When the house was empty of visitors, Dr Davenport directed Elizabeth back into the drawing room, guiding her to sit in one of the chairs. They remained in silence until her father spoke. 'I think it's very important we address what happened tonight, Elizabeth.'

'It's obvious, isn't it?'

He nodded. 'Yes, unfortunately it is. But we don't want to fuel the rumour mill, do we?' People were already starting to talk. Even in the shop last week she had felt the hush of a whispered conversation and knew somehow without hearing a word that it had been about her family. 'Sleep walking would be a much kinder story than the truth, for all involved.'

'Of course, Daddy. But . . .' she began, and then thought better of it.

'What is it, Elizabeth?'

'It's just . . .' she hesitated, licking her salty lips. The ocean was still loud in the distance, sounding now to her like a threat. 'This is as good as she is ever going to be from now on, isn't it?'

He sighed heavily, all his breath leaving him, and for a moment Elizabeth wished she could take her question back. The burden of it weighed heavily on her, but she had to know what to expect.

'Alzheimer's comes and goes in waves, Elizabeth. She will have good days, and there will be bad days. But when you are with the people you love there is nothing that one cannot find the strength for. One can always find the light through the dark when there is love, no matter what is expected of you.' His hand stroked heavily across her shoulders. 'Now go on, Elizabeth. Get yourself off to bed. It's been a long night.'

Moonlight illuminated the staircase as she climbed, her skin pale and cold in the grey light. Not only did she find herself feeling pleased to note the absence of an engagement ring, but also that she was thinking of Tom. Tonight, she realised that she had never been more grateful for anybody in the whole world. The image of him lingered in her mind, stumbling from the water with her mother under his arm, saving one of the people she loved most. She was still thinking about him when she slipped into her sheets, when she closed her eyes and eventually succumbed to sleep. That night she dreamt that she was the one who was struggling out at sea, fighting for breath, and that Tom was the one who came to rescue her.

Now

For a while Elizabeth sat at the table, staring at the basket of past wishes. For forty-nine years he had kept his promise, had always delivered. For the second time in as many minutes she got up to check that she hadn't made a mistake, telling herself that perhaps it had been windy overnight and that the pot had blown away. It was impossible to ignore the fact that Tom had always known how to account for that in the past, tucking his gift alongside the front step, just behind the rose planters. Never once had his gifts gone missing. Never once had he forgotten.

Could she have it wrong? The calendar hung above her from a pin tacked into the old plaster wall, so she ran a gnarled fingertip along the row until she came across the right date. September 7th. There it was, the little blue crocus she had painted in anticipation. Had she got the date itself wrong? Things like that happened lately, at her age more than she would have liked. Only last week she'd wandered down to the Roundhouse, the gallery in Porthsennen, to enquire whether any of her latest water-colours had sold. After waiting outside for the best part of an hour, watching as the surfers moved back and forth in the water, Old Man Cressa's grandson had walked past.

'Out for the last of the weather?' he'd called as his little spaniel scurried along a trail of scent on the ground.

'Waiting for them to open,' she'd said, pointing to the gallery, then tapping her watch. 'Am I running fast or are they running late? My watch says it's almost ten.'

'I'd say you're running about twenty-three hours too fast,' he'd said, laughing to himself. 'It's Sunday.'

Stupidity had swamped her at the realisation, and even more so over the thought of him laughing. If she'd have been a youngster it would have been a simple mistake, but when you're sixty-seven years old, she thought, it's a mistake of old age. And now, sitting in that robe and clinging on to a love that slipped her by, she couldn't have felt more foolish. What on earth was wrong with her? Who was she trying to kid?

The sight of the champagne felt like an insult, so she tipped what was left down the sink and put the dirty plates in the dishwasher. The basket of wishes was just as unfortunate, so that went back into the cupboard alongside the old bottle of champagne, his diary, and a few other gifts that he had left throughout the years.

'What are you looking at?' she asked Cookie when she saw him watching her. 'A silly old fool,' she offered quietly to herself. A single fat tear dripped onto the robe, the silk blushing as dark as her mood. 'What a senseless old woman you've become, Elizabeth.'

Pictures of Kate stared back at her accusingly from around the room. One in particular stood out. In the photograph, Kate was just twenty years old, wearing a harness with her feet strapped together and her arms spread wide, standing on the edge of a cliff surrounded by jungle greenery. Moments after that photograph had

26

been taken, she had thrown herself over the edge, her life secured by nothing more than the bungee cord and a large dash of hope. Born courageous, was what Elizabeth always said of her. Even as a child she never feared having a go at things. Nothing like Elizabeth, not in appearance or character, instead following her father in both. Kate would never have sat around waiting for gifts from a man who'd left her. When she thought things were over, that was it, done. That's why Kate wouldn't speak to her anymore, not since last November. Best part of a year without so much as a hello. Elizabeth missed her so much, and her two boys. They would have grown so much in the time she hadn't seen them. Elizabeth wished she could take back the things they had said, but that wasn't how life worked. It didn't seem to matter how many messages she left or phone calls she made, how many times she begged for forgiveness. You couldn't turn back the clock.

Standing at the window, she brushed the curtains aside, looked down to the coast and up the hill to where the old Mayon Lookout was positioned. A walk up there would have been her first stop in her plan for the day, and afterwards she would have driven out to Penzance to go to the theatre. That was Tom's wish in 1982; *I wish that I could take you to see a musical in the West End. Cats was good. I think you would have loved it.* Today she was due to see an acoustic guitar player, a woman singing. The closest she could get to fulfilling that wish. But she already knew she wasn't going to go. It wasn't 1982 anymore, and this wasn't the West End. Whosever life she had been trying to live all these years, it wasn't really hers. It was a life that belonged to another girl, one that stopped existing in many ways on the day that Tom left.

Heading upstairs, Elizabeth returned to her bedroom. Sitting on the edge of the bed, she opened the bedside drawer and removed a box of tissues. Underneath, she found a black and white photograph of Tom, standing without a shirt, his hands on his hips. The hardest thing was not that he didn't look like that anymore, but knowing instead that she had no idea of what he *did* look like now. Of knowing that he had changed, and she didn't know in what way. Fingers so old she barely recognised them as her own brushed across the image, before she placed it back into the drawer and covered it with the tissues. Sometimes it was best not to look.

'Pull yourself together, Elizabeth,' she told herself. Using a trick of old, she gave her cheeks a pinch for some colour, then fingered her hair into place. Grabbing a pair of walking trousers and a thick fleece from the wardrobe, she dressed, then picked up the robe from the bed. After a moment's hesitation she bundled it into a heap and tossed it to the bottom of the wardrobe. 'You're acting like a silly girl,' she said, dusting off her hands as if she had just completed a job well done.

Outside the house she found it was a perfect coastal day, bright and sunny with a light breeze. Clouds moved at speed overhead, and out near the horizon they lingered grey and heavy, offering the promise of rain. It was hard to ignore the old lookout behind her, the place she used to go to with Tom. The last time she'd climbed those steps to the lookout, it had made her knees ache. Was it so stupid to go there now? Pausing on the road, she stopped to look back over her shoulder, her gaze travelling up the green hill towards the small building on the top. What stopped her? A sense of regret perhaps, or even foolishness. Whatever it was, she continued along the road instead, reminding herself again that it was pointless to revisit the past.

With her plans for the day in ruins, she stopped at the café and ordered a cup of tea, sat to drink it at a small table overlooking the water.

'What are you doing sitting out here?'

Elizabeth looked up to see her oldest friend, Francine, just coming down the road with a newspaper tucked under her arm. Francine took her time thanks to a recent hip replacement. Balancing her weight on the table, she set her stick aside and lowered herself into a chair.

'Just an early morning cuppa,' Elizabeth said. The thought of admitting the real reason she was sitting there made her cheeks blush. Heat spread across her face, so she loosened the zipper on her fleece.

'Don't often see you wasting time like this,' Francine said as she helped herself to a sip of Elizabeth's tea. 'Why aren't you painting?'

'Oh, you know.'

Francine shook her head, waited for an answer.

'I just didn't fancy it.'

Her friend's eyes widened with surprise. 'What have you done with my Elizabeth?' Francine chuckled, before looking out to the clouds on the horizon. 'I would have thought a storm like that would have soon sparked your interest. What's up with you? Is it something to do with Kate again?'

Elizabeth loved Francine, and in all the time she had known her she hadn't changed at all. There might have been a few more wrinkles, but her hair was still dark chocolate brown and her lips as red as strawberries. Even her manicure was perfect. They had nothing in common really if you thought about it, but had shared a lifetime of highs and lows. Like a couple of sisters who bickered something rotten, they would have defended each other to the end. Elizabeth had learned early on that Francine was to be depended upon, and she had never forgotten it since. But although Elizabeth had told Francine some of her deepest secrets, she knew nothing of her ongoing connection to Tom and the gifts he left each year.

'Well, Kate's still not talking to me, but it's not that.'

'So, what is it then?'

'It's Tom,' Elizabeth said.

Francine thought for a moment, but the name needed no introduction. 'Thomas Hale?' Francine said with a smile. Elizabeth didn't like that smile one little bit. 'Now there's a name from the past. What about him?'

Was she really going to admit to this? Francine would think it silly, wouldn't she? Any lasting connection they had could be reduced to a concentrated version of life, forty-nine wishes that never really came true. It all seemed a bit daft now that she was preparing to say it aloud.

'It's the anniversary of the day we first kissed. That day he took me on a boat to the Brisons.'

Francine smiled at the memory. 'Never took you as the nostalgic type. What made you think of that now, after all these years?'

Elizabeth shook her head. Suddenly it felt hard to breathe, and she knew she just had to say it. 'I think about it every year.'

Francine glanced down at her hand, brushed her thumb against her wedding ring, loose on a thinning finger. 'A love that never disappeared, eh, even if he did.'

'Something like that.' Francine reached out, took Elizabeth's hand in her own. 'You think I'm silly, don't you?'

Memories of the past made her chuckle. 'I've always thought you were silly, Elizabeth, but it's got nothing to do with you loving Tom.' Her smile showed that she was joking. 'I wonder if he still thinks about you too. I bet he does.'

'I know he does,' Elizabeth said, before she had time to censor herself. 'At least I always thought he did.'

'What do you mean?'

Here goes, she thought. 'Because he never actually disappeared. He comes back every year.'

Francine shook her head with disbelief. 'What? Have you finally lost the plot?'

'I'm serious.'

'Elizabeth, darling, we haven't seen hide nor hair of him for what now?' she said, pausing to think. 'It must be fifty years.'

'I know we haven't, but he still comes. I know it's him. He leaves me gifts on the doorstep.'

Francine was quiet, trying to comprehend what she had just heard. 'What does he bring?' Her tone suggested she was humouring her.

'Don't say it like that, as if I've gone mad. Every year he brings me a blue crocus, just like he promised me he would. He always writes me a wish too, something we would have done together. And if you don't believe me I've got every one of those forty-nine wishes at home. It's him, I'm telling you. I even saw him once or twice.'

Something changed in Francine's tone, realising the seriousness with which Elizabeth spoke. 'OK, OK,' she said. 'I believe you.'

'Good.'

Francine sat back in her chair, her mouth hanging limp and wide with disbelief. 'Didn't he get married?'

Elizabeth closed her eyes, felt the same spark of guilt and jealousy that always stirred when she thought of his wife. 'He did.'

'And he still holds a candle for you?' she asked of nobody, shaking her head. 'Cheeky old bugger.'

'It's not like that.'

'Well,' said Francine, looking less than pleased with what she had learnt. 'I don't know what it's like, but it's obviously done you no good. Look how upset you are.'

Elizabeth pulled a tissue from her pocket and wiped her eyes. 'I'm not upset because he brings me presents every year.'

'Then why are you upset?'

'Because this year, he forgot.'

Francine drummed her nails against the brushed metal table. After a moment she shook her head. 'Unlikely if he never forgot before. Elizabeth, I hate to remind you, but none of us are getting any younger. I've just had a hip replaced, and your fingers are full of arthritis.'

'What are you saying?'

'Only that you don't hand deliver a gift to a girl you were in love with when you were eighteen, for forty-nine years, even when you're married to somebody else, and then not bother for the fiftieth.'

Elizabeth had been so preoccupied with how hurt she was, she'd never stopped to wonder why he had failed to deliver the present. 'You don't think . . .' The hairs on the back of her neck stood on end as the thought came to her, her mouth too dry to finish the sentence. Until today, Tom looked to her mind like the boy in the only photograph she had of him, but he'd be sixty-eight now. People she knew had died younger than that.

'Only one way to find out,' Francine said. 'Why don't you try to get in touch?'

'Well, I have his phone number, but what if his wife answers? Or his daughter?' Elizabeth had always kept his address and phone number written down, but she had never used it out of respect for the fact she knew he had a family. 'How would I explain who I am?'

'I'd say that doesn't really matter if it comes to the worst. Just tell them you're an old friend from Porthsennen.'

With some regret, Elizabeth realised that the truth was not all that different.

Her heart raced as she hurried along the road back to her cottage, the keys jangling in her pocket as her fingers fumbled to find them. Cookie arrived at the door, his cue the sound of the lock, his fur warm and his purring loud as he rubbed at her ankles.

'I haven't got time for your nonsense now,' she said, nudging him away. Her fingers wouldn't seem to grip the handle of the cupboard alongside the fireplace as she crouched down, too stiff from the cold, too arthritic from age. Taking a breath to calm herself, she focused, managed to get it open and pull out the basket containing every one of Tom's wishes. They scattered like autumn leaves on the floor. 'I'm so stupid,' she told Cookie. 'How could I not have even considered it?'

All her life she had been plagued by the thoughts of 'what if?' What if they could have been together? What if they had never argued that night? What if Tom had never gone to the lighthouse? Now the only 'what if' that mattered was whether something might have happened to him. They had had so many chances to put things right and never taken a single one of them. They had been so stupid. Panic rose as she rifled through the little blue notes, unable to find what she was looking for. And then, like a gem shining in the dirt, she saw the white piece of paper with his address and telephone number. Snatching it up into her sweaty palm, she moved across the room and grabbed the phone.

Her fingers shook as she dialled the number, looking at her face in the mirror as she waited for the call to connect. Her features had changed so much, grown so old. Why hadn't she trusted her feelings, that sense that he would never have let her down? After a while she realised that she was still waiting, that the call hadn't connected. As she looked down at the little scrap of paper, she noticed that it was an old number from the seventies, so she pulled out her phone book to find the new area code for London, before dialling again. Still she got nothing, so dialled instead for the operator. After a moment the call connected.

'Operator, how can I help?'

'Hello,' Elizabeth began. 'I'm trying to reach a number, but the call won't go through. Can you check it for me?' Elizabeth gave the number, then waited as the operator made whatever necessary checks. Gazing about the room she saw her past, felt the cold of the first night she had returned to this cottage with Tom, recalled the things they had done in his room. The pain of the memory forced her eyes tight shut, the earliest tears welling in her eyes. Then a noise on the line.

'I'm afraid that number is no longer in use.'

'If I give you an address?'

'I can try. What is it?' Elizabeth gave the last known address that she had for Tom, no clue if he was even still living there. What other choice did she have? If Kate was talking to her she might have been able to look him up on that Internet thing, but without her daughter's help she had no idea how to do it herself. 'I'm really sorry,' the operator said. 'The number for that address is ex-directory. I can't help you, I'm afraid.'

Her body crumpled into the nearest seat, the receiver still clutched in her hand. Too long had passed, too much life lived apart. Cookie gazed at her, indifferent to her pain. It had always seemed easy to live here on the furthest reaches of the UK coast, miles away from Tom when she knew that he would be coming back, even if it was only once a year. But what now? To miss this day meant he was never coming again. His absence implied that he might already have . . . 'No,' she said to herself, shaking her head. 'Don't think that way.' Surely she would have felt it, would have somehow subconsciously known if he had died. And as she had had no such feeling it meant there was still a chance that she could find him. She'd found him once before, so why not find him again?

Her steps thundered up the wooden staircase, her feet moving faster than they had in years. The suitcase smelt old and musty as she pulled it out from under the bed, dust making her sneeze. She hadn't used it in over a year, not since she had last visited Kate. The trip when she'd told her daughter the truth. After the initial buzz of activity, she found herself out of breath sitting on the edge of the bed, surrounded by clothes, toiletries thrown in the case at all manner of angles amenable to leakage. The thought that she was being stupid crossed her mind, but she pushed the idea away.

'Get it together, Elizabeth,' she told herself. 'You're not going to make it to London like this.'

The sun was warmer as she left her cottage behind, travelling in a taxi to the train station. And although she was relieved to finally be on her way, the fear of what she was heading towards almost made her turn back. All those times she'd told herself to go to the door when he delivered her gifts, and all those times she hadn't. The same fears gripped her now; what if it wasn't the same? What if she felt differently? What if too much time had passed and really there was nothing left? Those fears were still there, but now a different idea overpowered them, driving her forward. What if they had shared a whole life together? What if he did still love her, despite the fact they hadn't? And perhaps most important of all, what if they still had time for just one more wish?

Then

When she awoke from a fitful sleep, early before the sun had broken the monotony of the dark sky, she left her bedroom to find an atmosphere of regret hanging over the house. It was heavier than any winter sea mist that would soon embrace their part of the Cornish coastline. Her parents were still in bed, and she found that she didn't want to be there alone. Grabbing her bag and a coat, she headed from the house, down towards the sea.

The view that greeted her was quite different to the endless black of the ocean that had tried to claim her mother only hours before. Sunshine graced the coastal road, trimmed with thatched cottages and granite roofs as first light broke the night. Gulls swooped and cawed overhead, circling above fishing boats stuffed with pollack and mackerel. Drifts of smoke rose from the chimneys of fishermen's cottages, wives warming hearths to welcome their husbands home.

'Miss Davenport, would you do an old man a favour and come down here?' Elizabeth looked up to see Old Man Cressa. He was standing at the edge of his boat, the *Princess of the Sea*. It was a vessel built for one man, a lonely life of early starts, his working day over before most had begun. Two of his front teeth were missing, yet his smile was only enhanced by the depleted sum of incisors and the overgrown beard that skimmed the centre of his chest. 'I heard about what happened last night,' he said as he shook his head. His voice was soft, and seemed even softer as he asked, 'How's your mother doing this morning?'

'Much better, thank you. She was sleep-walking because of a fever.' He nodded, unquestioning of her lie. 'Was the catch good?' she probed, changing the subject.

'Not up to much if the truth be told. Last night's storm stirred up the waters. The weather that will feed a farmer will starve a fisherman. Seems summer's in for an early finish.' He tossed her the edge of a net, still wet with seaweed caught in the knots. He motioned for her to pull tight, while he set about bundling the other end into a bucket. He nodded to her satchel draped across her body. 'Isn't it a little fresh for you to be out drawing at this time of the day? Shouldn't you be at home helping your mother?'

'Perhaps,' she agreed. 'But it's about last night that I'm here. I was looking for Mr Hale. Tom,' she added, feeling a little foolish using his first name, as if they were friends. She didn't want to confuse Old Man Cressa with the implication she was looking for Tom's father. Everybody knew him. He was the local drunk, could often be found slumped on a bench, or sheltering by the moored boats. That was why her father was disappointed when he discovered that Tom was a Hale last night. His idea of what it meant to be a Hale coupled with Tom saving his wife just didn't fit. 'Is he here?'

'Still out at the moment.' He nodded towards the water. 'Why don't you come back later once the catch is in?'

'I'd rather wait, if that's OK.' It was only right to thank him again for what he had done, but Elizabeth also knew it wasn't just that. It was something she couldn't describe; thinking of him made her smile, made her wonder what it might feel like to have him smile back at her. What would it be like to meet with him in his own life, rather than embroiled in the momentary turmoil of her own?

'Then you'd better get yourself into the lifeboat station. You can keep warm in there until he's back. Doors are open.' He looked over at the gently rolling sea. The view was better now, the light already stronger. 'Shouldn't be too long.'

Elizabeth bid farewell to Old Man Cressa and did as she was told, entering the lifeboat station via the heavy front door and down the steps. It was dark inside, quite different from when she'd last been here, watching the launch of the *Susan Ashley* as part of the spring fete, a celebration of winter passing and the promise of calmer waters. But the smell was unchanged; the scent of sea and brass, old rope, the gentle hum of the ocean underfoot. It felt safe, and strong. Elizabeth could remember seeing Tom at that fete, dressed in an oversized yellow wax jacket and a hat too large for his head which kept slipping over his eyes. He was climbing the ropes, hauling himself on deck, along with a vast number of other kids who were there to celebrate. Tom's father was a volunteer then, part of Coxswain Nicholas's crew. Yet she could remember her own father making a comment, something about the Hale boys being as troublesome as their father. Elizabeth had thought it looked as if Tom was enjoying himself, his little brother Daniel too. Everything changed for the Hales after he died. Everything she supposed, except her father's opinion.

How much time had passed when she heard the door to the lifeboat station open? His feet on the steps? She was so lost in thought, she had missed his boat coming in. Tom appeared, wearing a blue jumper, worn and pulled at the cuff, a little large on his frame. His hair was wet, like it had been last night, falling in wavy clumps across his forehead. With feet as heavy as lead she stumbled from her chair, feeling awkward and clumsy as he arrived.

'Old Man Cressa said you were looking for me,' he said, seeming confused. 'Everything all right?'

Her fingernails pressed into her palm as she clung onto her satchel, taking a step forward. 'Yes. I just wanted to say thank you for what you did. You risked your life and saved my mother's.' While she had been talking to Old Man Cressa she had seen the seaweed tarnishing the beach, the driftwood that had washed up in last night's storm. It must have been a squally sea into which he had chosen to throw himself.

'And I'd do it again if the need arose.' He stepped out of his waders and went to slip his feet into his shoes, only to realise that they belonged to her father. 'I'm sorry,' he said, motioning to the brown brogues. 'I was intending to return them.'

'It's OK. He doesn't wear them.' Her satchel hung heavily between them as she offered it to him. After a moment he stepped forwards and took it.

'What's this?'

40

'Your clothes. I dried them for you.' Last night when she couldn't sleep, she'd got up and hung them over an airer in front of the dying fire in the drawing room. Now they smelt faintly of soot. He took the bag and peered inside, before pulling them out and tucking them under his arm.

'Thank you,' he said. He set them down and knelt to lace his shoe. 'How is your mother today?'

'She'll be fine,' she said, trying to soften the edge of mistruth. Lying to Tom felt awkward after what he'd done. It was a strange feeling to her, that disconnect in her loyalties; it was impossible to tell Tom the truth without betraying her family, and yet despite that understanding she found herself wanting to tell him everything.

'That's good then. But you know, it wouldn't have mattered to wait to return these.' He motioned to his clothes. 'It's chilly out this morning. I reckon summer's nearly over. You'll catch a cold.'

'Well it's just that I was hoping to get you alone.' He smiled at that, appeared surprised. 'Oh,' she said, realising the implications of what she just said, feeling heat flood her face. 'I didn't mean it like that. No, honestly,' she said when he began laughing. 'I'm engaged to be married.'

He looked down at her hand, becoming mock serious. 'I don't see a ring. Doesn't seem like a fair arrangement to me, to agree to marry somebody and not get a ring. Especially if the man is a doctor.'

A sense of disappointment washed over her, the realisation that everybody knew she was supposed to marry James. It was true, she liked him well enough, but the truth was that while she'd been quite impressed by his stories about London when he'd first arrived in

Porthsennen, now that she'd heard all those, sometimes twice, she wasn't sure what there was left that she liked so much anymore.

'Well, what would you know?' she asked, defensively.

'I know a bit,' he said, still smiling.

'Asked a lot of girls to marry you, have you?'

'Not yet I haven't,' he told her, laughing. 'But when I do, I'll make sure I do it with a ring.'

It was impossible not to feel foolish, being engaged without a ring to a man she wasn't all that sure about. Yet for some reason she still felt obliged to defend it. 'Look, if you must know, he hasn't been home to collect it yet. It's a family heirloom.'

He was still smiling, but this time sincerity shone from it. 'It's none of my business. But if I was marrying you, I certainly wouldn't be leaving you without a ring. I'd want everybody to know you were mine.'

'Oh,' she said, aware that her face was growing hotter by the second. A cool draught crept in from the window and so she moved towards it.

'But that's beside the point. You're marrying Dr Warbeck, aren't you?'

'Yes,' she stuttered. 'Yes I am.'

A moment of silence got the conversation back on track. 'So, jokes aside, you didn't just come here to say thank you or return my clothes.'

She shook her head. 'No, there was something else. I wanted to ask you about what happened,' she said. 'I thought it was better to do that in private, without prying ears. It's about how my mother ended up in the water.'

He took a heavy breath in, did up the buttons on his coat, all traces of that cheekiness lost. 'I know somewhere we can go, if you like. It'll be warmer there than it is here at least.' Picking up a small satchel of his own, he turned to the steps. A moment later he stopped, that smirk returning. 'Come on then. That is unless you think people will talk, what with you being as good as married and all?'

They left the lifeboat station behind and walked through the village, just stirring from the blustery night before. The small cottage in which Elizabeth knew that Tom lived with his parents produced a thin slither of smoke from its chimney. His mother was probably already working. Thoughts of Tom's brother came to mind. Gossip had reverberated around the village after Daniel's death, the women decrying what a terrible shame it was to lose a little lad like that, whispering of how he should never have been left alone, but Elizabeth couldn't remember exactly what had happened.

After a climb up the headland, they reached the old Mayon Lookout. It was a small structure, cubical almost, a granite buttress carved from local rock standing high on the craggy prominence. From here you could see across Longships Reef to the lighthouse of the same name, all the way to Cape Cornwall in the north and Land's End in the south. The building had lain derelict since it was decommissioned as a coastguard lookout in the forties, yet as Tom pulled open the creaky wooden door, she saw evidence of life before her in the shape of a small pile of black ashes in the corner of the room, a gas cooking stove, and a wicker fishing creel that looked to have seen better days. The crumbling window frames shook as the wind struck the glass.

The hinges on the fishing creel creaked as Tom lifted the lid, producing a handstitched quilt which he shook out into the space before him. It gave off a faint scent of the ocean as he passed one end to Elizabeth. 'It'll be much warmer if you get under here.'

She wanted to, but the story would travel faster than a coastal wind if anybody saw her sneaking away with a local boy like that. A Hale no less.

'Nobody saw us coming here,' he said, as if reading her thoughts. 'And you're quite safe. I'm not about to try anything.'

It felt adventurous in some way to be with Tom, independent and exciting. The door slammed shut behind her, and she found a position on the stone floor. Keeping his word, Tom draped the quilt over her legs, and Elizabeth was aware that as he did so his face brushed close to hers, his breathing audible. A smile crossed her lips when his gaze flicked to hers, and suddenly her mouth felt dry. When she thought of the gossip that would abound if anybody knew her smile faded, and with that Tom pulled away.

'Who sewed this?' she asked as she looked down at the quilt for a distraction. It was how she imagined the earth might look from above if she could see all the irregular rock walls and multi-coloured fields knitted together.

'My grandmother,' he said, pointing to some of the scalloped edges. 'And then my mother added these bits. It's kind of a family tradition. Something they hand down upon marriage. In fact, I think this bit might have been my great-grandmother's.'

'It's beautiful,' Elizabeth said. 'What are you doing with it?'

'It's the best quilt we have in our house. And it's cold up here.'

'You could just go home,' she suggested. 'That's what most people do after work.'

'Suppose it depends on the home.' It was an idea she could understand. Since her mother got sick she had wanted less and less to return home at the end of the day.

'It's very nice,' she said, not wanting to think of her reluctance to return to her own home.

'Grandpa was a herder, you see,' Tom said, his attention focused on the quilt. 'One of the landsmen. Kept sheep out near Kelynack.' It was a small settlement only a few miles from there. 'That's why Nanna chose browns and yellows. For the land. Mum added the blues for the sea, because Dad is a fisherman.' It was his turn for a moment of unease, as he tried to clarify what he had said. 'At least, he was a fisherman, before he started drinking.'

Elizabeth knew that Pat Hale's drinking corresponded to the loss of Tom's brother, but she didn't want to ask about it. So instead she watched as Tom set about lighting the small gas stove, after which he produced a pan from his fishing creel. He filled it with water and set it to boil before sitting down next to her. The warmth felt good, so Elizabeth held her hands close to it. When he opened the edge of the quilt, resting his legs underneath, it didn't feel wrong, but still her gaze flicked to the door to ensure they were alone. It surprised her to realise that she wanted that, to be just the two of them.

'Do you like being a fisherman?' she asked him.

Checking the water as bubbles began to rise, he shook his head. 'Not much, but it pays OK. I don't really like the sea.'

'I love the sea,' she told him.

'I doubt you would like it very much if you did my job. There's not much fun to be had waking in the dark and waiting for fish to catch every morning.' He dropped a tea-bag in the water and dabbed at it with a spoon. 'I'd have rather stayed at school like you did. But after Daniel died I had to leave. We needed the money.'

Was it all right to probe if he was the one who brought it up? The need to ask him about his brother swelled so fast that she began talking before she even realised. It was a personal matter, and yet after what he had done for her mother last night, she felt somehow as if it wasn't an intrusion.

'What happened to your brother?'

The light from outside was weak, but what was there cast his features in a golden yellow haze as he stared straight ahead. The sight of him thinking made Elizabeth want to reach out and touch him, hold him close to her body. His soft gaze spoke of a depth for the way he felt about the world, she could sense it. Even though she wanted to know his answer, know all about Daniel, she wanted even more to stop time right there and then so that the moment they were sharing might never end.

'He was sailing when he shouldn't have been. Winter weather, the sea too rough.'

'Oh, my goodness,' she said, bringing one hand up to her open mouth. It made what he had done for her mother last night even more commendable. 'And still you jumped in.'

He shrugged his shoulders. 'Like I said, anybody would have done the same.'

Elizabeth didn't believe that for a moment. A lot of people would have been too scared, would have called for help and decried what an awful tragedy it was without once getting a foot wet. 'My mother was so lucky you were there.'

'Well, you can thank my father for it. If he'd been at home my mother wouldn't have sent me out to look for him and I wouldn't have been there to see her slip.'

Elizabeth thought of the breakwater, the gently sloping wall that was built to withstand the power of the sea. It had a heavy footprint, and anybody who fell from the top would surely have hit his head on the way down. Was it possible that in her confusion, her mother had jumped?

'So, she did . . . slip?'

The tinny resonance as his fingers tapped the edge of the cup broke through the silence. The light intensified, streaming through the window as the sun breached the crest of the land. 'Of course, Elizabeth. What else could have happened?'

The truth was on the tip of her tongue, but she thought of her father and how angry he would be. Still, she wanted to tell him, because there in that shelter with Tom she found that for the first time in months she could breathe, when she had never even realised before that she had been drowning.

'She's been ill. Confused.' Guilt swamped her in the place of the truth. The betrayal of her family didn't feel good, and yet as Tom reached for her hand, she found that she wanted to keep talking. 'She tried to take a boat once before.'

'I'm sorry about that. But she slipped, Elizabeth. That was all.' And then he changed the subject. 'I seem to

47

remember that you once liked to paint. Do you still do it?'

'Yes,' she said, surprised he knew, relieved the conversation had moved on.

'Are you any good?'

'Some people say I am, and sometimes I think I am. My father just thinks it's a silly hobby.'

Silence lingered between them until Tom set the mug down. 'There's nothing silly about what makes you happy.' The sun was much stronger now and the heat under the blanket was becoming unbearable. The sound of the waves roared beneath her as they brushed the rocks of Longships Reef. It looked magnificent, the water bright with sunlight, but the beauty of it failed to raise her spirits. Since her mother had become sick, she found it hard to enjoy the world around her, conspiring as it was to take her away.

'Do you ever dream of a different life, where there are no expectations of you? Where you wouldn't have to fish to help your family?'

'Dreaming is a luxury of the rich, Elizabeth,' Tom said as he stood up. He set the tin mug back onto the floor, the wrong way up so that it might drain in his absence. 'My job is to put food on the table for my mother. That's all I know.' It was clear that their meeting was coming to an end. They were two people in the same place and yet they had two totally different lives. Wind blew in as he opened the door. 'But I'd like to see your paintings sometime, hear more about your dreams.'

That didn't make sense to her. 'Why would you want to? Doesn't sound as if you much believe in dreams.'

'Of course I do. And wishes, desires that people have for the future. It's dreams that make us who we are.'

48

The wind dropped a little as they descended the steps. 'I thought you just said dreams were for the rich. Surely you must wish for something if that's what you think.'

They walked alongside each other, slower than they'd ascended, as if perhaps neither of them wanted their meeting to end. Elizabeth knew that she didn't. 'I suppose I do. Just not dreams like you've got.'

'Like what then?' she asked, stopping on the trail. He continued a few more steps, then turned to look at her. 'Please?'

'A nice life. Enough food. Everyday things.' The idea forced Elizabeth's arms across her chest. How foolish she felt again. How selfish and grand her ideas really were.

His hair blew in the wind, and soon enough he turned and continued down the path. Was that it, their meeting was over? Disappointment flooded her; she wasn't ready for that. 'Can we meet like this again?'

He smiled as she rushed to catch up. 'You want to?'

It wasn't a good idea, she knew that. And getting away with it this time didn't mean she would again. People would love to gossip about her being out with Tom, a boy from a disreputable family, and she the doctor's daughter. People would think it improper, and James wouldn't be pleased. But still, she had enjoyed this morning, and liked the fact that coming here had been her own choice.

'Yes,' she said. Her heart raced a little, a sense of excitement tingling in her fingertips.

The moment of silence before his answer was excruciating. 'Well, then I'd love to,' he said eventually, much to her relief. 'Maybe you can show me your paintings later, let me see what your dreams look like.'

As they arrived outside his cottage Elizabeth could hear Tom's family inside, and other voices just up ahead. 'I'd better go,' she said.

'Before somebody sees you,' he replied with a smile. For a second he leaned in, and she thought he was going to kiss her. Her breath caught in her throat, but then he just brushed her shoulder. Following his movement, she saw dust from the old walls of the lookout scatter to the ground. 'Shall we meet at seven, or is that too late?'

'It's perfect,' she whispered as he pulled away.

Her stomach turned over on itself as she walked towards home, as if nerves had got the better of her. What was that sense of disappointment she felt? Was it because she was leaving, or because when he'd leaned in, she'd thought he was going to kiss her and yet he hadn't? Maybe it wasn't disappointment at all; maybe it was just nerves. The urge to glance back just one last time took control over her movements. And as she gazed over her shoulder there was Tom, still watching her. He waved, and her stomach turned again. No, she thought, it wasn't nerves. It wasn't disappointment either. It was excitement, the anticipation that for the first time in her life she didn't know what was going to happen next.

Now

The train was not an easy option, but it was the only option. Driving there was out of the question. Although Elizabeth knew that she was sailing into unknown waters, she also knew that she had no other choice. Her stomach was in knots, somersaulting with every twist and turn as the train rocketed through the countryside. The words on the pages of the book she had taken to pass the time seemed to dance around, and she was unable to get through more than a few lines before she was right back where she started. Eventually she closed her eyes, listened to the rhythmic pulse of the tracks, thinking about the boy she met when she was seventeen. The picture she had in her mind was as clear as it was then, standing on the stairs dressed in her father's clothes, completely out of his depth. Her thoughts wandered to the moment when he emerged from the water with her mother at his side, and how his voice on that night had calmed her more than anything else. His presence in her life had brought such freedom, allowed her to consider what she wanted, and who she was. Before Tom she had never considered how the dreams that burned inside her might come true.

After two changes the train pulled into Paddington station and she stood up with her suitcase, her palms sweaty and her grip on the handle poor. Her stop at Plymouth was nothing compared to this, the cacophony of announcements combined with the rumble of feet and stink of engines. Many years ago she had walked through this same station with such certainty and excitement, but now as she stood on the platform with the bustle of bodies moving all around her and no idea where to go or where to start, she felt as if she had been transported into a different world. Her little village was so quiet, a place where the hours felt endless, where you could hear the waves breaking against the shore even when it was busy with tourists. Here people moved as if the hours offered little more than minutes, their heads down, angled into the screen of their phone. Overwhelmed by it all, and with no clue where to go from there, she took a seat on one of the benches to give the crowds a chance to disperse, herself a moment to collect her thoughts.

By the time she got moving she realised that almost everything seemed different from before. It was over forty years since she had been to London, and even after ten minutes of trying she couldn't work out the map. The machine in the wall, from which if her observations were right, she was supposed to acquire tickets, was an even bigger mystery. People punching in numbers and inserting cards, rushing off at speed. Where were all the people who worked here? Why couldn't she talk to an employee? Through the sea of heads she came across a line, a huge bank of ticket sellers beyond, but between her and the cashier was a queue five rows deep. It made her think of rock concerts she had seen on the television. Things Kate liked when she was young. Her fingers brushed her purse, the phone just inside. Should she send her daughter a message, tell her what she was doing? No, she decided. There wasn't time for that right now. Hoping her legs would see her through the wait, she headed towards the line, but was stopped by a young man in the queue.

'Do you need some help?' Elizabeth looked up. His face was round, his beard a fluffy auburn mass that seemed strangely familiar. What a relief he seemed, appearing like an angel, and she wanted to reach out and hug him for suddenly making her feel that her inexplicable decision to come to London was not only right, but necessary. 'You look a bit lost,' he said.

'I am. I have no idea how to work those machines, and I've come all the way from Cornwall and now I don't know what to do or where to go.' Emotion was building, a mix of relief and anxiety, all of which seemed to work together to form a lump in her throat.

'Where are you trying to get to?' the man asked.

'I don't even know that,' she said, before reaching in her bag and rummaging for that slip of paper with the address from years before. The address she could only hope Tom was still living at. 'A place called Hampstead,' she said, reading the paper.

'Sounds like you've had quite a journey,' he said, reaching for her case, pointing towards the machines. 'Come on, I'll help you. It's easier than it looks.'

Perhaps it was the exhaustion, the anxiety, or just absolute relief, but she reached out and took the young man by the arm. 'Thank you,' she said, blinking a tear away. 'I would have been here all day in that queue, and I don't have the time to waste.'

'This is London,' he laughed. 'Nobody has.'

Less than half an hour later she found herself in the relative calm of Hampstead tube station, and thanks to the young man's help, only minutes from where she believed Tom's house to be. Feet drummed the corridors, the smell of oil and food thick in the station, but the help from the stranger had bolstered her. This was doable, she told herself as she stepped outside into the heat of the city. It struck her that there was no breeze, no saltiness to the air, yet life continued; mothers with pushchairs, men and women in suits. The little slip of white paper that she had kept for over forty years shook in her hand with the rhythm of her nerves as she tried to remember where to go.

'How have you spent your whole life here?' she said aloud, talking to Tom despite his absence, as she often did as a way of imagining him alongside her. 'So far from home.' It seemed impossible to think Tom had lived in this place for close to fifty years, but she hoped for her sake he had. This was the only way she was going to be able to find him.

Only once had she made this trip before, the occasion when she first acquired Tom's telephone number and address. The idea of a reunion hadn't gone as planned that time, but her memory of that trip had left her with a certain sense that she knew where she was going. But that was a long time ago, and life had changed. They had changed. Would he answer the door? Would his wife be there? She hoped not, but felt guilty for even thinking it. Would they understand her arrival? With each step it became harder to breathe as she wound down the street following the map of her memory. It was exhausting, and her fingers were sore from wheeling her case. And then, in the window of an expensive looking bakery the sight of herself – hair all limp, her face red and shiny with sweat – held her back. Throughout the whole journey, her mind had been focused on how Tom might have changed. But what about how *she* had changed? What in the hell was he going to make of her in the state she was in?

In her mind he had remained for ever beautiful, blessed by youth, but it was impossible to deny her own ageing. What others would call womanly things, moisturisers, fancy clothes, or stylish haircuts, had always seemed like a bit of a bother to Elizabeth. They were things for women like Francine. What did she need with frivolities like that when she spent her life in front of an easel painting? Even now there were traces of blue paint on her wrists. Her fingernails were never neatly shaped, just snipped practically so that she could work unhindered. If she was honest with herself, she had weathered much like the thatching on her cottage roof, which considering the bucket catching drips in the bathroom, was to say not that well at all.

The thought of standing in front of him like that took her breath away, and she had to take a moment for herself. Crossing the road, she took a seat in the bus shelter outside a Waterstones bookshop. Licking a tissue found in her pocket, she managed to remove some of the blue paint from her wrists. The zipper of her bag was a struggle for her gnarled fingers, but she got it open and located her toiletry bag, using the small attached mirror to look closely at her face. Crepey eyes stared back, red from tears shed on the train, born from fears over what she might find. The inside of the bag smelled of old cosmetics, and she found the remains of a lipstick that was no doubt as old as she was. It was probably something Kate used to play with as a girl, and Elizabeth was relieved to find that it was still moist enough for a dab of pink to rub into her cheeks. For so many years she had dreamed of this reunion, but now all she could think was that she wasn't ready. Not physically, and certainly not emotionally.

And she wondered then if she had ever really been ready for it. Because although she thought she knew why she had never opened the door, what about Tom? What had stopped him from knocking? Had he not wanted to see her? Perhaps they had both feared the consequence of reality. In their model of a shared life they couldn't get it wrong, couldn't hurt each other, at least no more than either of them already had. There was no disappointment, no mistakes. But the dream was finally over. Now she was here in London, and she couldn't fail to knock on his door this time. Now she had to face reality, all the things they'd said, and all the things they hadn't.

After a while she composed herself, continued down the street filled with different styles of home; Victorian, Georgian, cottages she couldn't date. London really was the melting pot people described it as. The streets all looked different to her, but eventually she found the house she thought she recognised. A man in his fifties opened the door.

'Yes?' he asked.

A portly face stared back at her, a soft body inadequately hidden by a stained white vest. It made her think of a poster Kate had in her bedroom as a teenager, that action hero with no hair who liked to swear a lot. 'I was looking for Thomas Hale,' she said, unable to hide her mounting disappointment. 'I'm sorry, he must have moved.'

'Think you might have the wrong house,' said the man, chewing on a half-eaten doughnut.

'Yes, my mistake,' she said, going to turn away. 'It was a long time ago.'

'No, lady, you don't get what I mean. I was born here, fifty odd years ago.' Elizabeth stopped, took another look at the man, before standing back to review the house. 'Before that it was me mum that lived here, so I don't think you've got the right place.'

Was it possible? Even on a second glance the house looked the same to her. 'What number is this?'

'Fifty-three.'

She sighed. 'That's what I was looking for.' She handed him the piece of paper.

'Got the wrong road, love. Just keep going that way,' he said, pointing down the road, 'and you'll come across it.'

And sure enough it didn't take long before she found herself facing the house she recognised as his. Although the previous house had seemed familiar, this time she knew she was right, could feel that she'd been there before in the nerves that simmered through her. She could see the bench she had once sat on, waiting for the courage to knock on the door. This time she wasn't going to let her fears get the better of her.

Her heart was pounding as she pushed open the gate, her mouth dry. The path was only short, and nowhere near long enough to give her the time she needed for last minute preparations. What was she going to find? As she stood on the step, her knuckles braced to knock, she realised she was on the cusp of everything she had wished for throughout her life. He was just on the other side of the door, or at least she hoped he was. When she heard a woman's voice she hesitated a moment longer. His wife? Oh, good Lord, she thought as her nerves took over. What on earth was she doing? What was she going to say to her? Her hand fell, her feet shuffling backwards, but before she could change her mind the door opened. And standing on the other side was a woman, just a little bit younger than Kate, who must be – undoubtedly if the black hair was anything to go by – Tom's daughter.

'Can I help you?' the woman asked.

Could she? Why hadn't she prepared anything to say? 'I was looking for Mr Hale, Tom. Thomas Hale,' she said, the tremor in her voice betraying her nerves.

The woman glanced down at the suitcase. 'And you are?'

'An old friend from a long time ago.'

The woman thought for a moment, seemingly nonplussed by the idea, before looking down to check her watch. 'I have to go now. He's not really up to visitors.'

But then she heard his voice. 'Who is it, Alice?' It was unmistakably Tom, and Elizabeth had to summon all her strength not to barge past and rush to him. 'Tell them we're not interested.'

That seemed to raise a smile on both Alice and Elizabeth's face. 'He's not at his best at the moment. Maybe you could come back later, or tomorrow?'

But Elizabeth hadn't come all this way to leave so easily, not now she knew he was right there. 'If I could just say hello. I've come all the way from Cornwall.'

'From Cornwall?' Something, Elizabeth wasn't sure what, registered on Alice's face then. 'OK, maybe it wouldn't hurt. Follow me.'

Closing the door gently behind her, Elizabeth couldn't believe she was in his house. Nervous shakes took control over her body, and for a moment she became that same awkward girl who first stepped foot inside his cottage. 'What did you say your name was?' Alice asked as they headed down the hall, but she didn't have time to answer.

'It's Elizabeth,' Tom said, standing with a stick in the doorway, his hair grey, his frame small. Smaller than she remembered, at least. Tears welled in Elizabeth's eyes; she felt unable to breathe, and despite all the things she had longed to say, all words failed her. He smiled then, and the thought that he was pleased to see her made her heart pound against her chest, her fingers tingle. A moment of absolute relief. 'How did you know where to find me?'

Alice stepped closer to her, her mouth limp with shock as if she'd just seen a ghost. 'You're Elizabeth?' She turned to her father. '*The* Elizabeth?'

'Yes,' said Tom to Alice, although his gaze never once left Elizabeth. 'I was hoping you would come. I never thought you would, but I'm so glad you did.'

'Why don't we go through to the living room?' Alice eventually said. Despite his appearance, which was that of an old man, Elizabeth could see the eighteen-year-old boy she had fallen for all those years before as she followed, feeling Alice's eyes on her all the way. Her hands shook with wanting, desperate to reach out, hug him, kiss his lips. But she did none of those things.

'Elizabeth,' he said, stepping forwards. His hands hovered close by; little white tufts of hair sprouted from his knuckles, speckled with liver spots on the back. She wanted to touch him, but Alice's presence held her back. 'I'm so pleased to see you.'

'Me too,' she said after a moment, her voice shaking. He reached up and moved to touch her cheek, yet without warning she pulled away. Just for a second, the reality of what was happening was all too much. His hand dropped and the moment was lost.

'Does one of you want to explain what's going on?' Alice said as she followed them into the living room. 'Did you call her, Dad?' Elizabeth felt like an alien just arrived on Earth, unwelcome in the shadow of the photographs on the wall, images of a life she knew nothing about. Where was his wife? What would Mrs Hale say when she came home to find Elizabeth here? How could she explain what had brought her here today?

'No,' Tom said. 'I didn't have her number,' he said, as if that was an excuse. 'I'm sorry I couldn't make it this year.'

'Oh, that's all right,' Elizabeth said, as if she hadn't spent most of that morning in tears over his absence.

'Then how did you know how to find him?' Alice asked.

Only the truth served her in that moment, so she told it the only way she could. 'I've always known,' Elizabeth said, feeling somehow ashamed that she both had the address and had never visited before. 'But I didn't know whether you were still living here.'

'It's a long way to come on the off chance, isn't it?'

Elizabeth wished it was just the two of them, and then felt guilty for the thought. What right did she have to such expectations?

'Alice, love,' Tom said, moving to his daughter. 'You needed to get going, didn't you? Weren't you heading off when Elizabeth surprised us?'

'Well I was, but . . .' Elizabeth realised her visit had thrown the young woman, upset the foundations upon which her life was built. Her voice was soft, just for Tom. 'I can stay if you want.'

Tom shook his head. 'I think we'll manage. And anyway, we've got a lot to talk about after all this time.'

With a degree of reluctance, Alice nodded. 'OK, well I'll be back tomorrow.' Turning to Elizabeth she said, 'It was nice to meet you,' although Elizabeth doubted the sentiment was true.

After Alice left, Tom guided her to the settee, and took a seat in the chair by her side. 'She's quite protective of me. Especially now.'

'Daughters,' she said, and he smiled knowingly.

'Cup of tea?' Tom eventually asked.

Elizabeth nodded, and after he left for the kitchen she took the chance to look around, glad for a moment to herself. The house was much grander than anything she expected before coming inside. The ceilings were high and corniced, and a fireplace crackled with a golden log molten in the centre. It was otherwise silent, but she couldn't help but wonder about the presence of his wife. Where was she?

Drawn like a moth to light, she moved towards the pictures on the wall, each an image of a life well lived, his family throughout the decades they had spent apart. In some he was engaged in fatherly duties; teaching Alice to ride a bike, erecting a tent. In most of the pictures he was with his daughter at various stages of life. Elizabeth had always imagined him being a good father, and it seemed that she had been right. The photographs transported her back to 1975; she never could forget that year, or the wish he left her. *I wish we could raise a family together.* How she wished that one could have come true.

'Is she still standing today?' he asked as he returned from the kitchen with two cups on a tray. He nodded to a painting of Wolf Rock lighthouse hanging in the centre of one wall. Wolf Rock was the lighthouse that sat roughly seventeen nautical miles from Porthsennen shore, the final testament to man's attempted reign over the oceans before the vast wastes of the Atlantic. Elizabeth's great-grandfather had been one of the first keepers almost a century before.

'Yes,' Elizabeth said, turning away from the picture. She could never work out quite how she felt about Wolf Rock. It plagued her dreams, an obelisk to her greatest loss, yet throughout her life she must have painted it more than a hundred times. Thoughts of that isolated monolith roused fear and hatred, yet when she saw its light skipping across the water it still brought her closer to Tom, even after all those years. 'Nobody lives on it nowadays. Everything is automated.'

'Probably for the best. Nothing good comes from living that far away from the people you love.'

'I don't know,' she said with a shrug. 'It's not so far when you think about it. London is a lot further away from Porthsennen than a lighthouse just off the coast.'

'Not as dangerous though.'

'No,' she conceded with a smile. 'I suppose that's true.'

They were quiet for a moment then, fifty years apart a chasm too difficult to breach. So much needed to be said, although still she found it was impossible to say any of it.

'It's changed a lot over the years, hasn't it?' Tom ventured when the silence became too much.

'What has?'

'Porthsennen.' Easing into the settee, he handed her a mug of tea, and her heart skipped a beat when his fingers brushed hers. She sat down too, right on the edge as if she didn't really belong there. 'I didn't put any sugar in. Is that still how you drink it?'

'Yes.' The intimacy of his knowledge of her, there in his house, surrounded by images of his life and family, stirred a deep-rooted sense of her own mistakes. So much had happened to him during the time they had been apart. Her life remained small in a way his wasn't, and she felt a sense of shame for the part she had played in their separation, and began to wonder what she was doing there.

'I saw what they did to the roundhouse,' he continued. 'A gallery now, eh?'

'I sell my paintings in there,' she said.

'Oh, I know,' he said, smiling. As he pointed over her shoulder, her gaze followed, and there she saw a small watercolour of the beach that she had painted several years ago. 'I'm always thinking about the place, and you too.'

The sight of her work, there on the wall alongside images of his life, lived without her, suddenly shattered her cool. They were dancing around fifty years of estrangement as if they'd seen each other last week. All the things she wanted to say were stuck inside, making it difficult to breathe. 'I shouldn't have come here,' she said, setting her tea down, standing from the settee. 'When you didn't come, I should have just left it at that.'

'What?' he said, following, his mouth wide as he followed her towards the door. 'Please don't go now?' he begged.

To feel his hands touch her arm as she made to leave only made her want to go even more. 'I don't know what I was thinking.'

'I do,' he said, his grip firming up. 'You were thinking of me.'

His cheeks were flushed from the hurry to stop her. 'Well of course I was,' she said, raising her voice. 'But why? Fifty years, Tom, and not once did you knock on the door.' This wasn't how she had imagined their reunion, but now she found she had to say it. How could she forgive herself if she kept quiet? 'Why keep coming if you never wanted to see me?'

'I had to,' he said, and she sensed he too felt ashamed.

'How did you even know where I lived after I moved?'

'Porthsennen's a small place, Elizabeth. Wasn't too hard to find you.' She knew that must have been true enough. 'But in all fairness, you never opened the door either. You could have, but you didn't.'

'I did once,' she said, unable to stem the flow of tears. 'Did you?'

'The first year. I saw you. I ran after you.'

He hung his head. When he slumped onto the settee she sat down beside him. 'I didn't hear you,' he whispered. She could see that he was embarrassed. 'Still, you were married then, had a little baby. And you also knew where I lived it seems, and you never came either.'

'Actually, that's not quite true,' she said, feeling as if it was a confession of sorts. The truth of the situation depleted her, the memory of that day a painful recollection that left her with a deep sense of resignation. 'I sat on that bench across the road. I saw you with Alice, and then I suppose when it came to it, I couldn't knock on the door any more than you could.'

'We had other lives, other responsibilities,' he said sadly. 'But I always regretted it, Elizabeth. I always wished that it had been different.'

A sensation of fear and foreboding hit her, and she recognised it as the same fear she'd had on the night he left Porthsennen. When she watched him walk away that night, she had never believed it would have been for ever. Had she known then what she knew now, how differently might she have done things?

'Are you going to tell me what happened? Why you didn't come this year?'

It was hard to watch him as he walked away, his shoulders hunched and frame slight, like seeing a man she had never known. Time, she saw, had betrayed them. Her hand shook as she took an envelope from his outstretched hand, already able to see the headed paper was from a hospital. By the time she reached the end of the letter her throat was sore with emotion, as if there was a lump of pain that she could neither swallow nor bring up.

'An oncologist?'

He nodded.

'But isn't that . . .' She couldn't bring herself to say it. Her mouth was painfully dry, unable to articulate anything she wanted to say.

'Cancer? Yes. They tell me I've got it in the lung.'

'Oh Tom, no. Don't tell me anymore.'

To his credit he was quiet for a moment. The sun was setting, and the kind light of late afternoon, which softened skin and muted age, dappled through the window. After a while he dared join her, resting his hand on her shoulder, and this time she didn't flinch.

'I have to go on Monday to see the specialist.'

'Maybe they're wrong,' Elizabeth offered. 'It's possible. Doctors are wrong all the time.'

'I don't think so, Elizabeth. Not this time at least.'

'I can't believe it,' she said, turning once again to look outside. A man walked by, talking on his phone, smiling and laughing. Life, she thought, was cruel, and shorter than anybody realised.

'I'm so sorry,' he said. 'I wish the news was different. I hope you see now why I couldn't come. I would never have managed the trip on my own this year.'

'I do.' A look crossed his face, one she thought she recognised. 'What is it?'

'I was going to ask you something, but I don't know whether it would be right.'

'Well that never stopped you before.' Things had eased a little then, a good feeling from the past edging its way forward, a memory of how close they had once become. 'What did you want to ask?'

'Whether you might consider coming with me to see the specialist. It's a lot to ask, especially after so long, but I'd love to have you there.'

Instinct told her to say yes, but sense held her back. 'I don't know, Tom. What would your family think? Your daughter didn't look too pleased to see me here, and I doubt your wife will want me hanging around either.'

'My wife?' The wrinkles of his face deepened with confusion. 'She passed away twenty years ago now, and we weren't together for a long time before that.'

'Oh, I thought . . .' She held back, unsure what she really thought. 'I'm sorry. I didn't know.'

His hand felt heavy on her shoulder, reassuring and grounding. 'There's a lot I suppose we don't know about each other by now.' The idea that they had both been alone for years made her want to ask for details, like why they separated and how she died. But now wasn't the time. 'And Alice was just taken by surprise, that's all. She'll come round.'

'You told her about me, didn't you?'

The smile that passed his lips was a curious mix of pleasure and sadness. 'Of course I did.' It amazed Elizabeth that they could find something to smile about then. 'How could I have kept you a secret? So,' he said, reaching for her hand. She didn't pull away this time, and as his fingers slipped between hers, she felt her body relax. 'Will you stay?'

'Well, it's not like I can go back to Porthsennen tonight, is it. But I'll need to find a hotel.'

'Why would you need a hotel? I've got plenty of spare rooms.'

'What would Alice say?'

'Leave Alice to me. I've spent years rattling around in this great big house. It's been pretty lonely, Elizabeth,' he said as she felt his grip tighten, 'but none of that matters now if you say you'll stay.'

Not long after that he showed her to one of the spare rooms. It was a pleasant space which overlooked the back garden, along with about twenty others. It made her feel as if she would be sleeping in a dormitory, all those people in such proximity. After he left her alone to unpack, she pulled the curtains shut, leaving the room in a subtle darkness. Soft light trickled from the lamp at the side of the bed as she lifted her suitcase and opened the lid. After taking out a couple of items she couldn't face doing the rest. Tears flowed but she kept it quiet, didn't want to upset him. And then, nesting in amongst her clothes she saw the little basket that she had grabbed at the last minute, filled with every wish he had ever written. Why had she brought it with her? Perhaps because for years she had been existing in Tom's wishes, always searching for the reality where their life and dreams met. Right then she would have done anything to go back to the dream, but knew that was no longer possible; the dream was over. This was their new reality now, and she was devastatingly awake.

Then

That evening Tom and Elizabeth sat in the old lookout with the small gas stove lit against the cold, the sound of birds singing the melody of a passing summer. Tom browsed her sketchbook with much greater care than he did the two canvases she had taken with her, which she had to admit was a disappointing response when she had chosen them so carefully. After a time, he placed the book down and turned to Elizabeth.

'I think you are quite good.' He pointed to the canvases stacked against the wall. 'But I'm not so sure about those.'

It was unfortunate, but she gave herself a mental reminder how much she hated it when her father gave her unburnished praise. 'What's wrong with my paintings?'

'Nothing,' he said, shrugging.

'Then why don't you like them?'

Hope rose within her as he viewed them again, as if he was giving them a second chance, quickly dashed when he shook his head. 'It's just,' he said, closing his eyes to think. 'They're not very adventurous.'

Elizabeth was more than a bit put out. 'Not adventurous? They took me hours to complete.'

'Maybe that's the problem.'

How could that be? Everything needed time and effort, that's what her father had taught her. Like getting ready for tonight, trying on nearly everything she owned before she settled on the pale yellow dress. 'You will have to explain what you mean, Thomas Hale.'

'It's like when I left school. If I'd have taken ages over the decision the choice would have felt harder than it was, because I knew leaving wasn't what I really wanted. But I had to leave; my brother was dead, my father was a mess, and I was the only one left who could do something to help.' The space created as he stood up felt like a void, and she missed his presence as he moved to pick up the smallest canvas, a painting of the local church. 'When have you ever seen a wall that straight?' he asked, pointing to the bell tower. 'It looks as if you used a ruler.' Admitting that indeed she had was not an option. 'You've painted what you thought you saw, not what was there. The painting doesn't tell the true story at all.' He set it aside and sat once again alongside her.

Her focus remained on the quilt, wondering who would sew in the next pieces, but eventually she looked up. 'You're right, I suppose.' Disappointment weighed on her shoulders, and she pulled the hand-stitched quilt up to her waist in defence. She had really wanted him to love her work.

'Don't be like that,' he said, giving her a nudge. 'You just have to learn to let go, be adventurous.'

'Adventurous?' she scoffed. What did he think she was doing now? 'Do you know what would happen to me if people knew I was here with you?'

'I can't imagine your father would be too pleased. Or your fiancé. But,' he said with a smile, 'you came anyway.' Heat from his body pulsed against her as he pulled the quilt over his knees, his legs alongside hers. A shiver rippled down her spine as he reached out, stroked her cheek. Thoughts came to her that she had never experienced before today. It took her breath away to think what it would be like if he kissed her. 'And I'm glad you did.'

Her lips were dry, so she wet them with her tongue, acutely aware that his hand was still on her face, close enough that she could feel his breath. 'I'm glad too,' she told him, having already forgotten about her paintings' failings.

Sleep was impossible that night for the thought of his touch. It had been so unexpected, so . . . wrong. Up until that point she had been telling herself that meeting him was a perfectly reasonable thing, even for somebody close to marriage. But when she considered telling the story of their meeting to James or her father, she found herself hiding the details, like the way they shared a quilt and the way his hand felt large against hers when he held it. Yes, they'd done that too, only letting go when they reached the bottom of the steps on the way back to the village, as if they had both somehow known they were stepping back into the real world where the rules were different.

Tom made her feel something that day, something about herself that nobody else did. With him she started to believe in things that had once seemed impossible, as if she had choices and a blank sheet in front of her to be filled as she saw fit. As if life was an open ocean and Tom was her vessel upon which she could sail. He made her believe in an unwritten future. He made her believe in herself.

For weeks they met like that, every day and sometimes twice. They shared the heady weeks of summer, and as the days shortened, their time together seemed to take on an ever more precious nature. It was so exciting to meet, arranging their dates when nobody would find them, sneaking off together to places they wouldn't be seen. They never visited each other's houses, but walked the coastal trails, huddled together in the shelter, and once walked into Sennen village for ice creams. Often her thoughts ventured towards the lifeboat slipway, the rocks underneath where she knew boys and girls of her age sometimes went to be alone, but he had never suggested taking her down there, and she wouldn't have dreamed of suggesting it herself.

'What are you smiling about?' he asked one time as they met to go for a picnic.

'Nothing,' she said, still thinking about when he might try to kiss her. That's what being around him did to her, made her smile for nothing, because the truth was their time together was beginning to feel like everything.

'Looks like you're smiling to me,' he said. His fingers clasped around hers in that familiar way, her smile intensifying as she leaned into his body. 'Anyway, I like it,' he said, standing back to look at her. 'Whatever it is, long may it last.'

Following the picnic that evening, they sat in the old lookout, drinking tea from a shared cup, and he asked her about painting and she asked about his family. He never liked to talk all that much about his own, content instead to listen to her. And what she came to realise in those stolen moments was that she could have spent a whole lifetime sitting in that lookout station telling him about herself, and still there wouldn't have been time enough to tell him everything she wanted him to know.

The deep indigo of the night sky was fading as she arrived at the harbour, chased away by the pale blue light of morning. Wet, grey streaks mottled the horizon, a watercolour of early September. They'd been meeting up for close to six weeks now. The cold ground chilled her body as she sat down on the edge of the sea-wall. Pulling out her sketchbook, she set about passing the time while she waited for Tom.

'You're a glutton for punishment,' he said as he neared only fifteen minutes later. His hands were pink and chafed, felt rough and cold as he took hers in his. Watching as he gazed about to make sure nobody was looking, he leaned in and pressed his lips against her cheek. Her stomach knotted, excitement and danger and something else all muddled together. That feeling was like a drug, one of which she thought she could never tire. 'It's freezing out today.'

'It's the coldest day yet.' She smiled, amazed by how cold his hands were from the sea. 'What are we going to do when it's the winter?'

'I'll think of something,' he said.

'I brought something for you.' She pulled out a rolled up canvas from under the fastenings of her satchel. 'I hope you like it.'

'What is it?' he asked, as he shuffled in next to her. He began to uncoil the roll, his fingers struggling at the string.

'A painting,' she said, and saw him smile. 'Here, let me help.'

'What's it of?'

'You'll see in a minute.' Her heart was pounding with anticipation. 'Don't be so impatient.'

Warmth flooded her as he stole another kiss on her cheek, let his lips linger as he whispered in her ear. 'It's hard to be patient with you around.'

'Well try,' she said, unable to stop giggling as she wriggled away, shivering from the cold, or something else she couldn't describe.

'Oh, believe me, I'm trying.' A shudder passed through his body too, as if they'd shared the same physical manifestation of their emotions, and she didn't dare let her imagination go where it wanted.

Once the roll was open, he held it out in front of him, turning so that the weak light from the lifeboat station shone in his direction. 'It's my house.' With wide eyes he glanced at the painting, then along the road towards his home. 'I love it.' He motioned to the sketchpad. 'Am I in there, too?'

'Might be.' As he went to reach for it she played with him, hiding the sketchpad behind her back. With one arm either side of her he struggled for it, bringing their faces close, only backing off when they heard a car's engine just a short distance away.

Once all was quiet she handed it to him, and watched as he flicked through the pages. A gull cawed at their side and she felt Tom's hand slip into his pocket. He tossed a small chunk of dry bread onto the beach which the gull chased with enthusiasm. 'Is this me?'

Struggling to stifle her laughter, she said, 'Do you think

you look that old? That's Old Man Cressa.' The paper rustled as she turned the page. It required her to move in closer still, and she could feel the warmth of his face against her cheek. That sensation was something she had come to crave, wasn't sure she could make it through a morning without it anymore. 'This is you,' she said quietly.

The sketch was of Tom standing tall with fishing nets at his feet, one hand up against his face to wipe a salty brow. It was the most detailed of all the pieces he had seen, something she had completed a week before while she had watched him working.

'It looks like me,' he said, pleased with himself and her. 'But you have made me bigger than I really am. I think you wish I had more muscles.'

'Your muscles are just fine,' she said, blushing.

'Can I keep it?' There was a quality to his voice she had never heard before. At first she wasn't sure what it was, but then began to realise it was humility. The urge to stand up and shout for anyone who could hear what she was feeling right then surged through her. Instead, she took the sketchpad and closed the cover.

'Maybe. But only if you can help me with something.'

'If I can, I will.'

Elizabeth looked out to sea, across the choppy waters to the nearby islands she had never seen up close. They were still in silhouette, but visible against the increasing light. 'I have never been on a boat, not properly. I want to know what it feels like to be out there, on the water.' It heartened her to see him both smiling and nodding. 'I want to go there.'

His gaze followed her arm towards Cape Cornwall. 'To the Brisons?'

'I don't know. Those two rocks,' she said, pointing again.

He nodded. 'Yeah. They call them the Brisons.'

'Will you take me?'

'No,' he said, shaking his head, much to her disappointment. 'I doubt you could even put a boat aside it to stand on the rock, and they rise a good fifty feet tall. Only things that can get on there are crabs, seals, and stranded ships.'

'Oh,' she said. The idea had stayed with her for days; she'd been eyeing up those distant rocks and felt sure he'd take her. Only now she had plucked up the courage to raise the idea of a proper adventure with Tom and he didn't want to go. 'Couldn't we just try?'

'You just said you've never even been in a boat.'

'Well that's not strictly true.' If it was her experience that was the problem, she could fix that. 'I have been on the water. When I was a child, in a dinghy.'

It didn't seem to help much. 'We couldn't go from here. We'd need a punt with a motor for that distance, and everybody would see us, say we were a pair of bleddy idiots. So, we'd have to get to Cape Cornwall first, take a boat from Priest Cove. It's still a good mile from the coast, mind. That's a fair distance in a rowing boat.'

'Could you row a mile?'

'Of course I could,' he said, his words trailing off into quiet contemplation. 'But I'm not so sure I should.'

'Why not?'

'Come on, Elizabeth. If your father found out, what would he say? And Dr Warbeck, too. Don't you wonder what they would say if they knew about us meeting like this?'

76

'Yes,' she said, wrapping her coat tight around her chest. 'But this has got nothing to do with either of them.'

'I think it probably has.'

'Where are you going?' she called as she scrambled to follow him, aware that if anybody drove past, or if Mr Boden from the shop came out to collect the milk they'd be seen.

'I just don't know what this is, that's all. What would people say?'

'I thought you didn't care about what people might say?'

'I don't care what people say about *me*.' His face softened as he stepped towards her. His hands were cold as he touched her cheek, but she leant into that touch because when it wasn't there, she missed it. 'But I care what they think about you.'

Standing in full view of anybody who walked past, she realised that she didn't care. Not anymore. Before she could talk herself out of it she moved into him, wrapped her arms around his body. His head pressed against hers, and she heard him breathing deeply, sure that he was taking in the scent of her hair. 'I only care about being with you,' she whispered.

Words like magic, an unexpected gift, and as she held onto him, she felt his body soften against hers. For a moment it was as if he was melting into her, but then he pulled away. Despite her feelings, Elizabeth knew it was no good for them to be seen together like this. Not yet. From his actions she assumed that Tom knew it too.

'OK, look. The sea is too rough to go now,' he said, already mentally planning the trip. 'Tides are all wrong, you'll end up bringing up your breakfast, and your father will have my guts. But Old Man Cressa says it'll be a millpond later according to the forecast for the next few days. Never usually wrong when it comes to launching the *Stella* to Wolf Rock. It's due to sail on Monday.'

Dreams of their adventure came to her as she followed his gaze, roaming wild as sheep over the grassy lands that rose high above the sea. 'So, you'll take me then?'

'We'll take the coastal path over Carn Olva.' It took all his effort to keep his smile hidden, she could see that. He was as excited as she was. 'It's no easy path, and you won't make supper, so make sure you cover it with your father. I don't want him knocking on my door tonight.'

'I'll sort it all out. I'll tell him I'm seeing Margaret. Shall we say 5 p.m.?'

'No. Too late. 4 p.m.'

After a quick look around to check they were alone he kissed her on the cheek, and she wondered how long it would be before he kissed her differently when he had the chance. Because she wanted him to, but not under the slipway of the lifeboat station like she'd heard he had taken a few other girls. She already knew she wanted something more than that.

'I'll see you later then. Don't be late.'

The distance between them grew as he made his way towards his cottage, and as she watched him walk away, she hurried a pencil from her satchel, sketching the lay of the land with Tom in the very centre. It was imperative she capture that moment exactly as it was, knew she would never want to forget it, although at the time she still had only a limited understanding as to why.

Now

Waking up in Tom's house left Elizabeth confused and uncertain. As her eyes adjusted to the light she remembered where she was, and the ramifications of her rash decision to come to London became clear. That first morning, as she tiptoed down the stairs like a burglar, snooping around where she didn't belong, she wondered what the hell she had done. Never in her life had she been so spontaneous before. The photographs still seemed to stare back at her, especially those of his wife with Alice, but as she made tea, the faces of his past didn't seem quite so judgemental anymore.

Tom woke late, and they ate a quiet breakfast together which she prepared. Later, Elizabeth called Francine and asked her to feed Cookie and water her pot plants, and having those necessities taken care of helped her feel a little more relaxed. They talked about the old characters they remembered from Porthsennen, and Tom told her about his life as an architect. They danced around the subject of their separation, Elizabeth not mentioning it at all, and at the one time she thought Tom was going to raise it he seemed to think better of it too. Silence and space lingered between them, neither sure of the rules. So, to break the tension they shared happy stories, a version of the past in which their separation barely played a part. Most of the stories were Tom's.

'I wish you'd tell me more about your life,' he said as the day drew to a close. 'I feel like I've been rattling on all day.'

'Ah,' she said with a smile. 'There's not that much to tell. You know Porthsennen. Nothing much happens there.'

Alice didn't come by that day as she said she would, although Tom spoke to her on the phone. Elizabeth heard him reassuring her, and it made her think of Kate. In the afternoon they took a slow walk through Hampstead Heath, watched a woman taking a swim in water that must have been freezing. Elizabeth thought about holding Tom's hand, but somehow it felt inappropriate. Still, by the time they went to bed that night, Tom to his room and Elizabeth to hers, the effortlessness with which they once used to talk had eased back into their conversation, and when she heard him being sick in the middle of the night she thought nothing of going to him.

'What would I do without you here?' he asked as she helped him back into bed.

'You seem to have done all right for the last fifty years,' she joked, trying to make light of it.

'I don't know about that,' he said as he turned over to get comfortable, his face away from hers. 'Appearances can be deceiving.'

The warm morning was uncharacteristic for early September, the hospital waiting room stifling. The nurse's shoes clicked in time with the clock on the wall, her feet striking a confident note as she paced up the corridor.

Unnatural light stung Tom's eyes, so he let his lids rest shut. Elizabeth watched as the nurse drew her finger down the list of names, each one a patient, each one here for the same and yet altogether different reasons. The nurse gazed out into the waiting room, her smile neat but somehow not in the least bit friendly.

'Mr Kerridge?' she called into the crowd of expectant faces. A man stood up with the assistance of a young woman at his side. Her hair was long, blonde, and bothered at her eyes; her fringe had drooped in the heat. Elizabeth wouldn't have noticed it if it wasn't for the fact that the man with her had lost his hair, a side effect of treatment, she guessed as they disappeared through a door. For the tenth time in as many minutes she read the sign. *Oncology Outpatients*.

'How long have we been waiting now?' Tom asked as the doors swung closed. 'I've seen two go in since we arrived.'

'I doubt that,' she said. 'You've had your eyes shut since the moment you sat down.' Elizabeth drew her sleeve back from her wrist. 'It's only just eleven, and our appointment isn't for another ten minutes.'

'My backside hurts,' Tom sighed. 'I can't sit here all day. I'm not young like I used to be.' Tom was thinner than he looked in even the most recent of photographs on his living room walls, and she'd noticed that he could barely keep his trousers up, even with a belt.

'Why don't you go for a walk or something?'

'With this thing?' He held up the walking stick he had taken to using, gave it a strong tap against the floor. 'I can't be bothered.'

It was as if somebody had flicked a switched that sent him into old age. Add to that the vomiting and insomnia, and Elizabeth could understand his falling asleep in a waiting room. Her hand reached for his without a second thought; how quickly things had changed.

'What about Alice – where is she?' They had spent a lot of time talking about Alice and looking at his old photographs yesterday.

'She couldn't get out of work, but she'll meet us at home,' he said. 'Anyway, what about your daughter? What did you say her name was?'

'Kate. After my mother.'

'What's she like?'

Her breath shook as she thought of where to begin. 'Well, she's a live one, I'll give you that. Married now, two little lads. They are beautiful boys, really they are. She works as an engineer. Big builds, that sort of thing. Does quite well I believe.'

'Very nice.'

'Loves to travel, too. Trekked through South America, did that Picchu thing in Peru.'

'That what?'

'Or was it Paraguay? I can't remember. I've got a picture of it at home. It's quite famous.' Memories came to her of Kate's youth, things she wanted to share, but where should she even begin? 'You know what kids are like nowadays, they have all these ideas and go off and do it all. Nothing stops them.'

'Not like us.'

'No,' she said, hit by a wave of sadness. 'Different generations. To them, anything is possible.'

'I bet you're a fantastic mother.' Was she? She had put Kate first in many respects, there at every event, giving her everything she could. Tears at the graduation, then at her wedding, and when her two grandsons were born. Never once had she feared Kate would get into any trouble that she wouldn't reach to her for help. That's what had made Kate's decision to exclude her even harder to bear. But she hadn't given up on a reunion yet, and never would.

'Mr Hale?' Neither of them had seen the nurse approach, but as soon as she heard the name Elizabeth was up on her feet, helping Tom to find his balance. It was a different nurse, and she was smiling, holding the door open. Older than the first, plump about the waist. 'Sorry to have kept you, my love,' she said as she touched Tom on the arm. Elizabeth liked her straightaway. 'I'm Lynn. Head through to that first room on the right. We'll get you weighed and ready for Dr Dawkins.'

Tom propped his stick up against the wall before stepping onto the scales to have his decreasing weight and blood pressure recorded. The effort of that alone seemed to take its toll. Another plastic chair squeaked with heat as he sat down into it, positioning his stick between his knees. Elizabeth took the chair alongside him. The plastic was hot, and stuck to her legs.

'Well, you've lost a few kilos since your visit to the GP, Mr Hale, at least according to our scale. Do you think you've lost more weight?' Lynn asked as she filled in a chart.

'What's two kilos in old money?' he asked.

'No idea.' She laughed, and Tom rolled his eyes. He wasn't in the mood for it, not surprising really, but Lynn took no notice. Perhaps she was used to it. Elizabeth imagined that a lot of cancer patients were like Tom, especially when they first learned of their diagnosis. It must be devastating to hear you had something growing inside you that had the capability to kill you. And as she looked at Tom then, his grey hair cropped close, his skin wrinkled and hands bony, she said a simple prayer; please let them be wrong. Perhaps Lynn sensed her fear because right then she leaned down, touched Elizabeth on the arm.

'Dr Dawkins will be with you in just a mo,' she said as she left, still smiling, despite it all.

As she shut the door they sat for a while in silence, the only interruption the occasional sound of feet and cheerful voices in the nearby corridor. 'She seemed nice,' Elizabeth said, short of something better to say.

'They all are,' Tom replied. 'They have to be, don't they?'

A moment later Dr Dawkins came through, his head almost brushing the door frame. Elizabeth tended to compare most doctors to her father, who by anybody's standards would have been an anachronism should he have been there practising today. But she recalled that he did instil a certain confidence that she would have appreciated right then. Dr Dawkins was nothing like her father; too young, with not a wrinkle of experience in sight.

'Nice to meet you both.' Tom took his hand regardless and shook. Elizabeth did the same, noticing that he had slim hands, covered with soft skin.

'Nice to meet you too,' Elizabeth and Tom mumbled in near unison.

The chair creaked as Dr Dawkins pulled Tom's notes in front of him. The pages whispered their secrets as he leafed through. Elizabeth noticed Tom sitting up a little straighter. 'I understand the GP has informed you about what we think is the problem.'

'Yes,' Tom muttered, his voice quiet. 'She said I've got lung cancer,' he continued, wincing as he swallowed. 'Probably.'

Dr Dawkins left the notes and swivelled in his chair to face Tom. 'Well, your X-ray and history are highly suggestive, yes. It would explain your symptoms of pain when you breathe in, and the blood you have been producing when you cough, but it's not the only possibility. Tell me, when did that all start?'

'Couple of months ago. First time I noticed it I was on a walking holiday in the Lake District with a group I'm in.'

'And it persists, correct?'

Tom nodded.

'Well, for a start we need to get you booked in for some extra examinations such as a bronchoscopy and a CT scan. Get a closer look at the lungs.' Dr Dawkins crossed, then uncrossed his legs. 'But first off, tell me a little bit about how you're feeling now. Are you still managing at home well enough?'

'My daughter's been helping me, and Elizabeth too,' Tom said. 'I've been struggling on the stairs a bit.'

'And are you keeping any food down?'

'Some of the time,' he admitted. 'Less so in the last week.'

'That would explain the rapid weight loss.' Dr Dawkins sat back in his chair, leaning against the desk. He turned to Elizabeth. 'Any dizziness?'

She nodded to the stick. 'He tells me that he wasn't using this last week.' Dr Dawkins jotted that down.

'Well, I'm keen to get things moving as quickly as we can. I don't want us to waste any time. I have scheduled a bronchoscopy for two weeks tomorrow, where we'll put a little camera through the nose and down into the lungs, and we will try to get the CT scan done on the same day. You'll be here with us overnight, and we should have you home by the following morning at the latest.'

'OK,' said Tom. 'And what then?'

'Well, we have a lot of options available to us, but it's difficult for me to suggest the best way forward until I have the results. I don't want to talk about things like surgery, or radiotherapy and chemotherapy until after that. Let's see what we're dealing with for starters.'

Tom was quiet for a moment. 'I'd lose my hair,' he said, turning to Elizabeth. Her friend Margaret had undergone chemotherapy last year. All she'd been able to talk about were her eyelashes, and at the time Elizabeth couldn't understand why their absence became so important. His hand was clammy as she took it, and it didn't feel strange or awkward, only intimate and right.

'With chemo some people do lose their hair,' Dr Dawkins said. 'But try not to worry about the unknowns just yet. First, let's focus on getting all the diagnostic information together so we have the full picture. Is that all right?'

He nodded. 'So, there's still a chance I might not have cancer.'

The doctor licked his lips. Above them, a clock ticked on the wall. 'Yes, but I think it would be very unlikely that we don't confirm what the GP thought, Mr Hale. Let's focus on the test results first, eh? The nurses will get you all the information you need, and I will see you then. Unless you have any questions for me, there's nothing more we need to cover today.'

Silence descended for a moment. Elizabeth's eyes were beginning to hurt. All her effort was going into keeping them open so that the tears didn't fall. 'Tom?' she probed, pushing her own thoughts aside. 'Anything you want to ask?' He shook his head. The doctor was still smiling in that reassuring fashion when Elizabeth turned back. 'It's a shock. We're not sure what to ask.' One idea came to mind, but she didn't want to ask that now. Not in front of Tom. 'We will have a think and ask you when we come in for the tests.' Yesterday they had agreed that she would stay until tomorrow, get the early train back if everything was OK, but she knew already that she wasn't going anywhere anytime soon.

Then

James was in the waiting room talking to Francine, a girl a couple of years older than Elizabeth who possessed certain charms that local boys found attractive. His suit was fine, London tailoring, single breasted. Savile Row, he had told her once, as if that meant anything in Porthsennen. Francine always seemed impressed, even though Elizabeth doubted she had any more of an idea than she did about what Savile Row meant. Francine wore dresses that showed the shape of her body, painted her lips and nails red, and her hair hung coiffed on her shoulder. The crown was full of volume and it was set with so much hairspray that the whole thing barely moved. Elizabeth watched her sometimes; the way she walked, the way she crossed her feet. What she wouldn't do for some of that confidence, the guts to dress as Francine did. Dr Davenport would never have allowed it though, even if she could have found the courage.

The door gave off a soft clunk as Elizabeth closed it behind her and they both turned to stare at her. The sound of the ocean softened as James removed his hat and paced towards her.

'Where have you been?'

'I was at the coast,' she said, slipping her arms from her jacket. 'What of it?'

Things had been awkward lately, and she was increasingly aware she couldn't make eye contact with the man she was supposed to marry. Shrugging off her coat with his unsolicited help, she moved quickly towards the cupboard located to the side of reception and made herself busy with some filing.

'It's a bit chilly for that, isn't it?' James said, following. 'What were you doing there?'

'Drawing,' she said, picking up a small pile of papers. Her father insisted that an understanding of running the practice would help in her wifely endeavours once James took the helm.

'Well, your father was looking for you. As was I. I've missed you.' How different his lips felt as he kissed her cheek. At twelve years her senior, he felt like an old man in comparison to Tom. He reached for the sketchbook. 'Is this today's?' he said, turning the pages. The book opened to the drawing of Tom standing on the beach. 'So, who is this muse of yours?' he asked. 'I haven't got competition, have I?' His question was laced with derision, and in some way, she realised, despite his constant support for her love of painting, he was mocking her.

Or testing me, she wondered.

'Old Man Cressa,' she replied, taking the sketchbook and closing it firmly shut.

'Doesn't much look like him,' Francine chipped in, snatching a glance just before Elizabeth could stop her. 'Looks more like Tom Hale.'

'Ah,' sighed James, stroking Elizabeth's hair into place. 'The unsavoury boy who saved your mother.' Another cold kiss, this time on her forehead. 'Sweet, wonderful Lizzy. You should give him one of these drawings. He might like it.' Her teeth clenched to hear him shorten her name, a nasty habit he had picked up. She suspected her father wasn't too keen on it either. 'I was thinking,' he said, already moving on, his smooth hands taking hers; how neat they seemed in comparison to Tom's, like the hands of a little boy. 'We should visit the Minack Theatre. It's quite a sight, and the headland of the Porthcurno coastline is a perfect backdrop for your sketches. I think you'd like it.'

'Sounds nice,' she said, just wanting to get back to work. Every touch, every kind word, all felt like a betrayal to Tom.

'What about tomorrow?'

'Tomorrow?' she almost shouted. The first thought to come to mind was Tom, and when she might see him if she was out all day with James. 'It's a bit far, isn't it?' Perhaps that would put him off. 'And anyway, how would we get there?'

His touch was gentle but definite as he led her towards a seat. 'I'm taking delivery of an Austin Morris today.' His smile lingered in anticipation of her approval, fading only when it didn't come. 'Well,' he said, a little disappointed to have had the wind whipped from his sails, 'you just wait to see it. The weather should be fine, and we can take a picnic. You can draw to your heart's content. I'll arrange it all with your father,' he said, just as Dr Davenport arrived in the waiting room with Mr Bolitho in tow, nursing a bandaged hand.

'Elizabeth.' Her father stopped when he saw her, his eyes flicking to the clock on the wall, saying nothing more before turning to Francine. 'Could you please book an appointment for Mr Bolitho to see me next Tuesday? And Dr Warbeck, if you would be kind enough to see Mr Anderson and his good wife through to my office,' he said, motioning to the couple on the far side of the waiting room. 'I'll be with you all in just a moment.' The implication was that he wanted some time alone with Elizabeth.

Once the Andersons and James were in the office, he turned to his daughter. Francine was sitting at the reception desk, trying to hide the fact she was still listening in, but doing a poor job of it. It appeared her father noticed that too, and a slight hesitancy softened his voice, cushioning the forthcoming reprimand. Elizabeth wasn't fooled.

'We missed you at breakfast today, and I might add, on a number of other days since that business with your mother. Is everything all right?'

'Yes, Daddy.'

A breath shuddered through his lips. 'I do hope so,' he said, pausing. Elizabeth's pulse quickened at his hesitation. 'Let me be clear, Elizabeth. I've heard some disconcerting rumours about where you've been sneaking off to.' Had Francine seen her with Tom, dropped her in it? They hadn't been careful enough. 'Is it true that you have been meeting the boy who saved your mother?'

'Would it be so bad if I had?' she asked, despite knowing that nothing about her meetings with Tom was appropriate anymore. Not even her thoughts about Tom were appropriate anymore.

'Elizabeth,' her father said, his tone changed. He licked at his lips, deciding how best to proceed. 'I don't want you talking to that Hale boy.'

'I've done nothing wrong, Daddy.'

'No, you haven't, not yet at least. But you don't understand how these local lads think. And what in heaven's name would James say if he knew? Why would you risk your future on a whim such as this?'

Elizabeth could feel her face flushing because she knew the answer to that; she couldn't help herself. The time when she was so eager to please her father and James seemed like a different lifetime. Tom's presence created something within her, like a spark, an energy that could start fires. It made her want to light up the world. That was how you knew somebody suited you, she thought; they made you feel something good within your soul about the kind of person you were. James, she had since realised, did nothing to make her feel that way.

Dr Davenport straightened his white coat and placed one hand on her shoulder.

'Elizabeth, I know you're not like a lot of these other local girls; you have always wanted something more than a husband and a home, and I know you aspire to be an artist with those pictures of yours. But don't you want to settle down with a family, have children of your own, and create a home as your mother did for us? Trust me when I say that you have brought the most pleasure for your mother and I.'

'Of course I want those things,' she said, hesitating. Her voice dropped to a whisper. 'But I'm not sure I want them with James.'

'So, what? You want them with this Tom lad? A fisherman? How would you survive, darling? Your little pictures aren't going to clothe your children or put food on the table. James is a decent man, he'll let you keep at it if you so wish. Please consider what I have said, OK?' She nodded. There was nothing else she could do for now. 'I need to get back to work. But I assume we can expect you at the dinner table tonight?'

It wasn't really a question, and Elizabeth had to think quickly. 'Actually, I was planning to go out with Margaret. We were going to walk to Land's End, watch the sunset. Is that all right?' It caught her breath to think how easily she had learnt to lie.

'I see no reason why not,' he said after studying her face for a while. 'Speak to Mrs Clements.' Mrs Clements was their housekeeper, and since Elizabeth's mother became sick, integral to the daily running of the house. 'She will make you a nice supper to take with you. But I want you home by eight-thirty. The sun should have set an hour or so before then, so it should give you plenty of time.' He kissed her cheek. 'I'm very proud of you, and James is too. Let's not do anything to change that, OK?'

Her heart was still pounding when he retreated to his consulting room, and when she felt Francine arrive at her side. A small black tube appeared on the notes in Elizabeth's lap. It rolled towards her body, settling against her stomach.

'What's this?' she asked, picking it up, answering her own question by pulling off the lid to see a slick of cherry red lipstick emerging as she twisted the end.

'You should wear it,' she said. 'He'll like it.'

Elizabeth tossed it back to Francine. 'James doesn't like me to wear any make-up. He says it's cheap.'

Francine caught it against her chest. Laughing to herself, she tossed it straight back. 'Perhaps he does, but I wasn't talking about James.'

Now

Alice arrived a short while before they were due to sit for dinner, while Elizabeth was still laying the table, the keys rattling in the door, the sound of heels against the tiled floor. Nobody else had a key. Only family. It worked well, Tom always said, having a daughter living just a few roads away, who could let herself in if anything happened.

'Hello,' Elizabeth said as Alice arrived in the doorway. Her eyes moved first to Elizabeth and then to the table, to the chair upon which Elizabeth had left a cardigan early that afternoon.

'Hi,' she said, a smile forming which appeared uncomfortable, as if it made her face sore. 'Where's Dad?'

Alice had been there a few times since their hospital visit. The first occasion was brief, and Elizabeth had stayed upstairs as Tom had asked her to. She'd heard Alice crying, and then the door opening as she stepped outside. Noise had drawn Elizabeth to the window, where she saw Alice with tears on her cheeks, glistening like morning dew on the overgrown grass. When she looked up to see Elizabeth she wiped her face and eyes before turning away to light a cigarette. That evening Tom had explained that one of Alice's problems was that

94

she was supposed to be moving to Hastings within the next week. Alice insisted she was moving in search of a better job, but Tom said she was running away from the difficulties of a dissolving marriage. Decisions taken before Tom got sick, and now everybody wished, deep down at least, that she was staying.

Alice was standing in the doorway where she had as a child scratched an A into the paintwork. In the kitchen there was a mural of the sea that she'd painted on one of the cupboards. Reminders of Alice's childhood, things that Tom always refused to repair. Things that made Elizabeth feel like she didn't belong.

'He's having a lie down,' Elizabeth told her. 'We were having a game of cards earlier on and he got a bit tired.'

Alice peeled away her jacket, her cheeks red from rushing to get there. It still eluded Elizabeth as to what it was that Alice did for a job, but she was always well dressed. Something about selling and currency. Or stocks, maybe. Definitely money. Kate was always in boots and an overcoat, working on building sites. The thought was bittersweet, and she took a mental note to message her daughter again that night.

'How has he been today?'

Elizabeth appreciated the question. It made her presence here useful, something she always felt less of in Alice's presence. 'Well, he wasn't sick last night.'

'Something positive. And his mood?'

Elizabeth shrugged. What could she say? 'He has been quite down today. Not very talkative to be honest.'

It came in waves, like it did for all of them. His moods swung between wanting to make the most of each day, denying that he had anything wrong with him, to utter devastation over the fact that time was going to be shorter than he had hoped. Often Elizabeth felt she was at a loss for what to do.

'I don't suppose it's much of a surprise, is it? None of us are strong all the time.'

Alice slumped into one of the dining chairs. Elizabeth's instincts were to offer comfort, the same as she would have done for Kate, but it was clear to her that this was not the kind of person Alice was. Still, she took a seat in a chair alongside her, let her motherly instincts take over, and rested one of her hands on hers. Alice's skin was dry and cracked. Only a few days ago her manicure had been impeccable, now it was all chewed to bits. Elizabeth understood; the little things that once seemed important had paled. Like her winter roses that she doubted had been watered properly since she left. How she had been looking forward to their bloom. Francine was feeding the cat, but Elizabeth doubted she'd bother with the plants, even though she'd asked her to tend to them. Still, she was sending Elizabeth a package of things she had requested for her extended stay, and for that she was grateful.

'When is the appointment?' Elizabeth looked up from her daydream to see Alice setting her phone aside.

'A week on Tuesday,' Elizabeth replied, getting to her feet.

'It seems like for ever away.' Elizabeth was on uncharted ground; Alice was never usually chatty like this. Her gaze fell somewhere beyond the window, in the garden. Elizabeth wondered which memory had caught Alice's thoughts. 'Another week of waiting feels like a year when it's about cancer,' she eventually said.

Elizabeth didn't want to say the wrong thing, so instead she motioned to the kitchen. While she was aware they weren't family, she wondered whether perhaps her presence could help facilitate some simple familial ministrations like a good meal shared together. Moments like that were important, especially now, and she knew how much she had missed Kate's family coming over for Sunday lunch. 'Would you like to stay for tea, love? I've made pork chops and roasted vegetables. There's plenty as your dad won't eat much.'

Alice glanced at her phone. 'I can't. I've got work to finish for tomorrow, and still have loads to pack. If Dad's going to sleep for the rest of the night I might as well get going.'

'You just sit right where you are.' Neither of them had heard him creeping down the stairs. On the 1960s stair carpet you couldn't hear him coming.

'Dad,' Alice said as she stood up and moved toward him, supporting his arm even though he didn't seem to need it. 'How are you feeling?'

'Bloody marvellous, Bab,' he said, and they all detected the irritation in his voice. Bab was his nickname for his daughter, had been since she was two years old. He was grumpy and short tempered in a way he wasn't usually. Elizabeth had read that sometimes cancer could have that effect, start to change a person's mood or manner. Alice helped him settle at the table, and because Elizabeth didn't quite know what else to do she went to the kitchen and pulled out another placemat and plate, then grabbed a stout from the fridge and emptied it into a glass with a slim head just the way Tom liked it.

'Now,' Tom said as she returned to the table. 'While I've got you both here, I want to tell you that I've been doing some thinking.' His hands were placed flat against the table, but still Elizabeth could tell they were shaking. 'I want to go and see the place I grew up just one more time.'

Elizabeth thought of her basket of wishes upstairs, and all those they might be able to fulfil together if they were in Porthsennen again. How she would love that.

'What?' asked Alice. 'Don't you think it's a bit far for you at the moment? You'll wear yourself out.'

'You're a fine one to talk,' he said. 'Running back and forth like this, coming here every spare moment and working every other. You're the one who'll wear herself out.' Tom took a small mouthful of potato, but from the look he gave the plate afterwards it must have made him feel sick, and he pushed the rest away.

'Don't you want me to come here?' Alice asked.

'Of course I do, but not at the expense of your own life. What about Brian? Have you even spoken to him about all this yet?'

Elizabeth noticed Alice set her jaw as she turned to face her father. 'I haven't seen him, spoken to him, or thought about him. At least not until you brought it up. We're not together anymore, Dad.' The plate clattered as she pushed it away. Elizabeth had served her some food regardless of the fact that she said she wouldn't stay. 'You just have to get used to that. And as for coming here, I want to be here with you,' she said, stealing a glance at Elizabeth, 'so stop worrying about me.'

'Well I do worry. You've got your own life to live.'

'Don't you think you're more important than anything else right now?'

He shook his head. 'One day you'll understand what I'm telling you, my love. I don't want you to look back in another fifty years and say you could have done it differently. I'd never change having you, but there are plenty of other things I should have done better.' Her face softened at that, just the reminder that his mithering came from a place filled with good intentions. 'Does he still call, at least?'

'Leave it, Dad. It's done.'

'OK, I'll leave it alone,' Tom said, reading her silence. He took another small mouthful of potato, forced it down. 'Still, I'm sure he would be there for you given a chance.'

'Is that what you call leaving it alone?' He held up his hands in surrender. 'So, about Cornwall,' Alice said, changing the subject. 'You want to go back to Porthsennen.'

He looked to Elizabeth with a smile. 'It's about time after all these years sneaking down on my own, don't you think? And part of me can't believe that we never took you, love. Wouldn't you like to see where I grew up?'

Alice smiled at that. 'I see where this is going. I remember asking to go to Cornwall once and you said over your dead body.'

'Well, if we don't go soon that might very well be the case.'

'Dad,' she shouted, and he looked sheepish enough to keep whatever retort that came to mind to himself.

'I'm sorry, love.' He reached for her hand and held it tight. 'I know it's a lot to ask, especially considering I've just told you to focus on your own life instead of mine, but it would be lovely to go there together. The old cottage where I was born is right on the seafront, thatched with a view of the little harbour. If we can make it up to the headland, you'll even be able to see Wolf Rock.'

'The lighthouse?' She looked to the painting, to the place where her father had once worked.

'Yes.' Elizabeth could see how much the trip had come to mean to him. How long had he been thinking about it? She thought of her cottage, the very cottage Tom had grown up in, and how it would feel to be there together again. If he didn't go now, he might never go again if the worst came to them. Alice must have seen it too, because her face softened in that moment. 'I would really love to show you.'

Elizabeth watched the smile spread across their faces. It was a good plan, coming together. 'I'll drive us, but only if the doctor says it's all right.'

'You're a good girl, Bab,' he said, taking her hand in his. He held on tight and took a deep courageous breath, or at least as deep as his damaged lungs would allow. 'Now, about Brian. We could call him together if you like.'

'A girl can change her mind, you know.' He didn't suggest anything else.

At Tom's request they put the television on and listened to a game show in the background while they ate the rest of their dinner. Tea steamed in mugs on the table, one of which remained largely untouched. They sat back on the settee, Tom in his threadbare chair. After a time, he drifted off to sleep, his mouth open and eyes only half closed.

'Is that it for the night?' Alice asked, nodding towards her father.

'Most likely,' Elizabeth told her. 'He doesn't have much energy what with not eating his dinner. Sleeps ever such a lot.'

'He always fell asleep early, even when I was a kid.'

Elizabeth smiled. 'It's Porthsennen in his blood, love. He was up every morning at three or four, out fishing. Used to have bags under his eyes sometimes before it was even midday. Was always the most handsome man in the whole of Porthsennen, mind.'

Alice laughed, but stifled it so as not to wake her father. 'Not the whole of Cornwall, then?'

'I have no idea,' Elizabeth said, smiling to herself. 'I had never left Porthsennen.'

They were both quiet for a while, watching Tom as he slept. Elizabeth thought of their past, and the times they stole away together. Of later times when he was angry with her, and times after that when she feared she might never see him again. All those wishes he made, and the time they had wasted. There was one thing she could say about cancer, and that it was a brilliant leveller. Nothing else seemed important right now.

Alice broke the silence. 'Can I ask you something?'

'Of course.'

'Do you think I should call Brian?'

Elizabeth turned down the volume on the television. 'I can't answer that, my love. Only you can know what the right thing is. I've never even met him.'

'But what would you do, if you were in my shoes?'

Elizabeth paused, thinking back to when she was younger, and all the stupid decisions she'd made. All the times she was weaker than she should have been or let herself believe a lie because it was simpler than the truth. She supposed it was near impossible to get to sixty-seven and not have regrets, but by God did she wish she could go back and change a few things.

'All I know is that you really don't want to get to our age and wish things had been different.'

'He still calls all the time, you know? But we used to fight so much, and wanted different things. How am I supposed to know what the right choice is?'

'You just have to try your best, love. The only way you can say that is if you've exhausted all possibilities. Same as going to Porthsennen. I know you're worried about the trip, but we'll never know if he can do it if we don't try.'

Alice nodded. 'He was very disappointed not to have gone there this year to deliver the flower to you in person.' Elizabeth must have looked shocked, because then Alice said, 'I know all about it. All those wishes he made for you both.'

The thought of Tom telling Alice about his dreams with Elizabeth left her feeling a deep sense of loss for the life they could have lived. Yet without his marriage Alice would never have been born. Life was confusing, she realised. Even after all those years of experience.

'I'm sorry I was a bit off at first,' Alice said. 'I'm not at my best just lately.'

'Please don't apologise, love. I'm the one here in your house. A stranger. And it's not exactly an easy time, is it?'

'No, it's not, but you're hardly a stranger. Dad used to talk about you, when I was old enough to understand. All those wishes and not one of them came true, eh?'

Elizabeth smiled; all she could do. 'Do you really think he can make the journey?'

It would be tough, Elizabeth knew that, and she had her own fears about whether the long trip would make Tom worse. But he had cancer, and she knew she had to do everything she could for him now. If going back to Porthsennen would make him happy, then they had to go.

'I think we could try,' Elizabeth said, just as Alice's phone beeped.

'I best get going,' she said, standing up and reaching for her coat. 'I've got a lot to do.'

'OK, love. And think about what I said about Brian,' Elizabeth whispered as she followed her through to the hallway. 'I appreciate you asking me about it, really I do.'

'And I appreciate the advice.' Alice opened the front door and stepped out into the fading light. 'You know something, Elizabeth? I know we don't really know each other, but I'm really glad you're here.'

'Where else would I be?'

The cold was biting, so Alice braced against it, wrapped her scarf around her neck. 'The garden is looking dreadful. You should let Jim from next door know. He always puts the mower around when Dad asks him to.'

Elizabeth looked at the overgrown grass. 'I'll speak to him in the morning.'

After watching Alice disappear around the leafy corner that Elizabeth had first walked around so many years before, filled with hope and love for a life with Tom, she closed the door to a quiet house. Alone again, Tom sleeping and unaware. Her eyes fluttered closed as she held onto the door handle, listening to the troubled sound of Tom's laboured breathing. Was there still time to put right the things she had done so wrong, and make his wishes come true? With her eyes closed for just a moment, she dreamed of a different life. But when she opened them again, she found that nothing had changed, and the cancer settled back over the present like a winter fog blanketing the coastline of Porthsennen, drenching everything in its path.

Then

True to his word, Tom was waiting for her when she arrived at the foot of Cove Hill, his feet dangling over the sea-wall. Trails of smoke drifted skyward as he puffed on a small hand-rolled cigarette, and when he sensed her behind him, he tossed it towards the shiny granite rocks beneath his feet.

'I thought you'd changed your mind,' he said. After stopping to speak with Margaret, who wanted all the details pertaining to the need for a cover story, her arrival had been delayed. Well, that, and because she had changed her clothes multiple times before deciding to stick to the same trousers as she had been wearing that morning. They were most practical and were her only pair, but also, she didn't want to overdo it. The slick berry glow of Francine's lipstick had seemed like a good idea too, but it felt so strange that eventually she had wiped it off again. Still it had left a subtle stain on her lips that suited her mood of adventure.

'Of course I didn't change my mind.' His eyes wandered up and down the length of her body, lingered a little on her face. 'I'm really looking forward to it.'

'What have you got there?' he asked, pointing to the roll under her arm.

'Paintbrushes and some watercolours.' The brushes rattled inside as she patted the satchel slung across her shoulder. The strap cut across her chest in a way that made her self-conscious of her own body, deeply aware of the shape of her chest. The material shifted as she adjusted the strap, but there was little to be done. 'Hadn't we best get a move on?' she said.

'You mean before somebody sees us?' Stealing a glance over her shoulder she got close to him, caught his scent, heat and tobacco as his body met hers. It would have been a lie to say she didn't wonder about being seen when she planted a kiss on his cheek, but she did it anyway. The smile that grew on his face made the risk worth it. 'Let's get this show on the road,' he said, before turning away and heading towards the path.

They gained in height quickly, the pace fast and eager as they crested Carn Olva and passed the old wartime pill-boxes. Goosepimples rippled across her clammy skin as she reached for his hand, glad to be away from the scrutiny of her father's wishes and the villagers' prying eyes. His stature seemed larger somehow as she held him, or perhaps she just felt smaller, pressed up close with his fingers clasped around hers. The heat from his body warmed her, realising that what had seemed like a fine day in the shelter of the cove was quite different up high on the peninsula.

Tom stopped, placed his hands on his hips to catch his breath. Setting his bag on the ground he knelt, unclipped the buckles and pulled out a jumper. 'You're shivering,' he said.

'Is it yours?' she asked as she took it.

'Who else's would I bring?' The bag looked heavy as he slung it back over his shoulder, the pack landing against his hip. 'It's a bit big for you, but it'll do.' It smelt of him, of the sea, and a little of tobacco as she slipped her arms through. In the light of the weak afternoon sun she noticed the brilliance of fish scales like soft pearls of morning dew woven into the stitches. 'But when those shoes start giving you gip, I don't have any suggestions.' They were her favourite pair, but she had to admit they weren't the most practical choice. He brushed his hair from his eyes and winked. 'I suppose I could always carry you. Come on,' he said, heading off without her. 'Last one to the bottom's a stinky old fish.' His arms flailed left and right as he stumbled forwards. Her shoes pinched as she followed, and secretly she hoped she might begin to develop a blister so that being carried became a necessity.

The Brisons grew steadily in size and stature, as did Elizabeth's anxieties as they arrived on the brow of Cape Cornwall. From the elevated vantage point she could see waves breaking at the foot of the mighty sea stacks. Up close they were perhaps smaller than she expected, but the terrain appeared rougher than it did from the safety and distance of Porthsennen. The thought of putting a small boat alongside the angular volcanic rocks and treading the irregular surface seemed fanciful if not complete folly. The rocks jutted out from the water like the fins of a giant sea creature, and as she stared at the distant landmass she couldn't help but wonder what lay beneath the surface.

Following Tom's lead, she took his hand as they navi-gated the meadows of gorse and heather, past land cleaved by old mining works. After dropping down to Priest

Cove, a small beach littered with dilapidated fishing huts and heavy black boulders, they arrived in the shadow of a giant chimney that still rose from the headland above. A small hut had been built into the rocks, and as they paced towards it a frail old man emerged. His clothes were too heavy for the weather, a bright yellow waterproof, and waders up to the thigh. He seemed almost Poseidonian, with great lengths of wavy grey hair, and a rich matted beard in which he could have been hiding any manner of things. Tom approached but Elizabeth hung back, clutching her satchel close to her chest.

Thoughts of James came to her as she watched Tom organising a boat, edging it down the slipway, and setting his bag inside. Tom was at ease in her presence, as if it didn't really matter to him what she thought. Yet she had spent her whole life watching men trying to create an impression. Only today James was telling her about his new car. Then there were his Savile Row suits, his promises to take her to London, organise her an exhibition and create an art room in their new house. There was always something for him to achieve on her behalf, whether she liked it or not. Tom was the only person that had so far in her short, charmed life, done something for her just because she wanted it.

Gentle waves lapped the shore as Tom prepared the boat for their adventure. 'Careful not to get those shoes wet,' he said as he coiled the rope into a loop, before placing it into the vessel. The ground chilled her feet as she reached down, pulled them off. They clattered against the hull as she tossed them into the boat, then leant down and turned up her trousers. The surging sea water comforted her sore toes. One last look at The

Brisons did little to calm her nerves before she took the offer of his hand, and stepped in.

Watching him row raised a smile, and he looked at her with that silent questioning half-smile of his, the one that asked, *What?* Knowing she would have been embarrassed by the answer, she crawled across the boat and sat so that she was sharing his little seat, her back pressed up against his chest, enclosed by his arms. His hands were tight and strong against the oars as she placed hers on top of his, following his movements, while her weight rested against his body. It was the closest she'd ever been to him, physically at least, watching as the shore shrunk away. Just the two of them, exactly how she wanted it to be.

The boat came to rest against a rocky shelf which connected the mass of Great and Little Brisons. In a fluid movement he tossed a rope onto the closest thing that resembled land and leapt from the boat. For a moment her heart pounded at being left on the boat alone, but the water was calm enough, their landing spot sheltered from the currents of the Atlantic. He soon had the small boat tethered to a sturdy looking spur.

Reaching underneath her arms, he lifted her out. Her thoughts returned to James, and what he would say if he knew where she was. It was a moment laced with guilt, but still she knew she wouldn't change it for all the Savile Row suits and exhibitions in the world.

'Climb up there a bit,' Tom ordered as he set her down on the rocks, and she did as she was told.

The ropes pulled tight as Tom put his weight behind them, tethering the small boat with a second line, gripping onto the rocks with both hands as he climbed to her. Glancing over the edge towards the open water she saw the currents chopping back and forth, spray from the waves hitting her feet. But it didn't scare her, and as Tom sat down in the small nook alongside her, both glancing out to sea, she had never felt freer in her life.

'If you follow my finger,' he said, leaning in close and pointing out to sea, 'those silvery slithers on the horizon are the Scillies. You should just about be able to make out St Martin's.' The sun was bright, so she shaded her eyes. Her other arm looped through his without a second thought.

'I see it,' she confirmed.

'And there,' he said, angling his finger towards the south. 'That's Wolf Rock.'

'The lighthouse?'

'Yes.' It was the last outpost before the vast Atlantic Ocean stretched all the way to Nova Scotia. 'One hundred and thirty feet tall for close to a century now. Three beacons were washed away before they built the lighthouse that stands there today.'

'Really?' He nodded. 'I wouldn't want to go there, miles from land and other people.'

'Somebody's got to do it.'

'Would you do it?' she asked.

'Maybe. It would be easy enough. The sea's what us Cornish lads are good for, or so my ma says. Our grandfathers and their grandfathers before were all fishermen or smugglers. It's passed down to us, like bones and blood; we're nothing without it.'

'My great-grandfather worked on Wolf Rock. He was one of the first people to light the lamp.'

Tom's eyebrows rose with surprise and she liked the fact he was impressed.

'I think the men who go there must be very brave.'

'Or desperate.'

'Well, maybe that too, but being desperate doesn't mean they're not brave as well.' They were quiet for a moment. The sea fizzed and foamed at her feet, the rush of the tide. The support of his arm held her firm when a large wave wet her feet.

'Mr Pommeroy offered me a job there, even did some training, but I think I'd rather stay in Porthsennen.' He turned to her and smiled. 'Would you like that?'

'You know I would,' she said, letting her head rest against his shoulder. 'So, you don't really want to be a fisherman, and you don't really want to be a lighthouse keeper. What do you want to be, Thomas Hale?'

The sun began to dip as he gazed towards the horizon. If only she understood that in that moment all he really wanted to be was hers. 'I've told you before, Elizabeth. Dreams are for rich people, like you. Lads like me don't get the choices you get. We don't get to go off to London and come back as doctors.'

If it wasn't for fear of falling, she might have pulled away from him then, aggrieved as she was by his assumptions. 'You think dreaming is for rich people, but I'd say it's for men like you. You are the free one, able to do whatever you want. If you wanted to go to Wolf Rock, you could. Nobody would stop you, just like they didn't when you left school. I can't do that. My father wouldn't let me.'

'And he'd be right too. Who wants to live on a lighthouse?' His laughter did nothing to raise a smile.

'At least you get to choose for yourself. Every day you do whatever you want, like take boats out and land on rocks like this.'

'Land? We didn't fly here.'

'Don't play the fool,' she said, wincing a little as her words reminded her of her father's. Her mouth was dry, from either the salt or the surprise of her quick response. She wondered for a moment if she might have offended him. But he was enjoying himself if she had judged his smile correctly, and she softened. 'I don't get to choose any more than you do.'

They were both quiet then, watching the sea with their arms linked. The urge to tell him everything she was feeling swelled in her chest. How could she keep to herself the fact that since she'd met him, she felt something she never had before, and that the way he sailed and fished made him stronger to her than any London education ever could? That she liked the simplicity of his life, the lack of expectation, and the way he never tried to be anything he wasn't in front of her? Fear over what he might say in response held her back, and instead she focused on the way his fingers brushed unconsciously at hers.

'Do you think we best get back?' she asked after a time.

'You haven't even done any painting yet.'

The water continued to foam at her feet, the little boat rocking back and forth. 'It's not what I imagined. I didn't think it would be this uncomfortable.' The rock was really starting to dig in. 'And those waves look like they're picking up to me. I don't want to get stranded.'

'At least we'd be together,' he said, and she felt herself blush. 'And even if the worst comes to us, everybody has to die sometime,' he said as he helped her into the boat. He was quiet for a moment, swallowed hard before his gaze met hers. 'It might as well be alongside the one you love.'

The small boat chopped back and forth as they made the crossing. They thanked the old man as they left Priest Cove behind, then set out to cover some ground. Tom led her to a vantage point overlooking Gwynver Beach, a small grassy embankment surrounded by granite pinnacles which sheltered them from the wind.

'I had a wonderful afternoon,' she said after a while, a soft cushion of grass beneath her. It was only then that she noticed Tom hadn't brought anything save a small flask of tea, so she reached into her bag, offered him a sandwich, and he took it without question. Then she picked up her sketchbook and found the drawing of him that he had liked at the beach. It flapped in the breeze as she tore it out. 'Just so you know that I keep my promises.'

'Thank you,' he said quietly. His fingers brushed at the page, his face a mixture of both surprise and repletion. He carefully rolled the sheet of paper, making sure to protect the edges, before slipping it in his bag. 'Honestly, I was a bit concerned for a while back there,' he admitted. Her eyes widened. 'I was so lost in talking to you I forgot to keep an eye on the sea. Those waves had really grown.'

'Are you serious?' she asked, her mouth full.

He nodded sheepishly. 'Stupid of me, especially after what happened to Daniel.'

But she was the stupid one, she realised then, asking him to take her out on a boat like that when he had told her what happened to his brother. 'Oh, Tom,' she said. 'I'm so sorry. I didn't think.'

'What are you sorry for?' he said, surprised.

'For suggesting the trip. It wasn't fair.'

The casual shrug of his shoulders eased her discomfort at what she perceived as her mistake. 'Elizabeth, it's fine.

What happened to Daniel was an accident, despite what my dad thinks.'

'What?' she asked, clambering towards him. 'He doesn't think so?'

'No, not really.' What was worse than his answer was the look on his face, as if some distant memory had a hold of him, digging in its claws. 'He thinks I'm to blame.'

'No,' she shouted, wanting to touch him and not knowing how. 'That's not possible.'

The moment before he spoke was one of the most painful of her life. How could Mr Hale blame Tom for his brother's death? 'You see, Dad had built that boat, but I wasn't watching when Daniel took it. Do you remember him before; Dad I mean? No? Well he was a pretty decent guy. Member of the lifeboat crew, excellent carpenter. But the snow the previous winter had rotted the hull of that little boat, and when Daniel took it, I was in the bath. Should have been watching him, but I wasn't. He knew how to row good enough, but once he hit the choppier waters past the reef the boat capsized. Wasn't strong enough to make it back.'

Her hand found his shoulder. 'You can't be blamed for that.'

'Doesn't matter either way. All our lives changed after that. My mother held herself together, how I don't know, but she did. But my father got stuck in the mud of it, numbed himself with drink, and finds it easier to blame me than accept that Daniel's gone. He's never been the same since. Don't suppose any of us have, really.'

Her mind was all over the place, thinking of the risk they had taken, and of Daniel, the life unnecessarily lost. How quickly it could be taken from you, how little time they really had. Tom's eyes shone blue as the sky overhead, the clouds casting shadows at their feet. And then all Elizabeth could see was her own future, married to a man she didn't love. How could she live and die in that life she didn't want?

'Are you OK?' Tom asked, sensing her discomfort. 'I didn't mean to upset you.'

'I don't love James,' she blurted out without really thinking. 'But I'm supposed to be getting married to him.'

'Yes,' said Tom, nibbling his thumbnail. 'I haven't forgotten about that.' His fingers were surprisingly warm as he rested a hand onto hers. 'If you don't love him, why would you marry him?'

The vista was as wide and great as anything she had ever seen. A big sky under which small decisions were taken that changed the course of whole lives. So much life out there, just waiting to be lived. All those risks she was yet to take. Tom's eyes shone like sapphires as she gazed at them and wondered.

'I don't know,' she said. 'I don't even know if he loves me.'

'What if I told you I loved you?' Tom said. 'And that I could love you until my dying day, whether that's next year or next century.'

It made her want to cry, the easy way in which he spoke of love, aware still that his hand was resting on hers, his fingers touching the spot where she should have been wearing an engagement ring.

'Next century?' she asked. Her breath had become quick, her voice shaky. 'That's a long time, isn't it?'

His weight shifted towards her as he took his hand from hers. As soon as it moved she felt as if something was missing. Tingles raced across her skin as his breath struck her cheek, and despite their proximity, his body over hers, she thought for a moment he seemed shy. 'It's a whole lifetime, Elizabeth,' he replied after a while. 'But if you can't love somebody for ever, what's the point in loving them at all?'

Now

The ringing of the doorbell was a welcome interruption to the banality of morning television. It was a routine they had slipped into, something neither of them could have imagined doing just a few short weeks ago.

'I'll get it,' she said, pressing the standby button on the television. The rubber gloves snapped off as she pulled them from her hands, setting them down on the side next to the bowl of warm soapy water that she had been using to clean the mantel and the trinkets on it. The faint odour of cigarettes still permeated the room, drifting from every surface, and until it was gone, her work was unfinished. 'It'll be Jim here to cut the lawn.'

His form was just visible through the dimpled glass. As she opened the door to the cool air of a bright autumn day, she saw him nibbling his lip and pulling at his fingers. People didn't know how to act in the presence of cancer, she realised, or what to say. But sometimes saying nothing at all was better than rattling on and on until you said the wrong thing. Only yesterday they had been in a café for a quick stop on the way down Hampstead High Street when Tom saw an old friend he used to work with when he first moved to London.

Elizabeth had listened politely as the man called Graham regaled the story of his own mother, and how cancer, in his own words, had ravaged the very bones of her until there was nothing left but skin. Afterwards Tom had turned to Elizabeth, had simply said, 'Well, that made me feel better,' and they'd had a bloody good laugh about it until tears pricked their eyes and dripped onto their untouched toasted teacakes. Why did people think you needed to hear their horror stories when you were already living through your own?

'Do you want to come through?' she asked Jim, leading the way. 'I've got the kettle on if you'd like a cup of tea.'

'That'd be great,' Jim said, setting his hat on the coat stand before following Elizabeth through to the living room. Tom was asleep in his chair.

'Give him a nudge,' Elizabeth suggested. 'I'll go and get that tea.'

Moments later she could hear the soft mumble of their chatter as Tom and Jim moved through to the garden. It was good to hear Tom speaking, nice to hear his easy conversation with a friend of many years. The cups felt heavy as she pulled them from the cupboard, her fingers aching and muscles sore. Too much cleaning for want of something better to do. Tom was asleep so often she had to keep herself busy. The leaflet she had picked up at the hospital was on the side, so she picked that up while she waited for the kettle to boil. It was about lung cancer, and she had read it cover to cover. It claimed that ninety per cent of people who got lung cancer were smokers, and it was the main reason why she was still doing her best to remove the evidence that a smoker had ever lived there, trying to polish away every trace of the enemy as if it might make a difference. But still, even with all the information from that little book she felt none the wiser. It couldn't tell her whether she would lose Tom, and that was all that mattered.

'Said she'd find me, didn't I?' Tom said as Elizabeth arrived in the garden. Jim looked up with a smile, a smudge of mud already across his cheek from where he was weeding one of the rose beds. An early frost had gripped the ground last night, and it had melted in the morning sun, wetting everything in its path. 'She always does,' Tom said as she sat down. His hand reached for hers, and as she nestled in alongside him, she felt like an eighteen-year-old girl on her first date. The cool weather meant she really needed a coat, but didn't want to leave him to fetch it. Sometimes she couldn't even bear to go to sleep because it meant she had to stop watching him as he slept in the chair, checking every few minutes that he was still there. The old dream kept coming back to her, the same one from the night he saved her mother; that she was drowning, and he was saving her. Only now they were older in the dream, and she always woke up before they made it to shore. 'Look at those,' he said, raising the end of his walking stick. 'Aren't they magnificent?'

Under the tree in the corner of the garden grew speckles of blue and purple, white tips sneaking towards the light through a carpet of golden leaves. 'Croci,' she said. 'My favourite.'

'I know,' he said. 'Why do you think I planted them? I needed a good selection to choose from. Every year I chose the best, which wasn't always easy as by September most of them are already fading.'

'You're an old romantic, Tom,' Jim said, leaning back on his heels, an appreciative smile on his face. He wiped his brow, sweating despite the chill, then sipped his tea.

'You weren't really thinking of me when you planted them, were you?' she asked.

'Sometimes I think you forget the way I love you.' Warmth flooded her then as he squeezed her hand. 'I was always thinking of you.'

Elizabeth listened as Tom and Jim talked of the old days for well over an hour; how the street had changed, and how it was near impossible to get a parking space nowadays. After a while Tom got cold, and with Jim's help he went for a rest in his chair. Jim's sigh was deep and weary as he joined Elizabeth in the kitchen.

'He'll be out like a light, I reckon.'

Elizabeth handed him another cup of tea. It was the fourth since he'd arrived. The man sure could drink. Crumbs fell to the table as he helped himself to a second slice of Hevva cake, a Cornish favourite that Elizabeth had made for Tom the night before, and which she had managed to burn at the base as usual.

'He sleeps a lot just lately.'

'Bloody awful disease. Lost my first wife to it years before.'

'I'm sorry.' The sound of Tom's snoring came as an immediate comfort. 'I didn't know that.'

And then it was as if he suddenly had to let it all out, speaking with a full mouth, his words fast but barely more than a whisper. 'Over thirty years ago now. I was only twenty-five. Thought we had a whole life ahead of us, didn't I.'

'I'm so sorry,' she said again, not coming up with anything better.

'Nothing you can do to change the hand you get dealt, is there? When I talk about her now people always assume it's a fairy tale I'm painting. That she couldn't have been as wonderful as I say. But she really was.' The kitchen chair creaked as he leant back, took another bite of the cake. Elizabeth followed his lead and took a slice for herself. 'Of course, after that I met Phillipa, and she's been a fantastic wife and mother to our two. But there's something about first love. You can go on to love again, but it's never the same. It's not the new person's fault or anything. It's just when you first fall in love you have no idea of just how hard it is to lose somebody. You don't leave yourself open to it a second time. Don't you think?'

'I do,' she said, not looking up. 'I really do.'

It was a strange mix of relief and disappointment when she saw Jim off not long after that. The bags of garden waste were heavy as she helped him carry them through to the front ready for recycling, along with a bunch of cut roses which he said he would drop off for Alice when he went into the city later that afternoon because he knew they were her favourite. Waving as he entered his house, she looked up the busy city street on which she was living; the trees, bare in places, still clinging to leaves in others; the cars too numerous; the background din of normal life, whatever it was that normal meant. A place like this could never really be home for her, and she doubted it was for Tom either. The coast ran through her like a mountain spring, even though as a young woman she had always dreamed of coming here. Porthsennen formed in her mind as she looked up at a sorry chink of blue sky, that wide coastal vista and how small what she saw now seemed in comparison. Lives had come and gone, with young wives lost, children raised to adulthood in the time since they had first fallen in love. Was it true what Jim had said, that the first love is always the strongest? Maybe it was. And she knew, like Jim knew, that if she was forced to lose Tom soon, she could at least say that she had spent a whole lifetime loving him. Many people didn't get that.

That afternoon after Tom woke up, Elizabeth made them tea and set a couple of slices of Hevva cake on a plate. He was impressed by her efforts, even though it wasn't as good as what he could once make himself. How good it was to have her in the house, puttering about, as if she had always been there. And the reality was that he didn't feel all that different from back when he'd first met her. But all he could think about these last few days was that if they did confirm that he had cancer next Tuesday, there might only be a little bit of time left. Suddenly it was finite. How could he die, if he never saw the cottage in which he was raised again, or if he didn't ask Elizabeth the question he wanted to ask? About the things he thought he knew, and that had kept him returning to Porthsennen year in year out? Returning during his years of marriage had been more complicated, yet his wife never questioned his excuse of a fishing trip to see old friends. He had always felt as if he was betraying her as she waved him off, yet equally felt that sense of betrayal towards

Elizabeth when he considered no longer going. So, every year he had been back, delivering those flowers and wishes, each visit a chance to knock on the door and put things right, uncover the secret – if there was one – and yet he hadn't taken a single one of them. He was a bloody coward; he knew that all right. But if there was something to amend for, he wanted to do it now while he still had the chance, not think about how one day life would just be over, snuffed out like a candle flame, nothing more than a faint smoke trail that would, like memories, fade over time.

'I was thinking,' he said as he picked off a small piece of cake. It stuck in his teeth, his mouth too dry. 'We should go to Cornwall sooner rather than later. Maybe even before the bronchoscopy.' Cornwall was the place to have those important conversations. 'It's about time Alice saw where all this began.'

'Where all what began?' she said, muting the television. Crumbs settled in her lap as they fell from her lips.

'This,' he said, flicking a finger back and forth between the two of them. 'And maybe we should see it too. Together one last time in the place where we met, so that if there was something we needed to say to each other, we would have the chance that we never got the first time round.'

'Well, that's because you left without word or explanation, Thomas Hale. Even now it amazes me to think of it.'

'What was I supposed to do? Stick around and watch you and James play happy families?' he said without looking up. 'I can't believe you married him as quick as you did after I went to Wolf Rock.'

Her tutting cut through his indignance. 'And I can't believe you still believe what he told you.'

'What?' he said, his eyes narrowing.

'He wanted shot of you, so he told you we were married, but we weren't. I only married him because you left.'

'You mean to tell me . . .' The weight of the news caused him to deflate in his chair. 'That bloody lying bastard,' he said after a while, and then, 'What a fool I was.'

'No, Tom. Fooled, but not a fool. He lied to us both, and we were too green to see through it. When he told me the truth, we separated.'

'When was that?'

'Seven years after you left. After that, it was just me and Kate. There was never anybody else.'

A heavy sigh shuddered through his lips. 'How I wish I could go back and change things. All these years on our own, and we could have been together.'

'No point thinking like that. We had our chances. Still, I do think it would be lovely to go back together now. Perhaps see about a few of those wishes you wrote me.'

'I can't even remember what most of them were now,' he said, still amazed at the revelations. He watched as she got up and headed through to the hall. 'Where are you going?' he called.

'I'll be back in a moment.' And sure enough, just a short while later he heard her descending the stairs. When prompted he moved across in his chair, his bones aching as Elizabeth eased in beside him. There wasn't much room, but it was enough. The springs in the cushion creaked, and if he was honest, from the way she winced as she assumed position, it seemed as if perhaps her hips were telling her it was a bad idea too. But when she rested her head back against his shoulder, the sensation of her body against his overcame any pain he might have otherwise felt.

'What's that?' he asked, nodding towards the basket in her hand.

Her fingers fiddled at the clasp and she removed the lid, angled it so he could see inside. Breath rushed from him as he realised what it was. 'It's the life you wanted us to live together. I was thinking, now that I'm here with you, perhaps we could try our best to live it now.'

'You kept them all,' he whispered, reaching into the basket and fingering through the little blue notes. Paper rustled, stirring his memories. For a moment he thought he could smell the sea.

'Sometimes I think you forget the way I love you,' she said, repeating his words from earlier in the day. Heat rose in her cheeks, and he could feel himself getting choked up. Pulling one of the notes out, he read aloud.

'"1992: I wish we could fly kites together across the sand of Whitesand Bay".' A tear broke free which he quickly wiped away. 'So, you really did care that I came each year.'

'Of course I did. That one might have to wait for Porthsennen.' Her fingers rifled in the basket, and there it was again, that scent that was unmistakably home. 'Here's one we can cross off the list though. From 1970. "I wish that I could stroke your face and kiss your lips".'

It was a struggle not to cry again, his chin quivering at just the idea. 'There wasn't a year that went by that I didn't wish for that.'

His cheek was damp as she turned his face towards hers. Whispering, she said, 'Then what are you waiting for?'

As his lips touched hers it was as if not a day had passed since the last time he had kissed her. He felt her weight as she sank against his shrunken body, nestled in alongside him, everything they had ever needed right there. Just before he fell asleep, she whispered, 'I'm going to make all these wishes come true, Thomas Hale,' but he didn't hear her. Sleep came, and that night he dreamed of being back in their cottage, their first night together, Elizabeth wrapped up safe in his arms.

Then

The distance from home garnered an edgy sort of freedom, but with each step back to Porthsennen it weathered a little. Although Tom's mother had warned him against it, just the thought of getting to spend a few hours away from the village with Elizabeth, away from prying eyes like those belonging to Mr Bolitho whom he had seen watching them only that morning, had been too much of a temptation to resist. Joy swelled inside him, greater than anything he had ever felt. It had been the perfect afternoon. Being with Elizabeth outweighed everything.

'Still got a bit of a way to go,' he told Elizabeth as they crested the brow of the hill overlooking Gwynver beach, going as slowly as he could. At his feet he noticed a small crocus flower growing against the odds in the shadow of a rock. The petals were blue, bright as amethyst crystals in the coastal caves. The stem snapped easily as he held it at the base, presenting it for her to see.

'My favourite,' she said as she took it into her hand.

'Then I shall bring you one every year to mark this day,' he said as she held the flower to her chest. His hand brushed the soft curve of her back, the day behind them emboldening his touch. All the effort to hold back over the last six weeks felt foolish now; it was the right time. How could he not kiss her in that moment? But just as he was about to move in, he caught sight of a sparkling Austin Morris, red with a chrome trim, parked at the end of the track just the other side of the trees. The sunlight dazzled him as it danced off the grille at the front.

'Isn't that James?' he asked as she pulled away, turning to see.

'God, what's he doing here?' she whispered. 'You best let me do the talking,' she said, pulling Tom's jumper over her head as they descended the last few steps on the rocky path. Moments later they were standing in front of James Warbeck in the small clearing. The sea was rough, and Tom could feel the spray of it on his cheeks.

'James,' she said, smiling. Her voice sounded different, affected in some way. 'Whatever are you doing here?' Tom had to look away as Elizabeth kissed James's cheek. The young doctor took one of her hands into his without once looking away from Tom.

'Looking for you.' A jagged tooth jutted from his smile as he draped his arm around her shoulders. 'Mrs Clements told me that you went to Land's End with Margaret, but I saw her in the grocer's, and I thought to myself, if Margaret is back from her trip then that must mean that my Lizzy is also back.' An elaborate show exposed what looked to be an expensive wristwatch. Tom wanted to push his arm away from Elizabeth's shoulder. 'I have been looking for you for over half an hour. And here you are.'

'Yes,' she said, a little quieter, less sure than she was before. 'Here I am.' Tom saw the crocus flower fall from her hand.

'I have been itching to show you this. I thought to myself, my Lizzy would just love to see it.' An arm swept wide in the direction of the vehicle. 'Your carriage to Porthcurno tomorrow. Have you ever seen such a fine example of a car?' he asked, looking at Tom.

'It's very nice, sir,' Tom said, hanging back. But he wasn't thinking about the car. He couldn't shake a sense of anger over James's insistence on referring to Elizabeth as *my Lizzy*. He had no right; she wasn't a possession. She wasn't his.

'Come closer,' James insisted, beckoning them both forwards. 'Take a look at the interior.'

Tom took a few hesitant steps as a wave crashed over the sea-wall and the sun dipped behind a heavy cloud. Even from a distance he could smell the warmth of the new leather. He couldn't deny that the red seats and the slick black dash were beautiful. It was spotless, like nothing Tom had ever owned. Jealousy stirred and it felt like sickness, a rousing disappointment that he knew he would never be able to offer Elizabeth such things.

'It's a very fine car,' Tom said. Waves continued to strike the sea-wall. Was that sea spray or the first drops of rain? Elizabeth would be cold, and he thought to give her his coat, but he doubted it was appropriate.

'Yes, James. Really, it's lovely.' Elizabeth had a quick nose in the car, then took a step back. James watched them both then, his gaze flickering one to the other.

'So, tell me. Where have you been?'

'Tom kindly agreed to show me the path that leads to Gwynver beach. Margaret had told me that the view was quite spectacular, and I wanted to draw it.'

'Wonderful,' James said, taking a step towards her. She handed her book to him when he reached for it. 'What happened to your walk to Land's End?'

'Margaret couldn't make it. Tom saw how disappointed I was and offered to cheer me up.'

'What a kind fellow you must be.' James gave Tom's upper arm a slap. Cordial enough if you didn't know the truth. 'Keeping her entertained while I am otherwise engaged, saving lives. So, what have you been drawing?' The pages fluttered in the breeze as James struggled to turn them. 'I don't see anything new.'

Tom knew he had to do something when he saw Elizabeth stutter. 'It was too windy, sir,' he said, stepping in to cover their tracks. 'She drew a wonderful landscape of the coast, but the wind picked it right up and tore it away.'

'Art critic as well as a hero, are you?' James looked up to the sky. 'Well, the weather certainly has turned. Come on, Lizzy. Let me drive you home.' Tom could do nothing but watch as James ushered her into the car, his hand on the small of her back. Every muscle in his body felt ready for a fight, as if he was about to rush towards them and tear them apart. Eventually the sight of that car and the soft ticking of the engine forced his eyes away. The petals of the trampled crocus were already turning brown as he picked it up from the ground, yet he carefully slipped it in his pocket and made his way towards home.

James pulled up outside the practice in the sheltered spot alongside a rampant honeysuckle bush. The drive had been silent, uncomfortable in every way despite the soft leather seats which smelt new and luxurious, a little like vanilla. The engine quietened as Elizabeth arrived back to her reality, and she felt a weight in her chest, making it harder to breathe. Out with Tom in a place she had never been before she felt like herself, and here, in a place she could walk around competently in total darkness, she felt like somebody she didn't know, or even like that much. Tom made her feel safe even when she wasn't.

'Lizzy, are you listening to me?'

'What?' she said, realising that James had been speaking to her while she was lost in thought.

'You were miles away. What were you thinking about?'

'My lost drawings.'

'Oh,' he replied, licking his lips, pulling a piece of thread loose from the steering wheel. 'I thought perhaps you were thinking about that boy. You seemed awfully close when I saw you.'

There was a sadness to his voice that stirred her earlier guilt. But she couldn't find the courage to admit to her feelings. 'My feet were sore,' she lied. 'He was helping me.'

'Oh,' he said again, and she wasn't sure this time whether he believed her or not. 'Well, if that was all it was, he sounds like a suitably helpful person to have around. Maybe I could ask him to clean this for me twice a week,' he suggested, patting the dashboard. 'He looked as if he might need an extra bob or two.'

Her jaw locked, and an acrid taste flooded her mouth. 'He has a job,' she said. 'He doesn't need your money.'

Air vibrated at the back of his throat. 'If you can call it that.' It was a side of James that she had never seen before, built from snide, belittling intentions; gratitude for Tom and his simple life rose within her at that moment. 'It's hardly taxing pulling fish from the sea.'

'Not everybody has the opportunity to go off to London and become a doctor,' she said, her voice cold and curt. Her fears for what he might tell her father diminished in the shadow of his cruelty. 'And this *is* a fishing village.'

'Yes,' he said, going back to the stitching on his steering wheel. 'I suppose it is.' His hand settled on the door handle, the first drops of rain falling fat against the windscreen. 'Let's go inside. Your father is expecting us.'

They walked into the house together, much to her father's delight, and her mother's too once he alerted her to their presence. Elizabeth sat alongside her, but a vacancy hung between them. The kettle whistled to a boil, and from the seat on the other side of her mother James asked about her day. Elizabeth listened as she tried to tell him what she had been doing but couldn't really find the right words. It broke Elizabeth's heart a little, both for her mother and for James as he listened so patiently. Once the tea had brewed, her father asked Elizabeth about her walk to Land's End. She tried to catch a glimpse of James's expression as she told her father it was too chilly to really enjoy it. James kept his face turned away, but she was thankful for his silence until the conversation moved on.

Would she pay a price for his collusion? Perhaps, but it didn't matter right now. Even her mother's confusion couldn't wipe the day clean. The taste of salt was dry on her lips, and the fine grains of sand scratched at her skin through her clothes. Knots tangled her windswept hair.

It was a detail that didn't slip her mother's attentions, who every so often reached up to tuck a few strands back in place. With Tom, time ceased to exist in the form she knew it. It felt as if hardly any time at all had passed while they were together, yet she felt as if she had known him for a lifetime. Anything less than that could never now be enough.

'Elizabeth, dear,' her father said. 'Are you here with us, or somewhere else?'

'Sorry,' she said, lost in an idea of what her life could be, of the choices that she had. 'I was just thinking about something.'

'Excited for tomorrow,' her father said to James.

'What's tomorrow?' she asked.

'Don't tell me you've forgotten,' said James. 'I'm taking you to the Minack Theatre. I'll be here bright and early, before eight.'

'But I've got plans,' she said, even though it wasn't true. Going on a day trip with James was unthinkable now. Tom had all but told her he loved her, hadn't he? The courage was in her somewhere to tell the truth, and wherever it was hiding, she had to find it fast so that she might stop this charade.

'Surely nothing that can't be changed,' suggested her father. 'What could be more important than a day with your fiancé?'

'Nothing, I suppose,' she said quietly. Only she didn't believe it, because now she knew that Tom was more important to her than anything else in the world.

Now

His eyes flickered open to a brilliant light, disturbed by the sound of the front door closing. For a moment he was disorientated, even though he was in his chair, positioned in the house in which he had been living for the last forty-six years. Only in that moment there was something different; a scent, something familiar yet as unexpected as the sight in the mirror that gazed back at him now. That was when he felt her, remembered that she was nestled in his arms, her feet stretched out behind his. Memories of Porthsennen came to him, and then the present caught up when he opened his eyes to see Alice standing in the doorway, wrapped in her winter coat.

'Look at the pair of you,' she said, her smile at odds with the look in her eye. It was hard for her; he could see that. Setting her bag on the sofa, she started to remove her jacket. 'Have you been there all night?'

Tom whispered, didn't want to do anything that might make Elizabeth move from his side. 'That depends on the time.'

'Close to eight in the morning,' she said, checking her watch.

'Then I suppose we must have been.' The buzzing of her telephone cut through the silence. 'Anything important?' Tom asked as she slipped it back into her pocket.

'No,' she said, shaking her head. Alice picked up Elizabeth's almost untouched sandwich from the night before and stacked it on Tom's plate before moving them through to the kitchen. The rhythm of Elizabeth's breathing intensified as she roused.

'Oh, my goodness,' Elizabeth said, shuffling up in the chair. Her hair was all out of place, her eyes puffed with soft grains of rheum in the corners. 'We fell asleep.'

'We must have been comfortable.' Breathing her in, he felt her soften as he held her body close. 'And now we have completed another one of these wishes.' The blue note had become creased overnight, and with only one free hand each they unfolded it together and he angled the paper for her to read. '"1974: I wish that the first thing you saw today was my face".'

Skin crinkled around her eyes as she smiled. 'Only another forty-seven to go.'

'Well, we managed to complete two wishes in one night. I'd say we're off to a good start. And I think there's good news. Tony has called.'

'Who?'

'Tony. Alice's husband.'

Elizabeth sat forwards and rested one hand onto his. 'I thought his name was Brian.'

'Is it?' Confusion etched wrinkles across his forehead, his face scrunched up like one of those designer dogs Elizabeth had seen being dragged around the streets. Too much money and not enough sense for her liking as far as she could see in Hampstead. What could anybody do with a dog like that? They couldn't round sheep or manage the ascent of a steep coastal trail. 'Where did I get Tony from?'

'No idea, love.' Cups rattled on the tray as Alice came back, and the smell of hot butter permeated the air, drifting from the small silver rack set with a few slices of toast.

'Morning,' she said. Tom could see the shock of seeing them together like that had passed. It had been years since Alice had seen him with her mother, but he understood it was still strange to see this other woman in her mother's home, a woman of whom she had heard so much and yet knew so little.

'Good morning,' replied Elizabeth. Alice handed her a mug of tea as she sat forwards, squinting against the early morning sunlight, the sun low in the sky and too bright to see. 'Your father was just telling me that Brian called,' she ventured.

'Was he now?' she asked, stringing out her words sufficiently so that even Tom, who it seemed was playing the transient deafness card, would understand her dissatisfaction at the perceived intrusion.

After a moment of silence, he decided to reply. 'Well, he did. Didn't he? I saw you checking your phone.'

Alice sat down on the arm of the settee, took a deep breath in before she spoke. 'Actually, I called him, let him know what was happening.' The moment of shared understanding between his love and his daughter didn't go unnoticed, and he wondered what he'd missed. The barrier that had seemed to exist between them the last time they were all together had been brought down, an ease and comfort taking its place. 'That's what you thought I should do, wasn't it?'

'I think it was; yes,' Elizabeth said.

Alice turned to her father. 'He wants to come over. I said I'd check with you first.'

Tom was lost in a daydream until Elizabeth gave him a nudge. Was he feeling confused? He had been at times, forgetting simple facts or the date and day of the week. Like the name of Alice's husband just now. Perhaps they were just getting old, and this was part of the deal.

'That would be lovely,' he said. 'I would like to see him.'

'I'll find out when he's available.'

Tom knew there was something else on his daughter's mind from the way she was focusing on details around her, like the speck of fluff on her trousers and a tuft of hair that suddenly didn't seem to conform.

'Want to tell me what's on your mind?' he asked.

Her eyes glistened as she looked up, tears forming, threatening to fall. 'I'm thinking about not going to Hastings.'

Tom shared a look with Elizabeth. 'Where did that come from?' he said, turning back to Alice.

'How can I go now? You need me. I can't help from miles away, can I?'

Years ago, she had sat on this same couch, her eyes red with tears then too. In the memory she was barely a teenager who had made a mistake, cigarettes found under her mattress. The only thing that had calmed her then was a cuddle from her dad, telling her that things were still OK, and that he still loved her. Pushing with all his strength from the chair, he moved across to Alice. The sight of his effort shook loose a tear.

'You can't change anything by being here, Bab.'

'But I want to be here. I want to help.'

He rubbed her arm like he had when she was small. 'I know you do, but it's not your job to look after me.'

'I thought you wanted me to stick around so that I could fix things with Brian.'

'Well, what do I know?' he said as he shrugged his shoulders. 'I only want that if it's what you want. I'd hate to pry.'

His last comment elicited a smile. 'Well that *would* be a first. I just thought it would be best for you if I stayed.'

'It's always best for a parent when they have their child close.' That idea broke Elizabeth's heart, and she began to cry too. Guilt forced her to turn away, desperately trying to hide it. 'But I want what's best for you, whatever that is.'

'OK,' she said, drying her eyes. 'I'll think about it. And I'll tell Brian to come over anytime he likes after we get back from Porthsennen. Is that OK?'

'Of course, Bab.'

He kissed her on the head, and she managed a little smile.

When Elizabeth walked back in from seeing Alice out, Tom was just finishing his cup of tea. A new ease about things comforted her this morning after waking up together for the first time in a long while, and so she positioned herself alongside him on the settee, wanting to be as close as she could get.

'She tries so hard to be strong, poor thing.'

'I know.' His hand brushed against Elizabeth's knee, his fingers distorting the dappled light streaming through the trees in the front garden.

'Has she always been like that?'

'Ever since her mother left.' Elizabeth wanted to ask more about that but wasn't sure it was her place, and the conversation was already moving on. 'But sometimes being strong gets you nowhere though. I've been strong for years on the subject of Porthsennen.' He pointed to the picture of Wolf Rock on the wall. 'What happened between us, and the way I left . . . it's never left me, you know. I thought it was for the best, but looking back, I'm not so sure it was.'

For a while neither of them said anything, both remembering the past and what they had left behind. Silenced by things that remained unsaid. 'Do you think Alice will work it out with Brian?' Elizabeth eventually asked.

He shrugged a little. 'I don't know. I do hope so.' He reached for the basket of wishes. 'Now, what do you say about trying to see if we can do a few of these today? I can think of one or two I'd quite like to bring to reality.'

Her cheeks flushed bright red to think of the ones he was referring to. Embarrassment hit her as hard as it had when she was young, before she knew anything of the world or what her life would hold in store. 'You're a cheeky old bugger,' she whispered, his laughter breaking her awkwardness. But when she looked up his expression was deadly serious. 'Do you think you still can?' she whispered.

'Well I'm not dead yet,' he giggled, 'and I seem to remember having a few good ideas back in 1980,' he said, waving the slip of blue paper at her. What he had written in 1980 had made her blush then, and it seemed little had changed. And with that he reached over, took her in his arms, and kissed her again.

'I don't look like I used to,' she said, breaking away. 'Neither of us do.'

'When I found that wish, I thought you must be having a midlife crisis,' she said, laughing again. He began stroking her hair, his fingers fiddling at the way it curled underneath at the ends. How she had missed that touch.

'Maybe I'm having an end of life crisis now.' He tried another laugh, but neither of them really found it that amusing. She struggled to hold back a tear. 'Come on, what do you say we go upstairs, spend the day in bed together like we should have done back then?'

And just a moment later she followed, Tom leading the way with her hand in his, like the young woman she once was who fell so endlessly in love.

Then

The warm water came as such a relief that she felt like spending hours in the bath that night, soaking her sore feet and blistered heels. Thoughts of Tom came and went while she lay there, his arms and all that rowing he had done. How tired he must have been. The memory of the waves, and his confession that he had forgotten to keep watch. The water chopped against her pale skin as she swished her hands back and forth.

Standing in her bedroom, dressed in the fluffy comfort of her robe, she could hear her father downstairs, turning the pages of a book. Light shone from her mother's open bedroom door, and as she approached Elizabeth could see her sitting up in bed with a reading light casting a subtle golden glow. The pink damask sheets of childhood. When she saw Elizabeth in the doorway, she beckoned her forwards.

'Where is your father?' she whispered as Elizabeth sat down on the bed. It was a good sign; she understood the people that linked them together. Was there a moment of mental clarity to be enjoyed here?

'He's reading downstairs,' Elizabeth said. 'Do you need something?'

'No, dear. It was you that I wanted – to show you

this.' She picked up a book from her knees and offered it to her.

Elizabeth took it, sitting on the edge of the soft bed. As she opened the cover, she saw that it was a photo album, the first image her mother as a child. They bore a striking resemblance, the same slanted nose, the heavy brows. The same plump lips and deep cupid's bow.

'It's you,' she said to her mother.

'Yes. It's an album that my own mother gave me on the day I married your father. It's a strange day, leaving home that morning as a child, leaving the church as a married woman. Two totally different lives. Even the best mother in the world cannot adequately prepare a child for such an event.' Elizabeth clung to her every word. 'She created this album as a guide, something to show me what I was supposed to do. Here, you see. Look at this.'

Together they leafed through the pages, images of them at various stages of Elizabeth's mother's life; a changed nappy, playing in the garden, her grandmother alone. Cooking dinner in clothes that appeared more suitable for a Sunday trip to church.

'It's an instruction manual, Elizabeth, for a life I never asked for. Of course,' she said, holding onto her daughter's hand tightly, 'I love both you and your father a great deal, and would never change a moment of the life we have built together. But at the time when your father was presented to me, I didn't want what he was offering.'

Elizabeth didn't know what to say for a moment. The idea of her father being presented didn't sit well with her, as if her mother had been given little choice. Yet

142

despite the many thoughts running through her mind she could think of only one question to ask.

'What did you want instead?'

Holding open the sheets, warmth diffused from the bed. Elizabeth slipped in alongside her mother, facing each other like they did when Elizabeth was small and had woken from a nightmare. They held the covers close under their chins.

'Everything. I wanted to cruise on a ship to America, see the Statue of Liberty, and eat a proper Italian pizza in Naples. I wanted to see the ballet in London. Pick at French bread while sitting on the grass of the *Jardin du Luxembourg*.' Elizabeth had never even heard of it.

'Did you ever do any of those things?'

'No.' Elizabeth saw it in the flicker of her eyes, the regrets that she had stifled over the course of her life. Pity for her father surfaced too. 'But what I did do is something so much more wonderful than all of those things, and that was that I had you,' she said, reaching out, stroking Elizabeth's cheek. 'Without your father that would never have been possible. Sometimes our biggest dreams are the things we don't even know we want. Life is not really about the fun and adventure, or the moments of excitement, but the people you love and the family you create; that's what I'll miss when I can no longer remember who you are.'

Elizabeth could feel the tears coming, but her mother's stoicism forced her to fight them back. 'Don't say that, Mum.'

'But I must, because already you are slipping away from me. Don't tell me you don't feel it. Last week I struggled to place your name, and there are times when I think you are still a small child and then I see you and I realise how wrong I am. I can't stand it, Elizabeth. And now, here you are, faced with a predicament that troubles you, and which I understand all too well. I know you are struggling with the decision to marry James.' A tear escaped, streaking hot across her cheek. 'Life is short, too short to take chances on what may make you happy.'

'I don't understand. Do you think I should marry him anyway, even if I'm not sure?'

'I'm trying to tell you that if you choose to marry him, you will be just fine. But if you have other dreams and you know what they are, you must chase them over a marriage to James.'

This was her moment to tell her mother. 'What if my dream was to be with somebody else?'

'If he made you happy, then I see no reason not to approve.'

'What if I made a choice that I knew you wouldn't like? That Daddy wouldn't like.'

The saddest smile crossed her lips. 'Your father might understand more than you realise. We've all had to make difficult decisions at some point, Elizabeth. And sometimes the decisions we must make are beyond the comprehension of other people. So, try to remember those words when I'm not around, darling, and always remember to be brave.'

Tom stood in the shadow of the gable end of the house, the spot where the light didn't catch his face. His fingers sifted through the stones in his pocket, the small grey pebbles he had taken from the beach. Moonlight bounced from the windows above in silvery halos. He counted the windows again. If he got the wrong one, it would be a disaster.

'Here goes,' he told himself, and with a breath in for luck he launched the first pebble. It hit the wall, clattered all the way back to the ground, coming to rest in a small gully by the side of the road. Nobody stirred.

After giving a second pebble a kiss for luck, he launched it. This time it hit the pane of glass. Finding his courage along with his aim, he quickly launched two more in close succession until he saw a light illuminate the bedroom beyond. The surf roared in the distance, his constant companion, carried by a rough sea breeze. Retreating into the shadows, he saw somebody draw the curtains.

The creak of a hinge cut through the night air and he dared a look skyward. Elizabeth was standing at her window, looking to the street for the source of the disturbance. Relief flooded him. Tom knew that he wasn't good enough in so many ways for a girl like her. But the way he felt around her, and the way he made her feel, if he had read it correctly, was impossible to ignore. His mother had warned him not to get involved with the likes of the Davenports; after all she should know. But Elizabeth was worth the risk, worth betraying his family for. She was worth everything, so he had to be prepared to risk everything for her.

Her mouth hung wide as he stepped into the light. 'What are you doing?' she asked, her voice half a whisper, half a shout. Her lips twisted into a slight smile. That gave him hope, and he clung to it.

'Well, right now I'm praying that nobody sees me here talking to you. Go and get your coat. I've got something to show you.'

'I can't,' she said, incredulous. But out of view she was already using her big toe to pull her feet from her slippers. 'It's almost midnight.'

'Which is why you need to come now.'

'But my parents are at home. My mother's in bed, and my father's awake. If he catches me . . .'

'Didn't you tell me that you wanted an adventure?' He left only a moment's pause for thought. During it, she remembered her mother's words, the reminder that she needed to be brave. 'I'll be waiting at the bottom of the steps. Don't take too long about it.' Seconds later he was gone.

When he saw her hanging from her window, the subtle smile, her hair undone and draped about her shoulders, it was as if he was seeing his own future before him. Thoughts came to him as if they were already memories; early mornings as she rose from bed; the days when she was unwell and how he would care for her. He hadn't witnessed any good example of what to do as a husband, but he sure as hell knew what he *shouldn't* do, and he prayed that was enough. He wouldn't be out late drinking. There wouldn't be other women. He wouldn't use his fists when a gentle word would suffice. Damn it, he wouldn't use his fists at all. If his best financially wasn't enough, he'd compensate for his failings with gifts more valuable than any possessions; his time, love, consistency. They were his riches, and he would give them gladly. Her wish was his command.

And then he saw her hurrying along the path, wrapped in her coat, looking around to see if anybody was watching them. Her shoes were the same as from that afternoon, the same as she had been wearing on the night when he'd pulled her mother from the water. Laced and dainty with a heel. He liked them. And those legs. He liked those too, although he did his best to keep his eyes off them. Porthsennen was a small place. Girls had been tarnished with a label before; poor Edith Ball was the latest, had given birth to a little girl only a couple of years ago when she was just sixteen. Poor Edith. How some people talked about her now. And she wasn't the first. He felt a sense of guilt in that moment, but despite it he stayed. He didn't have a choice. Not when it came to Elizabeth.

'You must be mad, throwing stones up at my window. Can you imagine what my father would have done if he'd caught you?'

'But he didn't, did he?' When that didn't settle her, he relented. 'I knew it was your window.' He heard the call of a voice then, and it was a reminder to him that they were still out on show. Reaching for her cold hand, he led her into the shadow of the Old Success Inn. With the weight of his body he pushed her against the wall, covered her as if they were kissing, and he felt something shift in his belly, his body tighten. Elizabeth's heart was pounding too, a sensation of being both trapped and excited all at once. Then they heard a man stumbling from the pub. He staggered across the road, vomited over the sea-wall, before slowly meandering away.

'Who was that?' she whispered. The cool air chilled her as his body pulled away from hers, and she had to stop herself from pulling him back.

'Don't know,' Tom said, his attention on the road. 'Probably a tourist from one of the holiday lets.'

'What a disgusting thing to do,' she said, motioning to the sea-wall. 'I can smell it.'

'Then we better get out of here,' he said. The cool wind hit him as he nosed out from behind the wall, looking left and right. 'Come on. Let's make a dash for it before anybody else comes along.'

'I don't think anybody saw us,' he said when they were away from the village, his hands resting onto his knees, his tongue loose on his lips. They were soft and red, his hair messy. Heat flared from her face as she mirrored his stance.

'Well if they did, we'll soon know about it.'

'Do you care?' he asked, hopefully.

'No,' she said. 'I don't think I do.'

He pointed past the fence towards the rocks where the sound of the waves echoed beneath them. 'Let's cut through there. Nobody will be down by the rocks at this time of night. It'll just be you and me.'

From the moment they left the path the land was uneven and difficult to negotiate. Rocks sharp and shaded jutted from the ground, and she stumbled more than once. He held onto her tightly, and she liked the way he touched her, the certainty of his hands on her body. He didn't wait for an invitation, and that self-assurance made her feel completely safe.

'Just over here,' he said. 'I want to show you something.' They found a small hollow in the rock and she slipped her body in. He sat down beside her, guided her head back with his hand softly placed at the back of her neck. 'I want you to close your eyes, and make a wish,' he said, just before she was flat. 'Are you ready?'

'For what?' she asked. She wondered if he was still watching her. He was.

'Just trust me. On the count of three, open your eyes. One. Two,' he said, resting his head back to gaze at the sky. 'Three.'

The dark this far away from the village was as thick as oil, the only light the moon which itself was off hiding somewhere else. In its place before her she saw a lucent smudge streaking through the sky. In places it was silver, in others purple with brilliant light coming from within it. It was as if the sky had revealed a view to another world beyond. She thought of her grandparents then, how they were in heaven, and thought that perhaps in this place just moments from home she had found a way to be closer to them. Her breath caught in her throat, and she felt a tear prick from her eye. A cool fingertip brushed the tear away. For a moment her muscles stiffened with self-consciousness, lying there on the rocks like that, letting him wipe her tears. But then she relaxed again, aware that it felt as if he was returning to her, as if somehow, he had until then, been missing.

'There's no light from the village this close to the sea,' he told her. 'At least not when the lighthouses go quiet.' Both Wolf Rock and Longships winked from a distance. Every time the light faded, she had the clearest view of the sky above.

'It's beautiful,' she said. 'What is it?'

'It's called the Milky Way.' He might not be able to give her a car, but he could give her the stars. 'It's our galaxy. And there are constellations too. Look, over there is the Plough. Cassiopeia just below. Next month you'll be able to see Orion. Just look for the three bright stars in the south sky near the horizon.' He spread his hands wide like an offering. 'Now it's all yours.'

'How do you know about things like this?' she asked softly.

'My grandfather,' he said, resting a hand onto her stomach. His fingertip trailed absently along the lace edge of her blouse where her coat had fallen open. 'He taught himself to read because he said clever folk didn't get taken advantage of.' He frowned. 'Sliced off half of his hand when a wave struck his boat one day. Not too clever, was it?'

Despite her trying to hold them, her giggles erupted. 'Sorry,' she said, calming herself. 'Do you read a lot too?'

'Yes, I suppose so.' He paused. 'For a fisherman.'

'There's nothing wrong with being a fisherman,' she said.

'Maybe not, but it's hardly my dream to catch fish for ever.'

'I thought you said you didn't have any dreams,' she said, nudging his arm. 'You're not a liar, are you?'

'Everybody has dreams, Elizabeth. I just meant that only certain people's dreams get the chance to come true.' As he turned their noses were only inches apart. 'But I'm starting to believe that maybe I'm luckier than I thought I was.'

He didn't feel uncomfortable like he had in the past, like when he was with Francine in his bedroom and wanted her to leave. God, he hadn't known what to do afterwards. This time it felt easy. Her silence didn't fill him with fear, and he felt no rush to fill it.

'So, what is your dream?' she asked after a while.

Shyness kept him from speaking. 'You first.'

'My dream? You know it already. I want to paint. I want people to hang what I create in their homes, let it be a part of their lives.' The night air was cold, yet she sucked it in, remembering how much her father thought it a folly. 'It's not that easy though. My father doesn't think it's a good idea.'

'He also thinks you should get married to James.'

A certain resignation lingered in his voice, the same she had felt since the engagement was arranged. 'Yeah,' she said, wondering. But she didn't want to think or talk about James. 'Now you go.'

Shadows from her eyelashes stretched across her cheek as he moved to look at her from above, long and curled and beautiful. It was possible to imagine her old in that moment, the lines of shadow as wrinkles. Any kind of life would be good enough for him, dreams fulfilled or not, if that was the face waiting for him at the other end of it.

Placing a large flat pebble on her tummy, followed by a second so that it was perfectly balanced on top, he began. 'I want to build,' he told her, placing a third. 'Modern buildings, nothing like what we've got here in Porthsennen. I want to be an architect.'

'So why don't you do it?'

He shook his head and removed the stones from her body. 'Can't do it here, can I? I'd have to leave Porthsennen. That's not easy for me.' She realised he was lost in the thoughts of a dream that seemed unattainable. How easily she understood. 'Maybe you can hold one of your exhibitions in a building that I design.'

The idea of that future seemed comforting to Elizabeth. That version of their lives, away from Porthsennen, together and pursuing what they loved; it felt right in a way that nothing ever had before. Even the simple things, like cleaning and cooking dinner for when he returned home from work felt like a treat to savour; doing the same for James felt like a sentence for a crime she wasn't sure she had committed. Looking at Tom, she wondered if she was on the cusp of committing it.

'Why is this so easy?' she asked.

'What do you mean?'

'Being with you. Talking to you.' The wind struck her as she edged forwards, their faces realigned. 'Why do you make me feel like anything is possible?'

'Is that how I make you feel?'

'Yes,' she said.

He wanted to kiss her so much then as she licked her lips, wetting what the salty air had dried. But he didn't get a chance to because she reached forwards and kissed him instead. It was an inexpert effort, but he didn't mind, and he didn't want it to stop when moments later she pulled away.

'I didn't expect that,' he said.

'Neither did I,' she replied. Her body shook. 'But I've wanted to do it all day.'

'Me too,' he said, leaning in to kiss her again. Her hair tickled his face as she moved, her lips, falling into rhythm with his. They stayed like that for some time, but even when she pulled away it was as if she was still on him, her touch imprinted on his face.

'So that's how you do it,' she said coyly, her voice soft and apologetic. He could barely hear her over the sound of the water striking the rocks below. 'Perhaps I shouldn't have done that after all.'

'Why not?'

'It wasn't right.'

'It felt right to me.'

The stars twinkled as she gazed up, then the dark was broken by a flash of bright light guiding ships to safe passage. Her eyes met his, then she looked away. In truth she didn't know where to look. 'What are we going to do?'

'That depends, Elizabeth.'

'On what?'

'On whether you love James or not.' He paused, faltered just a little. 'And also, maybe whether or not you think you could love me.'

'I barely even know you, Thomas Hale.' Her words were soft, fearful, but she knew the answer. 'But I know I love you.'

'You know me better than anybody else knows me.' In that moment when she felt so vulnerable, she couldn't have imagined a better answer, and she welcomed it when he kissed her again. 'Tell James that you don't want to marry him and marry me instead.'

Be brave, she thought. *Please be brave.*

'How are you supposed to tell somebody that you no longer want to marry them?'

'It's like what you are looking at,' he said, pointing to the inky sky and the streak of luminance bleeding through it. 'You can't see what's up there most of the time. Even just a short walk back to the village would make this part of the sky look totally different. But just a subtle change, just a short distance from what you know, and look what you find. All that, just waiting to be found.'

'That all sounds simple enough now, but what about in real life? You're full of nice words, but do you think my father is going to let me gad about with you?'

The untimeliest smile crossed his lips. 'Gad about?'

'Oh, would you stop it. You might know all sorts of fancy things with your books and facts about the sky, but don't tell me you know my father better than I do. He's going to be angrier than I've ever known him.'

She was up on her feet, moving ever closer to the edge. Tom jumped up, followed her. 'What are you getting upset about?' he asked.

Fat, hot tears streamed down her cheeks, filled with her worries as she pulled away from Tom's touch. It was foolish to think of her father accepting this. He could barely accept her wearing trousers and had been so mad when he knew that she had seen Tom in a companionable fashion. What was he going to say when she told him that she loved Tom? Loved him? Oh, God, she really did. She could feel it all through her body, from her racing heart to the throbbing of her feet.

'We don't need his permission, Elizabeth.' Despite the fact Tom was right, and the anger her father's ideas and insistences often raised, she wanted his approval. As his daughter she wanted him to be proud. 'And if you're so worried about it, then I'll speak to him myself. I'll ask his permission to marry you.'

Water washed beneath her in foamy sprays as she sat down on the edge of a rock, her feet dangling towards the sea. 'And what do you think he'll say?' she asked as Tom sat alongside her. Gulls called in the distance.

'I don't care if he doesn't approve. We'll leave, go where he can't find us.'

'How can I when my mother's not well? And there's your family too, remember. What would you say to—' she began, but she didn't get a chance to finish. They heard the crack first, but it all happened too quickly. Her balance was lost as the shard of rock shifted beneath her, and moments later she fell forwards onto the ledge below.

'Elizabeth!' he shouted into the dark, swinging himself around to look down over the edge. Dark stared back at him, her body just visible, half in the water, half out, all splayed out. Her fingers clung to the edge of a wet, slippery rock. All it would take was one large swell and it could sweep her into the sea. His muscles pulled tight as he reached towards her, but the drop was too far for him to pull her to safety.

'I'm coming,' he shouted as he snaked left and right for a path down. Tested each step as he weaved closer, the sea growing louder as he descended, almost growling by the time he reached the ledge. His first step proved too slippery to cross by foot, so instead he laid his body down onto the stone, wedging his feet behind a rock to secure himself.

'Can you reach me?' he called to her, stretching across. A wave broke the surface of the rocks, cold water rushing in through his clothes. Elizabeth yelped as her body surged forward, stumbling as the sea washed around her. It brought her closer to him and he saw she had lost a shoe. 'Can you reach?' he called again, more desperate this time.

Her fingers were splayed out as far as they could go, as another wave breached the rocks. A dribble of blood ran from her forehead down the edge of her nose. The sound of the water was deafening, but the wave brought her just close enough that he could clasp her hand in his.

'Hold on,' he called, and he felt her fingers tighten against his. His arms were strong but still he doubted himself as another wave rushed towards them. Memories of his brother surfaced; he had hated the water ever since the day Daniel drowned, hated it even more in this moment when it threatened to take Elizabeth from him. The heavy burden of his father's blame weighed him down, but fighting against it, he pulled as hard as he could and with a gasp and cough Elizabeth emerged from the water. Doubts continued to bother him, but he had little choice other than to do his best. As Elizabeth held on, praying to be saved, she didn't doubt him for a second.

Now

The first thing Elizabeth did the following morning was collect the basket from the settee and set it down on the table. All was quiet besides the gentle lull of Tom's breathing, so with a smile over the thought of what they had done the night before, she made a cup of tea and sat with the wishes. It was like being seventeen again. Somehow her fingers felt flexible this morning, so she leafed through the wishes with ease, beginning to sort them into three piles. Those that could only be done in Porthsennen, those she could manage to recreate in London, and those they had already achieved. Placing the wishes in that pile brought a smile to her face, and she was glad there was nobody there to see her blush.

Putting the wishes in order, she found that they had already done more in the last few days than she realised. But the more difficult wishes, including one very important one that would require a considerable degree of soul searching of her own, weighed heavily on her. It was best not to think too much about those she thought, so she placed them back in the basket along with those they had already achieved, folded so they would think they were complete. Then she added those that could only be achieved in Porthsennen, like flying kites at Whitesand Bay. And what she was left with was a handful of wishes that were possible in London, but with very little idea of how best to achieve them. Cool air drifted into the house as she stood at the French doors overlooking the garden, and the sight of the croci brought a smile to her face. Help was what she needed, from that Internet thing Kate and her grandkids were always using. Knowing she couldn't ask her daughter for help, she picked up the phone and called Alice, and explained what she was trying to do.

It was just the next day when Alice knocked on the door to begin their grand plan. Elizabeth hadn't been able to sleep much the night before, but her adrenaline was working overtime, and she hoped that would be enough to see her through. Tom was too tired to notice her anxiety and had spent most of the day asleep. That night they had lain alongside each other in the bed, spooned up close, and she had mused how right everything felt with the world. For a moment she had even forgotten about the cancer. At least he was well rested; he was going to need all the energy he could muster for today.

'Come on, Dad,' Alice said as she blustered into the living room. 'Get your coat on.'

Tom looked to Alice, then Elizabeth. 'What for?'

'We've got things to do today,' Elizabeth said, unable to control her smile. Alice reached forward and helped herself to a mug from the table, poured herself a tea from the pot. Tom watched her every move as if he'd found himself in a strange house and was trying to work out what the hell was going on.

'What's she talking about?' he asked Alice.

'Got nothing to do with me, Dad. I'm just the facilitator. You have more unfinished business together than anybody realised.' She winked at him. 'But you'll have a bit less by the end of the day.'

Tom turned to Elizabeth. 'What have you gone and done now?'

Her heart was racing, as if she'd been running like one of those crazy types she'd seen in the streets. It felt too hot as she slipped her arms into her coat, the adrenaline of excitement on double time. Apprehension too. 'You'll see,' she said. 'You'll see.'

Alice dropped them off at a corner restaurant on Drury Lane. '1972,' she said to Tom as they were seated at their table. 'You wished we were eating Eggs Benedict in a fancy restaurant.' His eyes widened as she pulled out the small slip of blue paper from that year. He took it with a smile, and after reading his words he propped it up against the saltshaker.

'My writing was a bit neater back then,' he said, eyes still on the paper. 'I used to eat it at a small café near the Barbican. I was sure you'd love it. I think that place is a Costa now.'

'And you were right, I do, so let's place our order. We've got a fair bit to get through today.'

Breakfast was better than anything Elizabeth had ever cooked for herself, two perfectly poached eggs with bacon on toasted muffins, and the smell of it made her mouth water. Nearing the end of her meal, she realised Tom had barely touched his.

'Don't you like it?' she asked.

159

'It's not that,' he said, taking another small morsel. 'It's just that too much makes me feel queasy.'

Despite her disappointment regarding the implications of food induced nausea for the rest of her planned day, she managed a smile before setting her knife and fork down. 'I'm not that hungry anyway. Why don't we head off? We have plenty of other things to do.' She pulled the wishes from her pocket and waved them at him. 'Just a few special moments to share together. We missed out on so much. We can at least try to recapture some of the things you wished for over the years.'

'What about what you wished for? I never stopped to ask, did I?'

'No, you didn't,' she said, slipping her arms into her coat. He was grateful for her help in dressing in his own. 'But never mind that now. I'd say you didn't do a bad job of knowing what I'd like over the course of the years. You just wait until we get to Porthsennen.'

'Have you still got that robe I sent you?'

'You'll have to wait and see.'

'I'd like to see you in it, that's for sure.'

'Steady on. It's not even ten o'clock.' The waiter arrived at their table and she paid the bill. 'Now come on, your chariot awaits.'

They stepped outside the restaurant to find a black limousine pulled up alongside the kerb. The chauffeur was standing at the passenger door, waiting as if they were royalty or celebrities, and stunned into silence, Tom stepped inside. When the door was closed and it was just the two of them, he said, 'How did you manage to organise all this?'

Bubbles tickled her nose as she raised a flute of champagne to her lips, poured by the driver moments before. 'I didn't do it on my own. Alice helped.' The arthritis made everything heavy, the bottle included as she reached down to turn it so that he could see the label. 'Recognise this?'

'Is that the one I bought you all those years ago?'

'It sure is. If you manage to have a sip of this, I'd say that's 1999 and 1978 just about taken care of.'

He sipped, then quickly spat the champagne back into the glass. Some of it sprayed over their knees.

'What year did you say I got you this?'

'1978. Why?'

'Just taste it.' Her taste buds flinched, like sucking on a lemon.

'I thought wine was supposed to get better with age.' Her shoulders dropped with disappointment at the thought of all the years she'd been keeping it.

'Apparently not all of them,' he said, brushing his wet trousers. But he liked the sentiment. 'Let's say it still counts.'

The city rose around them as they pulled into the traffic. Buildings towered above them. Elizabeth couldn't hear what was said as Tom leaned forward and spoke to the driver, but when he sat back, he turned to her.

'Are we on a time limit?'

'Sort of. Why?'

'Can we spare thirty minutes? I've got something I'd love to show you.' He watched as she checked her watch. 'It would take care of 2004.'

The earliest of wishes were imprinted on her memory, but some of the later ones were harder to recall. What was 2004?

'I suppose half an hour is fine,' she said.

'Great. Driver,' he called through to the front. 'We are a go with the history tour. Fasten your seatbelts,' he said as if there was a car full of people. 'Let's get this show on the road.'

They started with an office building, then a bridge, followed by part of a school. All places he had in some way helped build. That year, along with the flower and the wish, he had left her a little model of a house. They finished up parked in a narrow lane in the shadow of the Barbican Estate, and had been driving around the city for much longer than half an hour.

'And you built all that?' she asked as they peered up at the towering apartment blocks.

'Well, not really. But I worked on the central tower.'

It was so tall she couldn't see the top from her position in the car. Everywhere felt so different from their village, but somehow with Tom there with her it didn't feel strange. It was perhaps, how she had once imagined her life would be. 'You came a long way, Thomas Hale.'

'Not bad for a fisherman, eh?' he asked.

'You finally got to live your dream.'

'Well, one of them.'

'And we still have a lot of little notes to get through.'

'Yes,' he said, and she wondered for a moment what was wrong. Was he sad? Tired by it all? Fearful of his own mortality? She couldn't read him. 'But some of those wishes might be harder to fulfil than others, wouldn't you say?'

Her aged hands shook in her lap. 'Yes, Tom. Some of them will be almost impossible.'

That afternoon he found himself in a private cinema screening – *Armageddon*, the movie and his wish, from 1998. At the time he had thought it was wonderful, and although he was fighting back a tear as the credits rolled, Elizabeth seemed distinctly unmoved. 'It was totally unbelievable,' she said, and left the building shaking her head, hurrying as best they could to get to their next stop. But even though they hadn't done all that much to expend energy, he didn't have much to spare. The limousine pulled up on Fleet Street and moments later the driver's door opened.

'Are we there already?' A weary breath fluttered through his lips. 'I thought we might head home for a rest soon.'

'A rest?' she said, pulling on her shoes. 'You've been sitting down all day, and we've just been stuck in this car for the best part of forty-five minutes thanks to traffic.'

'It wasn't that bad today.'

'Well it's not like Porthsennen. I didn't expect it to take us so long to get from one place to the next.' When he didn't relent, she sighed before asking, 'Do you want to go home instead?'

'It's not that I'm not keen. I'm just a bit tired, love. That's all.'

'It was a mistake, wasn't it? I should have known we couldn't fit forty-nine years into a few hours.'

Her expression made him feel guilty; she had gone to so much effort, and all he could do was complain that he was tired. All those years he had let her down by never once knocking on her door, and now he was struggling to make it through a few hours.

'It wasn't a mistake. We might have both made mistakes over the years, but this certainly isn't one of them.'

It was so warm and genuine that her disappointment eased.

'Am I forgiven?' he asked.

'Forgiven? For what?'

'Being a spoilsport.'

'There's nothing to forgive.' And she didn't just mean today; although he was the one who left, she was the one who needed to ask for forgiveness. 'I could never be angry at you.'

'Then let's get to it,' he said, edging her out of the car. 'I'm guessing we're about to see 1984 come to fruition judging by our location,' he said as he stepped into the sunlight. It was such a lovely day, a light blue sky with fine wisps of cloud. It made everything seem easier, and somehow it helped him find the energy he needed. The driver helped steady him, and soon enough they were on their way down the narrow lane that would lead them to Temple Church.

'I thought that you couldn't remember all the years so well,' she said.

'Well, maybe I can remember them better than I let on. After all, I had all year to think about what I wanted to wish for us. It wasn't that hard to remember fifty wishes, and the order that they came in.'

They steadied each other, Elizabeth gripping his arm as the ground sloped down. 'I think you mean forty-nine,' she said with a hint of sarcasm. 'Remember you never made it to Porthsennen this year.'

'No, I don't suppose I did, did I. Let's call it forty-nine.' The ornate circular church appeared before them, and as they descended the steps into the vestibule Tom watched as she gazed up at the ceiling. The architecture was awe inspiring, and she was floored just as he knew she would be. 'I'm right though, right? It was 1984.'

She handed him another wish, a crumpled piece of blue paper from her pocket. He read the date and the wish. *1984: I want to take you to Temple Church, one of the most beautiful places I have found in London, where we will listen to evensong by candlelight.*

'Just like you said.'

'I knew what I was doing that year, all right. And listen,' he said, holding his hand up to his ear. 'I can already hear them singing.'

The acoustics were wonderful as they stepped inside, surrounded by interred Templar Knights. Vaulted ceilings rich and echoey loomed above, drenched in flickering shadows. They took their seats to listen to the choir, and he watched Elizabeth get lost in the music, transcended for a while by the feelings the singing could stir up. He had first walked in here by accident, drawn by the dulcet voices that reached him on the street. That night he had argued with his wife, which was nothing new, but this time she had accused him of seeing somebody else. She had told him that she had a feeling in her heart that he wasn't really hers. And although he wasn't having an affair, and was in every practical respect a loyal husband, he also knew he couldn't promise his wife that she was the woman he truly loved. And when she had asked him outright if he was in love with somebody else, he saw little option to lie. He told her the whole story of Elizabeth, and she left the same night.

He knew his feelings would never change, and so Alice began to share her time between them both, but it had taken only six months for the natural shape of things to form, spending more and more time with her father in their family home until one day her mother stopped coming back to see her altogether.

That evening after they left the church, they boarded the boat from Embankment and began their sail along the river, just as Elizabeth had planned. They stood outside, the breeze cool against their skin, London Bridge itself lit up a soft shade of blue. When they started to feel the cold they took a seat at their table by the window, where they watched the boats, buildings, and lights paint the moving cityscape all around them.

'All the lights look like the stars,' she said as she gazed out towards the city. The food had been perfect, the atmosphere incredible. Even Tom had eaten. Now a pianist was beginning to play, and a woman was singing along too. 'It reminds me of the night we were down by the rocks.'

'You mean the night you fell in.' He shook away the memory. 'What a disaster.'

'I should have been more careful.'

'You weren't to know,' he said as he sipped the last of his wine. 'I took us down there, so really it was my mistake.' He was feeling a little bit tipsy. 'But a mistake is as good as an accident. Nobody means to make them. And it's never the mistake itself that's the problem, but rather how people act in response. You slipping in would have only been a problem if I hadn't managed to help you to safety.'

'You think it's always possible to put right a mistake?' she asked.

'I think so. That's what we are doing here, isn't it?'

'I suppose so.' The grand structure loomed above them as they passed through the turrets of London Bridge on their return leg of the journey. 'It really is magical here,' she whispered to him as they sailed through. 'London is as beautiful as I once imagined it to be. It's just different to Porthsennen, that's all.'

'There's beauty in every place, Elizabeth. Just like there's beauty in every life. But the really magical moments are few and far between.'

Her hand felt the warmth of his forearm. 'Like this one?'

He shook his head. 'Not just this one. Like every moment with you.'

'Oh, I almost forgot,' she said, pulling back. Elizabeth pulled a small electronic tealight from her pocket and set it down on the table. '1987,' she told him.

'The wish for a candlelit supper?' She nodded. He looked over to the small dancefloor, saw a couple of people getting up to enjoy the music, a song he recognised. Pain shot through his arms as he balanced his weight against the table and stood up, but he held out his hand and waited.

'I thought you were tired,' she said.

'Well, I can't promise you dancing the night away like I could in 1983, but I could offer you at least one dance. Especially to this song.' It was 'Can't Help Falling in Love' by Elvis Presley. He had played it to her once before, the most romantic night of her life. Back to when they were kids, when everything seemed possible. With her hand in his they moved onto the dancefloor, began to sway along with the music, his hands on the back of her waist, his breath warm against her ear. 'I'm sorry,' he said eventually, and tears pricked into her eyes. 'I'm sorry for every mistake I made that made things harder for you.'

The strength that had held her together since her arrival was fading, and all the feelings that she had been trying to supress since he first told her he was ill, her unreasonable certainty that blood on a tissue didn't have to mean anything; well, she just couldn't hold them in anymore.

'It's so unfair,' she said. 'After all this time.'

With his arms wrapped protectively around her body, thinner than they were just a week ago when she arrived, he began to sing a softly whispered melody. It made her tingle, feel things she hadn't in a long while. 'I can't help falling in love with you,' he sang to the tune.

They danced, their eyes on each other, eyes in the room on them. But it was in that moment as if nothing else existed in the whole world. No broken promises, no mistakes, nothing that either of them was desperate to undo. No cancer. They could have been anywhere, a time long ago, a place that belonged only to them. Instinctively she bore his weight and he held on tight. Neither of them wanted to let go. And as the song finished and they stayed right where they were, they both realised, perhaps for the first time in their lives, that neither of them ever had.

Then

Taking her into his home was a dangerous option, but as he turned to look at her, that beautiful face with a cut still oozing blood on her forehead, he figured he didn't really have much choice. Not if he wanted to be the man she made him wish he was. Made him believe he could be.

'Mum is asleep, so,' he said, holding a finger tinged pink with cold up to his bluish lips. The door creaked as he opened it, just enough to peer around the edge and into the room, breathing a sigh of relief when he saw the empty chairs before him. No doubt his father was still out; Tom certainly hadn't gone looking for him tonight. Probably down by the water, asleep in one of the boats. Old Man Cressa would find him in the morning and turf him out, no harm done.

The timorous whistle of the wind tickled past the window frames, and Tom was aware of it in a way he wasn't usually. He viewed the room with fresh eyes, an outsider like Elizabeth; the small table in the centre, the chipped crockery set out for breakfast, and the flaking paint of the kitchen cabinets which bubbled like the rusted paintwork on the harbour trawlers. Their eyes met and she understood his concerns.

'I like it,' she whispered.

It was nothing like her grand house with the big bay windows and high roof. Did she really like it, in all its shabby glory? It didn't really matter in that moment because all he could wonder was whether she wanted him to kiss her again. He was struggling to read her; for all the books he'd read she made him feel embarrassingly illiterate.

'We'd better clean that cut on your face. Come on, follow me.' His grip was firm as she led her up the stairs.

Standing on the other side of his bedroom door, she heard the click of the latch behind her. Elizabeth took in the details with eager eyes while Tom went to fetch some warm water. The wardrobe in one corner, dark wood and half open, a belt hanging over the door. On the inside surface both the drawing and painting she had given him were displayed like a little gallery of her work. Next to the single bed stood a two-drawer chest unit, white and worn in places, much like the kitchen cupboards. In her room not a single item was out of place, and even her paintbrushes were always neatly lined up on a soft towel because she liked to take care of them. Tom's bedroom was in disarray, with books in piles, and clothes in heaps in just about every direction you looked. Yet she liked it. It felt homely and snug under the ceiling which sloped down to the floor like the hills that rolled gently into the sea. On the floor she saw a small black and white photograph, Tom minus his shirt. Before she could talk herself out of it, she picked it up, slipped it into her pocket.

After returning with a steaming bowl of warm water, he pulled off his wet shirt, changing into the thick jumper that was draped over the end of the bed. It was the same one she had been wearing only that afternoon. Nerves forced her eyes away, but as he pulled the jumper over his head she glanced back, catching a glimpse of his naked torso.

'You'd better give me that,' he said, pointing to her shoe, snapping her out of her trance. 'I'll put it by the heater to dry.' It was a relief to remove it, her toes cold with the wet. Tom placed it near a small aqua coloured heater underneath the window. He turned a dial on the front, and she felt the room heating up. 'What about the rest?' he asked, pointing to her clothes.

'You'll have to turn around,' she said, remembering her own wild thoughts while he was changing. And so he did, turning to face the window. Her movements were awkward, her fingers struggling either through exposure or fear. Not that she didn't want to be there, but still, it was one thing to want something and another to get it. After pulling off her coat and the rest of her clothes she reached for one of his shirts, slipping it over her head. It was so long it almost reached her knees.

'Get under the sheets.'

'What?' she cried, a little louder than she had intended.

'Listen,' he said, pausing in his task of laying out her clothes to dry. 'If I was going to try anything, I'd have already slipped my trousers off.' Her eyes shot to his bottom. It was very shapely, she thought, like two of Mrs Anderson's eggs in a handkerchief. 'But if you get under, I won't see you in your underclothes.' Her heart was pounding as she lifted the cover and sat onto the bed. It was soft but lumpy, the sheets cold. Watching him lay out her clothes was calming, arranging them as he was across a chair by a small wooden desk. That too was covered in books, pushed up against the sloping ceiling, as if it were playing its own part in holding up the side of the house.

Within just a moment he was sitting on the edge of the bed. 'So why do you always call me by my full name? Should I be calling you Elizabeth Davenport? Is that what posh people do?'

'If you were calling me by my full name it would be Elizabeth Margaret Beatrice Davenport,' she said with all seriousness.

'Four names?'

It went without saying that it warranted explanation. 'Elizabeth after our queen, and two names from my grandmothers. It's quite normal when you think about it.'

'I'm just Thomas Hale.'

'And yet you make such a fuss when I call you that.'

He shuffled up the bed and took a small cloth to dip into the water. With the care of a mother cat over her kittens, he dabbed it at the cut above her eye. 'It's a bit formal, don't you think, considering that you're half undressed and in my bed.' He deserved a slap across the arm for that one, and he got it. 'My shirt suits you though.'

'Why do you always make jokes?' she asked, trailing off as the water rushed into the cut. A sharp stinging sensation caught her, the water dribbling over her eye and onto the sheets.

Her thoughts raced as he moved up and over her body, shuffling on his elbow. Just a short distance from her face she could feel his breath mingling with hers. 'I could stop making jokes if you like.'

'I thought you promised not to try anything.'

'I don't recall making that promise.' He shrugged, smiling, as if he didn't care either way. 'Can't blame a bloke for trying, though.'

Goodness knows where she got the courage to kiss him before, because although she wanted to again now, she couldn't bring herself to do it. But the kiss on the rocks was different. It wasn't going anywhere. A kiss in that room could lead just about anywhere, and while she was happy to get lost with him, she was anxious about the journey.

In the end it was easier to change the subject, so she pointed to the desk filled with books. 'You like to read a lot, don't you?'

'Yes,' he said, scampering across the bed. He let his feet splay out behind him, close to her face. It felt so personal, so intimate. 'This is my favourite,' he said, handing her a dog-eared book.

The pages were brown and tatty, smelt of fish and the sea. '*Pride and Prejudice?*'

His fingers fussed at the bedsheets, moved over the chenille bobbles before working their way towards her covered feet. He traced the outline of her toes. 'Please tell me you know what it's about. If you don't, I can't see you anymore.'

On the inside cover she saw that he had written his name. She thought of her father and how Tom would be able to hold a discussion about books, how maybe he would be impressed that Tom was well read. 'What do you think it's about?' she asked, closing the book. Even though she was sure he was joking, she didn't want to risk admitting that she had never even heard of it. Her foot tingled where his hand continued to rest on it.

'It's about love.' For a moment he was quiet, as if he was thinking. 'And us.'

'Us?'

'Yes. About how I'd never be good enough for you, not really. About how people think I am one thing, when really I am many.' His fears were coming to the surface, washed up like flotsam in a milky surf. He wanted to share everything about himself, even the bad bits, like the fact that sometimes he was quick to temper like his father, or that when he ate fish he got terrible wind. Even that. He wanted to know everything about her, and for her to know him in the same all-consuming way.

'You think that people look down on you?'

'Maybe.' He took his hand from her foot. 'That I'm just a Hale. Like my father.'

'Does that bother you?'

'It used to. But now all I care about is what you think of me.'

'Well, you should know the answer to that by now.'

He rose from the bed and moved over to one of the bookcases on the far wall. He leaned over, giving her another fine view of his backside, then stood up holding a vinyl. He set it on a turntable and it began to play, keeping the volume low so as not to wake his mother. It was Elvis Presley, one of her favourite songs.

Once he came back to the bed, he was close enough that she could feel the warm air breeze from his mouth to her face. 'I've never met anybody like you before, Elizabeth. Most people just get on with things, but you do and say what you think is right. You've always been like it, right from when we were at school.'

'At school?'

'Don't you remember when we were about six or seven, and they walked us down to the beach?' He stopped for a moment, remembered that walk. 'We were supposed to be making a beach scene back at the school, but all you came back with was a dead bird and a tuft of yellow gorse. You told Mr Nance that it wasn't right for God's creatures to die alone, or to be forgotten. That you were going to bury it in the churchyard. He made you throw it away.'

'You remember that?'

'Of course. I took the bird from the bin for you. I buried it in my garden.'

It was hard to believe, but he was nodding to indicate his truth. 'But it was just a dead bird.'

'That's not how you felt at the time. You're rare, Elizabeth. You care about life, about dreams.' He swallowed hard. 'About me. You make the impossible feel possible. You make me feel brave, even to the point of coming to your house and throwing stones at your window. Telling your father that I'm going to marry you.'

'Maybe I'm not so good,' she said. 'I'm supposed to be engaged, yet here I am with you, in your bed, wanting things I'm not supposed to want.'

'Who says you're not supposed to want them?' he whispered.

The room had warmed up, the heater on full. With a gentle push the covers slid from her arms, and she noticed his eyes following the curves of her body, visible through the thin material of his shirt. He opened his mouth again, but for a moment no words came out. He was so close that the outline of his features was blurry. They were merging together, becoming part of each other.

'I don't ever want this to end.'

He smiled then, a little crease forming by the side of his lip. 'Then I promise you it won't. We can spend the rest of our lives in this room together, forget about the rest of the world.'

'I think I already did,' she said. And instead of answering her with words, he placed his lips on hers and pulled her body close.

Now

When Elizabeth opened the door and saw Alice it was with both relief and concern. Dark bags hung under her eyes, the skin tissue-paper fine. Her time away in Hastings had drained her. And Elizabeth feared that what she had to tell her was only going to make things worse. Since her day out with Tom, which even as she thought about it now was near perfect, everything had become steadily more difficult. Only yesterday she had found Tom leaning on the door frame of the kitchen, looking out to the rear garden. When she asked him what he was doing there his answer had been simple enough but concerning nevertheless; pulling in the nets. It reminded her of her mother in the months before her death, the spontaneous uncoupling of her mind from the reality of the surrounding world. There one minute, gone the next, like a little puff of smoke.

'Hello, love,' Elizabeth said as Alice moved into the porch. The chill of an early autumn day came with her, the summer already starting to fade. It did little to settle Elizabeth who was already shivering with nerves. 'How was your trip?'

'To be honest I didn't enjoy it much,' Alice said as she removed her coat. 'I just wanted to get back.'

Everything about her looked ready for some unknown event, like one of those antelopes Elizabeth had seen on a documentary last night, a perpetual awareness for the possibility of attack. 'But I'm back now and today's going to be great. Can't believe we're finally going to Cornwall. Is he ready to go?'

Dread coursed through Elizabeth like ichor in the veins of gods. Her body weak, vibrating to the rhythm of trepidation as the words took shape in her thoughts. 'No, love, I'm afraid he's not. You better come upstairs.'

Only when she saw Alice's expression did she realise just how much Tom had changed over the course of a few days. He had slimmed down, his cheeks were sunken, and one of his lower eyelids had drooped. It looked wet and pink, as if it was sore. Was his mouth also drooping? Elizabeth had been denying the changes, but now it was impossible to pretend. When she lay alongside him the bottom edge of his ribs poked into hers. All night she stroked them gently, as if perhaps she could smooth them back into place, as if her love was enough to mute the blades of bone. But love was never enough. She knew that of old.

'He looks terrible,' Alice whispered. Elizabeth had no verbal response that could soften such truth and so she rested a hand onto her shoulder. 'He doesn't look like Dad anymore.' Sheets, hot with the sweat of the night, crumpled as Alice sat down on the bed and picked up his hand. He barely stirred.

'I called an ambulance already,' Elizabeth said, hoping it came as some reassurance.

The bedside table, normally so well ordered with a picture of Alice when she was small, was covered in a carpet of used tissues, like little pink gauze ghosts. The sheets were all chaotic, the pillows askew, positioned in a way that any able-bodied man would have corrected for himself. And a scent hung in the air, something Alice couldn't place but that was without doubt bodily. It was a sensory reminder of the illness that had stormed their lives, taken everybody prisoner.

'You don't look very comfortable, Dad,' said Alice, her voice breaking, coarse and tearful. Elizabeth thought it to her credit that she had managed to come up with something that sounded relatively normal. His eyes flickered open; a wry smile passed his lips. Elizabeth realised she was right; one side of his mouth wasn't responding as it should.

'What are you doing here?' he said, his voice croaky.

'I came to see you. And Brian's coming too. He's really looking forward to it.' His eyes closed again and Alice turned to Elizabeth. Her voice dropped to a whisper as they both stepped away from the bed. 'Look at his mouth. And his eye.'

'It started like that last night,' Elizabeth whispered. 'But he was talking normally then. Perhaps a bit confused, but I could understand him. This morning he seems a lot worse.'

'What time did you call an ambulance?'

'Just before you arrived.'

Alice moved to leave the room, beckoning Elizabeth to follow. After a quick look at Tom, she did.

'I don't like the look of him,' Alice said. 'I'm calling them again.'

As Alice descended the stairs, Elizabeth hurried for a glass of water from the bathroom, offered it to Tom in the hope that she could break his fast. He wet his lips but that was about it. Alice's raised voice as she called for the ambulance rumbled in the background, leaving Elizabeth feeling that she was somehow to blame, even though she had no idea how.

'You all right, love?' she asked, rubbing Tom's hand. It felt different from a few days ago, stiff somehow, the ridges of his knuckles sharper and more prominent. To see him like this was a shock that played on repeat, as if every time she dared to look, the picture before her worsened. If he couldn't answer, could he still hear the things she said? It took her back to the days she spent waiting for him to return from Wolf Rock, the way she would sit and watch the light shining every thirty seconds at night. Even then, with so much distance between them, she had always felt as if they could communicate. Even when he was in London and she was in Porthsennen the space between them had felt tangible. Now, sitting at his side, he had never felt more unreachable in their whole lives.

Then

Afterwards, they didn't speak for a while, their heads sharing a pillow, their fingers intertwined like the weave of his fishing creel in the old Mayon Lookout. Elizabeth couldn't stop looking at his face. Every detail felt like something necessary to imprint on her memory, so that she might convince herself that it had really happened. But despite her shock, the biggest surprise was the sensation of absolute normality. When she had considered the idea of intimacy with James, the very idea of being naked with him, it felt extraordinary. With Tom, she hadn't given it much more than a second thought. When he looked at her it was as if she was looking at herself. They were mirrors, Tom her own reflection. Even when he pulled back the covers and eased her onto her back, kissing her neck, trailing all the way down until he arrived at her bare tummy.

'You are the most beautiful woman I have ever seen,' he whispered, before resting his head into the crook of her arm, letting one hand settle across her chest. Instinctively, she wrapped her arm around his bare shoulder, cradled him close. His breathing deepened, the soft lick of air across her chest as his rose and fell. Her eyes flickered shut, blithe to the insurmountable complications that their union would trigger. Little hope existed that she could lie or explain her way out of an overnight absence any more easily than her father would be able to decipher the complexities of her feelings for Tom. But it seemed to her that nothing was as important as right there and then. Perhaps that was what love was, she thought to herself, when nothing that came before or after seemed to matter anymore, when the world could be on fire, but you didn't fear the burn. Moments later, she drifted into sleep.

Tom was the first to wake, and he watched her sleeping for a while. It wasn't the first time he had observed Elizabeth like that. Her presence in the village had become something for which he searched when he left his home in the afternoons, or when he was returning to it after a morning fishing, his eyes exploring the coastline in search of the girl who liked to paint. How many times had he watched her since then? Last night, as much as he had wanted to kiss her, what he wanted to do even more was curl up next to her, touch her face, listen to her talk and feel the rush of her very presence. That would have been enough. It wasn't like he only had a few stolen hours to enjoy, or that he was going to lose her; he could never lose part of himself, and he felt sure that was what she was.

The bedroom door opened before he had time to appreciate what was happening. His mother's eyes widened then narrowed, an animal with prey in its sights. They flicked between her son and the soft blonde mass of hair stirring in the bed. Elizabeth roused, saw the look of concern on Tom's face. 'What's going . . .' she began but he shushed her with a finger set tight against her dry lips, before she saw the shift in light as Martha stepped into the room and closed the door.

Elizabeth had seen Martha Hale before but only vaguely knew her face. Either she had a wonderful constitution, or she visited a different doctor, because she never attended the practice, and neither did the rest of the family. Up close Elizabeth realised she was a beautiful woman; Tom shared her pale skin and dark hair, which she had scraped back in a loose knot at the base of her neck. The sight of her staring at them, which she did – it seemed – without any great discomfort, made Elizabeth's throat go dry and her heart race.

'What in the name of our Lord are you thinking, Tommy? I said that no good would come of this. Have you forgotten everything I told you?' She picked up Elizabeth's dress and placed it on the bed. 'I thought you were engaged to be married,' she said, her hands on her hips.

'She fell,' Tom said, trying to distract his mother.

'Into your bed?' Mrs Hale took in the cut on her forehead, and the single shoe still drying in front of the heater. 'I mean no disrespect, Miss Davenport, but you've no business being here.' Her attentions turned to Tom. 'If you needed to help her, you could have woken me. We could have explained whatever might have happened to her father together. Last night.' Disbelief and perhaps something else, maybe despair, crossed her face as she glanced to Elizabeth. 'Not much explaining it now, is there?'

'Mum, it's not what you think,' he began, but she interrupted him.

'It's exactly what I think, Tommy. But I'll hear it from her. I don't need any of your clever lies.' Elizabeth was going redder by the second. 'Just how do you expect to explain your whereabouts to your father? And there's no use looking at him,' she said as Elizabeth looked to Tom for support. 'He's not going to be able to help you. Goodness knows what the young doctor is going to say. So, tell me. Are you still engaged, or did I miss the latest village gossip?'

'Yes,' she eventually muttered. 'I suppose I am.'

Martha picked up Elizabeth's underclothes and handed them to her. 'What a bloody mess. Would the pair of you just get dressed? I'll be in the kitchen waiting.'

'Do you want to go out the window?' he asked once his mother had left. That was how Francine had left months before. 'The ground isn't all that far.'

'There's no point running away, is there? We'd better just get this over and done with. People might as well get used to it now rather than later.'

Despite their predicament, he couldn't help but smile. 'So, you still want this?'

Her face turned ashen, a cloud passing under the sun, taking away the light. 'Have you changed your mind?'

'No,' he said quickly. 'Absolutely not. I love you, Elizabeth Margaret,' he paused for thought. 'Oh, I can't remember all your posh names. I love you, that's what counts.' His movements were becoming quick and purposeless, his mind a bit of an overexcited fog. 'I'm going to come with you now, speak to your father. Like you say, we have to face this head on.'

His fingers were cold and palms sweaty as she took his hand. Giggles shook loose, inspired by how keen he was. How brave he was. Had she been brave? Not yet she hadn't, but she knew she would have to be soon. 'No. Don't do that. There are some things I'd better do alone,' she said, thinking ahead. 'Best my father meets you after he knows.'

Tom's grip tightened. 'I'm not going to hide, Elizabeth.'

'Good,' she said, stroking his face. 'But my father is nothing like your mother. And it's different for boys and girls.' They shared a kiss and some of that certainty from the night before returned. 'It's best this way. Plus, I also need to speak with James.' Heaviness over what they had done settled on his shoulders. It hurt him, she saw, that he had to hurt another person to be with the one he loved, and she loved him all the more because of it. More than the night before. What a way to spend a life, she thought, enjoying an exponential increase in the loftiest feeling she had ever experienced. Within seconds she had kissed him again, all thoughts of their families temporarily lost.

'When will I see you next?' he asked as they pulled apart.

'I don't know,' she said, shaking her head. Was that apprehension she could see on his face, the creased brow and pursed lips? She noticed his favourite book on the floor, kicked from the bed last night by their feet. 'But I'm going to take this with me.'

'I seem to remember telling you that's my favourite.' He didn't look too sure about letting it go.

'I remember, Thomas Hale,' she said, her fingers flicking at the edge. 'Just like I can remember your names. All two of them.' With a gentle tap she bopped him on the nose with the back of the book. 'This is my insurance. You'll have to come and find me if you want this back.'

It didn't really hurt but he wanted to play along, so he rubbed the edge of his nose. 'You just try stopping me.'

Tom's mother's fingers drummed against the table as they arrived downstairs. It hit Elizabeth more then, than it had the night before, the differences between their homes and lives. It looked as if a breakfast bomb had gone off. Was this normal, she wondered, not just for Tom, but in general? Was this what a normal household without a housekeeper was like? His mother was sitting at the table with a cup of tea by her side, a cigarette clasped between her fingers. Smoke drifted towards the ceiling like a distress signal.

'You've missed work,' she announced, as if that was the worst problem of all. The cherry fizzed as she sucked on the cigarette. Confined in the small room, the smoke stung Elizabeth's eyes. 'And at least now I know why your father never made it home. You were too busy off gallivanting to bother to find him.'

Elizabeth felt Tom tighten next to her. A cold draught slipped beneath the door and brushed her feet, wearing only the odd shoe from the night before, one foot still bare.

'He's big enough to look after himself, Mum.'

'And I suppose you are big enough too, are you? You plan to go and admit it all now, do you? Expect Elizabeth's father to offer you his daughter's hand?' An incredulous look passed across her eyes, as if Tom had suggested he might fly there. 'You think he'll let the likes of you marry his daughter?'

'Not now, but eventually. I love her.'

Elizabeth felt his hand clench tight around hers. It wasn't possessive like James's touch often was. It was reassuring, unifying. It was a touch she would never forget.

'I feared as much,' said Mrs Hale. Her fingers worked hard to stub out her unfinished cigarette, then stood up. 'We've all been *in love,*' she said, like it was a disease or something equally distasteful. 'Even Edward Davenport has been in love, Tommy, but look where that got me.'

And just then they heard the door opening, footsteps on the other side. Cool air rushed in, the smell of seaweed sweeping through the house, quickly followed by Tom's father. His hair was all rough in a ratty plait that ran down the length of his back and which looked not to have been washed in a good long while. Goosepimples rippled across Elizabeth's skin as his eyes skipped over the two lovers. They all watched him as he sat down, not a word spoken, yet a thousand looks passed between Tom and his mother.

'Where have you been?' his mother finally asked. Elizabeth felt Tom's hand pull tight against hers, and when he edged her towards the door she followed his lead.

'Out where I shouldn't have,' he said, looking up at Tom, then Elizabeth. 'Aren't you that Davenport girl?' he asked, but didn't wait for an answer. 'Two Davenports this early on a Sunday,' he said. 'I am a blessed man. What's she doing here?'

'Nothing,' said Martha. 'She was just leaving, wasn't she, Tommy?'

Tom pulled her closer to the door and opened it.

'If you're looking for her father, you'll find him down at the harbour.'

Tom and Elizabeth turned to look at each other. Dr Davenport was out looking for her, they both knew it. If she'd had her sketchpad she could have made something up, but if he was already looking for her there was every possibility that he knew her bed hadn't been slept in.

'I told you,' said his mother. 'I told you both. This is a bad idea. You know why, Tommy.'

Mr Hale picked up some toast, shovelled it into his mouth. Then slowly, after glancing at his wife, he met Elizabeth's gaze. His eyes were the blue of Tom's, and quite striking if she was honest. But the skin around them was red and wrinkly. He could have been handsome once, but now his skin seemed loose on the bones, his teeth all brown and crooked like the gravestones in Saint Sennen's cemetery.

'Dr Davenport didn't see me,' Mr Hale continued. 'But I saw him all right. It rained last night, so I'd crawled under one of the upturned boats, made myself a shelter.' That at least explained the sand on his sleeves and the wetness of his attire. 'I'd say he wasn't looking for you, that's for sure,' he said, turning to Elizabeth.

Tom stepped back into the room. 'So, what was he doing?'

Mr Hale wiped his hands on a napkin and stood up from the table. He was taller than Elizabeth anticipated when he closed the space between them. She didn't like the way he looked at her, and it would seem neither did Tom, because when he got too close he pulled Elizabeth away. The scent of stale alcohol filled the air, made Elizabeth feel queasy.

'Pat, would you just tell the poor girl what you saw,' said Tom's mother.

He took one more look at Elizabeth, his face giving nothing away, before he turned his attention to his son. 'You want to be careful of this one. When a Davenport sweeps you up in their plans, folk get hurt. Isn't that right, Martha?'

Martha Hale said nothing, turned away from the scene, and set about clearing the plates. Silence descended over them, and moments later Tom pulled Elizabeth through the door and quickly away from the house.

'I still think it best I go alone.'

They were sitting in the roundhouse, the old capstan wheel redundant beneath their feet as they sat on the first floor amongst the fishing nets. When they left Tom's house neither of them was ready to say goodbye, or face Elizabeth's father.

'If we explain things together, I think he will take it better. He will see how serious I am about you. Come on, my parents know now,' he said, dragging one of the nets over her body. 'I'll only let you go once you say yes.'

'This is no time for jokes, Thomas Hale,' she said, pushing him away. 'You don't know what he's like.' A look crossed his face that she didn't understand. It was the way he pursed his lips, averted his eyes. What Mr Hale had said that morning came back to her, about how the Davenports were trouble, and she wondered what she was missing. 'Is there something you're not telling me?'

'No,' he said, pulling absently at the floats on the nets. 'It's not important.'

'So, there is something.' To Elizabeth, as she reached to turn his face to hers, he still felt like the same boy from the night before, and yet she already sensed that something was changing, something she could never have predicted. 'What did your father mean back at the house? If we are going to be together, we can't have secrets.'

'It was years ago,' Tom shrugged. 'Before either of us were born.'

'Then it shouldn't matter, should it?'

Tom gazed about the storage barn, focused on an old orange bucket so that he didn't have to see the look on her face when he told her. 'Your father, and my mother . . . they had a thing together.'

'A thing?'

'They were in love, but he left her not long before he married your mother. That's why Mum ended up marrying Dad. People thought she was ruined, and he was the only one that would have her.'

Thoughts rocketed back and forth, nothing tangible in all her mind. Memories came to her, things her mother had said, like the fact that her father would be more likely to understand than she would have credited. Is that what she meant? 'You must have it wrong,' she said.

'It's the truth.' And then she remembered something that Martha Hale had said just moments before; *look where that got me,* referring to Elizabeth's father being in love. Could it really be true? 'And to make things worse, after that our fathers worked together. They were both fishermen. That's when it got really bad.'

'My father was never a fisherman.'

'He was, just for one summer, before they started shipping the industry out to the larger towns like Newlyn. It was my father's first proper job with a fishing crew, and your dad was there for the fun of it I suppose, on a break from his studies. Your father had this nice Thermos flask, had taken hot water to make tea while at sea. It rolled out of his bag, and my father picked it up. He was just admiring it, or so he says. Anyway, your father told him to keep his hands off and they had a fight. By the time he got back to shore your father complained that his flask was missing, and when they did a search it was found in my father's bag.'

'Why did he take it?' Tom was quiet for a moment, and she understood the implication. 'Hang on, you think my father planted it?'

He shrugged. 'That's what my father says.'

'I know my father, and he is no liar.'

'And after seeing inside our house, does it appear as if mine is a thief?' They were quiet for a moment then. It was strange, she thought, after such a perfect night that they should find themselves defending their respective families over an incident that she had never even heard anything about until just a few moments ago. Her father a fisherman, in love with Tom's mother; it was a past she could barely even begin to imagine.

'I'm going to go and try to sort this out,' she said. The wood scratched at her skin as she descended the ladder. Tom followed. They stood alongside each other, their arms brushing together, before they opened the door to another world, one tainted by reality and the history of their families.

'So, is this it, do you think? Is this goodbye?' he asked. There was a truth in his question that she couldn't even let herself consider, already wondering what he would do when she left; bathe, sleep, or maybe walk out somewhere near the coast. It felt almost painful to think of him living life without her intricately woven into it now.

He saw her hold up his copy of *Pride and Prejudice*, the paper yellowed, crisp on each turn. She thought of his photograph in her pocket. 'I've got this, haven't I?' Though she kissed him on the cheek, he still felt the gravity of uncertainty pulling at him. 'I'll see you later, alligator.' And moments later she was out through the door, into the brisk morning as it played out under a clear blue sky, the sun so close to the horizon that it would soon skim past the Porthsennen rooftops for the last time before next spring.

'In a while, crocodile,' he eventually said, but she was already heading up the hill, almost out of view, already too far away to hear.

Now

Elizabeth was pleased to leave the chaos of the Accident and Emergency department behind. The bed they found for Tom was on the chest ward, and despite the sound of coughing which resonated down the corridor, the place was altogether a relief. Only then did Elizabeth allow herself to think of the previous days at home, the difficulties they had faced in the simple effort of existence. How many dirtied clothes had she washed when Tom had failed to get to the toilet in time, and how few hours had she really slept for the fear? Fear of what? Losing him? It didn't do to say it, not even let herself think it, but that was how bad his chest had sounded to her over the last forty-eight hours. Being on the ward, at least she felt as if she was no longer fighting alone.

The relatives' room offered some calm as she waited with Alice while the nurses checked him in. They didn't speak, instead passed the time following along with the morning's television which was already playing when they first opened the door. Brian was there by then, sitting with his arm across Alice's shoulder, stroking gently at the side of her neck. His eyes looked tired, swollen with tears, a strange comfort for Elizabeth from a smart-looking stranger. After a while he offered to get them a cup of coffee and Alice said she wanted one too, which served as a decent enough excuse to follow him out of the room. It was a welcome respite, Elizabeth realised once she had the room to herself. Reaching into her bag she pulled out her phone and typed a message.

I'm not sure if you received my messages the other day, but I would really love it if we could talk. It's important. Love you, Mum xx

In a second bag on the floor she saw folded clothes, pyjamas, and a wash bag. When night settled, she would have to leave him here, return to that house. Had she spent her last night with him? It was hard not to cave into the Murphy's Law of thinking; they had hardly fulfilled any of their wishes. They had so many things left undone. Tears filled her eyes. There hadn't been enough nights together yet. But there never could have been, she realised. Not anymore.

A moment later a nurse with a kind smile popped her head round the door. 'He's all settled now. Want to sit with him?'

Her feet clip-clopped down the corridor until she reached his bed space, found him wearing a pair of hospital pyjamas that seemed to make him look even more unwell than he had when they'd arrived. His left eye still seemed droopy, but there was a softness to his features that elicited some relief for Elizabeth. He didn't look to be in pain as he was before.

'Is he asleep?'

'No,' the nurse said, giving Elizabeth a quick rub on the arm. 'But we gave him some painkillers, and they seem to have taken effect. You take a seat just there. The doctor will be along soon.'

Tom was resting in one of the six beds that made up the communal bay, and considerable noise rattled from one wall to the next, like wasps trapped in a jar, unable to escape. Yet the environment was remarkably reassuring after a few days alone at home.

'I'll just be glad when the doctor arrives, eh love,' Elizabeth said to Tom. Some of the wishes were still in her pocket. One she knew was from 1988; he wished he could take her up a mountain. Well, they were certainly climbing their own mountain now. Although he didn't respond to what she said, she continued with the charade of conversation. 'And when they get the CT done. The nurse in A and E said it might be later this afternoon.'

'I doubt that,' Alice said as she arrived in the bay, drawing back the curtains. 'You know what the waiting lists are like.'

'People don't wait if it's urgent. Not even in the NHS.' There was a certain relief to see Alice nodding, as if she had decided to agree. 'Where's Brian gone?'

'He'll be back in a while.' That was all she said about that, and Elizabeth didn't ask again.

The doctor's name turned out to be Dr Nathan Peterson, and he was South African. Did he have people he missed, Elizabeth wondered, all that distance from home? Tom slept throughout the consultation, but Elizabeth felt a lot better for Nathan's input, and even Alice seemed more settled by the time he had finished.

'So, we've added a steroid tablet which will help with his co-ordination, and I'll be in a little bit later as well to see how you're all doing,' Nathan said. Alice stood up, shook his hand. 'Until then, if there's anything you need, the nurses will have it covered for you.'

'Thank you, Nathan. Thank you so much,' Alice said. Elizabeth was a little worried that Alice had called him by his first name. It felt a bit familiar to her, but he didn't seem concerned. Time had changed more than just their appearances. Alice sat back down, smiling to herself. 'I can't believe that the CT scan has been pushed ahead of the list.'

'Yes,' she said, smiling the best smile she could muster. 'At least now we'll know the full picture,' Alice said, seemingly pleased.

For days now, all Elizabeth could think about was knowing; first of all knowing that it was really cancer, and then how far it had spread, or whether the type of cancer he had was amenable to chemotherapy. That was the predicament they were in. They were hoping for the right kind of cancer. There was only one thing worse than the disease itself, and that was how fast it might take him from her. How long had they got left? It had become a thought she couldn't shake.

Dreams remained unfulfilled; a walk out to the shops, or through Hyde Park. More of his wishes that were yet to be realised. Time was the only thing that might bring Kate and Tom together, and how was it possible for it to run out before the two people she loved most in the world had met? And yet all those hopes seemed like such empty wishes now. It didn't matter what the doctors told her about the prognosis. Not really. Her dreams were fading whether she liked it or not, slipping through her grip like water through fingers. Tom was right after all; dreams were for rich people, and she had never felt poorer in her life.

Then

Her tread was light as she entered the house, the soft sounds of chatter and the rattle of breakfast plates coming from the kitchen. Why wasn't her father waiting on watch, ready for a confrontation the moment she opened the door? Voices intensified as she headed towards the kitchen, leaving the book on the stairs, the conversation light and easy. Her father was serving tea, his hair wet and clothes casual. James was sitting in her mother's usual seat.

'Where have you been?' her father asked, casually, before spotting the cut on her head, the missing shoe. 'Oh, darling, whatever happened to you?'

Her first thought was one of relief as he rushed to greet her; it was impossible from his reaction that he knew she had been out all night. James stood up, took her hand. She stiffened at his touch.

'Lizzy, darling, tell us what happened.'

'I went to do some sketches and I slipped, knocked myself,' she said, thinking on her feet. 'My shoe got swept away.'

'Oh, my goodness, Elizabeth,' said her father, taking her in his arms.

'We should clean this,' James added, going to work

right then and there, cleaning it with a strong-smelling solution that he found under the sink.

'I have told her time and time again to be careful,' said her father, glancing to James with a certain look of resignation. Something exchanged between the two of them, and she recognised it as a handing over of the baton, as if she was James's problem now.

'I'm fine. It's just a little knock, that's all.' In truth her ribs hurt, and she was bruised all the way down her leg. Only now she felt it, returning to this house. Her ankle was quite swollen too.

'You must take it carefully, darling. Whatever you were doing, it's not worth risking your life for, is it?'

'No, of course not,' she said, although she didn't believe it.

'Well, sit with us, let me get you a drink,' he said, collecting a cup and pouring her some tea. 'James, will you take a top up before you go?' James held his cup agreeably, steam rising as her father poured.

Elizabeth felt a little sorry for them both, knowing what was coming. They had no idea how an ordinary moment like this would be impossible in just a few short hours, that she was going to change everything they thought they knew. She was half tempted to blurt it all out right then and there, but despite her eagerness, she knew there was a way to handle this, and urgency was not it. And even if she had wanted to, she was finding it a bit peculiar that her father was here alone, serving tea. It had thrown her a little.

'Where is Mrs Clements?' Elizabeth asked.

'She'll be in later.'

'And Mum?'

'A headache. Still in bed. She said not to wait for her.' He set down his cup and checked his watch. 'In fact you'd best get to it, otherwise you're going to miss the best of the day.'

'Quite right. Come on, Lizzy,' said James, waiting for her to stand. After a moment he took the teacup from her and set it on the table.

As Elizabeth headed towards the door with James behind her, she couldn't believe her father had accepted her lie so easily. He didn't believe her truths with the same enthusiasm lately. He hadn't even questioned the whereabouts of her sketchbook. What was he doing down at the harbour if he wasn't searching for her?

They arrived in Porthcurno to the sound of gulls, not another person in sight. The wind was strong as it chased across the headland, and as they stepped from the car James draped his arm around her waist and kissed her on the cheek. Feeling certain he was aiming for her mouth, she turned away just in time, managing to avoid it. The sea was rougher here, the blend of Atlantic currents with those of the English Channel disturbing the surface, as if invisible mythological giants were stirring below. The grey cliffs dripped with emerald pastures, kissed at the bottom by the luminant sands of Porthcurno beach. And there before her, the theatre, built in a deep amphitheatric bowl that from where she stood seemed almost impossible to negotiate. It was as impressive as any sight she had ever seen.

'It's quite something, isn't it?'

'It is,' she said softly. It was years since she had been here.

'I knew you'd like it.' Uncertainty lingered in the pit of her stomach, and it felt wrong to take any joy from such beauty. 'Come on,' he said, reaching for her hand. 'Let's make our way down. I know the perfect place.'

They secured a spot on the southernmost point, glancing back over the headland towards Porthcurno. It was a small grassy knoll with ragged knots of rock protruding skyward like the lumps in Tom's mattress. The act of sitting with her pencil in hand provided the balance she needed, her nerves steadying with each stroke. Across the expanse of sea, she could just make out the distant Wolf Rock lighthouse, little more than a speck of dust in the vast ocean. At some point in the future she would come here with Tom, maybe at night, watch the stars like they had yesterday. What a day it had been. It would be possible to live that day over and over and never once tire of the repetition.

'What's funny?' she heard James ask.

She hadn't realised she had been smiling to herself. 'I was just thinking how bad this bit was,' she said, pointing to a perfectly passable interpretation of the stage on the sketchpad in her lap.

He stood up and found a spot on the grass alongside her. 'Looks good to me,' he said, shooing away the gulls. He let his hand linger just a little bit too long on her shoulder for her liking. *Not too long for a fiancé*, she thought to herself, and with that she folded the cover of her sketchpad and set it aside. The time for games was over. 'Would you like one of these?' he asked.

Her gaze followed his hand to see that while she had been drawing, he had been preparing the picnic. It was the most extravagant picnic she had ever seen, with china plates, sliced strawberries, and a pot of tea steaming on a little stand. He held out a plate of cheese sandwiches and she took one, setting her pencil down.

'You've gone to a lot of effort,' she said.

'It's my pleasure.' He took a small bite of a sandwich. Crumbs settled on his chin. 'It's just how I imagined it, a beautiful day, you drawing as you are, a perfect setting. Don't you think?'

'It is a beautiful place,' she conceded, unsure what to add.

'You see, this is what I do, Elizabeth.' He took a breath, seemed a little nervous. 'I make my plans a reality. When I was small, I wanted to be a doctor, and now here I am close to having my own practice. Your father keeps asking me if I am ready; it won't be long, I'm sure of it. And yesterday I promised you a wonderful day of drawing, and that's what we've got. If I promise something, I deliver,' he said, taking another bite.

'Well, that's very impressive,' she said. He nodded. His manner failed to reassure her, and there was an uneasy feeling taking shape, like when her father questioned her about Tom, or when Tom's mother had walked in on them that morning. A sense that something was afoot that she could not control. 'You've had a lot of good opportunities, I suppose.'

'Or perhaps I created them, Lizzy.' Edging closer to her, he upset the edge of the picnic blanket. He paused to straighten it, mopped up a splash of spilt tea. All Elizabeth could do was watch before he continued. 'Dreams must be fulfilled. They are what set us apart from the animals. I know you have dreams too, and despite what your father tells me about what a wonderful wife you will make, I don't want to marry you for your housekeeping or cooking.' He winked, lowered his voice. 'I'd hazard a guess that neither will be much good. But you see, the truth of the matter is quite simple, Lizzy. I am in awe of you.' He nodded as if she had disagreed. For a second she could hardly breathe. 'I have been ever since the moment I laid eyes on you. Of course, I took you for a beauty, but you are so much more than that,' he said, taking her hands in his. 'That's why I like you so much. Why I . . .' he continued, stumbling. 'Why I love you.'

Inside her stomach was bottoming out, curdling like milk left out on a hot day. His confession had shrunk the world around them so that only she and Tom and James existed in that moment.

'James,' she said softly. 'We barely know each other.'

'Sometimes you don't need to know somebody well to know they are right for you.' That was something they could agree on, she realised. 'I know your love of art will always come above a clean house or cooked meal. I know your Hevva cakes are dry and always burnt at the bottom. But that's OK,' he said, smiling to himself. 'I did my two years' national service. I know how to clean, cook, and shine my own shoes to a standard that won't get me in trouble with my seniors.' His face changed, turned serious. It was coupled with a movement to touch her face. Still frozen, she didn't move as his fingers brushed her cheek. 'And I know that when your mother's confusions worsen it hurts you on a physical level, and that some days you can barely stand to talk to her for the fear she will forget your name.' Elizabeth couldn't look at him then, couldn't believe that in the short time they had been together he had seen so much of who she really was. 'But perhaps most importantly of all in relation to this conversation, I know that you don't love me.'

Their eyes met, Elizabeth drawn like a magnet. He was pulling at the open neck of his shirt, fussing at the blanket. The smile that seemed to exist on a near permanent basis was still there, but it was an effort now, and his neck was blushing purple as a summer grape.

'James, I . . .' she began, but when she got lost for an answer, he stepped in.

'It's OK. I don't expect you to deny it, and if the truth be known I don't want you to either. Your father pushed us together, and I understand your hesitations. And I'll be quite honest with you, Lizzy, I went along with meeting you to please him in the first instance. It was important for me to impress him, and if meeting his young daughter did that, then I was game.' A memory of that first dinner stirred, his smart suit the colour of sand, and how impressed by him she had been. Every word of his stories felt wild and exciting as they dripped from his tongue, languid and sanguine and exotic. But it had never crossed her mind that they were being pushed together. How naïve she was then, how silly. 'I assumed I might take you out and that we would laugh together about how we had been set up and call it a day. But his daughter turned out to be you, and I felt things for you that I couldn't ignore. And I knew then I could spend my life with you, Lizzy, if only you would give me a chance.'

The guilt she had felt on the journey there had receded, but in its place came a sense of sadness. Why would he want this for himself? He knew that she didn't love him, yet still he pursued this marriage. She had always assumed that he wanted her so that he could access her father's teaching and patients, but now that she knew he really did love her, how could he accept knowing that she didn't feel the same way? Was there anything worse than to love and not be loved in return?

'Why do you even want to marry me?'

'Because I know in time you will grow to love me, Lizzy.' He shuffled closer still, reached into his pocket. 'I'm not sure how long it might take, but I'm asking you to take pity on a good man, Lizzy, and give him a chance. I accept your current feelings, both for me and perhaps those you harbour for another, in the certainty that in time you will learn that to love me is the right thing.' Was he telling her that he knew about Tom? That he knew and still wanted her? 'We forget what it means to face consequences, or struggle, or even the existence of hardship when we feel love. But I promise you that love alone is never enough. I trust one day you will see that and be happy with your choice to marry me. I will always support you and will provide all that you need.'

His words left her speechless, but before she could protest, he produced a small black velvet box from his pocket. The wind had picked up, yet she noticed his brow had started to sweat, wetting the roots of his floppy hair. He carefully opened the lid to reveal a Deco style ring, a single solitaire set in a gallery of smaller stones. The ring itself was etched and engraved all the way down the sides. He took it from the box, carefully as one might handle an insect worth saving.

'I wanted to wait, wanted it to be a special moment, one in which you truly knew how I felt about you. I believe that is now.' His gaze flicked to the ring. 'It's from the twenties, belonged to my grandmother.' He didn't try to place it on her finger, instead handed it over, setting it in her palm. 'As soon as I got the car yesterday, I went to collect it. Now it belongs with you, just as you belong with me.'

A lot of what he said seemed reasonable enough, and there was no doubt that a lifetime with James would see her well provided for. But while James claimed that love could never suffice, neither could mediocrity. It wasn't enough to be satisfied, when she knew there was a greater prize to be claimed. How could she settle for companionship when she knew the beauty of love, the sweet unique taste of it? Love wouldn't fade because life got hard. It existed in a place beyond such complications. Love was a type of magic; not sleight of hand or trickery like some performers exhibited, but a mystery of the world that could never be solved. No logic existed behind it, yet it was a tangible element of life; like fire, air, water, earth, so real you could taste it, and see its colours when you put the right two people together. It was the reason the sun rose in the sky, and the force that caused the sea to roll with the tides. What was life if there was no love? What was there to live for if not for that? It was completely beyond her explanation, and yet one of the most certain things she had ever known.

'I can't accept this,' she said to James. He shrunk before her eyes. 'It wouldn't be right.'

'It's the boy I saw you with, isn't it?' he asked quietly as he took the ring. 'I knew it straightaway. But Elizabeth, are you quite sure?'

So, he did know. 'I'm sure,' and even as she said it, the words underlined her feelings, the act of admission making her even more certain.

'The wisdom of the fool and the folly of the wise. Could you just answer me one thing?'

There wasn't much that she wouldn't have done then to ease his upset. 'Of course.'

'If he weren't around, do you think you might have been prepared to give me a chance?'

'Yes, James. I think I might have.' Sitting very still, she wasn't sure if she meant it, but what she did know was that she wanted to. If it was possible for him to understand that she realised he was a good man, she wanted that. And in that moment a hope grew inside her, a hope for him to meet somebody who made him feel as Tom made her feel. She could never have known that he already had, and that indeed she had been right when she thought it earlier; to love and not be loved in return really was the worst feeling in the world.

Now

Tom was a picture of compliance as two cheerful porters wheeled him down the corridors and into the radiology department. He had lost some of his spirit, but Nathan was right when he said the steroid would help. In the hour they had been waiting, Tom had woken up and seemed a little livelier.

'Do you want me to get you anything from the vending machine?' Alice asked as they watched Tom's bed disappear into one of the scanning rooms.

Elizabeth shook her head as she took a seat. 'I'm all right thanks, love. I'll have a cuppa once we get back to the ward.' Goosebumps ran up and down her arms, chased away by her hands. 'It's a bit chilly down here, isn't it?'

Alice looked to the corridor, then back to the empty chair. The seat scraped the floor as she sat, and from somewhere in the distance a patient called out in distress. 'It's bloody freezing. I'll have to ask for another blanket for Dad when they wheel him out. We can't let him catch a cold on top of everything.'

Elizabeth doubted the severity of such a minor ailment, but she liked Alice's way of thinking. 'You're a good girl to him. You like taking care of him, don't you?' Only last Tuesday when he was feeling weak, Elizabeth had stood aside while Alice lathered soap on a flannel, washing her father's back as he sat on the edge of the bed. Tom had looked so small in those moments, so vulnerable as she watched his head hanging low, the roll of skin over his pyjama bottoms. That tanned neck and white torso, and all that extra hair he never used to have. How time had whittled him down, no more difficult than a small piece of oak on a lathe.

'Since Mum left, it's just been the two of us. I always needed him, and now he needs me.' Elizabeth wasn't sure what to say. Sometimes she caught Alice looking at her, watching her as she made a drink or straightened the sheets on the bed. There was no malice in those looks, but rather wonderment, perhaps over how something could last so long, when everything else was crumbling all around them. 'That's why Brian is here. Dad needs to see him, too.'

'Of course, love.'

They watched a mother carrying a small child, his face buried in her neck, closely followed by another radiographer. 'It wasn't his fault, you know? Brian, I mean,' Alice continued. 'It was me who ruined things. I told him I didn't want kids.'

'Oh,' Elizabeth said, wracking her brain for the correct response. 'Well, if it wasn't what you wanted, it was for the best.'

'I suppose,' she said, doing up the buttons on an over-size cardigan. 'But I'm starting to wonder if I was wrong. I see Dad in there, and you here with him. It's about family, isn't it?' An intense urge struck Elizabeth then, a need to tell Alice everything about Kate. 'That's the point of life. Not promotions and money and Michelin starred restaurants on a Saturday. It's family, and being together. I didn't understand that before.'

Elizabeth needed to break the tension, Alice close to tears. 'Michelin starred restaurants seem like a good part of life to me,' she joked. 'Not that I'd know, mind. I've never eaten in one.'

'You're not missing much.' Alice shrugged. 'Just the same as anywhere else really. Only less food.' They both smiled, shuffled to get more comfortably positioned in their seats.

'Regardless, your dad will be pleased to see Brian soon.'

'Yes,' she said, before a moment of quiet. 'And I never thanked you, did I? Not just for convincing me to talk to Brian, but for being here too. The truth is, Dad needs you. And I think this would be a lot harder without you.' Tears streamed down Elizabeth's cheeks. 'I'm sorry, I didn't want to upset you.'

Without thought Elizabeth reached for Alice, patted her arm. It was a simple touch, but a sign that something had shifted in their connection. 'You didn't. You just made me think of something, that's all.'

'Of what?'

'Not what. Who,' Elizabeth said. 'You know, a long time ago, I didn't want children either. Couldn't imagine it, and thought that having a family would ruin all my plans to be an artist.' Alice twisted in her seat. Elizabeth didn't look up in that moment, her cheeks growing hot. 'Then I had Kate,' she said. 'I love her more than anything, but we're not on speaking terms anymore.'

'I'm sorry, I didn't know. Families are not always easy, are they? I didn't speak to my mother very much in the years before she died.'

'I'm sorry to hear that.'

The resignation in Alice's shrug was hard to witness. 'When I was a kid, I worshipped her. She was so glamorous, you know, had all these amazing clothes; I used to dress in her heels, and she'd do my make-up. But she was fickle, too. Volatile.'

'Your dad didn't mention that.' Tom didn't seem to want to talk about it much, and what he had told her never once painted the woman he married in a bad light.

'He would never speak badly of her. But after she and Dad separated, when she asked me to go and live with her, there was never any question in my mind that I preferred to be with Dad. She died almost twenty years ago now. Caught an infection that went to her heart. I did try to reconnect towards the end, but it seemed too much time had passed. If it helps, I regret we lost touch like that, but I regret it more that she let it happen.'

It was beyond Elizabeth's comprehension that a mother wouldn't want her daughter in her life. She would have given anything to get Kate back. 'I'm sorry it was like that. I try all the time with Kate, but she won't forgive me.'

'What did you do?'

Only then did she realise she'd said too much. 'She feels wronged by something I kept from her.' Keen to get it back on track, she returned to the subject of Brian. 'But my point is this; even though things are difficult now I would have bitterly regretted not having my daughter. So, if you think you've made the wrong choice, just tell him. Don't get another ten, or even twenty years down the line and wonder where your chances went. It's a horrible place, hindsight.'

For a while, they watched the radiographers coming and going. They both shifted to stand when the door of the room Tom had disappeared into opened, but the nurse who came out said they would be another ten minutes because of a computer having frozen, or something like that. Elizabeth wasn't sure what she meant. It was cold, but not that cold.

'I'm still thinking about cancelling the move to Hastings, you know?' Alice said.

'Is that what you really want?'

'Sometimes I think so, and then I remember life with Brian, and how awful we were to each other before I told him to move out. Can things ever really get better between people if they were so bad before?'

'I think so.'

'But I said some terrible things; that he was selfish and lazy. Unambitious,' she said, horrified, as if that was the worst one of all. Perhaps just the one that hurt the most.

'Time changes things though. You could just tell him you're sorry.'

'He says he wants to make a go of it, but how am I supposed to put things right?' That was something for which Elizabeth knew the answer. Pride was a terrible thing, it kept a lid on all the things that needed to be said.

'You just say it, love. You just have to take a moment to be brave and do it.'

Elizabeth had rather hoped the conversation would lift Alice's spirits, but it seemed to have had the opposite effect entirely.

'The house in Hastings has got these two downstairs rooms,' Alice said. 'A second lounge and a bedroom. I thought maybe Dad would come and stay.' She reached into her bag and pulled out a tissue. 'Doubt that'll ever happen now.'

'You never know,' Elizabeth said, even though everything she had seen over the last couple of weeks told her that it was unlikely. 'Look at the fact I'm here. I would never have thought that likely a few weeks ago.'

'Well, he's always loved you. Just like you've always loved him.'

Elizabeth couldn't quite meet Alice's gaze then, but she did squeeze her hand a little. 'We both love him, Alice.'

'It's not the same though, is it? It's different for a parent and child. You two are lovers. You've loved each other for a lifetime.'

'Anything else just isn't worth it,' said Elizabeth.

It was 5 p.m. that afternoon when the knock came on the door. They had been moved into a side room, and Tom appeared to be settling in quite well, ordering Alice and Elizabeth to position his belongings in wakeful moments, and giving instructions for a list of shopping to include his favourite biscuits and sweets; Hobnobs and Jelly Babies. Some Bourbons too if they could be found. The new drugs had made a huge difference, and every now and again Alice shared a look of optimistic surprise with Elizabeth. It was quite the turnaround, but she didn't want to hope for too much.

From the window you could see a garden, planted with roses, accessible from the canteen. It was quiet in comparison to the shared bay they had been in before the CT, and with a gentle trickle of autumnal sunlight through the window it was warm and comfortable, nature's beauty propping them up. Elizabeth would always remember the soft smile of the nurse as she entered, asking if it was all right to come in. A second nurse was carrying a couple of extra chairs, and just behind them was a doctor they had never seen before. An older man, maybe in his fifties, wearing a nice suit that didn't fit very well. A tie tucked into a space between his shirt buttons. Hair as bright and white as the moon when the skies above Porthsennen were clear.

'Good afternoon,' he said. He was quick to shake hands with both Alice and Elizabeth, even quicker to reassure them that there was no need to get up. Tom was sitting in his chair, his dinner almost untouched. Somebody had been in earlier to shave him. It made him look tidier which Elizabeth liked, but also slimmer in the cheeks which she didn't. He pushed himself up, used his frail hands to smooth his hair into place.

'Afternoon, Mr Hale. I'm Ricky Jones, one of the chest doctors.' He slipped his arms out of his jacket and draped it over the end of the bed. 'I'm the consultant in charge of your care.'

'Nice to meet you,' Tom said, his mouth dry, his words croaky. His voice was quiet and soft, almost childlike with nerves.

'I'm sorry that we haven't had the chance to speak before now, but I know that Nathan has been keeping everything in order.'

'Yes.' Dr Jones sat alongside Tom on the edge of the bed. They all watched, Tom included, waiting on his next words.

'I wanted to come and tell you about the results of the CT scan.' He turned to Alice. 'This is your daughter, I assume.'

'Yes,' Tom whispered. His voice shook. 'And my Elizabeth.'

'And we can talk freely in their presence?'

'Yes,' said Tom. Elizabeth felt her pulse racing. Alice thumbed at a wedding ring Elizabeth had never noticed her wearing before. One of the nurses smiled at her; Elizabeth didn't like that smile in the least.

'Right. Well, as you know, prior to this CT scan the chest X-ray was highly suggestive of a cancer growing in the lung.' Tom nodded. 'The CT scan identified that quite clearly, and now there can be no doubt about what we are facing.'

Elizabeth watched Tom. He was doing all the right things, humming and agreeing in all the right places, but he wasn't there with them. His fingers were fiddling at the edge of the table, and there was a lack of focus in his eyes, micro movements, darting about left and right like a small animal looking for escape.

Dr Jones spoke clearly, every word considered. 'Additionally, the CT scan also provided us with some new information.' He paused; his voice softened. 'We found evidence of the cancer in the adrenal glands, the kidneys, and the brain.'

Tom registered something with that. 'The brain?' The brain was bad, they all felt it. Maybe you could be all right if they took a kidney, maybe even one of the other glands, whatever they were. Adrenal something. You could even endure an uncomfortable existence with one lung, Elizabeth suspected. But you couldn't live without the brain. One of the nurses took a step towards her and rested a hand on her arm. She didn't flinch, waiting on the doctor to continue.

'Yes,' Dr Jones confirmed. 'The nurses tell me that you have had some problems with your co-ordination, with the fork and with walking.' He pointed to a Zimmer frame that somebody had brought up earlier as proof. 'What we found in the brain explains these additional symptoms. Also, the neurological findings, like your eye and lip being a little weaker than usual.'

'The brain,' Tom said again, but this time to himself. He looked up at the doctor. 'Will I need surgery?'

Despite all his experience, it looked as though the doctor took a moment to compose himself. Elizabeth snuck a glance at Alice, who she could tell was trying her very best not to cry. She fished a tatty old tissue from her pocket and dabbed it at the end of her nose, her gaze all the while fixed somewhere permanently ahead.

'At this stage, with what we know from the tests and about what's been going on with you, we have some important decisions to make. One such decision, as you so correctly raised, is the possibility of surgery. Is that something you would have wanted to do?'

'Well I don't want cancer, that's for sure,' Tom said, just a little bit incredulous, as if Dr Jones was making a bad joke.

'I understand that,' Dr Jones said, shuffling on the bed. 'Such surgery, especially on the brain, is a big strain on the body. It is not without risk, and there are several severe complications associated with the kind of surgery that you would be required to undergo. The same applies for other treatments, like chemotherapy or radiotherapy. They all have benefits, but equally all carry risk. And with everything we know at this stage, I don't think that the best course of action for you would be to rush to undertake any more procedures that are going to potentially cause you discomfort. I don't want to put you at risk of any unnecessary complications. Surgery and even the bronchoscopy we had planned are not going to add anything at this point, or indeed make you feel any better. So, where does that leave us? Our aim now must be to focus on keeping you pain free and as mobile as we can, so we can get you back on your feet and home as soon as possible.'

Ironically, Tom got a burst of life, his voice raised, his arms up in disbelief. 'But what about the tumours?' Elizabeth loved him for it, she really did. Either he didn't want to see it, or just couldn't bring himself to accept what she understood the doctor was telling them. She stood up from her chair and moved close to Tom. His gaze weaved up to her, wide-eyed and a little teary. 'What does he mean, go home?'

'Mr Hale,' Dr Jones said, resting a hand onto Tom's forearm, 'the cancer that we have found presents us with a very difficult decision. It's not very amenable to an operation. We can't just cut it out, and I believe that the risk of other treatments outweighs any benefits they might potentially offer. I think to try to treat you would make you feel a lot worse, for a very limited benefit. You have an advanced cancer, and it has already had quite an impact on your physical abilities. There is no treatment that we can give you that is going to be what we call curative.'

It was the final word that did it. Curative. It made sense to Tom, the idea of a cure, or rather the lack of it. Now he understood what Alice and Elizabeth had understood right from the start of this conversation; not only did he have cancer, but it was going to kill him.

'There's nothing they can do,' he said to himself, but also to Elizabeth. He looked up at Alice, who was lost somewhere in a thought no child should ever have to contemplate. A single tear escaped to his cheek, which Elizabeth hurried away with her tissue.

'There's a lot we can do, Tom,' Dr Jones pushed. 'We can treat you with medications, pain relief, get you walking properly. We can really improve the quality of your life.'

'But not quantity,' he said.

'No, I'm afraid not.' The doctor leaned forwards. 'And because of that there is one more thing that I am obliged to raise with you, especially now while your family is here. It's important that they are involved in this decision. We must decide, on the back of what I've told you, about what we should do if an emergency with you was to arise. In your notes I see that you've had some heart trouble in the past, a heart attack if I'm not mistaken.' Elizabeth looked at him; he had gone ashen.

'That's right.'

'And do you ever get any chest pains now?'

Tom was struggling to focus. After a while he re-joined the conversation. 'Sometimes. I have my puffer spray and that helps if I get a twinge.'

The doctor took a deep breath. It was quick, but Elizabeth knew he was finding it hard. She didn't suppose you ever got used to having to tell people that they were going to die. 'Well, if while you are here with us you were to have any further issues like that, we would have to know in advance to what extent you would want us to treat you. For example, if you were to have another heart attack that led to a cardiac arrest, whether or not we should try to resuscitate you.'

Tom sat up a little straighter then, his shoulders back. 'I'd want you to do everything you could.'

Again, the doctor faltered. He had thought, as had Elizabeth, that Tom had begun to understand where this was going. He reached for Tom's hand; Tom didn't resist or try to stop him. That was an indication of just how out of his depth he really was. When you're drowning, you'll cling to anything or anybody.

'As your doctor, I would have to say that I believe it would be better if we didn't try to revive you should such a situation arise. With the location of the cancer you have in the brain, and the extensiveness of it, even if we were able to bring you back, you could be left with a serious deficit in your abilities.'

Tom snatched his hand away. 'Not do anything? Well, I'd like to know what my daughter has to say about that.'

All eyes flicked to Alice, who had remained until then remarkably quiet. She had been steeling herself, every muscle tense. Shards of tissue fluttered like winter snow to her knee from where she'd been wiping furiously at her nose. Elizabeth wanted so much to tell her it would be all right, but it would have been a lie, nothing but false placations. Although Alice was a forty-two-year-old woman, in that moment Elizabeth thought that she could see the fear of a little girl who had been thrust into a world she wasn't ready for, with decisions to make that were too grand for her to even begin to comprehend.

'I think . . .' she said, pausing for breath. 'I think that if the doctors could bring you back and you'd be you, then obviously,' she said, emphasising the word, 'I would want them to. But if you would be different, like not you, then maybe they shouldn't.'

Tom stared at his daughter, his eyes wide and wet. His words were soft and sorry. 'Shouldn't even try?' he whispered.

Alice was trying so hard to fight the tears, trying so hard not to let her father feel that she had given up on him. 'No, Dad,' she said, her voice breaking, the tears coming. A nurse stood up, rushed to her. Alice didn't stop her when she reached an arm across her shoulders. 'Not if you wouldn't be you,' she stuttered.

Tom didn't say anything for a while, then slowly turned to the doctor and spoke very quietly. Elizabeth could almost see the fight diffusing from him, like mist clearing after a storm. She thought of Kate again, how much she wanted her there, how time was running out. 'Then we should do what you think,' Tom told him, and with a quiet nod the doctor stood up to leave, stopping only briefly to reach for Alice's hand. She and the doctor shared a brief exchange, but nobody else heard what was said. In that moment Tom turned his head into the wing of the chair, closed his eyes.

'Shall I get everybody a cup of tea?' the nurse proposed, her words soft and well-intended. Elizabeth nodded, and the nurse left the room. Alice moved to the window, tears streaming down her face. Elizabeth reached for her hand, but Alice moved away at the last moment, knelt by the side of Tom's chair.

'I'm so sorry, Dad,' she said, burying her face against his arm. 'I'm so, so sorry.'

Elizabeth saw his eyes flicker open for just a moment. He glanced at his daughter as a tear broke free from his eye. And for a while after that nobody said anything else at all. Elizabeth turned to the window and gazed down into the garden where a young couple watched as their baby played on the grass, smelling the scent of a bloom of winter roses while her parents sat on a bench nearby.

Then

The first part of the journey home was completed in silence, their travel the slow speed of a funeral procession. Unapproachable space had grown between them, as if James was stranded on a calving iceberg, and she had no choice but to wait and watch as he drifted away into an arctic future of unknowns. His plans had been whipped out from underneath him, and the guilt smothered her. Without any intention of hurting him, she had ruined his future. But even then, amidst the pain of her choices she knew the only other option would have been to hurt Tom, and she could never ever do that.

'I am truly sorry, James,' she said as they turned back onto the road that would lead them to Porthsennen and the conversation she needed to have with her father. 'When I first met you, I really did think you were a lovely man.'

He nodded but it was with a sense of tenacity. 'It's not your fault. I always knew you were young. The young are notoriously frivolous.'

Elizabeth wasn't sure she fully understood his answer, but she had this sense that she wasn't entirely keen on the concept he was proposing. 'You think that I feel this way because of my age?'

The tyres skidded as he pulled the car over on the side of the road. It was just on the brow of the hill, overlooking the cove. The sea had picked up, whitecaps breaking across the shallows of Longships Reef like a bottle of spilt milk.

He silenced the engine and turned to face her. 'What could it be if not that?'

'Love,' said Elizabeth, without any of the doubt his certainty intended to raise.

The sigh that followed was deep and philosophical, conveyed all the weariness of an age he was decades from reaching. Raindrops appeared on the windscreen. 'I want to tell you a story, Elizabeth. I too was in love once.' It was strange to hear him call her by her full name. Something had changed between them, both a relief and bizarre at the same time. 'I was eighteen, halfway through national service, and ready to run away with a young girl I met near where I was stationed.' A little lost in the memory, he smiled to himself while his fingers played aimlessly at the wheel, stroking back and forth. 'The thought of her was the only thing that got me through my time away in Malaya.' He paused, and in that moment, she realised just how much there was she didn't know about him. Yet that silence granted her a brush with his history, the irrecoverable way that war could change a man. 'Wilhelmina,' he said wistfully. 'Her family wasn't wealthy like mine, but I didn't care. My father did, though.' When he looked up, all memory of that happiness faded. 'Her family used to own a farm, but after my father did what he did that all changed. I never saw Willie again.'

'What did he do?'

He paused for a moment, looked to the sky. 'In a small village, Elizabeth, it takes little effort for rumour to become fact. My father planted the seeds, said he'd seen something inappropriate happening between a young girl and Willie's father. I'm sure you can imagine the rest.'

'That's terrible.'

'Perhaps. But that doesn't change the fact that my father was right. How could I have built a life with poor Willie? We would never have survived London, my years of training. We were so very different. You and I are the same, Elizabeth. A life with you is everything it should be. Everything I want; secure, certain, predictable. We match, like a ship to water, or dark to the night. I only hope your father can help you to see that when you tell him of your plans.'

The thought of telling James that Tom was everything she could ever imagine needing in her future came to her as they drove down the hill. But then she saw the police car parked alongside her house. James slowed when he saw it too.

'What are they here for?' she asked him. They shared a glance of concern for what had transpired that might bring the police to their doorstep.

'We'd better go in, find out.' He parked the car and they hurried into the house.

Panting when they arrived in the living room, they happened upon Mrs Clements, her face ashen as winter snow, huddled next to Elizabeth's father who was sitting with his head in his hands. A police officer stood alongside him, broad shoulders, an expressionless face. He shifted as he saw Elizabeth and James approach.

At the sight of his daughter Dr Davenport stood up and rushed forwards, taking Elizabeth in a tight embrace. Tears streamed down his face and fear filled her, for she had only ever seen him cry once before on the night her mother had nearly drowned. Her hands hung like dead weights at her sides, unsure how to respond to the shift in current, the rip tide that had caught her and was dragging her out to sea. Then the slow mumble of James's voice broke through, his tones soft as he asked the policeman for answers, the words she would never forget.

'Found out on the reef,' said the policeman. 'Nothing they could do.' Her mother had drowned, and some-where inside her, like an almost undetectable expulsion of energy, steam rising from a cooking pot, part of her was irrevocably lost.

Her father had to go with the police. They needed to create a clear picture, even though the officer relented that it seemed obvious enough what had happened, especially when a couple of hours later an old fishing boat taken from the harbour had washed up on Gwynver beach, spat from the water by an offended tide, with one of her mother's cardigans still on the seat.

James strengthened the fire against the rain, waxing against the window which framed the greyest of skies. He drew the curtains against it, made tea and sand-wiches from the cold chicken, then insisted that Elizabeth needed to eat. Later, he positioned her on the settee with her feet on a stool and a blanket over her knees, his arm warm across her shoulders. And when the shadow of night descended on the earth, the sky little more than a spectre sinking into the sea, he went upstairs and ran a bath, guided her to it. He stopped short at helping her undress, closing the door softly behind him when he left.

James was still there two hours later when she went downstairs, unable to sleep. He looked shattered, bags under his eyes, the rims as red as Francine's painted nails. She had arrived not long after Elizabeth climbed into the bath. Her swollen eyes betrayed the fact that she too had been crying, her face flushed in a way Elizabeth had never seen it before. When Elizabeth arrived in the kitchen, Francine approached, hesitated a little before reaching out to hug her.

'If there's anything you need, just ask. Don't worry about any of the filing, or anything like that,' she said. 'I'll cover it all.' Her embrace softened but her hands lingered on Elizabeth's arms. 'I'm so sorry, Elizabeth. I'm so, so sorry.'

With the scent of her sweet jasmine and lavender perfume lingering long after her departure, Francine's visit left Elizabeth confused about their newfound friendship. But it was the sight of her father returning a short while later that left her most bewildered. The face she had known since her first days on this earth was barely recognisable; drawn, eyes rimmed with shadow, his hair greyer than she recalled it that morning. He looked as though he had aged ten years in as many hours. Elizabeth took a seat in the chair alongside him, his gaze following her until she was still. His eyes were watery, his lip trembling.

'I'm so sorry I wasn't here for you.' The melody of his voice was lost, little more than a single note left. The jumper he had been wearing since that morning smelt of ink and sweat. Hair slicked to his forehead in ragged clumps.

'James was here,' she said, knowing her father would like that. 'Daddy, what happened?' she asked.

He shook his head. 'I don't know, Elizabeth. They think she took a boat and got confused. Perhaps tried to swim. I can't believe she's gone. Oh, Elizabeth,' he exclaimed, his head falling to her shoulder. His body shook against her, so she wrapped her arms around him and held him tight, rocking as a mother would a child in the hope to make right his wrongs. She too had aged in the last ten hours. Losing a parent did that, made you question your existence for the first time in your life. Human mortality paraded before you, utterly unavoidable, the world changed.

'I don't understand,' Elizabeth finally said. 'Why would she take a boat?'

'All that time I thought she was upstairs,' he said, not answering her question. 'All that time she was gone. If only I'd known sooner, I could have raised the alarm. I could have saved her.'

'Dr Davenport, please,' she heard James saying behind her. 'You mustn't think that way. You could never have known.'

'I still don't understand why she was on the boat,' said Elizabeth again. She needed an answer. With it might come understanding.

The touch of James's hands on her shoulders grounded her. 'A terrible, tragic accident, Lizzy,' he said softly. His fingers needled at her skin. 'I'm so sorry, really I am, for both of you. And to think of what people have said. How somebody can strike a family at their worst moment, I just don't know. It goes to show the nature of some families.'

'It's the drinking that does it,' her father replied. He sat up, the tears gone, a determined look on his face that seemed out of place.

Elizabeth didn't understand. 'What are you talking about?'

Her father and James shared a look. He nodded, gave James the all clear to proceed. 'Elizabeth, I'm afraid somebody told the police that they saw your father at the harbour this morning, along with your mother. That they were taking a boat out together.'

Before he said anything more, she knew who was responsible.

'Pat Hale,' James said, unable to maintain eye contact. 'Tom's father.'

What was it that Mr Hale had said that morning, something about the Davenports, and about her father being down at the harbour? And then there was that story Tom had told her about the misunderstanding over the stupid flask, the possibility of her father jilting his mother, leaving her heartbroken. Was that what this was, a moment of vengeance? How could Pat Hale lie like that, at a time like this?

'The police might want to talk to you at some point, darling,' her father said, seemingly bolstered by his mounting sense of injustice. 'Perhaps ask you if you saw your mother when you woke up this morning.' Did she appear as guilty as she felt? 'Of course, it won't have helped much that you were up and out so early, but perhaps you heard or saw her? Here or close to the water?' There was such hope in his eyes which made her guilt run ten times deeper. 'Anything at all?'

It took all she had to find the words enough for the lie. 'No, Daddy. I'm afraid I didn't.' It was impossible to be sure, but she thought she recognised some level of understanding on James's face. What would she do when the police asked her about that? Was it possible to skirt around the issue as she had now, or would she have to tell the truth? Tell them where she was when she awoke?

In the house of the man who had lied about her father.

'I'm sure the police will get to the bottom of it. In fact, I'm afraid I must go back to the station quite early tomorrow to help them put together a proper timeline. Hopefully they won't need to bother you at all.' It came as a surprise to her to realise that you could fail to recognise a person you knew so well, her father no more her father than a stranger in the street as she watched him, his head in his hands as he spoke again of his responsibilities with the police. 'I'm afraid I'm not much support to you right now, Elizabeth.'

Years passed at speed; she felt older than she could ever remember feeling before. James's words stayed with her, what he'd said about being naïve, and she wondered if on some level he might have been right. In the last few hours she felt like a different person altogether.

'It's OK,' she said. 'James has been here.'

'And I can stay tonight if you like,' James added. 'I'll be fine on the settee, and I'll be here in case you need anything.'

'We have a spare room,' her father suggested. 'I would feel most comforted knowing that you were here. You will after all, be family soon enough.'

'It's not necessary,' Elizabeth said. Surely James understood this wasn't a good idea after what she had told him earlier on today.

'Allow me to help,' he said to Elizabeth. 'Even if it's just for company in the morning when your father goes to the station.' He lowered his voice, although it was pointless because her father was still within earshot. 'Let me help you now, when you need it the most. Nobody else can be here for you like this under the circumstances, can they?'

She stole a glance at her father and was relieved to see him with a vacant look on his face, not really listening, lost in some horrible vision of what had transpired that day. The thought of prolonging the debate offered even less comfort than the thought of James being there when she woke up.

'I'll show you to the spare room,' she told him. Then they stood up together and ascended the stairs, Elizabeth closing her eyes as they passed her parents' empty bedroom.

'Why did you tell the police?' Tom shouted across the table. In all the years, after all the fights and late nights and broken promises, he had never been angrier with his father. Not even those accusations following Daniel's death, the implication that he was to blame, had caused him to hate his father more than he did now. His father was still sitting at the table nursing a cup of tea when Tom shouted, 'Why couldn't you have just kept your mouth shut?'

Pat Hale stood up quickly, knocking into the table. Tom flinched, a habit formed over years of experience. 'Don't you tell me when I should and shouldn't keep my mouth shut, lad. Especially when I'm telling the truth.'

Setting his overturned cup straight as he sat down, he picked up his knife and fork. 'You should be thanking me. You've had your way with her, and now she'll leave you be. You're a free man again.'

A vision came to Tom of his father on the floor, standing over him, like Muhammad Ali growling over the dead weight of Sonny Liston. 'It's not like that,' he said, never more certain of anything in his life. 'I love her.'

Pat Hale laughed, looked to his wife in the kitchen. 'Sound familiar, Martha?' He turned back to Tom. 'You're as stupid as your mother to think one of the Davenports would be interested in you.'

Tom kicked back the chair and rushed towards his father, unable to contain his anger anymore, Martha only stepping in at the last minute.

'You leave her out if it,' Tom shouted, pointing his finger over his mother's shoulder. He felt his mother's body shaking, close to tears. How many times had Tom stepped in, how many times his mother? They had lost count. He pulled away, took a breath to calm himself. 'I can't stay here,' he told his mother. 'I'm sorry, but I can't do this. Not anymore.'

'Don't say that,' his mother begged as he grabbed his bag, already packed, before heading towards the door. He swung the pack over his shoulder, light with just a few clothes and special books. All he needed for a new life with Elizabeth. 'Please don't leave like this. We need you.'

Such words had stung before on the occasions when his father's anger and drinking or womanising had got too much. But now it was all he could do to leave. Somebody else needed him more, and he couldn't let her down. He opened the front door, pulled up sharply.

Mr Pommeroy was standing on the step.

'Can I come in?' he said, already stepping past Tom. He glanced at Pat Hale, his disapproval evident. 'We need to have a little chat.'

Later that night while she lay in bed unable to sleep, she heard the stones at her window again. It wasn't a gentle scattering like before. This time they came loud and heavy, a promise of broken glass. Pushing the curtains aside, she saw Tom standing in the shadow of their neighbour's house. He didn't wave or motion to her, just stared, his face wrought with a mix of what looked like sympathy and anger. His eyes shone in the faint light of a cloudy sky, filled with crystalline tears. She hurried from the room, the wool of her coat scratching her bare arms, the soft mumble of a hushed conversation between her father and James slowing her pace as it continued behind the closed living room door. Cigar smoke diffused the air, the night chill hitting her as she stepped outside.

As she rushed back into his arms, the pain of the day eased, his love softening the edge of her hurt. The scent of that morning comforted her, a mixture of warm skin and tobacco, and she buried her head into the worn leather of his jacket. 'I'm so sorry, Elizabeth,' he whispered.

He pulled back, one of his hands still cupping the side of her head. His fingers touched the back of her ear, reminded her of the way her mother used to stroke her face as she fussed for sleep as a little girl. Even last year when Elizabeth was sick with flu, her mother had traced circles on her cheek until sleep took her. Who would be there to nurse her now? A void had appeared in her life, and there was nothing that could fill the space. Not even Tom, she realised.

'I couldn't stay away any longer,' he said.

'I'm glad you came.' He held her again, listened to the sound of her breathing. His breath on her cheek felt like something of old, something she had never been without. 'I can't believe she'd do that,' she said. 'Why would she take a boat?'

'It doesn't make any sense,' Tom agreed. 'Your poor father, out looking for her like that.'

'What?'

Tom pulled back a little, inhaling as he lit a cigarette. 'This morning, when my father saw him, remember? He must have been searching for her even then.'

It was for only for the briefest moment that her anger outweighed her grief, but it steered the conversation on an irrecoverable tangent.

'No, you've got it wrong,' she said, pulling back. 'He had no idea she'd disappeared. Your father was just messing with us because I was in your house. What?' she asked when she noticed his confusion. 'You don't believe me?'

'But my father told the police, remember? I don't think he'd take it that far if he was just trying to mess with us.'

Elizabeth took a step back, let Tom's words sink in, plummeting like rocks in water. When she looked back, his face was cast as a silhouette, his dark hair at one with the night sky, the cherry of the cigarette bright against the indigo night.

'Are you trying to say that my father is lying?' Elizabeth said.

'Of course not.' His skin was cold as he reached for her hand. The shift in the connection between them was tangible as she pulled away, and she couldn't ignore it any more than he could. 'I worded that badly. I'm not trying to blame anybody, really I'm not.'

'It sounds as if you're trying to claim that my father had something to do with what happened.'

'I'm not.'

'But you're defending what your father told the police,' she said, hugging her arms across her chest. 'He really dropped my father in it; you realise that?'

'Please, Elizabeth. Don't do this. This is not us. I didn't come here to defend my father.'

'Yet you're doing it all the same.'

'I'm not trying to.' The cherry of the cigarette sizzled until it fizzed out when he tossed it to the wet ground. 'I came here for you, not to talk about our fathers. I want to be with you. To ask you to come with me.'

'Come where?' she said, stunned by the shift in conversation.

'I don't know yet. But I need to leave Porthsennen.'

Nothing he was saying made much sense. 'What are you talking about? You want to leave now, after what's happened?'

'I know, I know, but I can't stay with my parents anymore, Elizabeth, not after this. And I can't stay in Porthsennen without a job.'

'You've got a job, and there are plenty of holiday lets you can stay in over the winter. They're all empty, and Mr Bolitho will give you a good price.'

'No, Elizabeth. I don't have a job anymore. Old Man Cressa saw to that.' When she reeled at the revelation he felt a need to justify it. Feeling as if he had somehow let her down considering his bad luck, he reached for her, was relieved when she didn't protest. 'Mr Pommeroy told me that because I missed work this morning, I'm out.'

'But that's stupid.'

'I know. It's all nonsense; I've missed work before and nobody said anything. It's only cash in hand. They're getting rid of me because of what my father said, but I won't find other work around here. Not after this.'

The image of life before Tom came to her, the engagement with James, the future that was planned. 'But you can't go.'

'But I can't stay here on my own without money, and my mum needs me to work, Elizabeth. I have to help her. After my brother . . .' he paused, eyes filling with tears. 'Dad would still be working if Daniel hadn't died. And if I'd been watching him . . .'

'It wasn't your fault,' she implored, before taking a breath and lowering her voice. 'You can't take on all the responsibility just because your father couldn't cope. It's not right. It's not fair.' Images of the future they had planned together flickered like flashbacks from a dream, parts of her life that felt like memory, in the sense that it felt both inherently as if it belonged to her, but was now also confined to the past. 'I need you too. You can't just go.'

Her legs felt weak, her body too heavy. It was as if every bit of her was having to work to stay on her feet. And with that she gave up, let herself slump to the cold ground, still wet with the earlier rains. Her eyes drifted to the sky, the faintest of stars just visible through a break in the heavy grey cloud.

'This is so unfair,' she said. His touch was strong and yet still gentle as he sat on the cobbles beside her, reassuring to the point where she found the courage for a suggestion. 'What about somewhere close, like Newlyn?' she asked. 'A lot of the fishing went there. Or Mousehole.' Neither were that far, she reasoned, wiping her eyes, the tears unavoidable. 'We could still see each other if you were close.'

Disappointment hit when she saw him shrug his shoulders. That movement spoke of indifference, lack of possibility. 'You're worth more than a cottage with no electricity and scraps on the table, Elizabeth.' Deep inside, he felt the stigma that he knew would follow them for ever. What was a bloke like him doing with dreams of a life with a girl like Elizabeth, raised on expectations with a possible future as a doctor's wife?

'All I want is you, Tom.' He felt her grip tighten against his hands. 'I couldn't bear it if you left me. You might never come back.'

'I will never leave you, I promise,' he continued. 'But after what has happened between our families, I don't think we can stay here either. We need a fresh start, away from here.'

'You mean after the lies your father told.' Her voice broke at the very idea. 'What kind of person does that?'

'Elizabeth,' he said, his voice quiet. Every bone in his body told him to abandon this conversation, but he knew that one of the things she liked about him was his simple honesty, and if he kept his feelings inside, he was likely to lose her anyway. 'I know my father is a lot of things. But he's no liar. Your mother was found early this afternoon, remember?'

'What's that got to do with anything?'

'Everything. My father told us about what he saw before breakfast. I was there when he told the police. He said he saw your father down by the water, taking a boat while it was still dark. Your mother was with him. He saw him staggering from the water later alone.'

'What are you trying to say? That he killed her?'

'No, no,' Tom begged. 'I don't know what happened. Only that my father saw them leave on a boat together, and that when your father came back your mother wasn't with him. My father couldn't have made it up, because the village didn't even know that she was missing then.'

A lump swelled in her throat, the painful burn of impending tears. She blinked them away, not giving in this time. Only this morning she had woken in his arms and it had all seemed so perfect then, so easy. How by the end of the day had so many things changed that his touch no longer felt certain? It was as if a freak wave had capsized her boat, that everything she once held dear was floating on the surface of a choppy sea. 'I know exactly what happened, Tom. She was confused, just like on the night she slipped in the water and you saved her.' Her footsteps were quick as she started back towards the house, Tom chasing to catch up behind her.

'Please don't go. Not like this. I don't want you to be alone.'

'I'm not alone,' she said, pulling away from his touch. 'My father and James are inside.'

'What? James is in there?'

Part of her wanted to apologise, but a larger part of her still angered over his insinuations regarding her father. But to look at him, the hopeful eyes and anxious hands softened her.

'I thought after last night . . . I'm sorry. I have no right to demand anything.' His eyes filled with tears and he went to turn away.

The thought of him leaving that night, while not the worst thing to happen that day, was as unimaginable to Elizabeth as it was possible. 'You've got it wrong,' she said, and he stopped. 'He was just being kind. He stayed even after I told him about us.'

'You told him?'

'Everything,' she said. 'But it makes no difference now, does it? How can we ever be together after this? You believe your father over mine, and even if you didn't, you're planning to leave. Even though I need you here. I was a fool.' James's words rang out like a warning bell in her head. 'I was a stupid fool to even think we could just wish for something and it would come true.'

'No, no,' he said, trying to reassure her. 'You were brave. It's not foolish to love somebody, Elizabeth. When you told him you did the right thing. And we can still be together.'

'How? You're leaving anyway, aren't you?'

Only one option existed close to Porthsennen, offered to him by Mr Pommeroy not an hour before. At the time he couldn't imagine taking it, but if it kept him close to Elizabeth maybe it wouldn't be so bad.

'There is one way I could stay.' Her eyes widened and that hope gave him the courage to make the decision. 'Some bloke from St Agnes took sick yesterday. He was due to go out to Wolf Rock. Mr Pommeroy has already squared it.' She waited, her silence the permission he needed to continue. 'He offered me a job out on Wolf Rock for the next couple of months. A sort of trial, he said.'

A light rain brushed against her face as her gaze was drawn by the lights flickering across the choppy sea, a hint at human existence in the farthest reaches of her vision.

'On the lighthouse?' The idea of the danger pitted against the proximity. 'At least you would be close,' she said, closing the gap between them. 'And it would give things time to settle down, perhaps?'

'Plus, Wolf Rock pays better. When I come back, we would have some money. Maybe then we could leave.'

'Maybe,' she said, but it still felt as if she was clutching at hopes that offered little promise. 'But it's so dangerous.'

'I'll be careful. And I only have to do this once, maybe twice if we need the money.' He felt her hands slacken in his, their fingers curling together. This was who they were. Not those people moments ago who couldn't agree. 'The relief ship comes into port tomorrow.'

'Tomorrow?'

When she broke down, he held her. He breathed in her hair, the soft touch of her skin against his. He leaned in, let his lips linger against her cold cheek. She closed her eyes, told herself to remember it; it was going to be the last one for some time.

'This doesn't change anything,' he said as he pulled away. 'I'll be home soon. Nothing is different, not inside.'

'Everything is different,' she said, her voice cracking. 'Except for how I feel about you.'

'And it's not for long. When I get back, I promise that I'll spend the rest of my life making your dreams come true. Every wish you've ever made. When I told you it was for ever, I meant it.'

'So did I,' she whispered, her voice breaking. His pace was slow and heavy as he walked away, all the time Elizabeth wishing that he would turn around for one last look. Her wish came true as he reached the corner, turning for one final memory. 'I'll come and see you off,' she shouted. 'I'll watch from the headland.' He nodded and waved, and then disappeared around the corner, leaving her standing on the empty pavement in the soft light of the streetlamp. But she realised then that for ever didn't mean a thing if the thing that you loved was gone.

Now

Three days had passed since the doctor had told them that there was nothing more they could do. For the first twenty-four hours Tom barely opened his eyes while Alice and Elizabeth sat vigil. Texts to Kate went unanswered. How Elizabeth wished her daughter was here now. An emptiness hollowed her out like hunger, a longing for her child's touch. Knowing it was the braver choice, she also tried to call, but unsure she was going to be able to get the words out she hung up before even dialling the number.

The nurses came and went, but there was nothing any of them could do that really helped. When it came to leaving, neither Alice nor Elizabeth wanted to go, and they had been grateful for Brian's visits delivering packed food and drinks, along with a respite from their self-imposed isolation. But on the third night the nurses insisted. 'You're no good to anybody like this,' one of them said. 'You're running yourself into the ground, and he needs you to be strong.' So, they kissed his head and prayed as they left. Not for a miracle, but instead just a word, a smile, something they could use to bolster their reserves.

It didn't come.

Alice broke down after they left, and despite her own feelings, Elizabeth found herself in the role of comforter. The thin frame of Tom's daughter shook in her arms and so, imagining it was Kate, she held her close, as tightly as she could. Alice always seemed so well put together, so in control of her emotions like Kate always was, that it was a shock to find themselves like that, pressed up against each other in the cold of night. Even on the occasions Brian had visited, to an outsider it could have been a total stranger sitting there in the room with them. No expressed love or need on her part. But leaving her father brought all those hidden emotions fizzing to the surface, and like a pot left gently simmering, eventually she boiled over while standing at the entrance to the hospital with the smell of the city all around them.

'I just didn't think it would be so soon,' Alice said, pulling away from Elizabeth after some time. Elizabeth pulled a fresh tissue from her pocket and handed it to her. Alice took it, almost involuntarily. 'It's like he's already gone.'

'He's just in shock, love. And remember, they didn't give us a time frame,' Elizabeth tried. 'We have no idea how long he has left yet.' In truth, it was all she'd been thinking about since Dr Jones had told them there was nothing they could do, but even when she asked, nobody seemed to want to give a definitive answer.

'Whatever time we have left, it won't be enough,' Alice said, wiping her nose and then her eyes. Elizabeth couldn't disagree there. She had tried not to cry but hadn't quite succeeded so took a moment to find another tissue. 'It's like they have written him off,' she said, breaking down again. 'And I gave them permission.'

'You had no other choice, love.' Elizabeth hoped to God that Alice hadn't been mulling the decision not to resuscitate over in her mind as if she was responsible for the doctors' decision. 'That kind of thing is down to them, not us. They just try to make us feel involved.'

'But he thinks I've given up on him. He couldn't even look at me.'

'He couldn't look at either of us,' Elizabeth said, wanting to ease her burden, make her see she was as out of control as the rest of them. But while her words were truthful, somehow they felt futile. No matter what she or Alice felt, Tom had given up; that was the only thing that held any importance as far as she could see.

They walked home through the quiet streets, silence between them, stars faint in the night sky above. Patches of cloud and the haze of pollution shrouded them; it was nothing like Porthsennen. Elizabeth looked down at her watch and checked the day. It was Tuesday. They should have been having the bronchoscopy today. Should have enjoyed a quick forty-eight hours in Porthsennen by now. Alice was right about the time; there wasn't enough of it.

'He used to love the stars,' Elizabeth said as they arrived at the gate, still gazing towards the sky.

'He'd often try to point out the constellations to me,' Alice said, leaning against the wall. 'I never could understand what we were looking at.'

Elizabeth pointed at the sky. 'That's Orion. The three bright ones that look like the edge of an arrow; his belt. Can you see?'

Alice nodded. 'Maybe. I think so.'

'And that one all the way over there to the north is the Plough. To look at the stars was one of the first dates your father ever took me on.'

'He told me about that,' Alice said, still gazing skyward. 'Said it was a magical night. That it was the first place he told you to make a wish.'

Elizabeth recalled that night, and all the wonderful things it had brought her. 'I wished for a lot then. I thought . . .' she began, but then trailed off without finishing her thought.

'Thought what?' Alice asked.

'No,' Elizabeth replied. 'It doesn't feel right to speak that way, not standing here outside your family home.'

'Come on,' Alice urged. 'My father loves you, and I've known that for years. What were you going to say?'

Elizabeth gazed upwards, tried to imagine the view of the sky from her home. 'That on that night I wished for a lifetime together. So many dreams that never came true.'

'And some that did. You still have time for some more.' Her lips were cold as she kissed Elizabeth's cheek. 'I best get going.'

'Will you come in first?' Elizabeth asked. 'I'll put the kettle on. You could even stay over if you like.' Elizabeth didn't really want to be alone. 'Your room is just as you left it.'

Alice shook her head as she fastened an extra button. 'Thanks, but I'd rather walk home. I think I need some time to get my head around this.' Elizabeth nodded, unlatched the gate. 'Plus, I'll probably go to Brian's.'

'Oh, really? That's great.' Elizabeth glanced to Alice's hands and saw that she was still wearing her wedding ring.

After waving Alice off, she headed down the path. The radiators were rattling in the living room as she stepped inside, removed her jacket. Without turning on the lights, she made a drink, wanted the dark, didn't want to look at the paraphernalia of a life gone by. The photographs that weren't hers. The family which she wasn't a part of. Maybe there really was still time for a few more dreams, some memories of their own. And as she sat in his chair, curling her knees up towards her chest, her tears soaked freely into the material worn by years of gentle use.

'I need a shower,' Tom said as soon as she walked through the door the following morning.

Elizabeth set her shopper down, her heart racing to hear him speak. Her bag was filled with a couple of books, snacks enough for a week, and a flask of tea because she didn't want to bother the nurses and hated those plastic cups in the canteen. Questions raced through her mind now that he was speaking, like how he was feeling and if the doctor had been to see him again. If they had told him how long. But now wasn't the time, so she reminded herself that she was grateful that one prayer, at least, had been answered.

'Shall I call a nurse? I think I saw Panny on duty when I came in. Isn't she the one you like?'

'No,' he said. Panny was in her forties, wore her curly hair loose in a style that had no doubt been super fashionable in the eighties. Eyes ringed with kohl. Some people could never move on, spent their whole lives living in the past. He stumbled for a moment. 'She's nice enough, but I don't want her help.'

Elizabeth recognised something in that look. 'You want me to help you?' she asked quietly.

'Do you mind?'

She took his hand in one of hers, patted it with the other. 'I'll go and see if the bathroom is free.'

Panny helped her to set up a plastic chair with holes in the seat in the corner of the bathroom, and Elizabeth found a clean washcloth and some soap from the bag she had packed days before. But while Tom had managed to find his tongue, it had been three days since he'd stepped from his bed, and when he did, he was as wobbly as a new baby deer.

'You need to stay off the sauce,' Panny said, propping him up as he wobbled along with his Zimmer frame.

'Nothing wrong with my walking, Panda. It's all that black stuff around your eyes. You just can't see me properly.'

Elizabeth wiped her eyes dry and followed them into the bathroom.

Moments later they found themselves alone. 'You'll have to do it for me,' he said, motioning to his pyjama bottoms while he clung to his frame. They both knew that something fundamental would change in their relationship after this, when she would go from being his long-time love to his carer. It was a privilege to do things for him that he could no longer do himself, but it was also a reminder of just how many things had changed. Still, his smile was a rare reflection from the past, genuine and cheeky. 'You didn't come over all shy, did you?'

'Get away with you,' she said, reaching down to unfasten his trousers. With one pop of the button she whipped them open and they dropped to his ankles. 'Nothing I haven't seen before, is it?'

He looked up; he appeared so vulnerable, slightly hunched with his trousers round his ankles. She had to admit they made for a comical sight, her all fingers and thumbs and him with his trousers down. If anybody could see us now, she thought to herself as Tom took a seat. As she slipped the pyjama top down his back and helped him slide his arms through the sleeves, she felt his loose skin moving under her fingertips, the edges of his bones. The body she once knew was changed even from a few nights ago when they'd last slept together. Everything was wrong with the image before her, from his hair being too long and sweaty around the hairline, to his back which was red in the areas receiving too much pressure in the bed. But as she lathered up the washcloth and began to smooth it over his skin, the sound of his enjoyment brought a sad smile to her face. Setting the washcloth down, she used her hands to glide over his back, kissing the top of his head, when he reached up and patted her hand.

'What made you want a shower, anyway?' she asked as she turned on the water and began to rinse the soap from his back.

'I've got to make a special effort today, haven't I?' It helped that she couldn't see his face, unsure how she would cope if she had to deal with his upset. The date had loomed on the horizon, even though none of them had spoken of it. 'Alice is leaving this afternoon if I haven't completely lost my mind. Am I right?' As he waited for an answer, she saw his face in profile. Somewhere under that loose skin, he was still the man she had fallen in love with all those years ago.

'You haven't completely lost it, no. Do you think she still intends to go?'

'Knowing her, I'll bet she does.' Elizabeth was surprised by the speed of her adaptation to her new role, could even say she was enjoying the process, her ability to care for a person she loved. Isn't that what love is, she pondered, being there for a person when they need you? How quickly things became normal. Even things like this.

'Maybe she'll change her mind,' Elizabeth said. 'She's wearing her wedding ring after all.'

'Is she?' He thought for a moment then shook his head. 'I doubt it. She starts her new job tomorrow, and she's a stubborn little madam.'

As stubborn as Kate, she thought. As stubborn as you, Thomas Hale. 'Wonder where she gets that from?'

'Very funny,' he said, a wry smile passing his lips.

'Just don't be so sure of yourself. People change.'

'Did you change?' he asked. With the spray of the water misting across her face, she knelt at his feet.

'No, darling. I didn't change. Didn't we promise each other once that nothing would ever change for us?'

'I believe we did,' he said with a smile.

'And I'm here, aren't I? Whatever happens we'll face it together.'

'Promise?' With the water on his face she couldn't work out whether he was crying or not. She thought he probably was.

'Never managed to forget about you yet, did I?' He shook his head. 'Well then,' she said matter of fact, putting an end to his concerns. 'Anyway, even if she still goes to Hastings today, she'll be back before you know it at the weekend.'

'Friday's a long time away,' he said quietly. 'You never know what could happen between now and then.'

Elizabeth felt the emotion stir in her throat again. 'Oh, Tom,' she said, reaching for him, taking his shrunken body in her arms.

'You're getting wet,' he exclaimed as she held him close. It was a moment for them, just theirs, when she was everything he needed. It was something to be cherished, she knew.

'I don't care about that,' she said eventually. 'I don't care about anything else anymore.'

And that was how they stayed for a while, her on her knees in the wet, him on a plastic chair with a commode underneath the seat. They could hear the commotion of the ward around them but to Elizabeth it was as if they were the only two in the world. She had felt like that before, once.

'You know,' he said, breaking the silence. 'No woman ever came close to you.'

When she looked up into his eyes, the skin grey and tired, that one on the left still a droopy reminder of what had landed them here in this spot, she realised in many ways they were unchanged. That bright blue still as vibrant as ever. He was still to her as beautiful as he ever was.

'And no man was ever a patch on you either, Thomas Hale.'

'And you know something, we need to be honest about one thing. Neither of us know how long we've got left together. If there was anything we needed to say, anything we needed to get off our chest,' he smiled, paused. 'Of course, I mean other than cancer.' It was a poor joke but still she smiled for him. 'I just mean that, well, now would be the time.'

She sat back on her knees. 'Was there something on your mind?'

'I suppose so, yes. I want you to know that I'm sorry, for any time that I let you down. For when I wasn't good enough or didn't support you.'

'Oh, Tom,' she said, touching his face. 'Nothing like that matters now.'

'I'm just looking back, that's all. Thinking about those wishes and hoping you might forgive me my failings. Wondering how different it could have been.'

'There's nothing to forgive. Not anymore.'

His lips were soft against hers as she kissed him. It was a kiss of old, that felt as if it was leading some-where, even though she knew it couldn't. At least that was what she thought until she felt his lips curl into a smile.

'What's up with you now?' she asked. He motioned towards his lap. 'Oh, you dirty old bugger,' she said as she wiped away a tear. 'The door isn't even locked.'

He was laughing, and she began to crumble into a fit of giggles too, getting steadily wetter until they heard Panny's voice.

'Everything all right in there?' Panny said, along with a knock on the door. 'Sounds like you're having a bit too much fun for a hospital.'

'Not as much as I'd have liked,' Tom sniggered, still laughing as Elizabeth slapped him on the arm.

'Would you stop it,' she hushed. 'We've got to go out there and face them in a minute.'

'What about if it was my last dying wish?'

'Oh, get away with you,' she said, pulling back, pushing herself to her feet. She kissed him on the forehead, still giggling despite herself. 'You don't half know how to pick your moments, Thomas Hale.'

Three out of five patients gave them a round of applause when they emerged, red faced and both more than a bit wet. It was like a club of teenage boys, and Panny was right there with them, tutting and laughing along with the crowd.

'I thought Tom was the one supposed to be having a shower,' she said, looking at Elizabeth's clothes. Elizabeth felt her face flush as Panny moved towards them. 'Let's get back to the room and I'll get you a spare towel.'

Tom eased into his freshly made bed, and Elizabeth looked down at her clothes. A towel would be no use.

'Would you like me to bring you something?' Panny asked, pointing to Elizabeth's clothes. 'I could find some pyjamas for you while they dry.'

Elizabeth shook her head. 'It's OK. I've got something else.' She picked up the bag and disappeared into the toilet.

Panny set a little pot of tablets on the table and Tom snatched it up. He gave it a good inspection, shaking it to get a look at each different drug.

'I don't know why I have to take these,' Tom said. 'Not doing me any good, are they? Make me feel sick every time.'

'We can give you something to counteract that if you want,' Panny said. Tom rolled his eyes at the thought of yet another tablet. As if one more made a difference. 'Because they're doing you a *lot* of good.'

'Not going to cure me though, are they,' he said to himself, before tipping the tablets into his mouth and washing them down with a sip of water. And just like that, the moment in the shower when Elizabeth had made him feel like the teenage boy he was when they first met, was gone. But just a couple of moments after Panny left the room, Elizabeth arrived before him, wearing the pink robe he had given her as part of one of the wishes.

'You still have it?' he said, his eyes wide and mouth soft.

The silk brushed against her bare skin as she stood self-aware in the doorway to the toilet. Francine had sent it to her along with the bottle of champagne last week. It was obvious from the easy expression on his face that he liked what he saw, and it gave her a sense that she was exactly where she was supposed to be, doing exactly what she was supposed to be doing. 'Of course I still have it. I kept everything you ever brought for me.'

'When was that one? I can't remember.'

Warm air billowed out as she lifted the sheets and slipped into the bed alongside his shrinking frame. From the robe's pocket she handed him two slips of blue paper. Holding the first at some distance in the absence of his glasses, he read.

'1985. I wish I could see you in this beautiful pink robe. And 2010. I wish we could take a long shower together.'

'I think it just about counts. Don't you?'

He rested his head on her shoulder. Another two of his wishes coming true. He had to hand it to her; even in this place filled with disease and death, she had found a way to help him experience what it meant to live. 'I dare say it does, Elizabeth. If only we could make them all come true, eh?'

'If only,' she said. But there was part of her that dared to hope that they might still find a way.

Then

On the day of Catherine Davenport's funeral, the sky was clear, the soft grey of cashmere rising from the ocean. Standing in the churchyard at Saint Sennen's, one hand in the loose grip of her father's, the other in the tight hold of James's, Elizabeth listened to the committal. Numb feet shuffled as they lowered the coffin, and then, when it was all over, she watched as her father retreated to the vestibule of the church to where she saw Tom's mother dressed in a simple black dress waiting almost out of view. Her hair was neat, a small hat perched on the top. Elizabeth's father held her in a brief embrace.

'Why don't we get out of here?' James said, almost as if he was trying to hurry her away.

But keen to see what was exchanged she waited, watching as they spoke. From behind her, she heard one of the village women in attendance mutter, 'Some things never die,' and Elizabeth knew there and then that Tom had been telling her the truth about their parents' past.

Porthsennen had quietened like a hibernating bear, adjusting to life in the new season. Fishing had all but finished, even the most experienced keeping well away from the rougher seas of autumn, and most of the tourists had gone home. The village was quiet, contemplative regarding the season it was leaving behind. Elizabeth had been walking up to the old Mayon Lookout most evenings since her mother's death, sitting amongst Tom's belongings, which almost made it feel as if he could return at any moment. The quilt stitched by his family kept her warm while she sat gazing from the window towards the light from Wolf Rock. When it turned colder still, she lit his small gas stove, read his copy of *Pride and Prejudice* in the soft light, wondering all the time what she was supposed to do without him.

One night not three weeks after he'd left, she was blessed by the silvery smudge of the Milky Way, streaking through the sky like the sunlight from a fish's scales. It made her feel closer to Tom somehow, even though he was a world away. Her efforts focused on trying to imagine him out on that tiny outcrop of volcanic rock. Fears for his safety stirred, the fog creating nightmares that sometimes made it hard to breathe. Other times the thought of his return, and all the things she had to tell him, made her feel even worse.

James positioned a plate of warm buttered toast on the table, but even just the smell of it was enough to make her feel nauseous. Since Tom left just over a month ago, that feeling had become a regular distraction. Still, she took a slice to please James; didn't want to negate his efforts.

'Have you written it yet?' he asked, turning to the countertop for a pot of tea. 'I have to go in a moment.'

In her father's absence from the medical practice, James had been manning the clinic, which had become busier than ever since her mother died. The whole village had sickened at once, an epidemic of intrigue. Half of them had nothing wrong with them. He also seemed to have taken on the role of head of the household in the most discreet of ways, paying the odd bill, ensuring that Mrs Clements took her pay at the end of the week. Elizabeth wasn't sure what to think as she watched him slipping effortlessly into her father's shoes as if he too was no longer there.

'It's upstairs,' she told him. 'I'll go and get it.' Elizabeth moved to stand but James motioned for her to sit.

'I have to go up anyway because my shoes are up there. Is it on the dresser?'

'Under the doily,' she told him as she bit into the toast. 'Thanks again for helping me like this.'

'What else was I to do? You need me to do this.' One night in the first week following Tom's departure, she had lost track of time. In a panic, James had set out to find her, and did so in the old Mayon Lookout, gazing out at a misty sky with tears in her eyes. When she explained that to be there watching both the stars and the light from Wolf Rock was the only thing that eased her loss, he had seemed so sad for her. 'If sending a simple letter to Tom can alleviate some of your pain, how could I stand by and do nothing?'

'Well, I really appreciate it,' she said. 'What time are they setting sail?'

'The Stella leaves around ten. Mr Pommeroy promised me that he would put the letter in the chest with the newspapers.'

'Please make sure he doesn't read it.' It was terrifying to wonder what Tom would do when he read what she had to say. But she told herself to be strong, that she was doing the right thing. 'It's just for Tom.'

'Of course, Elizabeth,' he said, patting her shoulder. 'A letter is a private thing. Mr Pommeroy would never be so indiscreet.'

Her father appeared in the doorway to the kitchen a short while later, a smaller version of the man she once knew, cut down by the blade of death. Tiredness gripped him, even when he'd just woken up, as if he no longer had the energy for life.

'Was that James I heard leaving?' he said as he moved into the room, collecting the newspaper before sitting down at the table. Elizabeth poured him a cup of tea from the pot and slid it towards him.

'He has a full clinic. Mr Bolitho has made another appointment.'

'Isn't that the third time in a week?'

Elizabeth nodded. 'I believe so.'

'He has nothing better to do than fish for gossip. He ought to be ashamed of himself.' It was strange to hear her father speaking that way. He never usually had a bad word to say about people. Still, what he said about Mr Bolitho was tame in comparison to the thoughts he had shared regarding Tom's father. 'I should really make the effort to go in. I cannot stay here for ever, festering in these pyjamas. Perhaps if I make an appearance, they will lose interest and leave us in peace.'

'Perhaps,' Elizabeth said, although she doubted a fast resolution. A strange death would take some getting over for most folk.

'Plus, I must put a stop to this indecorous intrusion of James being here before you're married.' Elizabeth thought that perhaps it was exactly the kind of gossip they needed to take the focus off her father. An unwed couple. Cohabiting. Simply dreadful, Mrs Anderson would say. But Elizabeth was going to have to get used to gossip soon enough. All that she could hope for was that Tom would be back in time to help share the burden.

'It's not like he is sleeping in my room, Daddy. He is here as a friend to help.' If he wasn't, she would be alone, and right now, with everything going on, she couldn't face that either.

Her father shook his head. 'The sooner the wedding takes place, the better. Plus, it'll give us all something to look forward to.' He finished his tea, took a long breath. It crossed Elizabeth's mind to ask him about his past with Mrs Hale then, but it was so close to her mother's death that she couldn't bring herself to do it. 'You have been quite wonderful these past few weeks, have taken such good care of me after the awful things that were said. I want you to know how much I appreciate it, and how very proud I am of you.'

'You're welcome, Daddy.' How she was going to straighten things out between their two families once Tom returned, she still had no idea. What Tom's father had suggested remained unforgivable. But once Tom was back, they had no other option but to try. Things did seem to have blown over a little. Elizabeth had overheard the whispers surrounding her mother's death, shock at her inexplicable presence on a boat, and over the terrible things implied by Tom's father. People, she was beginning to realise, loved to have something to ponder, extrapolating the how and why until they had their own, more exciting version of the truth. But the gossip had quietened now, and she thought perhaps enough for the unification of their families once Tom came home. The flame of hope was weak, but it burned still, and it warmed her.

'You are such a wonderful girl. You will make James a very happy man. Now,' he said as he stood up and drained his tea. 'I'm going to get dressed and have a walk along to the clinic. I think it's about time, don't you?'

It was about time, that was true. But it was also the time for something else; the truth. When she thought about telling him the tremor of trepidation hit her so hard, she sometimes couldn't breathe. Telling her father that which she must, left her even more anxious than the idea of telling James. But there was no going back now, because the letter was already on its way to Wolf Rock, meaning she had no choice but to await the most terrifying thing of all; what the hell would Tom say when he found out?

Dearest Tom,

It still feels unreal that I am here without you, and that I must resort to writing you a letter. It seems an almost impossible feat for it to reach you in your current location. But to write it is the only thing I can do until you return. Please tell me that you are coming back soon. I promise you that I am counting the days.

Since you left, I walk each night down Cove Hill and climb the steps until I reach the fork in the path that leads to the rocks. Although I admit it frightens me to go there after the fall I took, somewhere within the black of the horizon you are painted, as a flickering light to guide people to safety. I wait for the light each night to prove to me that you are still alive. When I see it shining, I can imagine you here, with me, as if the distance between us can be overcome. For now, the light from Wolf Rock acts as a reminder that we remain in this world together.

My love, it is with great courage that I write this letter. I wish you were here so that I could say these things in person, and part of me thinks I should wait. But the truth is that I cannot bear it. Because Tom, something quite wonderful has happened, although it is terrifying in equal measure. Tom, I think I am having a baby.

I cannot go to see the doctor to confirm this, but I asked Mrs Clements how she felt when she was pregnant and all the symptoms she described are exactly how I feel. She was most surprised by my questions, but I don't think she suspected anything. I hope you are happy with the news. I pray that you are; I know you will make a wonderful and loving father.

I am sure this must come as quite a shock. It has come as a shock to me too. I was very scared when I first realised but then I thought of you, and the promises you have made to me. I remembered that you promised nothing would ever change despite everything that's happened. I know we are young, and that our families have been tested against each other, but together I think we can do this. I was thinking about names. What was your grandfather called? I thought maybe if we have a girl, I could name her after my mother. Would you mind?

I think about you all the time and cannot wait for your return. Please stay safe. Until you are here I will watch the light and think of you.

Your ever-loving,
Elizabeth

Then

Tom had known it was going to be a long night when he saw the fog coming in. He had seen it descend within minutes out here. Sometimes it seemed to simmer up from the calm waters, blanket the lighthouse in a mist so thick you could barely see the breaking waves below. Every five minutes for the rest of the night he would repeat his task, or at least until the fog cleared. It wouldn't be the first night he hadn't slept since his arrival; some nights, despite the fact his bed on the third floor was comfortable and surprisingly warm, he couldn't settle for the thought of what he had left behind. The last time he'd seen Elizabeth and what he had said. And the things he hadn't. What good was withholding the truth about the night he saw her mother go into the water if he ended up losing Elizabeth anyway? He felt like the worst person in the world, and all he had tried to do was the right thing. But by whom? Not by himself. Certainly not Elizabeth.

Smoke from the first firing bled into the fog, then Tom descended the spiral staircase from the lantern room. The living room had a small gas stove to boil some water, and dressed in his winter woollens, he found Keeper Robertson already there, tending the pan.

'Thought you could do with one,' he said to Tom as he arrived at the foot of the steps. 'I heard the gun. Looks like it's set in for the foreseeable, don't you think?'

'You know better than I do, Reg.' Tom pulled his scarf tight, a cool draught licking at his skin, a dampness to the air. The mug of tea tingled as he took it, the steam welcome on his face as he sipped.

'That I do.' Reginald was in his fifties, had been manning Wolf Rock since he was Tom's age. To watch him maintaining the weights and the lenses was to watch a craftsman oiling his tools. He knew this place inside out, could work with his eyes closed.

'I don't know how Danny sleeps through it,' Tom said as he took up a seat alongside Reginald. Danny was the third keeper currently stationed on the lighthouse. He was due to leave when the relief boat sailed back in. It would bring letters and supplies, newspapers and fresh food.

'Always can. His first off-shore stint was Bishop Rock, and that takes the full brunt of the Atlantic's moods.' Reg chuckled to himself as he leafed through a three-week-old newspaper. 'It's only just October, and you got yourself until at least the beginning of November here. But don't worry, lad. She'll still be there when you get back.' Tom's eyes widened; he hadn't told them anything about what had happened with Elizabeth. 'Don't act surprised that I know about your girl back on shore,' Reginald added. 'You think they often send inexperienced lads like you out to places like Wolf Rock? Old Pommeroy was doing you a favour, told me all about it in a letter.' Cards flicked black and red between spades and hearts as Reg shuffled a deck. 'And your father has made quite the claim. Do you believe him?'

Something about his tone gave Tom the permission he needed for the truth. It was a genuine question, one that didn't already have an answer.

'I do,' Tom said. 'But I'm not saying anything about Dr Davenport,' he was quick to add. 'Only what my father saw.'

'I know, lad. Don't worry, just us here now.' He licked the tip of his thumb and dealt Tom a hand. Tom fanned the cards out in a tight palm. 'Elizabeth has a tough choice on her hands.'

'She already chose, I think,' he said, having spent the last lonely weeks mulling over their final meeting time and time again. 'She believes her father.'

'Of course she does,' Reg said, setting a queen of hearts onto the top of the crumpled newspaper. 'But I don't imagine it was easy for her to hear that her father had some hand in her mother's death. Plus, your old man's a drunk, and even though you know what I've just said is true, I can see your hackles rising. You want to defend him just as she did hers, so don't you tell me that she would find it easy to support you and what your father said over her own.'

Tom knew Reg was right. 'But what if I knew something that might change her mind?'

Reg eyed him above the cards. 'Such as?'

Never had he expected to confess what he knew, but what did he have left to lose? 'That night I rescued Mrs Davenport from the water.' Reg leaned in, waited. 'She didn't slip. She jumped.'

Reg shook his head. 'I don't think so, lad. You must be mistaken.'

'I was right there. She'd been confused for a while, wasn't well. What if she meant to take that boat out,

Reg? That would change things about what my father said, wouldn't it?'

The weight of the knowledge he didn't want settled on Reg's shoulders. 'Well, only you know what you saw.'

'I know,' he said, setting down his cards. 'And I saw her jump. After I jumped in the water she was shouting, "Let me go, let me go," until she passed out.'

'Good Lord.' He tossed the cards down, all interest in the game lost. 'I don't doubt your honesty, lad. Done nothing but a good job out here on Wolf. But others might, so think long and hard before you go saying anything.' The glass in the small window rattled against the wind, nothing but thick grey cloud beyond. 'The wind has picked up. Get yourself back up there to fire the fog gun. Last thing we need is a wreck on our hands.'

Tom was relieved to see the *Stella* arriving a week later, cutting a frothy trail through the sea. From the small table by the fourth-floor window, if he peeled back the frayed check curtain, he had a good view to watch the ship's approach. Seeing the boat was surreal in many ways; the five-day delay made it feel as if the rest of the world didn't exist. It was a little like he was adrift, even though he was stationary, his life suspended in uncertainty over what would happen next.

Tom rose to his feet, silencing the small radio and its songs which sparked memories of home, and span down the stairs to join the other keepers outside. Such was the relief to stand on the slither of land they called home, to feel the wind in his hair now that the waters had receded; it made him want to sing out loud and tell everyone of his love for Elizabeth. Still, as the *Stella* dropped anchor and the small relief vessel set course for the rock, he relented as such a display of madness would likely render him a liability and so he kept his mouth shut.

'It's been good to work with you,' said Danny McGreary to Tom. 'Do you think you'll be back another time?'

'I'm not sure,' he said, gazing first at the rocking motion of the boat, then the distant glimmer of the shore. It was like a mirage, there one minute, gone the next as the sea swelled and gave. 'I suppose that depends.'

'If she's got any sense, she'll be waiting for you. Decent lad like you. She'd be a fool not to.'

Tom reached out and shook Danny's hand, was surprised to find it sweaty. 'Thanks. I hope you're right.' He nodded towards Danny's little pack, draped over his shoulder. 'Have you got the letter I wrote?'

'I have. I'll get it to Pommeroy, who'll get it to her. I'll bet you two bob she can't wait to see you,' he said as his eyes followed an incoming barrel overhead, a new supply of paraffin which after the five extra days without relief was in sure demand. 'You'll see, all this trouble with your father will blow over.'

'You mean the trouble with her father, more like,' Tom corrected, reaching up to steady the barrel onto the ground. The source of his need to defend his father was a mystery to him. Yet he always did, despite the anger he harboured concerning his behaviour. It was unfathomable to him how the man who blamed him for the loss of his second son could simultaneously stir both hatred and longing in equal measure. He was not unaware that each emotion was intrinsically linked to the other.

'Aye, if you say so.' And with that, Danny McGreary attached himself to the winch and just a short moment later he was leaving the platform. With a salute and a smile, he was away.

It wasn't Keeper Williams's first time aboard Wolf Rock, and he kicked off his shoes and got his feet up on the table before the first cup of tea had even been poured. Tom could almost say there was a wash of relief across his face, satisfaction at the idea of returning home. It made Tom uneasy; he didn't like the thought of this place being more familiar than the home he planned with Elizabeth. Where would they live when he returned? Porthsennen was unlikely, but what about London? Maybe if he could find a decent job. He knew how much she wanted to go there. Would she be willing to leave by the time he was back on shore? He'd agreed to come to Wolf Rock in the hope it would give her enough time to realise that he could no longer stay in Porthsennen, that together they could make a fresh start. He only hoped she could see that by the time he got home.

The thud of a tea tin on the table shook him from his thoughts, precious cargo inside with news from home. He stared at it, craving the correspondence. Home, he realised was part of him, and he missed it; he even missed his father if he was honest. The tin made a satisfying pop as Robertson removed the lid, air rushing out, full of promise.

'Looks like this is for you,' he said, tossing a small bundle Tom's way. His heart skipped a beat as he fiddled at the ratty piece of string holding it together. 'Somebody is a popular boy.'

Tom held the parcel close to his nose, sensed the smell of home; the sea, mixed with the bread and tobacco. His name was written on the front of the envelope, a letter from his mother. Under that there was a small piece of cloth, wrapped around some of his mother's Hevva cake. The material was damp, and Tom imagined it still warm when she'd wrapped it up that morning. It stirred a yearning for the life he once knew, and resentment for the rock upon which he was stranded. Fear for his life ahead. He split the Hevva cake in two and bit into it.

'Anything else left in that can?' he called to Robertson.

With his feet up on the edge of the table, a newspaper in his hands, he shook his head. 'Nothing,' he said, without even looking up.

Nothing from Elizabeth. Could that be right? It was true that he hadn't left things on good terms, but he thought they had agreed that nothing had changed. That time was all they needed. He never once imagined that she wouldn't write to him while he was here. And he had been sure he'd seen her up on the headland, watching as he set sail for Wolf Rock, just as she'd promised weeks before. But now that she'd had the time to think it over, had she changed her mind? He had left the day after her mother died. He should have supported her, but instead he'd allowed himself to be hounded out of Porthsennen just because a few village busybodies made his job disappear, leaving when she had never needed him more. Oh, he had buggered it up all right, building a wall between them in the shape of seventeen nautical miles of rough Atlantic Ocean, one brick set in place for every whispered doubt and denial. And now he couldn't do anything to change it because he was so bloody far away. Not only that, he had sent that letter too, telling her all about how her mother had jumped. Was there any way to get it back?

With no other choice, he began to read his mother's words. The note was brief, but it was clear she missed him. Dinner times were lonely, she said, but she reassured him that they were both very proud of the job he was doing. His father had been inspired, had taken it upon himself to try to support the family and hadn't been drinking for over a week. Tom had to take a break for a moment there, couldn't believe the stroke of luck. But as he read on, his mother also wrote that Dr Warbeck had been to see them before the ship's departure, informed them that he had moved into Elizabeth's family home, and that they would be married before Tom had a chance to return. He had asked that they write to Tom, explain that there was no future for him and Elizabeth. And then, at the end of the letter, almost as if an afterthought, she wrote that Elizabeth was pregnant. Her final sentence read, 'And Dr Warbeck says it's his, and so I think you best leave it at that, Tommy. No point making things harder for anybody, is there?' She added, as if it meant anything, that she was really very sorry.

'Where you going?' Reg called as Tom headed towards the spiral staircase that led to the lantern room. 'Doesn't need lighting for hours yet.'

'Just need some air,' he said, the letter still in his hand, the taste of Hevva cake rich in his mouth. Stepping out onto the narrow shelf, buffeted by the intemperate Atlantic winds, Tom tried to bring Elizabeth to mind. Yet all he could picture was a child in her place. A baby. His baby, or could Dr Warbeck really be the father?

How could things have changed so unrecognisably in just the few short weeks of his absence?

But as he listened to the waves receding, the howling of the rocks as the raging waters drained through the fissures in their surface, he realised that even if it was his baby, she had chosen James. And why wouldn't she? What did Tom have to offer her? A useless fool, that's what his father had called him. How was he supposed to raise or provide for a child, fishing when the seasons permitted and scrounging for whatever work he could when they didn't? Elizabeth was doing what she had to do for security, for a better life for her child, but he couldn't deny it hurt to think of how little faith she had in him, her actions reinforcing every harsh word he'd ever heard about himself.

Part of him wanted to swim to shore, put a stop to her asinine plan. If that was his baby, surely he had rights too. But the other part of him wanted to plunge into the Atlantic waters, and if he survived the drop, begin swimming the other way, deep into the ocean until his arms weakened and he slipped, quite painlessly beneath the undulating surface to his death. Because losing Elizabeth and the future they once had planned reduced him to little more than a ghost, the shadow of what he once was, a remnant from a life that was already resigned to the past.

Everything about the thought of going back terrified him now. He couldn't return to shore only to watch his dreams unravel. After one more glance at the letter from his mother he let it go, watching as it skipped up and down on the currents of the wind. It landed in the water moments later, where it disappeared, along with his future, and all the dreams that Elizabeth had made him believe in, for good.

'Did you send it?'

James had barely stepped through the door after a difficult day. 'Of course,' he said. Her chest slackened as she let go of the breath she had been holding since he'd left the house that morning. So that was it; she had told Tom everything. A smile roused at the thought and she reached to touch her tummy. A baby? Tom's baby. 'Mr Pommeroy set it in the can in front of my own eyes. He should have it by now.'

After helping James remove his coat, she hung it on the rack in the hallway. 'You have no idea how much this means to me. To us.' His smile was strained, spoke of untold hurt, or so Elizabeth thought. Perhaps she was pushing it, gushing like that. But she had to ask, couldn't help it. 'Did he give you anything for me?'

James shook his head, patted her shoulder. 'I'm afraid not.' It was impossible to ignore her disappointment, but he tried all the same. 'I'm sure he was just too busy.'

'There are a lot of jobs to do on the lighthouse,' she said, trying to reassure herself. 'And what about my father?'

James pulled a face she didn't like much. It was sympathetic, but it didn't hide the truth of how he really felt. 'Not the easiest first day back, but I think it will have been good for him.'

'Where is he now?' By then they had moved through to the kitchen. Weeks together had taught her that he liked a nice cup of tea after a busy day at work, preferably with a shortbread biscuit if there was one available. Mr Boden's shop was out of stock after she'd snapped up the last pack that afternoon as a thank you for James's help with the letter. The tea was dark and strong as she poured, just the way he liked it, brewed in anticipation of his arrival. Offering a plate with three triangles of the Cornish shortbread arranged in a fan, she was pleased when he took one. Tapping away the crumbs, he sipped his tea, and ate.

'He wanted to stay late to finish some paperwork,' he mumbled, catching the escaping biscuit with his finger. 'He didn't get much of a chance with all the chatting everybody wanted to do. He'll be along soon.' He took her hands in his. 'If I'm quite honest I think he wanted to give us some time alone. You must remember that he knows nothing of your decision to end the engagement. He doesn't understand the truth of our situation here.'

Elizabeth sighed. 'I know,' she said, bowing her head as she sat down. 'We have complicated things.'

'I think we must tell your father what's really going on. He has all these expectations about our future. It seems so cruel not to tell him.'

'I know,' she said, sighing. 'But he already has so much to deal with. I appreciate that it's a lot to ask, but couldn't we leave it until Tom is due to return?' Even to continue with this charade just a little longer would buy her a bit more time.

Eventually he moved forwards and pulled her close. He kissed her lightly on the cheek and wrapped his arms around her. 'You are such a sweet thing, Elizabeth. Always thinking of others over yourself.' He held her there for a moment, and she could feel his heart beating against her chest. 'I hope to have a daughter as wonderful as you someday. You care so much about him that you would complicate your own life to simplify his.'

'I just don't want to hurt him. We can tell him soon, I promise.'

He smiled, clapped his hands together. 'Right then. I need to change out of this suit and put my slippers on. Why don't you make a start on some dinner? There's a lovely fresh bream I got from Old Man Cressa in the fridge.' It was such a relief that James had agreed to play along, but it was hard to extinguish the disappointment caused by the absence of communication from Tom. 'I'll freshen up and be down in just a minute.'

James closed the door to the spare room that had so far become his own. He set his briefcase down on the bed and clicked the two buttons. The clasps popped open and he stood up, removed his tie and jacket, set them across the back of a chair by the window. The edge of the bed creaked as he sat, then turned the briefcase so that he could see inside. Facing him was a small white envelope, the letters on the front spelling Elizabeth in simple, printed handwriting. It smelt of the sea. He tapped the edge against the case notes from the day's patients. He had to know what he was up against, so he used his finger to tear it open.

On the one hand he had no idea how he could continue lying to Elizabeth. He felt sick every time she questioned him, especially since he had read of the truth she had written to Tom that morning. Dizziness consumed him to the point of near fainting when she asked him whether Tom had written to her, knowing her lover's letter was right there in his bag alongside the one she had written to him, which he had failed to deliver. It had seemed such a good idea to tell her that he would deliver a letter on her behalf, but it was harder than he thought to lie to the woman he loved. Of course, he had never intended to send anything, but had hoped the idea of communication with Tom would be the end of it. When no response came, he had been sure she would tire, her affections reverting to him. He couldn't have positioned himself any better for it. But now there was a baby. He glanced down at the small white envelope and told himself that he really should give it to her. To let her go was the only kind thing, if that was what she wanted. But he couldn't do it. He wanted her for himself. He had so much more to offer that it simply wasn't fair to let her make such a terrible mistake. Not fair on anybody.

Elizabeth would always be the girl who'd fooled around with the local boy, he the fool who married her regardless, but if nobody knew then it was almost as if it had never happened. The truth was only the truth once it was known. Why should he let her throw her life away for a boy that could give her nothing, when he could give her everything? Surely, he would make a much better father than Tom. If he could just hold on a little bit longer, he knew he could convince her of the right way forwards. All he had to do was keep her away from Tom once he returned from Wolf Rock. Or find a way to ensure that he never returned. Either suited James just fine.

He reached into the white envelope and pulled the letter out. He began to read as the smell of frying fish permeated the room.

*

Dear Elizabeth,

Sometimes when I think of my location on this earth I feel as if I am a million miles and a thousand hours from the safety of home. Wolf Rock is a precarious place, Elizabeth, and it is true what Mr Pommeroy told me before I left, that one false foot could render me a thing of the past. I think I saw you on the headland as we set sail, and that lasting view of you I keep with me all the time.

The waves roar beneath us like a jungle cat here. But this lighthouse was built strong, and I am being trained well by experienced company. The other keepers have made me welcome and have shown me the ropes. I already know how to light the lamp and change the vapour tubes, and I am pretty good at cleaning the windows, or so they tell me. The waves are getting increasingly rough, and I am concerned that the supply boat will be delayed. However, Keeper Robertson has been teaching me to cook, so at least upon my return I will be of some use to you. Time is passing quicker than I might have expected, but I admit not fast enough.

If you have made it this far into the letter, I can only assume that you wish to know what it is I have to say, despite what happened. So, on that note, I will stop coursing around the issue like the ships in the distance navigate around this volcanic outcrop of land, and ask that you forgive me. Please, please forgive me, Elizabeth. I beg you to try to understand why I left. I am truly sorry for what happened, and that I am not there to support you when you need me. I lie awake at night listening to the gentle vibrations of the revolving lamp and all I can think about is you telling me that you still imagine a future together. I was such a fool, although, I also hope you can see, an honourable one. I had to think of my family, and us. I had to do what I could to protect us. I speak

272

the truth, Elizabeth, only that. And as it is the truth that led us here, I feel I must rely on it now. There are things I wish I had said in person while I had the chance, but sometimes the most important things are the hardest to express.

Elizabeth, I never told you this when we were together, but I have loved you for a long time. I would watch you painting, sitting alone and lost in your work, and imagine that we were together. And on that day you came to me and you agreed to go with me to the old Mayon Lookout, I felt as if I was the luckiest bloke in the world. But it was sadness that brought you to me on that day. And it was that sadness that prevented me from telling you the truth. I have tried hard to keep what I know inside. But I must tell you the truth if you are to understand what happened to your mother.

Sweetheart, she didn't slip on the night I pulled her from the water. It was no accident that I rectified, but a decisive act that I sought to reverse. She jumped. I called to her to stop, and I know she heard me, but she jumped in anyway. I dived in after her and she fought my efforts, telling me to let her go. You see, she didn't want to be saved, Elizabeth, and instead I believe was trying to save you from the hurt of her illness.

This is how I know my father is telling the truth. He saw your mother enter the boat with your father on the day she drowned, and once again I think it was what she wanted. He helped her fulfil her wishes, Elizabeth. I don't know what happened thereafter, and I will not make assumptions that might hurt you. I tell you only what I know.

I'm sorry to tell you this. I never wanted to.

Forgive me.

Your ever-loving, Tom

Now

'Did I wake you?' Elizabeth asked. The early afternoon sun was low. Alice had returned to Hastings after all, much to their disappointment. Tom shook his head.

'No. My bottom's sore, that's all,' he said, trying to turn. 'I want to go for a walk.'

'You can't go on your own,' she said. He had taken a tumble yesterday, bumped his head, despite the fact the medication seemed to have helped with his memory and co-ordination. 'You'll be in trouble with the ward manager.'

'I wouldn't mind being in trouble with the ward manager.' How he had the strength for a smutty joke she didn't know. His speech was still slurred, and it was getting harder to understand him. But the tone of his voice was playful enough, and she couldn't help but enjoy the moment of perfect mental clarity. It didn't happen often anymore.

'Like you were in trouble with Francine Matherson?' she teased. At first, he had no idea whom she was talking about, but then slowly, like the dawn mists rising, understanding came. 'Oh yes,' she said, lingering over the word when she noticed him smile at the memory. 'Don't think I didn't know all about that.'

He laughed to himself, slipped a hand from under the sheets and rested it on hers. It looked like such an effort.

'I got in more trouble with you though, didn't I?' he said.

His fingers were cold as she kissed them, his nails a bit too long, and she vowed to clip them later. 'Yes, love. I suppose you did.' His wriggling persisted, and it was hard to watch as he tried without success to get comfortable. 'Do you want to go up to the day room for a while?'

'I'd rather leave the hospital for a bit. What if you helped me get dressed? We could go out somewhere.'

'I don't think you're allowed.' He rolled his eyes; he always was the braver one. 'OK,' she said, testing her defiance. 'Where did you want to go?'

'Really? Well, there's something on that wish list I want us to do.' After Elizabeth relented, he dressed with her help, and once she managed to find a wheelchair, they were set to make their escape. 'Let's go,' he whispered once the coast was clear. 'But make sure you bring your purse. We're going to need a taxi.'

The wheels almost betrayed them as she pushed him out of the ward as fast as she could. But despite the whistling of a rusted bearing they made it out undetected. It didn't take them long to find a taxi from the rank outside the hospital, and soon enough they were on their way. Elizabeth kept thinking about what the nurses would do when they found his empty room, and the guilt was insurmountable, but Tom's eyes were fixed on the road ahead.

'I hope you're happy with yourself,' Elizabeth said, her heart still pounding.

A smile had been etched onto his face since the moment they exited the ward. 'What are you worried about? It's not like you broke me out of Belmarsh.'

'No, but they might put us there yet. If they go looking for you, what are we going to do?'

'Nothing. We won't even be there.'

'Tom,' she said, her voice raised. 'That's my bloody point.'

He turned back to the window, his smile widening. 'You never used to swear. You've become quite the rebel, Elizabeth Margaret Beatrice Davenport.' His smile made it feel as if she was looking at him fifty years ago. He winked. 'That means that what I've got in mind will be right up your street.'

They pulled up outside a corner shop, the light beginning to fade. Elizabeth glanced through the window and up at the sign. 'I'm not doing that. I thought you were crazy the first time you wrote that on your wish list.'

'I thought you wanted all the wishes to come true.'

'Well, maybe not that one. And definitely not at our age.'

'You're only as old as you feel, Elizabeth. Come on,' he said, urging her on. 'We can get the same one. Why not?'

Defiance wavered as she looked up to see that the shop looked clean and professional, but still she wasn't sure. 'Well, I'll come in and have a look but I'm not making any promises. A tattoo at my age; who'd have thought it?'

They left the shop a little over half an hour later. The tattoo was of Orion, the constellation, and it stretched across their wrists like two of those necklaces whose pendant was only complete when aligned with its other half. Elizabeth had half of it inked onto her right wrist, and Tom the other half onto his left.

'I don't know what you were thinking in 1995, Thomas Hale.' Admiring the little black lines and yellow dots that seemed to sparkle like real stars, she chuckled to herself as they got back into the taxi. She held out her wrist for him to see, and he aligned his arm alongside hers. 'I thought you were mad at the time, and I think you are even madder now. But the truth is, I quite like it. The man was an artist. Did you see some of the things he had on the wall? Really, very impressive. If only we could look up at the stars and see it now, but you can't see a thing in this city.'

The driver pulled away and into the flow of traffic. 'You can't see much, but there are other views that are beautiful. Would you like me to show you one? It's one of my favourites, and it's not far.'

'Don't you think we'd better get back?'

'Indulge me, Elizabeth.' He held her hand. 'We might not get to do this again.'

Just a short while later they were climbing to the top of Hampstead Heath. Elizabeth was doing fine on her own, and Tom had the help of their taxi driver, who after hearing their conversation offered to switch his meter off and push Tom up the heath himself. They sat down on the bench overlooking the city as eventide was falling. The lights from the skyscrapers twinkled in the distance, as close to the stars as they would ever get.

'It's beautiful, isn't it?' he said.

'You know something?' she said, nuzzling in close. 'It really is. And this sort of counts as a mountain. I'm sure you wrote one year that you wanted to climb one together.'

'Did I? Well that was a stupid idea.'

'Well, let's tick it off the list and be done with it. There are some others we could still do. I know you put a hot air balloon ride on there. I could try and organise that if you really want.'

He shook his head. 'We wish for all sorts of stupid things when we believe that time is infinite.' His cheeks were pink with the chill of winter, and she could see his eyes glistening in the city lights. 'But when you know it's not, those sorts of wishes don't mean much anymore. All I care about are the things that really matter now, which are the things that bring me closer to family, and to you. Like my wish that we could have raised a child together. Do you know how much I wished for that? Do you know how much it hurt when I realised we were never going to achieve it?'

'Oh, Tom,' she said, her voice breaking. She couldn't look at him then. Kate still hadn't responded, hadn't spoken to her since the day she'd learned the truth about who her father really was. Would Elizabeth hurt Tom even more by telling him the truth now, if it was only to be rejected by the daughter he never knew?

'I don't mean to make you sad,' he said. 'I understand what happened to us.' He reached up, turned her face to meet his. 'I failed you, Elizabeth. I let you down. I wish I could turn back time but neither of us can do that.'

'I let you down too,' she whispered.

His lips were cold against her nose as he kissed her. 'Maybe. But there is still time to put things right, you know. Every moment we spend together does that.' Angling his wrist in the air, he held it for her to see. 'And we have the same tattoo. Nowadays, that's as good as married.'

Aware of the taxi driver still lingering behind them, she moved in close and slid her arm through his. 'I love you, Thomas Hale,' she said.

'I love you too.' His grip remained tight, although she no longer knew if it was the strength of feeling or need for her support. 'Tell me, did you bring your phone with you?'

'It's here in my bag. Why? Do you want to call Alice?'

He shook his head. 'I was wondering if you had any photos of Kate on there. You told me about her, but I'd love to see what she looks like.'

Hesitating for a moment, sure that to see Kate was to understand her parentage, she eventually reached down to pick up her phone. 'I might have one or two old ones.' Painfully she scrolled through, a visual of good memories, before selecting the best one she could find. It was of Kate last year, on the beach, before she learnt of her true heritage. Gazing at the image, in which she was smiling and happy, Elizabeth handed it over. 'There you go.'

Even though they had just discussed the inevitable passage of time, it felt in that moment as if it stood still, the vibration of life quietened as he gazed at his daughter. A tear formed in his eye. 'She's beautiful.' Elizabeth nodded, couldn't find the right words to reply. 'And so much like Alice.'

Her hands were slippery with sweat as she took the phone, slipped it back into her bag. 'Yes, I suppose she is.'

'I think it would have been quite something to meet her,' he said, his eyes lost in some distant thought. 'Just to see what she was like.'

For a moment no words would come. So many things to say and no way to say them. 'Come on,' she said when she heard the driver behind them, shuffling his feet. 'It's high time we got back.'

Panny was waiting for them. After a quick dressing down and a check of his observations, Tom was soon confined to bed. Elizabeth could feel herself blushing with guilt, but Tom was unrelenting, flashing his wrist at Panny to show off his new tattoo.

'What are you two like?' she said, unable to sustain the pretence of anger when they explained the concept of the wish list. 'Have you got any more wishes that are going to make you disappear from my ward?' He shook his head, still pleased with himself. 'Good. Then you best get on the phone to Alice, because she's been calling near enough the whole time you've been gone.'

Alice was pleased to see her father upright and talking once they got the iPad working, at least until she saw the damage done to his face from where he'd fallen in the bathroom the night before. After telling him that he needed to listen to the nurses' advice, even reminding Elizabeth that she needed to be the voice of reason in her absence, she told him everything was fine in Hastings and that she would be back soon enough.

'That was nice, wasn't it?' Elizabeth said when they hung up, patting his hand. 'She looked pleased to see you.'

'Yes, she did,' Tom said, smiling to himself the best he could. He looked a bit shocked by the whole thing. 'I don't know how you did it.'

'Did what? Got the iPad working?' They had been trying for the best part of two weeks.

He tutted, shook his head. His patience was becoming increasingly limited, especially when he was tired. Only last night he had pushed his confectionery all over the floor when he couldn't finger the black Jelly Babies from the pack.

'It was a nice trick, that's all.'

Elizabeth sat back so that she could move him into focus. 'What do you mean?'

'Well she looked a lot like Alice.' He chuckled to himself. 'Brian arranged it?'

'What are you talking about? Brian didn't arrange anything.' When people say that their hearts skip a beat in a moment of turmoil, they were talking about moments like that one, Elizabeth realised. A life she had lived before with her own mother came into focus, but still she couldn't believe it. His worst fears had come true. How could he not recognise Alice after such a short period of time? 'Tom, love. That was Alice. Your daughter.'

He snickered, wiped his droopy lip. 'Don't try that one with me. It might have looked an awful lot like her, but I think I'd know my own daughter, don't you?'

'Yes,' she said. 'I suppose you would.' Had the photograph of Kate confused him? Her heart was beating so loud it was as if the walls were pulsating, constricted and stretching all at once. It was the first moment she realised that despite her determined vigil by his side, she had little choice but to accept their fate. Despite all the years that he had remembered her, soon enough he would forget her too. Tom was slipping away from them, just a little bit here and there, flaking away like decades-old paint from a weathered Porthsennen door.

The beeping of her phone distracted her, and she reached into her pocket to pull it out. Of all the nights, it was a message from Kate, the first in months. Her finger shook as she opened it.

> I'm sorry I haven't been responding. I found it too hard. But I want to see him. When can I come?

It was a small chink of light in an otherwise dark night. The relief was massive. Because she knew that Tom was, despite her desperate hopes for a miracle, slipping away. They were running out of time.

> Thank you so much, love. As soon as possible. Love you, Mum x

And she bargained then, with herself, and maybe with God, for two things; for enough time so that they could all be together, even if it was just once, and for the strength to tell Tom and Alice what she must beforehand. And she made a promise to whoever might have been listening, that she would accept having to lose Tom after that if it meant Alice didn't have to watch him slowly disappear. If she didn't have to dissolve into something unrecognisable to him. It was better to end it sooner rather than later, if they could escape the pain of all that. It was something she had learnt long ago, but perhaps only then had begun to understand.

Then

Like the gradual shift of the seasons, Tom's two-month stint on Wolf Rock reached its scheduled conclusion, but when it did Tom did not return. Rumours about his absence were rife and variable, and none of them satisfied Elizabeth. Atlantic winds battered her coat as she watched the *Stella* return to Penzance, apprehension and excitement turning over in her tummy. But when two hours later she saw Keeper Williams arriving in Porthsennen instead of Tom, all she could do was look on in dismay. 'I'm sorry, lass,' he said, a small bag slung over his shoulder. 'Don't suppose it's me you were expecting, was it.'

'Where is he?'

With barely a look in her direction, he said, 'You'll have to ask him when he gets back.' And then after a moment, 'Whenever that might be,' before heading up the hill to a home that would be as thrilled at his surprise return as she was disappointed.

That letter had been a stupid idea. The fact he was going to become a father wasn't news you blurted out in a letter. At first guilt crippled her, shame over the situation she had pulled him into. But after a time she began to reason that perhaps she was being unfair on herself as well. Wasn't she scared too? The pregnancy had come as a shock to her as well, but impending motherhood wasn't something she could escape, hidden on some rock in the shallows of the Atlantic. Not coming back was the most despicable thing he could have ever done, even more so than leaving right after her mother died. Thoughts that James had been right all along began to permeate her days, and the idea that perhaps she had been wrong about Tom started to grow.

Her father spent most of his time either at the practice or in his bedroom. Elizabeth was grateful because it made it easier to hide her increasing sickness. Gratitude didn't even come close to what she felt for James, who had proved a real stalwart when it came to matters such as the reading of the will and removal of her mother's belongings from the house. Until then she couldn't focus on anything that resembled normality. How could she when she was a single girl about to have a baby, and her boyfriend was ignoring her very existence? Her future materialised in her mind, life as a pariah, just like that poor Edith Ball. Out of desperation she started stitching odd ends of material together, planning to unite them with Tom's family quilt. It was the only way she could convince herself that their relationship wasn't over, yet despite her efforts it was becoming increasingly harder to believe.

In the day while James was at work, she took to hanging around the lifeboat station, had found herself a job of sorts even though there was little to no pay involved. Occasionally Mr Pommeroy gave her a small envelope with a little recompense for her time, which she kept in a box under her bed and told nobody about, something she thought of as money for her future. She also placed the photograph of Tom that she had taken from his bedroom in that box, so that nobody would see she had it. Mr Pommeroy always seemed to find a way to ensure they were never alone, as if he knew she had a thousand questions for him that he was not inclined to answer. Still, she liked it in the lifeboat station, alongside the *Susan Ashley*, the Watson Class lifeboat her constant companion. It calmed her to spend hours polishing the brass, cleaning the salt from the boat's hull. In some small way she felt that she was protecting Tom by doing so. Because as her initial anger faded, she found it was replaced by desperation. It was all she could do to ready the lifeboat in case it was needed, in case there was ever the call for a rescue.

Then, after weeks of waiting, one wet Sunday morning in December before the harsh reality of a coastal winter set in, she found her chance to question Mr Pommeroy. After arriving early, she watched him from the deck of the *Susan Ashley* as he set about boiling water, setting a tea-bag in his cup. Only once he moved deeper into the station did she make her presence known, for fear that he would nip out of the door to avoid the cross-examination. It wouldn't have been the first time.

'Good morning,' Elizabeth said. Mr Pommeroy jumped, spilt some of his tea down his leg. 'Sorry to startle you,' she said, handing him a tea towel.

'Christ almighty, Elizabeth. You scared me senseless.' More tea spilt as he set his mug down. 'What are you doing here at this time?'

In the early hours of that morning she had walked up to the headland to look out to Wolf Rock for the first time in a week. What had driven her there she didn't know, but it felt like a terrible dread, a sense of foreboding perhaps, something she couldn't explain. When she arrived on the rocks she had been met by a severe gale, the sea a swell of froth and foam, milky white along the coast. For what felt like hours she waited, praying for a break in the mists which clung to the choppy sea, anything that might show her that life still existed on Wolf Rock. No such prayer was answered. No light shone. So instead she had walked down to the lifeboat station and begun to ready the vessel just in case.

'The winds woke me,' she lied.

He nodded his understanding. 'They've woken most of the village. Old Man Cressa has lost a third of his roof, and one of the swells has flooded a few cottages on Cove Hill. Thank the Lord it's not tourist season and most of them are empty.'

'They're not all empty,' she said. Even though the reception she'd received the first time was more than frosty, and despite everything that had been said, she knew she had to call by to check on Tom's mother. She'd tried to see them a few times since Tom's leaving, but they never answered the door.

'If you're talking about Tom's, I'm afraid to tell you it is. His parents left a few weeks ago.'

'What?' Left? How could that be so? 'Where to?'

'Heard that Pat found work on the Tremayne farm, out near Releath. Now, it's not safe to be out here. Get yourself home.'

Even the idea of his parents leaving terrified her. Had Tom just disappeared too? Had he come back from Wolf Rock and just slipped quietly away? With the aid of one of the ropes dangling overboard she shimmied down to the ground. 'Mr Pommeroy, I have to ask you about the letter,' she said, swallowing hard, gulping at courage she was struggling to muster. 'The one I wrote to Tom.'

He opened his mouth to speak, hesitating she was sure. But before he could answer, the emergency line sounded, the coastguard calling in the lifeboat. Both Mr Pommeroy and Elizabeth knew there was no time to waste, and that awful sense of foreboding returned, along with a silent prayer for it to be anything other than something related to Tom. Mr Pommeroy picked up the call, Elizabeth listening to his mumbled answers as he scribbled down the most pertinent of details.

After hanging up the telephone he turned to face her. 'Fetch me the maroons, Elizabeth.' The need to ask questions held her back, but sense prevailed and she hurried away, while Pommeroy set about opening the doors. Lights blared against the black night still upon them, and almost as if in protest, the inimical sea roared loud and defiant, charging at the slipway like frantic hands clawing at the shore. Rain soaked him as he fired two of the rockets into the sky. The boom was loud enough to be heard up to a mile away, bright enough to light the whole of the bay for a second or so. He was soon back inside, completing a list of tasks that he knew as well as he recognised his reflection, readying the vessel the best he could before the rest of the crew arrived. They would already be rushing into yesterday's clothes, woken by the sound of the gun, the indication that somebody, somewhere was in trouble.

'Mr Pommeroy?' she probed, getting as close as she could without hindering him. The frayed ropes that tethered the lifeboat to the slipway strained against his might. He stopped only briefly, but it was a pause heavy with meaning, and she knew then that her worry across the course of the previous night hadn't been in vain. Tom hadn't left the lighthouse, she would have felt it if he had, and that meant he was in danger. 'Tell me.'

The grey pallor of worry spoke a million words before he could find the courage. 'A vessel has struck Wolf Rock. It's beached, and the crew are stranded.'

The waters off the coast of Cornwall were notorious and fierce. The crew of the *Susan Ashley* knew every hidden rock, every current that could take an outsider by surprise. Strangers to these waters had no such knowledge, but that was what the lighthouses were for. What had happened to Wolf Rock that a vessel could land upon its foundations? Why hadn't the sailors seen the light?

'And the lighthouse crew?' she begged, clutching at Mr Pommeroy's arm. 'Tom?'

His heavy hand pressed against hers. A misty rain waxed down the window, casting irregular shadows on the wall. 'The lifeboat crew will be here soon with a bit of luck. Let's get out there and see, eh? You've done your bit. Best thing you can do is get yourself home.'

Leaving the station as instructed, stepping out into the cold air with a wind that bit her skin as it burrowed through her clothes, she stood against the railings, watching a disquieted sea. Tom himself had told her that beacons had been washed clean away from Wolf Rock before that spike of granite dared house three brave men at a time. There was no way that she could go home. Not now.

The crew came rushing, hurried and poorly dressed. Not long afterwards, Mr Anderson came chasing down the road, still battling with the buttons on his coat. She hoped his blood pressure held out. The idea of Mrs Anderson alone and worried came to her. What would she do without him to fuss over for the next few hours?

'Yours out there too?' A woman arrived alongside her, wrapped in a thick dressing gown, her hair in rollers with a scarf tied around it. It was Mrs Nichols from down the road, who let her spare rooms out to tourists. Rain drummed on her umbrella, which she placed over their heads, but Elizabeth was already wet through. 'I can't stand it when I hear that bloody maroon.'

'He's on Wolf Rock. He's one of the keepers.' Mrs Nichols turned then, regarded Elizabeth with a keen eye, trying to work out what she knew, what she might have heard. A soft smile crept onto her face, recognition of what it meant to stand on the shore and wait for a person you love. 'I don't know anything,' Elizabeth said.

Mrs Nichols pulled her gown in close around her chest. 'I heard that the light went down sometime just after midnight.'

Elizabeth's breath caught in her throat, and she could feel her cheeks flushing with worry. 'How do you know that?'

'My Joe spoke to the station officer at Penlee last night.' That was the lifeboat station just a little way around the coast. 'Said he'd never been out in conditions like it. Pulled two men from a fishing vessel, but they lost a third.'

'That's awful,' Elizabeth said, her mind already elsewhere. Rough seas and a broken lighthouse. The waves would have to have been monstrous for them to break up parts of Wolf Rock. Only a sea boiling with fury. And how could a man withstand it, if a structure of that magnitude could not? And with that she couldn't hold them back, and tears began to stream down her face.

'Come on, love,' Mrs Nichols said, wrapping her arm around Elizabeth's shoulders. She looked close to tears too. 'Somebody called the coastguard, remember, and it's most likely the keepers on the light.' Elizabeth wiped her nose. 'It gets easier to watch them leave, you know? Easier to spend time apart.'

Elizabeth used the tissue to dab her eyes. 'I hope so,' she said, but she doubted that Mrs Nichols' words would ever be true for her.

Those who had managed to sleep through the events of the night before were waking to word of the storm. People were beginning to rally around, including a team of young men balanced on the upper rungs of precarious ladders, patching up Old Man Cressa's roof. Others were sweeping the sea's detritus from the streets, or bailing water from their homes, and Elizabeth made tea for the workers. Doors were opened for folk to come and go, a place for a brief hiatus, to get warm. James and her father arrived not long after first light, awaiting the wounded.

And right then she heard somebody shouting in the distance, the commotion of hurried feet before she saw the *Susan Ashley* returning to shore. The first accounts of what had happened began to ripple through the crowd; five crew members had been rescued from a beached fishing lugger, which had run aground on the plug of volcanic rock which housed the lighthouse. A sixth had been lost in a fall. Wolf Rock had failed; a rogue wave drenching the lighthouse, bringing with it all manner of oceanic debris, and a piece of driftwood no bigger than a teacup had taken out one of the windows, and subsequently the light. Two of the keepers had abandoned their posts to attend the stricken vessel, leaving another in charge of the fog gun, but who stayed and who ventured to help was unclear right up until the lighthouse crew came ashore. Rescued crew members from the lugger disembarked with a range of injuries; cuts to the face, a broken arm, and another with a severe looking wound to the leg which had drenched the lower half red. Only one casualty had cause to be transferred by stretcher, carried by the other two members of the lighthouse crew.

Elizabeth pushed her way forwards, elbowing the crowd.

'Tom,' she screamed, edging past those at the front. Water splashed her legs as she charged through puddles, and she could see Tom's face just peeking out from underneath a blanket. From the corner of her eye she saw somebody else rushing. It was Mrs Anderson, running to her husband. She flung her arms around him as if he had been gone for years, and he held her tight with relief. They were so in love, yet Elizabeth had never been able to see it. Love presented itself in all manner of different ways, even in places where she could barely see its existence. Love could be all but invisible, but still it was there, shaken to the surface by the strength of a sea storm.

'What's wrong with him?' she begged, close to tears as she rushed into the cottage where Tom was already supine on an old oak table. James was there, his hands poised over Tom's body. 'Why isn't my father helping you?'

James lowered his voice, leant in close. 'Elizabeth, your father's lost it. I found him crying about your mother, and I sent him home.' He motioned to Tom. 'He's broken his arm. I need you to let me get on with my job.'

'He doesn't look good.' Tom was panting, struggling for breath, yet seemed somehow unresponsive. 'Are you sure it's just his arm?'

'Elizabeth, please. Go home,' James pleaded when she didn't respond. 'Give me the room to help Tom.'

Knowing she had to leave, she took her chance. Tom's face was cold as she held it tight between her hands, planting a kiss on his lips. When she pulled away, she saw how he had changed, stubble where skin had been smooth, cheeks sunken where they had once been plump. His hair was long and unkempt, hanging in curls in the nape of his neck. He looked so frail, withered away.

'I love you,' she said, and for a moment she thought she saw Tom's eyes flicker, that his head might have turned to face her. Was that his lips parting? Then she felt the tug on her arm.

'Elizabeth, come on.' Francine was there, standing at her side. A smile crossed her lips, both kind and regretful. 'I'll help you get home. Let James work. He's going to be fine, isn't he, James?'

'Just fine,' he said, already turning to Tom. Elizabeth had no idea if she believed him, but she let Francine lead her away.

'Let's get you home,' Francine said kindly. 'You can wait there with your father.'

Not since London had James seen a patient looking quite so unwell, clinging to life by the skin of his teeth. It hadn't taken long to establish that his arm was broken, but what else was going on? Why was Tom so lost and struggling for breath?

'Get me some splints,' James said to the owner of the cottage, Mr Menhenick, a local carpenter which turned out to be a fortunate coincidence under the circumstances. 'And be quick about it.'

Mr Menhenick hurried to the rear of his cottage, while James stood back and looked at Tom. He was out of shape when it came to this sort of thing, hadn't got the stomach for it anymore. Broken bones had always given him the shakes, but it was more than that. Perhaps it was because Elizabeth had been there too, and he had seen the worry on her face. Something had stirred in him, guilt about the letters and the baby, and he couldn't shake it. He had been riding his luck, but now, even though nobody knew what he had done, he couldn't have felt any worse if the whole village knew his secret.

But he loved Elizabeth. When he first saw her with a smudge of blue paint underneath her eye, how she marvelled over his stories from London, he had felt something that he hadn't in a long time; like the person he'd been before he went to war. Memories of leeches and prickly heat disturbed his dreams, the killings he had witnessed, and worse still after that. Just the idea of a jungle could bring him out in a cold sweat. Yet that first night, as the moon crested in the sky and he listened to the gentle lull of the incoming tide, he'd understood that he could build a life there in Porthsennen. With her. That he could find peace with what he had done, what he had seen, and with the man he had become. For the first time in a long while he had seen a future, and when he'd proposed the following month at a dinner with her family, it had never crossed his mind she'd say no. Now, when he thought of that evening, recalling her silence and the fidgety enthusiasm of her father, he wasn't sure in fact, whether she'd said anything at all.

Leaning in close to Tom's chest, James saw the problem. The right side was flat, the same side as the broken arm. That lung wasn't inflating. Tom had a tension pneumothorax, and the realisation sent a wave of fear rushing through his body like the vibrations of the grenades that still exploded in his dreams. A single bead of sweat trailed down his temple, mixing with the blond hairs that softened to silk at his hairline.

'What the bloody hell are you doing?' Mr Menhenick said, his eyes dizzying when he saw James cleaning a small kitchen knife with some of his home-brewed spirits.

James tested the tip of the blade against Tom's chest, watched as the skin paled, before blushing pink as he released the pressure. 'It's either this, or a dead body on your kitchen table. Which would you prefer?' Menhenick licked at his salt-dried lips, and James took his silence as acceptance of the course of action that the blade implied. 'Find me a metal coat hanger, and some of the tubing that you used to brew this,' he said, shaking the dimpled bottle with its slick clear fluid sloshing about inside.

Despite the inexplicability of the request, Mr Menhenick returned moments later with the suggested items without further question. By then James had placed a chipped glass bowl of water on the floor underneath the table, had washed his hands and Tom's chest with the home-brewed spirit, and had a plan in mind.

'Tom, can you hear me?' A mumbled response came, but nothing discernible. 'OK, lad. I'm sorry, but this is going to hurt.'

Summoning all his courage, James jabbed the knife into the side of Tom's chest, making a small puncture wound along the top surface of one of his ribs. Tom barely flinched. Mr Menhenick had opened out the coat hanger as requested, and James guided it through the rubber tubing before inserting it through the incision, praying that he didn't end up puncturing the heart. Seconds later, he heard the rush of air coming from Tom's chest, and with it, Tom began to rouse.

'Sweet mother of Jesus,' said Mr Menhenick, sweaty hands pulling at sea-drenched hair. 'I've never seen anything like it.'

Tom groaned, squirmed on the table.

'Neither have I,' James admitted, a verifiable truth to which he would not have cared to admit given a moment for reason. His sleeve came away wet as he mopped his brow, removing the hanger from within the tube. Bubbles formed in the water with each exhalation as James inserted the other end of the tube into the bowl, the once trapped air escaping the space between Tom's lung and chest wall.

'What's going on?' Tom asked, his voice croaky and weak. 'Where am I?'

'You're going to be all right,' James said, as much for himself as Tom. He turned to Mr Menhenick, who was still shaking his head in disbelief. 'We're going to need to get him transferred to a hospital as soon as possible. The Priors have got the closest telephone, I think.'

Still trying to process the turn of luck following what had appeared little more than butchery, Mr Menhenick nodded his agreement. 'I'll go and call for an ambulance then,' he said, before stopping to dress in his coat and change into his wellingtons as if he had all the time in the world. As he was leaving he turned back, the door half open. 'You didn't really mean that you had never seen anything like that before, did you?'

James swallowed hard as he glanced at Tom, whose colour was slowly returning. Even his fingers looked better, no longer the cool blue of hypoxia they were before. 'Of course not. Saw the same thing a thousand times when I was in London.' The door slammed shut behind Mr Menhenick, and James took what felt like the first breath in minutes. 'Damn you Porthsennen,' he muttered to himself. 'You have made a liar out of an honest man.'

And as he looked at Tom, he realised that it wouldn't be the last lie he would tell that day.

Now

They managed, over the course of the next few weeks, when early frost blanketed the ground and where mist froze solid in their hair, to realise a few more of their unfulfilled wishes. It required a degree of imagination, but the urgency of the situation stirred reserves Elizabeth didn't know she had. Alice purchased a portable DVD player, and they dedicated a whole day to the *Godfather* trilogy, throughout which Tom mostly slept, managing, it seemed, to wake up only for the shootings and murders. They even passed a whole evening out in the common bay with the other patients where Elizabeth had organised a pianist. Because he was feeling particularly weak that evening, the nurses wheeled him out in his bed, and they spent almost two hours listening to a beautiful performance of 'The Well-Tempered Clavier'. Nurses huddled in doors, visitors overstayed their welcome, and even the lone man in the corner lacking visitors and concentration paid attention. Elizabeth was sure she saw a tear in his eye, although it could just have been the heat. Afterwards, Tom turned to her and smiled.

'It was perfect,' he said, and that night, just as they planned, Elizabeth stayed in the room with him, squeezed up into the bed. It was breaking all the rules, but nobody seemed to mind, and if they did, they turned a blind eye. As the ward quietened and the lights dimmed, she looked at the slips of blue paper that remained, and realised that those last few were going to be the hardest wishes to fulfil. But they were, at least, now Kate was talking to her again, possible.

It would be easier to tell Tom the truth before Kate got there, but that knowledge didn't get her any closer to understanding how one might go about explaining to a dying man, whom she had loved her whole life, that they shared a child. Possibilities charged through her mind, but eventually it was taken out of her hands. Because one minute he was chatting about Formula One with the changing faces of the ward staff, and the next all was quiet. It was as if night descended and dawn never broke.

It was later that evening when two women stood at the end of the bed, mumbling to each other, talking about things she didn't understand. The senior of the two doctors introduced herself as Dr Helen Sanderson, a small epicene woman who, despite her skittish movements, spoke with an authority that made Elizabeth nervous as she explained the diagnosis. The time she had spent at the hospital so far had prepared her well, and even before the doctor spoke, she knew it wasn't going to be good news.

'It's not causing him any discomfort,' Dr Sanderson reassured her. 'But I have him written up for morphine in case he experiences any pain later. We have asked the neurologists to come and take a look, but I'm fairly sure about what I think is happening.'

Dr Sanderson's diagnosis was an insult to a bad situation, and Elizabeth had little strength left to indurate herself for yet more bad news. 'Just pain relief? Is that all you can do for a stroke?'

Dr Sanderson whispered, as if they might wake him up if they spoke too loudly. 'I think in Tom's case the most likely explanation is that there is some compression from the tumours in the tissues of the brain. As you know, the findings on the CT scan showed that the tumours were extensive and inoperable.' Elizabeth glanced at Tom. He was oblivious to it all with his head tilted back, one eye disconcertingly half open. His snoring was deep, tremulous, and otherworldly. Somebody had removed his dentures and it gave him a pained, hollow look, as if part of him was already missing. 'I'm really very sorry that there is nothing more in the way of treatment that I can offer you. But if there's any family you'd like to call, we can help you sort that out.'

Moments later, the two doctors left the room, and Elizabeth found herself alone with Tom, wondering what she was supposed to do next. Minutes ticked by, and in the still immovability of the night, stretching endlessly before her, she did the only thing she could and remained at his side. Comfort came in the simplest forms, stroking his hands, the fingers curled in on themselves, rearranging the sheets when she couldn't bear the stasis. 'Alice will be here soon,' she told him, even though she had no proof he could hear. 'It won't be long now,' she whispered, and as the words left her lips, she realised just how true that statement really was.

*

Tom didn't flinch when Alice burst through the door before first light. No words were exchanged, explanations already given over the phone. Together they sat, Brian bringing tea and breakfast pastries that remained untouched by the time Dr Jones arrived, along with the neurosurgeon whose hair struck Elizabeth as too dark to be natural at his age. Funny, she thought, the observations we make, when we don't want to acknowledge the most important things right in front of our eyes.

'And the facilities?' Alice was asking when Elizabeth snapped out of her daydream. 'He doesn't like those air mattresses.' The conversation had moved in a direction Elizabeth hadn't followed. Yet she got the gist of it; he was being discharged. 'You know him here. Why can't he just stay?'

'The thing is, Alice, there is very little more we can offer you,' Dr Jones was saying. 'Our hope was always to get him home, but despite early improvements he hasn't responded to the medication as well as we would have liked, and the most recent changes, I'm afraid, alter the picture a little. We have to consider whether there is perhaps a more suitable environment for your father to live in.'

To die in, Elizabeth thought as she listened to the discussion. She rested her head on Tom's chest then, feeling the rasp of his breathing, hoping that nobody saw her cry.

Later that day, during one of Brian's trips to the canteen, Elizabeth knew she had to raise the idea of Kate with Alice. There was no time left to leave it any longer. 'Love,' she said, 'there's something I have to tell you.' Alice rested her chin on a slender hand, her elbow propped up on the bed. 'There is somebody I'd like to bring to see your father.'

'Kate,' Alice said, her face unflinching. 'Your daughter.'

Elizabeth's breath caught in her throat. 'Yes. She would like to come and meet him. I've told her a lot about him, you see.' The tears came. It was over-whelming, all those secrets trying to find a way out. She hadn't realised just how deep within herself she would have to dig. 'I must tell you something before-hand though. I wanted to tell your father, but now,' she said, gazing at his face, lost in a place she couldn't reach, 'I've left it too late.'

'You don't need to say anything, Elizabeth,' Alice said. 'He knew, he told me all about it.'

Elizabeth shook her head. 'You couldn't possibly know . . .'

'That Kate is his daughter too?' Elizabeth's skin contracted from head to toe. How, when she had never told a soul, could Alice know? Only James had ever known the truth. 'He always knew.' Elizabeth couldn't believe it. How was it possible? 'Dad told me that she looks just like me.' Elizabeth nodded, picked up her phone, unable to speak for shock. She scrolled to the pictures and handed it over. Alice took it, staring so hard it must have been like looking in a mirror.

'He wasn't wrong. She should be here,' Alice said, handing back the phone.

Elizabeth sobbed. Questions of how and when ran rampant through her mind, yet all she seemed to be able to grasp from those myriad ideas was a fateful cry of hopelessness. 'But I left it too late.'

Alice stood up and placed her arm across Elizabeth's shoulder, comforted by a person in such pain herself. 'It's never too late, Elizabeth. You and Dad taught me that.'

Then

Elizabeth returned to the house with Francine, cold without a lit fire and everywhere dark. Through the dim light she could see a letter on the dining room table, her name written on the front in a classic elegant scrawl. There was something ominous about the way it had been left there, ascetic against a vase of decaying flowers, foreshadowing the irrecoverable truths written inside.

'What's that?' Francine asked as she closed the door behind them. The sea quietened as they stood still for a moment, then Francine's footsteps echoed as she walked forwards, picking it up. 'It's your father's handwriting.'

Elizabeth took the envelope and slid her finger into the small opening to pull out the paper inside. The letters were elegant and calligraphic, the way her father wrote when he thought about it, when he took his time, when he wanted to create an impression. In that case, a lasting impression.

'Well?' said Francine, eager when it appeared that Elizabeth had read the letter. 'What does it say?'

'Nothing,' Elizabeth said. Her voice broke, her throat sore from trying not to cry. 'I'm all right now, Francine. You'd better get back. James probably needs you.'

Francine left under protest, bound by a promise to return. Elizabeth found herself hoping that she stuck to her word, because she was going to need familiar faces around her now if the contents of the letter spoke the truth. In the still house she read it again, her father's words describing how sorry he was that he didn't have the strength to tell her in person that he was leaving. He confessed that he had indeed taken her mother out on that boat, just as Tom's father accounted, and just as her mother had wished in the face of her mounting confusion. Unable to accept her fate, he had at her request provided her with enough medication so that it was painless enough as she let herself drop half-conscious into the water somewhere between Longships and Wolf Rock. As he signed off, he apologised again for leaving Elizabeth when she still needed him, and she realised with her father's confession that he never intended to be found.

The letter also detailed James's knowledge of events after he had raised concerns over missing morphine. Knowing only two people had access to the opiates and that he himself hadn't taken it, James's suspicions were raised. When he discussed it with Elizabeth's father, Dr Davenport had begged for James's compassion, and promised to make his silence as easy as possible with a swift and complete departure. On one condition. It was a condition that James was more than willing to fulfil.

For his part in it all, James really did wish that he could undo the letter he had written in Tom's name after seeing him leave for Truro Hospital, never having expected Elizabeth's father to have left on the same day.

Guilt gripped him as he watched her read the words he himself had written, claiming as Tom that he no longer loved her, and that he would never be returning to Porthsennen, for her or their child. And James knew that he wouldn't; not now that he had told Tom that he and Elizabeth were already married.

For two days afterwards she didn't eat or dress, and he nearly caved more than once. But on the third day when he returned to the house, he found a different picture awaiting him. Finding her dressed in a fine skirt and blouse, something quite beautiful that clung to her hips and skipped out just below the knee, he knew something was changed. The blouse was tight around the bust, and it stirred a sense of desire in him that he had tried to pacify for a long time. They were her mother's clothes, he realised, as she stood in the hallway to greet him. Taking his coat, she led him through to the dining room where there was a dinner table set with two plates and two wine glasses.

'We need to talk,' she said. 'My father always said that alcohol was a lubricant for the larynx.' After handing him a glass which contained a healthy measure of brandy, she picked up a second for herself. With one swift movement she drank it back, and so he did the same. 'I don't suppose he meant it favourably but seeing as he's not here we don't need to concern ourselves with what he might think. And besides, I don't believe anything we have to say to each other is going to be all that easy.'

'No?'

'No. I know you know what my father did. You understand the implications of that knowledge without the need for my explanation.'

'I do.'

'The police will no doubt question his departure, but we will tell them he is travelling. I have burnt the letter, and we will speak of its contents no more after this night. His actions might have been an act of mercy, but they are no less criminal for it.'

'You have my word,' James promised, and took her hand in his. 'I'm so sorry for what he did.'

'It was what she wanted,' she said through gritted teeth. 'If a person doesn't want to be around anymore, there is nothing you or I can do about it, is there?'

He knew there was more than one meaning hidden within her words, and it was a struggle not to confess to everything he himself had done that had forced Tom from her life.

'I'll be here for you,' he promised instead, hoping that was enough. 'And the child.'

Her fingers stiffened in his. 'How do you . . .'

'I'm a doctor, Elizabeth. It's my job to know. But I promise that I'll raise this child as my own if you stay with me. It'll never want for anything, and it'll never doubt my love.' He took the ring that had never once left his pocket since the day of their picnic and held it out for her. Tom was gone and she was having a child; what other choice did she have? This time she placed it on her finger.

They were married within the month. James wanted to order her a dress from France, and when she refused he insisted on a trip to London in the very least, but Elizabeth said she didn't want to waste time waiting, which helped settle any lingering concerns. Mrs Clements stitched a fine example of an elegant tea dress, and underneath fashioned net curtains to give the skirt volume to cover up the burgeoning bump. Elizabeth had insisted on no invitations or reception, but word had got out and still a fair number of people turned up from the village. Elizabeth suspected that it had all been planned.

That night when they found themselves alone, they retired to their separate bedrooms. But once James was asleep, Elizabeth left the house and walked to the lookout, cut down to the rocks, carrying her simple posy of white roses and cream ribbons in a tightly clenched fist. Spray brushed her face as she stood on the edge of the rock from which she had fallen only three months before, listening to the power of the sea. It had claimed her mother, in many ways her father, and now Tom. She wouldn't let it claim her too. The posy broke apart as she tossed it into the water, sent it crashing against the rocks. It was the only way she could tell Tom, and herself, that it was done.

James knew that she had married him out of a sense of duty, to both her father and her unborn child. But he told himself he didn't care and tried his best to maintain the visage of a contented newlywed. As for Elizabeth, she had found the juxtaposition of her feelings and her outward persona a difficult beast to tame. The idea of consummating the marriage loomed over her, because as kind and generous as James was with his patience, that, just like her time with Tom, would eventually expire. And so, one night in the second month of marriage, she ventured to his room and slipped under the sheets. He went to speak but she placed a cold finger against his lips, followed by a kiss. James was a gentleman, and she knew roughly what to expect, but that was also half the problem. Making love to Tom had felt natural, with no hesitations or shaky, diffident touches. He hadn't questioned himself or what Elizabeth had wanted. Poor James knew her mind was elsewhere, and he spent most of the time trying not to make the experience any more unpleasant than he felt it must have been for her, especially what with her growing bump. Afterwards they slept alongside each other, but that was the extent of their connection, tangled roots but still not part of the same tree.

Things would have perhaps remained that way if she hadn't found him alone one night, crying in her father's study. Surprised he didn't try to conceal his tears, she took a seat on the desk alongside him. It was an unexpected comfort to witness his unabashed emotion, because it meant he was nothing like her father, whom since the day he'd left she never allowed to enter her thoughts.

'What's the matter?' she asked as she handed James a handkerchief. He blew his nose then wiped his eyes, reddened from tears and dark with grief.

'I am wondering if it's going to be like this for ever,' James asked. Nervous fingers busied at a pot of pens. 'If this is all we will ever have, or if you will ever find it in your heart to give me a chance to be your husband.'

His efforts had been admirable; always a kind word; a gentle touch; home on time, and often with gifts. She spurned them at first, didn't want to betray Tom, crediting James with little to offer other than materialistic tokens. Paints, brushes, baby clothes from trips to Truro. But in that dark office which smelt faintly of cigars she didn't know he smoked, she realised that she had given him little chance to offer her anything else. At least he was trying. Was she?

'It hasn't been easy, has it?' she said.

His tears had pooled in the fine lines around his eyes which she had never noticed before. Their union had aged him, both of them tired. 'You could say that.'

'I haven't been fair,' she said. 'You deserve a lot better than this.'

Tears struck the desk as he closed his eyes. 'I'm not sure I do.'

Turning his head with the flat of her hand, she pressed gently against the side of his face. Did she make him feel as Tom made her feel? Doubtful, she thought, but perhaps she could try. Would that be so bad, to give him a taste of what she had felt, once? After all, he was her husband and he had promised to raise her baby as his own. Perhaps she would find something for herself too, a form of companionship and unity in their secrecy, or if she was lucky, some form of love. But if she never tried, she would surely never know.

'You have stood by me as you said you would. You are the only person left who cares.' A deep breath shook her insides, hot as acid as she reneged on a promise they had made together. 'And you've kept the worst secret I have ever known, that my father helped my mother die. I know we said that we would never talk of it again, but I think perhaps we must, if we are to stand a chance of making this work.'

'I did it for you, Elizabeth. For us, and this little one,' he said, his hand warm against her stomach. 'Sometimes people do terrible things for the person they love. Things of which they are not proud, that cause them great pain about who they are as a person.'

It was a confession of sorts, but she would never have known it. She kissed him then, and for the first time in the months since Tom and her father left, she had wanted to. She didn't want to live in a time that no longer existed, sucked into a vortex underneath the waves. If she stayed there for too long, she too would drown.

Kate arrived just six months later, a beautiful, perfect little baby. Nobody knew the secret of her parentage at first, but when Kate's dark hair and pale skin began to mark her apart from her parents, the likeness to Tom became hard to ignore. He hadn't been gone long enough to be forgotten. Nobody ever said anything of course, not wishing to rake over old ground digging for secrets. But all Porthsennen knew the lie, nobody more so than Elizabeth as she watched her beautiful daughter grow throughout the years, into the ghost of a man whom she had never been able to forget.

Elizabeth never stopped painting during the earliest years of their marriage, but it wasn't until the seventh year came that she felt ready to exhibit her work.

'What do you think of the space?' James asked as they stood in the middle of the room, the ceilings high and walls wide and white. It was overwhelming, the whole experience of being in London and finally having her own exhibition, which would open that same evening.

The exhibition was only possible because of James – aged since the day they married, flecks of white peppering his temples, his trousers growing ever tighter. She could still see that handsome chap that she had once agreed to marry, but the years of marriage and parenthood had worn harder on him than it had Elizabeth.

'I think it's wonderful,' she said, taking his hand. 'Thank you. The whole day has been wonderful.'

Lunch had taken place in Sloane Square, consisting of the sweetest cupcakes, tea from bone china cups. They had walked hand in hand by the river, and she found joy in noticing how he watched her, glancing every few steps. Their love had grown, had been nurtured by the shared responsibility of parenthood, and through watching him raise Kate as his own.

'What are you looking at?' she had asked him that afternoon as they walked past Buckingham Palace.

'Just you,' he had said, causing her to blush. 'Sometimes I still can't believe you're mine.'

'Well, I am,' she had said, yet just as always, a little thought came to her, like a single candle flame in an empty church. Part of her wasn't his. When she watched Kate see through a difficult task she always thought of Tom. He came to mind when she observed the dwindling number of fishermen, and when Kate marvelled at the stars. He was there in everything they did, never more so than on the anniversary of their love, when the little flowers and wishes started to arrive.

The first year had taken her by surprise. Kate, only two months old, had been crying at the time, Elizabeth walking circles around the living room before first light trying to bounce her to comfort. Through the window she saw the flash of a coat, the profile of his face unmistakable. Pausing to find a blanket, wrapping it around Kate as she ran, she rushed outside, calling his name.

'Tom, wait,' she shouted, searching left and right. 'Tom, I know you're there.' Yet he didn't show himself. And it was only as she returned home, defeated, that she found the little flower pot and the attached wish on the step. Scooping it up, she hurried inside, settled Kate to sleep, and then sat with the flower, reading the wish over and over. Why would he come and not say anything, creeping around in the dark? Angered, she threw both away, but before the rubbish was collected a few days later she retrieved that slip of paper, beginning a collection that would take another forty-nine years to complete.

For several years she tried to forget, but on the same day each year those gifts would always arrive, dragging her back to their life unlived. Try as she might she couldn't erase him, imprinted as he was on her past and herself. Every year she thought about waking early, opening the door to ask why he hadn't stayed, why he kept coming back. Yet she never found the courage to open the door again, unable to face the possibility that perhaps, deep down, she and Kate simply hadn't been enough to make him stay.

After getting ready at the hotel, James and Elizabeth stepped into the gallery a little after seven. The room was filled with people she didn't know, in clothes she had often dreamed of owning. Her black knee-length dress felt frumpy in comparison to the full skirts and neat jackets worn by the other women, sunglasses covering their eyes despite the fact it was the evening and they were inside. Frank, James's friend and host of the exhibition, rushed towards her as she entered, taking her by the arm.

'I'm going to have to steal your lovely lady wife for a while. So many people are just dying to meet her. The artist,' he said, waving one hand like a rainbow through the air. His mannerisms and affected voice would have been so out of place in Porthsennen, and she had never met anybody like him before. Outside the light was fading, the ground wet from a late afternoon shower, but Frank assured her that it suited the mood of her collection, entitled *Enough for a Lifetime*.

'Feel free,' James said, nudging her on the chin with his fingers. 'Go and meet your public.'

She kissed him on the cheek and waved as Frank whisked her away.

'I have to tell you that people have responded most exceptionally,' Frank began as they headed towards the crowd. 'I have sold five of the ten pieces already, and there has been an enquiry regarding a future commission.' Stunned, she said nothing. 'When you work for a buyer, to their brief,' he continued as if she hadn't understood. To comprehend such an idea, that somebody wanted to pay her for a piece she hadn't yet painted, was a dream come true; where some failed unexpectedly, others flourished with unparalleled surprise. 'The interested party is a young socialite who has broken her daddy's heart by falling in love with an unsuitable young cad, and made my night by falling in love with your work in the same irrecoverable way.' The glint in his eye and devil's smirk on his lips unnerved her a little. 'She's quite dreadful if the truth be known, but she'll pay handsomely. Come and meet her, and at least try to appear as if you like her. She's a sensitive little thing, prone to spontaneous bouts of what some might call self-doubt, and what other, crueller types, might label as outright madness.'

Shelby Summerton, the daughter of a property developer in the business of building flats in the East End, was more extravagant than anything Elizabeth had ever seen before. Her wide leg trousers were so baggy that Elizabeth had at first taken them for a skirt, and her blue satin blouse was cut so low you could see a tiny promise of what was beneath. Her hair was long and inexplicably voluminous at the crown, with half of it swept back away from her face.

'You see, it's about community living,' Shelby was telling Elizabeth regarding the flats her father was building, her cigarette wafting back and forth, creating little trails of smoke. The patterns created reminded her of the Milky Way. 'Not a community like this village you have painted here, but one that makes a splendid profit.' The snort rose from her gut as she laughed at what Elizabeth hadn't taken for a joke. 'I will be buying this one,' she said, pointing to the painting of Porthsennen harbour, the boats with nets draped over the side. In the centre of the composition stood a sole figure of a man on the end of the breakwater, staring out to sea. 'And this one. It's my favourite.'

Shelby's favourite was of Wolf Rock itself. It was painted in a storm, the waves crashing against the sides, swallowing the structure into the tempestuous mass. Although it was almost undetectable when you viewed the work from a distance, if you got up close your eye was unquestionably drawn to a small yellow brush-stroke depicting a torch at an open front door. If you looked harder still you could just see a man, supine and injured on the surface of the rocks below. Elizabeth's collection told a story she kept close to her heart, one she had told not a soul about, but that was, if you looked hard enough, there for all to see.

'And about the commission?' probed Frank.

Shelby threw her cigarette to the floor, stamped it out with a platformed heel. 'You worry too much, Frankie, and work as if you need the money. Don't be so crass.' She looked to Elizabeth, winked. 'We have all the time in the world for the details, don't we . . .' She paused. 'What's your name?'

'Elizabeth Warbeck.' It didn't matter how many times she said it. Even seven years after her marriage it still sounded wrong.

'So, tonight was a success,' James said as he met her at the door. Most people had left by then, just a few lingering in a corner talking with Frank.

Elizabeth gazed about the room, noticing the little tickets tucked alongside each painting. 'It was. I sold everything.'

'That's great.' He nudged at the rubbish on the floor with the toe of his shoe. 'What did that awful woman want?'

'To pay me an equally awful sum of money to produce a painting of Porthsennen so that she might have it printed and hung in her father's apartment blocks.' He nodded approvingly. 'I will be paid for each print. And there will be one in each flat. All two hundred and fifty-six of them.'

'A fine and charming lady,' James joked.

'I'm sorry if you were bored,' she said. 'You seemed it at one point.'

He shook his head, reached in his pocket for his cigarettes. Cravings for the habit he'd picked up during his tour in Malaya had returned not long after their wedding, and he hadn't been able to shake it since. 'I wasn't bored. I was proud of you.' He looked down to the floor. 'Very proud of you, in fact.'

'Shall we go back to the hotel? Maybe have a drink in the bar, make the most of a night away from being parents?' Any other time he would have taken her up on the idea. He loved her as much as he loved Kate, which was to say without limits. But after seeing her paintings all there together, proof of her thought processes for the last seven years, he had realised that she wasn't really his, never had been in fact. In some way he had achieved what he wanted; she did love him, he knew that. But she didn't love him in the right way. The lies inside him had swollen, were taking over like cancer. They required excision if he was to survive, find himself again.

'I'm afraid we can't do that, Elizabeth.'

'Why not?'

Her heart quickened as he took a step forwards towards the closest paintings. He stopped at the first, the old Mayon Lookout, Porthsennen just a dot in the background.

'I used to follow you sometimes when you were younger, did you know that?' She shook her head. 'I suspected as much. It amused me a great deal to be there without your knowledge, watching where you went. Remember, I was fresh back from this God-awful city and I thought a lot of myself back then. I felt quite untouchable because you were my fiancée. Quite entitled.

317

'Then one day I saw you leaving the old Mayon Lookout with Tom. I couldn't bring myself to follow you after that. I figured whatever it was that you had with him was a childish fancy. I doubted anything serious could occur to stand in my way. You see, when I first met you, you made me feel a thousand feet tall. I realise now it was this bloody city you were taken in by,' he said, raising his arms to the city of London, 'but at the time I thought you were enamoured by me.' He lit another cigarette, the first already finished. 'These last two days you've had the same foolish look in your eye as you did back then.'

'What does all that matter now? We've been married for seven years. We've built a life together.'

'But not a lifetime, Elizabeth. And we never can because you still love another man.' He swept his hand through the thick air, motioning to the paintings. 'I have tried to be everything you need, but I am not. Do I appear in even one of these?' He gave her a moment to answer, hopeful that she could defend herself, prove he was wrong. But her silence spoke volumes. 'I thought as much, yet he appears in every one, doesn't he? All this time we have been together, and not once did you ever stop thinking about him.'

'James . . .' she stammered, but he held up his hand, didn't want her to finish.

'Please don't apologise, for God's sake. You see, it's all my own fault.'

'No,' she protested, rushing to take his hands in hers. 'It's not your fault. Tom is the past, a memory.' It wasn't entirely true, but it was what she wanted to believe. 'I love you, James. And so does Kate.'

318

'And I love you both. I will always be her father, Elizabeth. Even considering what I'm about to say, nothing can change these last seven years. But you don't love me in the way you love him. He is a shadow over everything we have done together. A curse of my own creation.' He threw his cigarette down and stamped it out. 'I want to make this easier for you, Elizabeth, which is why I must tell you the truth.'

'What truth?'

'The truth about us.' It was necessary to turn away, because he couldn't bear to see the disappointment on her face. 'Also, about Tom and the letter you believe he wrote to you on the day he left.' He looked to the ceiling and Elizabeth was sure she saw a tear streak down his cheek. 'And the letter you wrote to him, telling him about Kate, that I never sent.'

Minutes became hours, hours without end spent alone in the Ritz suite which James had splashed out on in celebration of her show. Up and out by seven the next morning and hours before her train, she sipped a tasteless cup of tea in the café in Hyde Park and sat quietly by the water. Boys fished from the pavement, others dived from the high board. The sound of traffic was as inescapable as it was alien. Why was everything in this city so overwhelming? Nothing familiar, everything different to what she recognised as life, and yet everything she thought she knew was a lie. James had confessed to writing the letter she'd received on the day Tom left for Truro hospital, and to telling Tom that he and Elizabeth were already married when they weren't. To destroying the letters to and from the lighthouse, which was the worst thing of all as far as she could tell because it was the birth of his deception. Kate plagued her thoughts, all the lies she had told her, a tight painful knot in her stomach. All she wanted to do was get home, but when she went to the train station later that day, she found James on the platform waiting for her.

'I need to explain,' he said, taking her bag from her.

He looked dreadful, as if he hadn't slept. 'I think you've said enough, don't you?' But the soft pink eyes that spoke of shame and guilt forced her to listen as they shared the return journey. All the while he spoke she thought about Tom's little wishes left on her doorstep for years, wishes she had on occasion almost discarded.

'Please let us try again,' he said as the train pulled into Penzance station. 'If not for me, for Kate.'

All along she'd thought Tom had abandoned her, yet he had no idea about the baby and had left because of James's lies. And the previous year's wish had been for them to raise a family together. A horrible, painful coincidence. 'I think you'd better move out when we get home,' she replied. 'This charade has gone on quite long enough.'

Mrs Clements danced around the subject of James's departure for well over a week, hoping to ascertain what had happened. Elizabeth decided the best way forward was to focus her attentions on something that she could control, so set about painting the commissioned piece for Shelby Summerton, and was rewarded with a handsome royalty a little over two months later. The sale earned her enough capital with which she could leave the family home and move into one of her own. Mr Bolitho was reluctant at first, but she convinced him to let her buy the still vacant cottage that had once been home to Tom and his family. James helped her with the move, said it was the least he could do, and Elizabeth let him on account that she wanted Kate to see the only parents she had ever known working things through.

But she also knew that the truth had to come out before Kate got any older. In his continuing pains to make amends, James drove her to Tremayne's farm in the hope she might find Tom. They pulled up in a muddy patch of land, straw and rain ripe with the smell of manure. James stayed in the car, but Elizabeth rang the bell with the swell of hope tight in her chest. It was short lived; the Hales had gone missing along with a stash of smuggled whisky and tobacco not a month after they arrived.

'Never saw Tom in my life,' the farmer's wife said, hoisting up a skirt unsuitable for the manual labour her hands suggested she did. 'But I heard he took up a driving job in London.' Elizabeth returned to Porthsennen with the address of a forklift firm and renewed resolve that she was on the right track.

It took another year of joining loose ends before she found herself in an architect's office, the walls covered with wood panelling, the ceiling grimy and smoke-yellow. It was almost a dead end, Tom long gone, but they gave her his home address and wished her luck. From there she rode the sweaty Tube from Richmond to Hampstead, exiting into brilliant sunshine. Although she wasn't sure about the route, she did her best to follow the map she picked up in the train station, and eventually found herself standing outside the house she had been told was his.

Her first thought was that it was a pretty place, flowers creeping up the front, a square patch of lawn that she could imagine Tom mowing. Life, lived. The nausea of nerves rumbled in her stomach, so she took a seat on a bench on the opposite side of the road. It was facing away from the house, overlooking the overgrown perimeter of Hampstead Heath. Just a moment, that was all she needed, to think about what it might be that she was going to say. After all, it wasn't every day you were reunited with the only man you had ever truly loved after almost a decade of absence. Should she start with hello? An apology? A big toothy smile? No, she thought, not that one; her tea habit ensured that her teeth weren't that white anymore, a conclusion which at least helped to narrow down the options.

Just as she was getting up, dusting off her legs, she heard a woman's voice calling Tom's name. And the strange thing was the familiarity it aroused, the trill of it stirring a certainty that she had heard the voice before. Gazing over her shoulder, turning just enough to see, she saw Shelby Summerton standing at the front gate. 'Tom,' she said again, calling into the open front door. 'My parents won't wait for ever. Please would you get a move on.'

Moments later Elizabeth watched as he emerged from the building. His clothes were smart, his hair longer than it used to be, flopping into his eyes. Different, but undoubtedly Tom. And there, cradled in his arms with all the tenderness of a new father that she recognised from James, was a small baby, perhaps no older than a few months. Unable to move, she watched as he placed the baby in the car, then slipped in himself, before driving away without even realising that she was there.

In none of the possibilities of what would transpire had she ever considered he might have built a new life without her, yet now she understood the wish from the previous year. Perhaps he had hoped they would raise a family, but he was instead doing it with somebody else. As the sound of the engine faded, she watched the car disappear around a corner. And that was it; once again, he was gone, too late for second chances.

Not a week later, her breath tight, she pushed her way up the steps to the old Mayon Lookout, cutting down to the rocks as dusk fell across their village. Taking a seat in the spot where she had once lain with Tom, she unfurled the quilt, the one his family had been sewing for generations. Flickering in the breeze, the delicate white trim with colourful embroidery stared back at her. Her intention had been to save it for Kate, but now there was no point. Tom could never be her father. The rock was hard under her head, the quilt warm across her body, as she gazed up at the glistening edge of their galaxy. Everything had changed in that silvery stain, but to look at it now it was as if nothing had changed at all. She could have been lying there on the same night almost ten years before, when she and Tom believed they had a whole life ahead of them.

After a while she sat up and folded the quilt as neatly as she could, found a nook that she thought was protected, and poked it inside. She pulled the copy of *Pride and Prejudice* that Tom had given her from her bag and tucked that in too. She had to say goodbye, return Tom to her past so that she might be able to live her life without him in the future. Some secrets, she thought, were supposed to be kept. She stepped close to the edge, where she could hear the roar of the water, gazed across the indigo sea to where three more men were working in Wolf Rock lighthouse. The light danced rhythmically across the waves, the heartbeat of her memories. Nothing had changed, and yet everything was different. It was, just as it was before, the closest she could get to him now.

Now

Their arms were tired from hoisting boxes into the nursing home, belongings he wouldn't touch or use while he was there. Yet they helped create an illusion of familiarity which was surprisingly comforting. Alice and Elizabeth were watching Tom, listening to the harsh reverberations of his breathing, when the melody of Elizabeth's telephone broke the tension.

'It's Kate,' she said as she looked at the screen. 'She must be here.'

'Then you'd better answer it, hadn't you,' Alice replied, a reassuring smile on her face.

Descending the wide staircase of the care home, she took some deep yet insufficient breaths. Part of Elizabeth wanted to rush to her daughter, but the part of her that still felt shame over the lies told in the past held her back as she opened the door. Kate was standing on the driveway, dressed in a thick winter coat and heavy woollen hat. Elizabeth was wearing nothing warmer than yesterday's silk blouse, yet she didn't feel the cold as the cool air brushed her skin. To see her daughter again after so long made words and sensory perceptions impossible, but somehow tears fought their way out. Kate was nervous too, she realised, her breath fogging before her, one barely dissipating before the next cloud followed. Even through the heavy clothing Elizabeth could tell she had grown thinner since she had last seen her just under twelve months ago.

Elizabeth had always been the first person Kate called with news, like when she was pregnant, or when she secured another build at work. Elizabeth had kept the truth from her daughter for the duration of James's life out of respect for his dedication to the fulfilment of his promise, but after his death following a stroke the previous year she had known the truth deserved a hearing. After they separated, James had stayed in Porthsennen, and despite their differences they remained cordial for their daughter's sake; Kate had loved him as a father her whole life. And Elizabeth too had found an unusual sort of friendship at his side, support when it was needed, and a companion upon whom she could rely. When her father passed away at the age of eighty, living as a near recluse in the far reaches of Scotland, it was James who told her, and who understood the absence of grief. Elizabeth had expected upset, even anger when she told Kate the truth, but had never expected to be excised from her daughter's life. Elizabeth didn't know if Kate's anger ran deeper for the lie, or for the lost opportunity with Tom. But now there she was, standing before her.

'I've missed you,' Kate said as she reached out to hold her mother. 'I'm so sorry for everything.'

'No, I'm the one who is sorry, Kate. Sorry for the lies, and that it took me so long to get us here.'

'Well, we're here now.' The grand Victorian building rose up above them, Kate's eyes drawn to the details. 'I can't believe I'm going to see him. And Alice too. Will he know it's me?'

Elizabeth wiped her daughter's tears. 'I've done my best to explain to him, love, although he isn't very coherent. But rest assured he knew the truth all right. He was never sure, but he told Alice he felt it.'

'I shouldn't have taken so long to get here,' Kate said. 'I left it too late.'

'It's never too late,' Elizabeth said, guiding her daughter towards the door.

Their feet fell into step as they climbed the stairs. With shaky fingers Kate reached for her mother's hand. Looking at her daughter, the scarf pulled away from her face, Elizabeth saw the pale skin of Tom's family, and Kate's nervous nibbling of her lip that betrayed her fears.

'It's going to be all right,' Elizabeth said, even though everything about that statement felt uncertain.

Letting go of her daughter's hand as she reached the narrow corridor that led to Tom's room, she motioned for Kate to enter. Over her shoulder Elizabeth could see Alice, emotion claiming her as her half-sister arrived, tears welling in her tired eyes. Seeing them together was like seeing twins, albeit with an age difference. Alice came to the door, and without hesitating, she took Kate into her arms. Elizabeth felt like an interloper on the edge of their embrace, as if she shouldn't be there, but moments later she felt Alice's fingertips brushing her own. Alice was smiling at her as she held Kate with all her strength. She mouthed a thank you, before leading Kate towards the bed. Alice whispered something in Kate's ear just before they arrived, but Elizabeth couldn't hear what was said.

'Dad, Kate's here. She's come to see you.'

Elizabeth lingered in the doorway, watching her daughter be guided by Tom's daughter. Alice was younger, but in that moment it was she who seemed older, the one who offered support and led the way forward. Kate reached for Tom's hand and he opened his eyes a little, a flicker of a smile registering on the side of his face that was still working. 'All right, Bab,' he said, his nickname for Alice, but he was looking at Kate as he said it.

'I think he thinks you're me,' Alice whispered.

'Hello,' Kate said as she gazed at Tom, his eyes flickering shut. She wiped a tear away from her cheek as she leaned in close, kissing him on the forehead. 'We look like him,' she said, turning to Alice. 'I can tell that even now.'

'You're alike in more ways than you could imagine,' Elizabeth said as she stepped into the room. A sense of rightness joined her then, a peace that perhaps she had laid the first brick in the road to recovery. 'You have the same temperament, same determination.'

Kate stared at her father, her hand on the bony outcrop of his knee. 'I don't know what to say to him,' she whispered. 'I don't know where to start.'

'Would you like some time alone?' Elizabeth asked. 'Just you and him?'

Kate shook her head and pulled up a chair. Her fingers clasped Tom's, so tight it was as if she might never let them go. 'We've all spent enough time apart from one another, don't you think? Now's the time for us to be together.' And Elizabeth knew there and then that the only wishes left that really mattered had already been fulfilled.

It had been raining steadily all day, the window speckled with drops, kaleidoscopic light refracting through. Neither Alice nor Elizabeth had moved for close to forty-eight hours, except to go to the toilet or to make a cup of tea. The staff in the nursing home had been feeding them, and Elizabeth had a bag filled with fruit and crisps which just about kept them going between meals. If she never ate another ready salted crisp in her life it would be too soon for Elizabeth.

A Bulgarian nurse called Liliya popped in at least once every hour to straighten his sheets and touch his face. It was nothing really, in the scheme of things, but it was a regular show of compassion which meant a lot. Somebody beyond the door was thinking about them, and it really helped because most of the time it felt as if the rest of the world had ceased to exist. Whenever the nurse left the room one of them always commented on how nice she was, before they fell back into silence, broken only by the chesty rattle that resonated between them.

Tom's breathing difficulties intensified only a short while after Brian and Kate had both left for the day. Before that, if they ignored the facial droop and his slender frame, they could almost convince themselves he was sleeping peacefully. Elizabeth had even said it once, and Alice had agreed. That he seemed at peace. It was one of those things you said in the absence of having something of value to add. It was designed to make you feel better about things, and in a way, it did. But then everything seemed to take on an erratic energy, as if Tom was fighting the inevitable, as if he hoped there was still time left for one last hurrah before the lights went out for good.

Elizabeth lowered the lights and picked up a torch, something she used to get about in the dark without bothering Tom once night set in. Sometimes the sound of his breathing was overwhelming, and she would turn the torch on, that small beam of light just enough that she could see her own gnarled hands through the dark, enough to ground her in the present. But as she closed her eyes in the hope of sleep, she realised that all she could hear was Alice, the soft lull as she slept. The silence of the room. Flicking the switch on the torch, she shone it at Tom. His chest wasn't moving. And then suddenly it was, the rattling returning as a temporary relief. Lifting the heavy covers, she placed a hand against his, but found it cold, his fingertips blue.

'Alice,' she said, flicking on the main light.

Alice roused. 'What is it?'

'His breathing has changed.' They edged forward in their seats, both watching, both knowing, and yet denying all the same the inevitable as his breathing shallowed again. 'Liliya is working, isn't she?' Elizabeth asked.

'I'll go,' Alice said, knowing she would be faster. The door handle struck the wall outside as she flew through and down the stairs, as if they needed a witness, as if there was still something that could be done. Elizabeth huddled as close to Tom as she could, held his cold hand, let her head rest against his.

'It's OK,' she said. 'You've done all you had to do. It's OK to go if you're ready.'

Elizabeth was still at the bedside when Alice arrived back in the room with Liliya, her cheeks red, eyes wet. Tom's breathing had softened by then, had become slow and thin. Alice crept to his side, almost tiptoeing, and as she sat next to the bed she held his hand.

'I love you, Dad,' was all she said. Elizabeth couldn't find any more words, but she could have sworn that in the same moment he opened his eyes with a fright, gasped a little as he took his final breath, almost as if that time he knew it was over.

Liliya leaned in close. 'Alice,' she said. 'I'm so sorry, but he's gone.' Elizabeth looked up, saw Alice with her head flat against her father's chest, alongside her own. Tears flooded her face, her cheeks hot and red. Liliya held her as she led her away, already searching in her pocket for her phone, no doubt to call Brian. 'Elizabeth, do you need a moment longer?' Liliya asked as she stood at the door. 'I can come back in a while if you like.'

Elizabeth shook her head, sat up. She stroked Tom's hair and kissed his warm lips. 'No,' she said as she stood up. 'We've said our goodbyes.' But as she walked to join Alice, she stopped briefly to open the window. The sound of falling rain and a cool wind filled the room. The curtain breezed open like the rolling tide lapping against the Porthsennen shore. 'So he can find his way home,' she said, and that was the last time she ever saw him.

Dear Elizabeth,

As I sit at the dining table to write this letter you are upstairs in my house, taking a bath. It is such a simple picture, and yet one that I never imagined would ever come true. There are things I want to say for which I cannot find the courage, but let me start by stating something that I hope by now is obvious; I have never forgotten you, Elizabeth, and my love over the years has never waned. It is important to say that now, because I want you to know that when I asked you to stay here it was not a spur of the moment decision. I have wanted you with me my whole life.

But I have been a coward, Elizabeth. When I left Porthsennen to go to Wolf Rock I had every intention of returning to become the man I promised you I could be. I wanted so much to be your husband and call you my wife. But like a fool, when you didn't write, when I heard about the pregnancy, and then about your subsequent marriage to James, I made assumptions. Wrongly, we now know, after everything you explained about what James did, but I confess I found it easier to believe his lies than to trust that you could ever want me to be a father to our child. Even now as you talk of Kate you are yet to tell me whether she is really mine. You too must harbour your own fears, just as my old fears continue to hold me back. Perhaps you don't want me to know. Perhaps we waited too long. Perhaps for all these years I have been wrong. But I don't believe it. I believe, in my heart, that she is ours. I have to believe the love we shared came to something after all.

But my purpose in this letter is not to explain or excuse myself. It is to tell you that if what I believe to be true really is, then I forgive your silence. I want you to understand the joy it would bring me to know that our love brought something as beautiful as a child into this world. Yes, I have missed out, but this is not your fault. I am to blame, holding back through a fear of rejection. I had the opportunity to knock on your door forty-nine times, and through fear of my own incapability, I never took it. We may both have made dark mistakes, but they pale in comparison to the light we created together, and that I do not doubt for a moment Kate brings into this world.

So, I want to finish by thanking you, Elizabeth, for being here now. I always knew that if your face was the view I got to wake up next to during the final stage of my life, it would have been a life well lived. My last, and lasting wish is fulfilled; here you are with me.

Thank you for the present, for the past, and for every moment we still have left together. I have loved you greatly.

Tom

Now

Alice chose not to travel with Elizabeth. Elizabeth invited her, of course, and would have been glad to share a train carriage with her for the eight-hour return journey to Porthsennen. Elizabeth would have liked her company, would have welcomed Alice into her cottage, given her a chance to share her father's past. But Porthsennen and the memories Elizabeth had created there with Tom belonged to them, and it seemed that Alice was happy to let them rest along with her father now that the funeral was over. The memories that had kept Elizabeth in Porthsennen for all these years were from a different life that belonged to Elizabeth and Tom. It was a life that never really began, yet had never really ended either.

They did travel together to the funeral home, a small Georgian building with strange gothic lights on the wall and an atmosphere of library quiet inside. They knew Tom's wishes, and so Alice asked permission from Elizabeth to keep a small measure of the ashes, all that now remained of the man they had once loved so much. Elizabeth had no idea whether Tom would have thought it a pleasant or macabre idea that a small part of him would end up on a mantelpiece, and she herself couldn't think of anything worse than keeping him there, watching over her like that. Even the knowledge that he was in the green pot sitting on the table before her was almost too much. But she gave Alice the permissions she sought, and then helped her choose a small wooden heart, engraved with the word 'Dad' on the front. For her that was enough, just a small piece of him left, to take home to Brian's house when she moved in next week.

'I can't believe it took this to get us to realise how we felt,' she said to Elizabeth while the funeral director was off organising the paperwork.

'Sometimes it takes a tragedy to make us appreciate the treasures in our own lives,' Elizabeth said. Alice agreed, nodding. The shuffle of paperwork continued from the other side of the table as the funeral director filled out the necessary documents. They were nearly done, could almost see the line being drawn under this latest chapter. Not quite the last, but near enough.

Brian drove them the short distance to Paddington Station, and Alice insisted on escorting Elizabeth inside while he waited on the side of the road. Kate had already returned to her life in Truro a few days before, a husband and two children who needed her there. Elizabeth was going to visit next week; how she had missed her grandchildren and their noisy brand of company. This time the ticket machine posed no problem for her, and with the ticket in her hand they moved towards the gates. The travel bag, now heavy with Tom's ashes, cut deep into her fingers.

'You will keep in touch, won't you?' Alice asked as they watched the train pull in. Everywhere around them people rushed about; Elizabeth wouldn't miss that at all. But she would miss Alice. They had spent close to three months together. It had been Alice who had hand delivered Tom's final letter in the hours following his death, just as he had instructed.

'That would be nice,' Elizabeth said, trying to conceal her surprise. Elizabeth had expected that perhaps Alice would have liked to move on, not have a constant reminder of this small slice of life they had shared. 'You'll be welcome in Cornwall anytime.'

'And you with us. You're going to have to come back anyway, in about eight months' time. Without Mum and Dad around, somebody is going to have to be a grandparent to this baby.' Elizabeth didn't know what to say, and when she tried to speak the lump in her throat trapped all the words she could think of, her eyes shooting to Alice's tummy.

'You're pregnant?'

'I only found out a few days ago and couldn't wait to tell you. We're family now. I guess in some way we always were.' Alice reached forwards and hugged her.

'That's such wonderful news.'

'Well, I'm forty-two, so let's not count our chickens. But I want this. Always did, I think.' The announcement for the 10.03 for Penzance boomed over the tannoy, it would be departing in two minutes, right on time. 'Will you be all right with him?' Alice asked, looking down at the bag containing the pot of ashes. Elizabeth nodded. 'Try not to lose him this time, eh?'

Elizabeth pushed through the gate and lugged the bag onto the train, taking her place in the window seat. Waving to Alice as the train pulled away, she was comforted by a smile that confirmed for Elizabeth that it wouldn't be the last time she saw her.

Alice's words lingered with her throughout the journey, the uneasy responsibility of seeing a final wish come to fruition. Would there be anything worse than failing him now, losing him on the train? Elizabeth travelled with the pot on her lap, cursed the weight of his ashes for giving her sore knees as they coursed through the southern countryside. After arriving in Penzance, a taxi delivered her to Porthsennen. It felt like a lifetime that she had been away, the village changed during her absence. And as she approached her quiet cottage, the sound of the waves a welcome chorus, she noticed that all the roses in pots on the steps were dead.

'I hold you responsible for those,' she said as she heaved the bag into the cottage, kicking the dead heads that had fallen from the steps. 'And Francine. Last time I'll ask her to water anything.' All was quiet as she closed the door behind her. And in the dark of her living room she was hit by a smell, something she hadn't noted in a long time; the sea, tobacco, and heat. Tom. He must have been there with her all along, she had just never realised.

She set the bag down on the table with a thump. Cookie chirruped from the settee, but didn't bother to get up, although she was glad to see that Francine had managed to keep him alive. Next to her she saw her post, with it a small box with her name and address on it, a London postmark. Tom's handwriting, if she wasn't mistaken. Taking a knife from the kitchen she opened the edge and popped open the top. Inside was a small terracotta pot, and the remains of a dead crocus.

'You didn't forget,' she said as she lifted it out. Attached to the side was the wish.

2018: I wish this year that you would come back to me. That is all I want now.

Even though the flower was dead, she set the pot in the centre of the table and made a cup of tea. Unsure what to do, uncomfortable in her own life, she sat on the settee to drink it with her eyes on the ashes, stroking Cookie's head. 'I don't suppose there's any reason to put this off, is there?' she asked of herself. So after taking a thick woollen coat from the stand, and placing Tom in a satchel that she had found in the cottage when she first moved in, she opened the door. 'Let's get this show on the road, shall we?'

Forced to walk against the breeze, she strode up the path that would deliver her to the old Mayon Lookout. With careful footing she stepped out onto the rocks, the path even more precarious than she remembered it to be. It was further than she usually went nowadays, but it didn't take her long to find the small hollow in the rock that had been formed over thousands of years, and in which she had shared her first kiss with Tom. Her body still fit the mould as she slipped inside, and as she lay down she said to herself, 'Close your eyes. Make a wish,' imagining that she was still able to feel his warm hand on the back of her head.

As she gazed skyward, she saw the most lucent smudge streaking through the sky, just as it had before. In places it was silver, in others purple with lights coming from within. She thought of Tom, and how she hoped he was in heaven if such a place existed, and that if it did there was no place closer to him in the world than right there on that rock. Gazing briefly at her tattooed wrist, she smiled. Her breath caught in her throat as tears pricked her eyes. She could almost sense him looking at her. She brought a fingertip to the corner of her eye, brushed the tear away as she rose to her feet.

'Don't go anywhere, eh?' she told Tom as she set the satchel down. Until then the only light was that of the automated lighthouses flickering in the distance, but from her pocket she pulled a small torch. The beam shone bright, and she set off for the nearby rocks, hoping she could find that which she came here for. And sure enough, without too much effort she did. The space was tighter than she remembered, but her fingers soon felt the quilt just where she had left it all those years ago, along with the book that had once belonged to Tom. The quilt was damp, but in the low light it didn't seem especially damaged. The book had taken a battering. The paper was wrinkled, soft and brown about the edges. Parts looked barely readable.

'I was wrong about one thing,' she said aloud. 'It was never really over, was it? Not for either of us.' The quilt was almost too big to fit in the satchel, even once she'd taken Tom's ashes out, yet she managed to stuff it in along with the book and slung the bag over her shoulder. She hoped both would dry so that she might hand them down to Alice. It seemed only right they go to her. Kate had another family, linked to the man who raised her. 'We have loved each other for a lifetime, Thomas Hale, just as you promised we would. You did keep your promises, after all. Now I will keep those I made to you.'

The green pot was heavy as she picked it up, fiddling a fingernail at the seal. It took a while and required her to hold the torch with her teeth, but soon enough she had it open. It took only a moment for the wind to pick up the uppermost ashes, licking them upwards into the night sky. It was a struggle to hold the pot above her head, yet as she did, she watched the contents gradually escape, creating a silver arc that travelled up towards the stars. And just a moment later that was it. Done. She waited there a while, watching the light from Wolf Rock flicker across the sea. Then she turned to walk away, glancing back at the water only at the last moment. 'I'll be home soon,' she said, her voice breaking as she took the first steps in the direction of the cottage. For the first time in her life she felt ready for whatever came next, because finally, after fifty years of waiting, all her wishes had come true.

Author's Note

Thank you so much for choosing this book, and giving me the chance to share Tom and Elizabeth's story with you. I really hope that you have enjoyed it, and that it left you feeling as if it's never too late for love to find a voice. Of all the books I have written to date, this is by far the one that means the most to me personally, and I'd love to take a moment to tell you why.

The initial idea for this book first came to me during a seven hour airport layover, stuck in a cafe watching the snow settle on the runway. I wrote a few thousand words that evening, beginning with the scene when Tom and Elizabeth first attend the hospital together. I was trying to return to the UK from Cyprus on a last-minute flight, and the only one I could get included a substantial wait in Lithuania. But I had no choice but to take it; my dad was dying of stage four lung cancer, and I knew I couldn't wait if I wanted to be there in time.

The eve of that final trip came only four weeks after his diagnosis. I had been with him for that, but had returned home to Cyprus briefly, trying to manage a life that stretched across two countries on opposite sides of Europe. But he got sick very quickly. The shock of his diagnosis hit me hard, and sitting in the airport during that wait I knew it was going to be the last time to go there to be with him. Leaving the week before had been a hard decision to take, but possible because I knew I had been leaving him in the capable hands of his partner, Chris.

From the moment my father became sick she barely left his side. When I had no choice but to return home, she was there to care for him. Her presence made all the difference, the only constant in an otherwise uncertain world. Undoubtedly there were terrible moments during that period of our lives, some of which have been recounted in this novel. One such moment was his prognosis, when we found out that his problem wasn't something we could fix. But there were also wonderful moments. Jokes and movies. Music and memories. Support from places we didn't expect. And through it all, Chris was there. I witnessed so much love shared between my father and his partner during those difficult moments. Love given when there was no hope for the future, but when the present had never mattered more. I wanted desperately to capture that connection in a story, and that's how Tom and Elizabeth, and all their little wishes were born.

I loved my father dearly, and although this story is not based on his life, he runs through this book like a stamp through rock. For example, he loved lifeboats, Elvis Presley, toasted teacakes, and a shiny grille on a classic car. He had a lighthouse photograph hanging on his wall, my inspiration for putting that element in this story. And, sadly, like many people he was a smoker, who paid the heaviest price for that choice. He also, and perhaps most importantly, died with his loved ones around him, just as Tom did in this story. For that too, I remain grateful.

After writing the first chapter in the airport it took me another two years to finish the earliest manuscript for my agent to read. The original story has changed a lot since then. It brings me great pleasure to have written this tribute to my dad, John, and his partner, Chris. I hope in reading it, just like them, you might remember that it's never too late to chase a love you lost.

Acknowledgements

Four years ago, riding in a taxi with my agent before I'd even had a single book published, I told her that I wanted to write a love story. We were on our way to meet with my editor for my psychological thrillers, and the timing for a genre switch could not have been worse. I hazard a guess that not all agents would have reacted with such enthusiasm and encouragement, and so my first thank you must, as always, go to Madeleine Milburn and her incredible team. You keep on making dreams come true. I couldn't wish for a better team to represent me.

Thanks also go to Phoebe Morgan from Trapeze, who helped me craft the original book into something better still. I am indebted to you for your help and tireless effort in making this book what it is today. Also, to Lucia Macro at William Morrow HarperCollins USA, your enthusiasm for this novel blew me away. It is a joy to collaborate with you. And to all the other international editors who have shown faith in my work, I thank you for making me part of your journey. There are so many other people who play an important role in the publication of a novel, from assistants to typesetters, to designers and publishers who all work to make it possible. Thank you to every one of you for the part you play in all this.

A very special thanks goes to friends and family who have encouraged and supported me along the way, especially to my people, Stasinos, Theo, Themis, and Lelia; sometimes there are just no words. I'm grateful for you every day, and so proud of you all too.

But the biggest thanks this time must go to my father, who is no longer here to see this book achieve publication. However, he inspired this story in every possible way. Without him, and without the love he showed me throughout my life, it undoubtedly would have never been written. Perhaps this book was my way of keeping him here for just a little while longer, because I surely wasn't ready to say goodbye when the time came. He would have found it particularly strange I think, to imagine that he is behind the story in the pages of this book. He might be gone, but his memory lives on, and for that I am grateful every day.

Credits

Trapeze would like to thank everyone at Orion who worked on the publication of *Little Wishes* in the UK.

Agent
Madeleine Milburn

Editor
Sam Eades

Copy-editor
Laura Gerrard

Proofreader
Linda Joyce

Editorial Management
Sarah Fortune
Charlie Panayiotou
Jane Hughes
Claire Boyle

Audio
Paul Stark
Amber Bates

Contracts
Anne Goddard
Jake Alderson

Design
Loulou Clark
Rachael Lancaster
Lucie Stericker
Joanna Ridley
Nick May
Clare Sivell
Helen Ewing

Finance
Jennifer Muchan
Jasdip Nandra
Afeera Ahmed
Ibukun Ademefun
Sue Baker
Tom Costello

Marketing
Tanjiah Islam

Production
Claire Keep
Fiona McIntosh

Publicity
Alex Layt

Sales
Laura Fletcher
Victoria Laws
Esther Waters
Lucy Brem
Frances Doyle
Ben Goddard
Georgina Cutler
Jack Hallam
Ellie Kyrke-Smith
Inês Figuiera
Barbara Ronan
Andrew Hally
Dominic Smith
Deborah Deyong
Lauren Buck

Maggy Park
Linda McGregor
Sinead White
Jemimah James
Rachel Jones
Jack Dennison
Nigel Andrews
Ian Williamson
Julia Benson
Declan Kyle
Robert Mackenzie
Imogen Clarke
Megan Smith
Charlotte Clay
Rebecca Cobbold

Operations
Jo Jacobs
Sharon Willis

Rights
Susan Howe
Richard King
Krystyna Kujawinska
Jessica Purdue
Louise Henderson

Help us make the next generation of readers

We – both author and publisher – hope you enjoyed this book. We believe that you can become a reader at any time in your life, but we'd love your help to give the next generation a head start.

Did you know that 9 per cent of children don't have a book of their own in their home, rising to 13 per cent in disadvantaged families*? We'd like to try to change that by asking you to consider the role you could play in helping to build readers of the future.

We'd love you to think of sharing, borrowing, reading, buying or talking about a book with a child in your life and spreading the love of reading. We want to make sure the next generation continue to have access to books, wherever they come from.

And if you would like to consider donating to charities that help fund literacy projects, find out more at www.literacytrust.org.uk and www.booktrust.org.uk.

THANK YOU

*As reported by the National Literacy Trust